Lynne Francis grew up in Yorkshire but studied, lived and worked in London for many years. She draws inspiration for her novels from a fascination with family history, landscapes and the countryside.

Her first saga series was set in west Yorkshire but a move to east Kent, and the discovery of previously unknown family links to the area, gave her the idea for a Georgian-era trilogy. Lynne's exploration of her new surroundings provided the historical background for the novels, as well as allowing her to indulge another key interest: checking out the local teashops and judging the cake.

When she's not at her desk, writing, Lynne can be found in the garden, walking through the countryside or beside the sea.

By Lynne Francis:

THE MARGATE MAID
A Maid's Ruin
The Secret Child
The Lost Sister

THE MILL VALLEY GIRLS
Ella's Journey
Alice's Secret
Sarah's Story

THE SMUGGLER'S SECRET

LYNNE FRANCIS

PIATKUS

PIATKUS

First published in Great Britain in paperback in 2023 by Piatkus

1 3 5 7 9 10 8 6 4 2

A CIP catalogue record for this book
is available from the British Library.

ISBN 978-0-349-433-578

Typeset in Caslon by M Rules
Printed and bound in Great Britain by Clays Ltd, Elcograf S.p.A.

Papers used by Piatkus are from well-managed forests
and other responsible sources.

Piatkus
An imprint of
Little, Brown Book Group
Carmelite House
50 Victoria Embankment
London EC4Y 0DZ

An Hachette UK Company
www.hachette.co.uk

www.littlebrown.co.uk

PART ONE

MEG: 1813

PROLOGUE

The gloves are beautiful, but not for the likes of me. There are twenty-five pairs, come over from France along with a shipment of brandy, tea and tobacco. My hands are too broad, the knuckles too large, the skin too rough to think about slipping one on. The white kid is softer than anything you could imagine, the stitching so fine you'd think it done by fairy folk. I've wrapped them in the cleanest paper I could find and bound the parcel with oilskin and string – not so tight as to mark them but, I hope, secure enough to keep out the mice that have the run of the cavities in the walls, under the floorboards and the other secret places where we hide our precious goods. And these are very precious. I hope they'll be the making of us, our way to a fortune and a better future. They must stay hidden, until I can dispose of them safely. And I think I know how ...

Last entry, dated September 1813, in a diary found hidden in a wall cavity in a house in Prospect Street, Castle Bay.

CHAPTER ONE

It was only a few steps from her home in Prospect Street to the Fountain, the inn on the seafront, where Meg worked whenever the landlady, Mrs Dunn, sent word to say she was needed. The building was clad in weatherboarding, with a wooden terrace supported by timbers on the east side, commanding a fine view over the sea. The inn's name, painted on both sides of the building, came from the water fountain that fed the stone horse trough on Beach Street. Inside, low ceilings and alcoves half screened with dark wood lent themselves to hushed conversations and plans being hatched.

Meg loitered for a few moments outside and watched the moon rising over the water. It was a full moon, a perfect circle, trailing a silver path across the dark, still sea to the distant horizon. The inn would be busy that night, she thought. No wonder Mrs Dunn had need of her. The clear moonlight would put a stop to any smuggling: the French ships involved in the trade would be lying at anchor offshore, inconspicuous among all the other vessels there. Those were waiting for supplies, for crew, for a favourable wind to set them safely on their way to London or across the sea. Some of the sailors would have been given leave earlier that day to row over and beach their small boats on the shingle, tumbling over each other and wetting their feet in their hurry to gain land. The town of Castle Bay was well known for the quantity of taverns within two streets of the shoreline, and the number of pleasure houses set among them.

The smugglers out at sea would be waiting impatiently aboard their boats, hoping that the following night would bring clouds and the opportunity to offload their goods onto the galleys rowed out from Castle Bay. Meg, too, was waiting, although it wasn't rum or tea that she was expecting.

There was a stranger in the Fountain that night: she'd spotted him at once. He looked out of place. His dark coat was too well cut, his boots were fine leather, and his hands – when he accepted his tankard and handed over his coin – were smooth, the nails neatly trimmed. He was not a man who spent his days toiling to earn a wage.

She watched with amusement as he attempted to engage the other drinkers in conversation. They tolerated him for a few exchanges of pleasantries, then closed ranks against him, turning their backs so he was edged out. After four or five such rebuffs as he circled the room, he returned to the bar, a despondent expression on his face.

Meg served him with more ale. Then, as he lingered, watching the room, she said, 'You're not from these parts, I take it?'

'No, from London,' the man replied. He seemed wary of offering more information.

'And what brings you here from the city?' Meg asked, although she could guess. Others like him had tried their hand at taking a slice of the lucrative smuggled brandy or tea trade, and failed. The Silver Street gang had their distribution networks nicely set up and they weren't about to be impressed by the promise of riches from London.

'There's a gentleman in the city who asked me to find him some goods. The sort he can sell in his shop. Goods for which his customers would pay well.'

'Oh?' Meg lifted a tankard from its hook behind the bar and poured the ale for one of the regulars, William Huggett, who had just come in. She handed it over, giving him her best smile, then turned back to her city customer. 'And what sort of things are you looking for?'

She was unwilling to name the most obvious, wanting him to be the first to do so. It was as well to be cautious. He didn't look like a revenue man, but they could be wily. One evening, old Frederick Larkin had drunk more than was good for him and, on the way home, had fallen into the trap of believing the weasel words of a revenue man waiting in the shadows, pretending to be the go-between he was expecting. The lucky guess on the revenue man's part had seen old Mr Larkin lurching happily round to Market Street, to show him the trapdoor from the street that gave access to the kegs of brandy stacked in his cellar. The reward for his fool-ishness had been a hefty fine, the confiscation of his brandy and a cellar filled with shingle to discourage him from pursuing that line of trade again.

It had happened six months ago but was still fresh in the memory of everyone there, not least Frederick Larkin, who was sitting in the corner nursing the only jar of ale he'd be able to afford all night. Strangers at the Fountain, inside or out, were never good news.

This one, though, looked and sounded too well-bred to be a revenue man. He was gazing into his ale, apparently weighing up whether or not to explain himself. He lifted his head, and Meg saw that his eyes were drawn to the handkerchief she had just tucked into her sleeve. The fabric square was unremarkable – just plain white cotton cambric – but the edging was of the finest lace. Meg hadn't been able to resist it. She couldn't afford to keep any of the beautiful fabrics that came over from France – her working clothes were made of coarse wool and undyed linen – but, once

7

she'd measured and cut the lengths of lace, there had been a piece left over. It was too short to sell, but perfectly suited to edging a handkerchief.

'That's a fine piece of lace!' The man reached out and caught Meg's wrist. 'Now where would you be finding handiwork like that? From France, at a guess. My master would pay well for such things.'

Meg saw that some in the inn had noticed his action, among them Joseph Huggett. He was William's son, and without a doubt the most handsome of the regular visitors to the Fountain. She also knew him to have more than a passing interest in her. She disengaged her hand and made a show of lifting down another tankard, then picking up a cloth to polish it.

Speaking quietly, her head slightly turned away, she said, 'I can find you such things, and more. But we can't discuss it here. There's a corn mill called Oakley's to the north of the town. Walk out beyond the brewery and the timber yard, past a row of fine houses, and you will see it before you, standing to this side of Downs Castle. I suppose it's less than a mile from this spot. I'll meet you there tomorrow morning at ten o'clock. You can judge for yourself the quality of the lace and silk I have. But now I can't be seen to be speaking to you any longer. You'd do well to drink up and get back to your lodging. And watch your back.'

Meg turned back to serve newly arrived customers. When she turned back, the man had gone, his presence betrayed only by a trace of froth in the bottom of his tankard.

'Who was that?' Joseph was standing before her, his own tankard all but empty.

Meg shrugged. 'Someone down from London. Asking questions about houses for rent in Golden Street. I told him he needed to talk to the notary, not the girl who works behind the bar of an inn.'

She didn't like lying to Joseph, and his expression suggested that he didn't entirely believe her, but she was saved from further discussion by the arrival of a group of fishermen, their boats newly landed. They all arrived at the bar at the same time, bringing with them a strong whiff of fish and a desperate thirst.

She hoped no one could see how flustered she felt after making the bold arrangement with the stranger. Her heart was beating fast even as she laughed and joked with the men, while her thoughts were entirely taken up by the idea that this could be her chance to assure her family's future. As she walked home later that night, she glanced up at the star-filled sky, and imagined her father watching over her. She hoped he approved.

Chapter Two

⸎

The next morning Meg was at the meeting place near the corn mill well before the appointed hour. She gazed out over the broad sweep of the bay while she waited. The water looked almost green where the horizon met the blue of the sky, and the sun sparkled on the calm sea. The town of Castle Bay sat at the centre of the shingle bay, with three Tudor castles spaced along its stretch. Broad Castle, named after its builder William Broad, sat at the town's southerly edge, with Hawksdown Castle a couple of miles beyond it. France was visible when the weather was favourable, close enough for Henry VIII to have ordered the building of the castles to protect the coast more than two hundred and fifty years earlier. Downs Castle, now falling into disrepair, was out to the north of the town, along a little-used path. Few passed that way other than those with business at Oakley's mill.

Meg had folded her lace and fabrics neatly into the bottom of her basket, covering them with a faded cloth. It was her first venture in undertaking a little private business, in a town where the smugglers operated as a band, keeping each other appraised of their movements. She was wary of being suspected of operating outside the tight-knit group. In addition, if the revenue men should happen to be about she would need to appear above suspicion. And her mother would be furious if she knew what her daughter was up to: she believed she had gone out to buy flour from the mill. Her venture today was risky – a step into the unknown, which could either be the making of her or result in the loss of everything.

She saw the man she was waiting for toiling along the beach path and smiled to herself. She'd enjoyed the walk on such a bright, crisp morning, the sun barely warm enough to melt the frost on the grass. It was clear this man was more used to walking the streets of a city than the sort of rough track that lay beyond the town.

'I hope this is going to be worth the effort.' He was not in a good mood. 'I must be back in London this evening and I plan to take the next stage coach out of this place.'

Meg didn't waste time in placating him. Instead, she pulled back the cloth hiding the contents of her basket. His eyes brightened as he took in what he saw, and he was quick to lift out the differing widths of lace, the brightly coloured silks, plain and printed, and the fine muslin.

'I think my master will be happy to take whatever you can get of this quality,' he said. 'Provided the price is right, of course.'

He regarded her with eyes that carried no expression of interest in her. He would drive a hard bargain, Meg thought. But, then, she had the upper hand. She knew where to source these wares and he didn't. If he wanted her to supply him, he would have to pay her price.

The deal was surprisingly easily done. Meg reflected on it as she walked back to town, having taken the precaution of stopping at the mill for a small sack of flour. Her new customer would have been back in Castle Bay well before her, bent on getting the midday stage.

She had given him a sample of lace and a piece of silk, which he had tucked inside his jacket, and he had handed over a bag of coin to pay for the promised goods. They had shaken on it and exchanged names – Ralph Carter for Meg Marsh – but he had no other surety. She had said she would meet the carriage he sent to

South Street each Saturday, and that his goods would return on it. Her word was her bond, but in any case, he would know it was easy to find her in the town. She would prove to be good at this business, she thought. Once their trade was established, once he had customers eager for what she could provide, she would raise the prices. There'd be money enough to keep the Silver Street gang sweet, and she'd be able to buy more from Philippe, the French smuggler.

The bag of flour Meg carried was quite a burden but she was young and strong. The sunshine and the business had raised her spirits, and she bestowed smiles and greetings on all those she passed. More than one continued on their way reflecting on what an attractive young woman Meg Marsh had grown up to be, her long dark hair escaping from her cap, her brown eyes merry.

Back in Prospect Street, the bell above the door jangled as Meg stepped into the narrow hallway. The house was larger than it first appeared: the bow-fronted window on the ground floor housed her mother's shop, with the bedrooms on the floor above and in the attic. The family lived mostly in the basement kitchen at the back of the property and there was a cellar and a yard with a gate, which led into a discreet alley running off Beach Street. Although every house had a different appearance, the best-kept secret of Prospect Street was that all the cellars interconnected. Goods could be offloaded on the beach and, within five minutes, secreted in the cellars of the first house in the street before being moved by willing hands to emerge onto Middle Street a night or so later.

The red-tiled roofs, at different heights, also hid something from the unsuspecting revenue men. With them in hot pursuit, a man could slip into an alley, through an open gate into the yard of one of the houses, make his way from there up to the top floor and out through a window onto the roof. A narrow, hidden walkway at that level allowed him to continue to Middle Street, where he could climb down and settle himself in a corner of one of the inns, where everyone would swear he had been drinking all night.

Meg was about to make her way along the passage and down into the kitchen when her mother called, 'Is that you, daughter? Can you mind the shop for me? I must step out to see Mrs Millgate.'

Meg turned back and entered the shop, in reality little more than a display table in the window, and another table behind which Mrs Marsh stood and served her customers. Since the death of her husband, it had been hard for Meg's mother to continue the business. Mr Marsh had been the baker, getting up in the middle of the night to prepare and bake the bread. Mrs Marsh had made currant buns and scones – nothing too elaborate, for even when the smuggling profits were good there was not much call in that area for cakes and fancies.

Today two or three currant buns – whirls of baked yeasty dough studded with dried fruit – sat in the window. Meg suspected they were several days old. 'I've brought the flour, Ma,' she said. 'Shall I bake something for the shop this afternoon?'

'That would be nice.' Mrs Marsh was vague, throwing her faded wool shawl over her black dress in preparation to leave. Since the death of her husband, Esther Marsh had taken much comfort from the company of her new friend and neighbour, Rebecca Millgate. Meg suspected they would spend much of the next few hours on their knees at St George's, for her mother had become devout under the influence of Mrs Millgate. She tried to be pleased that her mother had found such comfort in God, but it was hard to ignore the bitter truth that devotion alone would not put bread on the table or keep the roof over their heads.

CHAPTER THREE

❦

Meg turned the sign in the shop window to read 'Closed', then removed the plate of buns. On closer inspection, they were older than she'd thought: traces of mould had started to appear among the whirls of dough. She made a face and carried them through to the kitchen. There was no point in throwing them out into the yard – they would attract rats. She would give them to their neighbour for the pigs he kept on the wasteland at the edge of town. And she would bake more buns, and a seed cake maybe, as she had promised her mother.

But a quick look at the shelves showed her that less than a handful of currants remained in the jar and not a single coin was to be found in the housekeeping pot, tucked behind the tureen on the dresser. Meg frowned. She suspected her brother, Samuel, of 'borrowing' the housekeeping to fund the time he spent at the inn.

Although Samuel chose not to drink at the Fountain, where Meg worked, he didn't lack for choice in the town – every street near the seafront was home to at least one inn, while Beach Street, overlooking the sea, was said to have more inns than houses.

The previous month, Samuel had lost his job at the boatyard due to his poor timekeeping. It was a job his father had found for him, and the change in their fortunes since Mr Marsh had died had made it all the more essential: the shop brought in very little now, and although Meg's work at the Fountain added to their income, it was barely enough.

It was the loss of Samuel's wages that had pushed Meg to think about how she might increase her involvement in smuggling. There was hardly anyone in town who didn't have some sort of part in it: from hiding goods, to transporting them or passing messages. Those who rowed the boats out to meet the French ships played an important role, but it was just the start of a lengthy process. When Meg had been a pupil at the Charity School, she had used the books there to teach herself a smattering of French. It had amused her father to have her write the messages the smugglers took to the french boats, or to translate the replies received. As Mrs Marsh's devoutness grew after the death of her husband, she had made it plain she wouldn't tolerate any involvement with smuggling by any of her household.

By then, though, it was too late. Meg had moved on from her role as occasional translator. Michael Bailey, who organised the Silver Street gang's smuggling trips, had taken her to one side in the Fountain to ask her advice about fabrics, having been offered some samples of muslin and silk. Meg had been delighted, even more so when her suggestions had found favour with those looking to buy, so Michael, confounded by the decisions to be made, had suggested she might handle that side of their business. As long as she paid the gang a proper share of the profits, she was free to do as she liked. It made her meeting with Ralph Carter doubly exciting – and all the more important that she kept it secret from her mother. She would note it all down that night in her diary – the money she had received, the promise made, and her future plans. Meg liked to record all of her transactions, but she kept the pages well hidden from prying eyes.

She saw that she would have to use some of the coins she had earned the previous evening at the Fountain to buy the currants and anything else she needed for the baking. As she left the house again, to go to Widow Boon's shop on Middle Street, Meg wondered about the whereabouts of her nephew Thomas, Samuel's son. He was a cheeky scrap of a boy with unruly blond hair (always uncombed), golden-brown eyes and a gap-toothed smile that had won over his aunt Meg on many an occasion – usually when he'd been hauled home by a shopkeeper who'd caught him pilfering. Thomas always maintained that he'd just picked up something that had fallen on the floor and Meg, exasperated and amused by his indignation, generally gave him the benefit of the doubt. He was only seven years old but, since Mr Marsh had died, he had been running around the streets of the town all day with no one to guide or control him. His mother Eliza, Samuel's wife, seemed to have given up.

Perhaps she could persuade the Charity School to take him on, Meg thought. Her attendance there had been due to her father's insistence, and she had learnt to read and write. Thomas might do well if his reputation in the town hadn't already spoilt his chance of being accepted. Meg had been sorry to leave – she hoped her own good record would help persuade the master to take Thomas. Maybe, if their business grew, she could employ him as a delivery boy after school, to keep him out of mischief.

By the time Meg was home again and sprinkling the currants onto a batch of prepared dough, she was once more filled with the enthusiasm she had felt that morning. The idea of developing a trade in run goods was more appealing to her than any of the other activities she undertook to support the family. It had become only too clear that Samuel didn't have the strength of character to step into his father's shoes, and her mother was still struggling to shake off her sadness over Mr Marsh's death. Meg knew that, for now, it was up to her to prove the Marsh family were capable workers in order to regain the respect they had once had, when her father was alive.

CHAPTER FOUR

Walter Marsh had been a big, burly man with a bushy beard and a pronounced limp, the result of an accident when two of the smugglers' galleys had been thrown together in heavy seas. Walter, flung backwards off his plank seat, had been unable to dislodge his oar, which had pinned his leg at such an awkward angle, and with such force, that it broke. The injury had healed, but badly, and despite his determination, Walter was no longer an effective crew member. He'd retreated into anger and, following in the footsteps of his father, had taken up baking bread. The early-morning hours spent in the basement kitchen, preparing the dough to go into the oven at dawn, had also made him useful to his smuggling friends. He was always there, alert and ready to spirit away a delivery of contraband if the revenue men surprised the smugglers at work. The alleyway leading off Beach Street, as well as the rooftops of Prospect Street, had saved the Silver Street gang many a time.

With Meg settled at the Charity School, Walter Marsh had spotted an opportunity for Samuel at the boatyard. He knew that the owner had no son to take over from him and he hoped Samuel might progress to managing the yard. Samuel, though, had had other ideas. He hung around the smugglers' gangs in the inns of the town, accepted by them because he was Walter Marsh's son. Yet, in appearance and temperament, they could hardly have been more different. Samuel was slight, and his attempts to grow a beard like his father's were doomed to failure. His fine fair hair produced patchy wisps on his chin, not the luxuriant growth he longed for, and although he talked up his bravery and prowess at sea, he was never included in the gangs' runs to meet French ships. Disappointed, his visits to the inns became even more frequent, and if his father hadn't hauled him out of bed in the mornings, he would have lost his job at the boatyard long before he actually did.

It was Meg who had found her father early one morning, more than a year earlier, slumped over the kitchen table, the loaves of bread neatly shaped and ready for the oven. She'd thought him asleep at first and laughingly shaken his shoulder. But although he felt warm beneath her hand, he didn't stir, and when she bent to look at him more closely, his eyes were open, unseeing, and his soul had fled. Her terrible cries brought the whole family running, in their nightclothes and still half asleep. Meg wondered ever after whether she could have saved him if she had risen just fifteen minutes earlier.

The pain of that discovery haunted her and the consequences were making themselves known still. Samuel, without his father to insist he got up in the mornings, had lost his job at the boatyard. His efforts to find more work were hampered by his lack of enthusiasm. Esther Marsh tried to continue with the baking, but bread-making proved beyond her. She couldn't adapt to waking at such an early hour and hardly had the strength to knead the dough. As a result, her efforts were rushed, the dough barely risen and the bread often burnt. Her customers drifted away to the bakeries along Beach Street, taking with them their custom for the buns once bought as a treat for the family when they had a farthing or two to spare. Meg had to leave off her education and find work, first trying her hand in the local laundry until she was glad to accept the irregular hours offered by Mrs Dunn at the Fountain.

The landlady saw how the family were struggling and, in the early days after Walter Marsh's death, she would send a dish of stew round for them. To avoid them feeling they were living off charity, it would be accompanied by a tactfully worded message, such as 'Just scrag end, but I didn't want it to go to waste.'

Mrs Marsh seemed bewildered by her husband's death and had lost the spark that had once made her a feisty partner to him. Widowhood had diminished her and she had abandoned the reins of the household. Of late, Meg had more than once caught herself wishing that her mother had just a fraction of Mrs Dunn's forthright manner.

CHAPTER FIVE

While the buns baked in the oven and the warm aroma of cinnamon filled the kitchen, Meg sat down at the table, still strewn with flour and scraps of pastry, and indulged herself in imagining how she might grow her trade in run goods. Michael Bailey had let her take an oar in the smugglers' galley on one of their runs, knowing that she had rowed frequently with her father from an early age and had more skill and strength than her brother. Philippe, the Frenchman they dealt with, had given her a glimpse of the more expensive fine fabrics and fancy goods he had and she had longed to be able to buy them. The silks and shawls were from India, he said, and she reached out to stroke the velvet and brocades, the likes of which she had never seen in Castle Bay.

She couldn't afford them then, and there was no local demand for them, but the London trade would be a different matter. The greedy look in Ralph Carter's eyes had told her that the ladies in the city would have an appetite for such things. If she bought and sold enough of the more regular items – ribbons and lace, muslin and cambric – she would be able to afford the purchases of the more exotic shawls and embroidered slippers, feathers and fine fabrics. And, eventually, maybe, a bolt of the beautiful silk in colours richer than her dreams. Then, if all went well, in five years' time, or perhaps less, she could have a shop of her own in London. She imagined it to be very like the shop in Prospect Street, but with sparkling glass in the narrow bow window rather than salt-streaked cracked panes. Instead of a sad display of dusty currant buns, it would be draped with cloth in rich reds and ochres, cream Indian silk painted with beautiful fruits and flowers, and fringed shawls sporting bold paisley designs, while the finest kid gloves, beaded bags and embroidered slippers peeped out among all the glorious fabrics. Her heart beat faster at the very thought.

Instead of sleeping in her cramped attic bedroom, where the wind rattled the window in the winter, bringing with it the sound of the crashing waves on the shingle shoreline, she would have a room just above the shop. It would look onto the street, where horse-drawn carriages would deposit fine ladies at her door, and she would retreat there at the end of the day to light the fire, recline on her brass bed and ... Meg's imagination failed her. She couldn't envisage how a successful shop owner might live, or furnish her rooms, or what she might eat. All she knew was that she saw herself alone in this rather hazy picture.

A husband didn't feature in Meg's plans for the future – for the immediate future, at any rate. She was only seventeen, after all, and there was plenty of time for that. Joseph Huggett, though, had made plain his attraction to her. He was at least five years older and a fisherman: as hazardous an occupation in its own way as smuggling. His earnings were dependent on his catch, which in turn was hostage to the weather and the tides. And even a good catch was worthless if the market was only interested in herring and the boat came home loaded with mackerel.

The smugglers and the fishermen had an uneasy tolerance of each other, threatened only once, a long time before Meg was born, when her father was a boy. He'd told her how the Lord Warden, who was responsible for the safety of the coast and the ports along that stretch, became furious at the amount of smuggling going on and the lost revenue associated with it. He'd ordered all the boats on Castle Bay beach to be burnt, employing the revenue men to carry out his orders. It was an indiscriminate burning: the fishermen's luggers were torched alongside the galleys the smugglers used. Just a few boats still out at sea escaped the inferno.

The only people to profit from this were the local boat-builders; they couldn't build new boats fast enough to satisfy the need. The smugglers, though, had money to spare – or they knew where to find it – and their willingness to pay more put them to the front of the line. The fishermen, who lived a much more hand-to-mouth existence, were reduced to trying their hand with nets off the beach. Even when they could finally procure a boat, they were forced to take out loans that reduced their income for years.

Then, just the previous year, the government had once more taken action – this time against the smugglers alone. They had seized the galleys – or at least the ones they could find: word of their intentions had got out and those who could muster the required number of men to handle the oars had put to sea. There they had waited, far enough out to be nearly invisible on the horizon, but close enough to see the signals that told them it was safe to return. This act by the government had damaged the large, organised smuggling operations, but left room for the small local gangs to operate. It was here that Meg saw the chance to make her profit. And although Joseph was undoubtedly the most appealing of the regulars at the Fountain, she reasoned that as a fisherman he wouldn't provide her with the sort of future she was looking for.

She wasn't entirely sure what that might be. Making a connection with the London trader had given her a glimpse of possibilities that lay far beyond her little patch of the Kent coast. Her father's death had taught her an important lesson. Money was vital if you were going to be able to pay the rent, put food on the table, fuel on the fire and clothes on your back. After the months she had spent increasingly taking charge of running the household, Meg vowed to herself they would never go short again.

Joseph Huggett might be the possessor of wavy brown hair and dancing blue eyes, slender fingers and strong hands, but his position was as precarious as the Marsh family's had been over the recent years. Six months ago, he had given her a necklace made from a shell caught up in his fishing net, a wink of mother-of-pearl threaded onto a leather bootlace. Hidden in the dark shadows at the back of the Fountain, he'd waited for her to finish work. He'd pressed it into her hand with a kiss on the cheek and his breath in her ear as he'd murmured, 'Wear this for me and make me happy.'

She'd blushed furiously, glad he couldn't see in the dark, and hadn't known how to reply. He didn't seem to mind, just strode away, whistling. Perversely, she'd made a point of wearing it only when she wasn't working at the Fountain, when she knew he couldn't see it. Early on in her time serving behind the bar she'd learnt to wear her demurest clothes: blouses buttoned to the collar, sleeves down to the wrist, plain colours. Even so, she'd caught him checking to see whether he could spot the tell-tale outline of the necklace beneath her clothing, and his quick flash of disappointment as he turned away.

She wondered what he would have thought if he knew she always wore it to bed: she liked the way the smooth shell nestled against her skin. As she drifted into sleep each night, she would turn its warm contours between her fingers, trying to imagine where it had come from before it had made its way to Joseph and then to her.

CHAPTER SIX

The aroma from the oven aroused Meg from her daydreams. The pleasing scent of baking dough and warm spices had been replaced by the acrid one of burning currants. She leapt to her feet, sending her chair crashing back onto the stone flags, and grabbed a cloth as she wrenched open the oven door. The trays burnt her fingers through the cloth but she held on grimly until she had deposited them on the still uncleared table.

'You're a fool, Meg Marsh,' she scolded herself, surveying the burnt offerings. The ones that had been on the top shelf of the oven were beyond saving but, if she picked off the charred currants, most of the second tray could be salvaged. She set them aside to cool, scraping the burnt ones into the pig pail, and began to clean the flour and pastry scraps from the table.

No more daydreaming, she decided. She would make the seed cake next, then think about preparing a meal for the family. Her mother would no doubt wander home shortly, and Thomas would return from whatever he was up to when he realised he was hungry. A rapping at the front door startled her. She'd bolted it on her return from shopping but if a family member found it barred against them, they would simply come to the back entrance. Who could it be?

Wiping her hands on her apron, she went along the hall and stood on tiptoe to wrestle with the heavy bolt. 'Who is it?' she called, but receiving no answer, she pulled open the door to find a man standing there, huddled in a greatcoat. She couldn't make out his features in the afternoon's gathering gloom.

'Can I help you?' she asked. She caught a glimpse of a uniform under the heavy coat; he must be one of the soldiers from the barracks.

'I'm glad to find someone in,' the man said, in an accent that reminded Meg of her London acquaintance from that morning. He glanced to the side, to the darkened window of the shop. 'Although it appears you aren't open.'

Meg didn't recognise him as one of their previous customers – not that they had many, these days. 'Did you want to buy something?' she ventured. 'The shop will be open again tomorrow.'

'The captain sent me out in search of Chelsea buns. He won't be pleased if I return empty-handed. I've been all over town – such as it is. I was told yours was the only place to sell the type of thing I'm looking for.'

Meg looked at him blankly. Whatever was he talking about?

'Rolls of pastry, studded with currants, and a kind of sweet paste filling,' the soldier added helpfully.

'Currant buns!' Meg exclaimed. 'Why, yes, I've just baked some. They were to stock the shop tomorrow but I could sell you some. How many?'

'A dozen,' the soldier said.

Meg was taken aback. 'A dozen?' she repeated. They normally sold in ones and twos. Did she have enough to sell? Her thoughts strayed to the burnt ones in the pig pail, before she dismissed the idea.

'You'd better come in,' she said. 'No point letting in the cold.'

The soldier nodded, scraping his boots on the doormat before he followed her down the passage. He sniffed appreciatively as he stepped into the kitchen.

'Something smells good,' he said.

'It's the buns you've come in search of,' Meg said, nodding towards the rack where they cooled. She scanned them: only ten had survived. 'I'm afraid that's all I have until tomorrow,' she said. 'Will that do?'

'It'll have to,' said the soldier. 'I daresay the captain will send for more if they meet with his approval.'

He looked young, Meg thought, as she fetched a roll of paper to wrap the buns, perhaps younger than her own seventeen years. 'What did you call them?' she asked.

'Chelsea buns,' the soldier replied. 'We were stationed in London before we came here, by the river, not far from Horse Ferry. Plenty of shops sold them around there,' he added, seeing Meg's puzzlement.

'Well, I hope he finds them to his liking,' Meg said, tying the package with string. 'I can send some more over with our boy tomorrow, if you like,' she offered, thinking to employ Thomas. 'Save you the journey.'

She offered him the package with one hand and held out the palm of the other. It was the soldier's turn to look blank.

'Payment? For the buns?' Meg prompted.

'Oh, I don't have money. I thought you'd have an account with the barracks.' The boy looked surprised.

Meg hesitated. She couldn't pass up the business, even if it was a risk. She handed over the package. 'I don't, but take it, and I'll make sure we do. And I'll send more tomorrow,' she said, determined to press home her advantage. 'A dozen?' she asked.

The soldier shrugged. 'Why not?' he said.

Meg showed him out, remembering at the last minute to ask him the name of his captain. She regretted not having a spare currant bun to give him, so that he could recommend the shop to the other soldiers in the barracks. She watched him go, shoulders hunched against the wind funnelling up Prospect Street from the seafront, until he vanished into the darkness as he turned the corner.

Would it cause trouble for her to be doing business with the soldiers? After all, they had burnt all the smuggling galleys and were always on the lookout for run goods. Although, from what she heard, quite a few barrels of rum and brandy made their way up to the officers at the barracks in return for their silence. She would have to tread carefully, she thought. Fired up by the prospect of business with the barracks, she carried on baking for the rest of the afternoon. She made two dozen currant buns – this time keeping a watchful eye on them as they baked – as well as a seed cake and a pound cake. The bag of flour she had bought that morning at the mill had come in very useful.

She had spoilt her own appetite by cleaning out baking bowls and eating currants while she worked. When Thomas came in, she gave him a bun that had come out smaller than the rest and he huddled by the range, eating it while he tried to warm up after a day spent outdoors. He needed some decent food inside him, she thought, seeing how his clothes hung off him, his knobbly wrists exposed by the frayed cuffs of his jacket sleeves. Eliza and Samuel had arrived in the kitchen too, reaching for the newly baked buns until Meg scolded them.

'You can't have those – I need them in the shop tomorrow.' She could smell the drink on Samuel's breath and she thought Eliza had been keeping him company at the inn. It was a situation that had become all too common over the last few weeks.

She put Eliza to work scrubbing and peeling whatever vegetables she could find in the larder and sent Samuel out into the yard to bring in more wood for the range. With them both occupied, Meg beckoned Thomas and extracted the few remaining coins from her pocket.

'I want you to go the pie shop and get a couple of pies – three if Mr Nash is feeling generous.' The pie-shop owner had been good to them in the past, letting them have pies with a burnt or broken crust at half price or less. 'Don't loiter,' she added, for it was a bitter evening. 'Run both ways. And bang on Mrs Millgate's door on the way back. If Ma is there, fetch her home to eat.'

Meg sighed as Thomas set off on his errand. Was she to manage everyone, as well as be the breadwinner? Thankfully, she hadn't been called to the Fountain that evening, but she'd have to organise the shop first thing in the morning. It needed a good clean. Then her mother and Eliza must be persuaded to take turns to keep it open through the day. She would restock with sugar and currants, then bake again. Thomas would have to be given instructions to make the delivery to the barracks before he tried to escape for the day. And she should go down there herself in the afternoon to set up an account. She'd need to find time to see Michael Bailey to discover when the next shipment of goods from France was expected. She had to fulfil her promise to Ralph Carter and, if everything sold well in London, she would need more stock to offer him.

Her head whirled at the thought of everything she must do, yet she was excited rather than daunted. The events of this one day – her meeting in the morning with Mr Carter and the soldier's appearance at the door that afternoon – might be the start of a change in fortunes for her family, and for herself. There would be even more to record in her diary that night.

CHAPTER SEVEN

The next morning found Meg in the kitchen long before anyone was up, while darkness still reigned outside. She had done another batch of baking – biscuits this time – and was heating the water to give the shop a thorough scrubbing. She was wondering when her mother and Eliza might make an appearance, until the creak of floorboards above her head told her that someone was up and about. Instead of the hoped-for help in the shop, though, it was Thomas who poked his head around the door.

'You've been baking again,' he said. 'It smells good.'

Meg set a plate on the table for him, cut a slice of bread and spread it with butter, then added a still-warm biscuit. 'I need you to do a job for me this morning,' she said, adding, 'It's important,' when he made a face. 'I want you to deliver a parcel to the barracks. It might become a regular delivery, so I want you to be on your best behaviour. I have to go down there myself later and I don't want to hear you've given them any cheek.'

She looked him up and down, checking whether he was presentable, and came to a realisation. 'You've outgrown your clothes, Thomas. Your jacket's too short in the sleeves and those trousers can't take another patch.'

Some of the money she'd planned to use for ingredients and more run goods would have to be spent on clothes for Thomas. She couldn't afford new – they would have to come from Mrs

Voss, who sold second-hand items at the back of her hosiery shop in Lower Street. If she was able to get him a place at the Charity School, she'd prefer him to go there looking presentable, not as though they didn't have two farthings to rub together, even if the latter were true.

She wouldn't mention the school just yet to Thomas, she decided. He'd kick up a fuss, and there was no point unless she was able to get him a place. Instead, she put another biscuit on the table in front of him, then gave him his instructions for the delivery to the barracks.

'Go the guard room,' she said. 'It's on your right as soon as you walk through the big gate. Tell the soldier on duty that you have a delivery from the Prospect Street Bun Shop for Captain Clements.'

Thomas looked puzzled. 'From where?'

'The Prospect Street Bun Shop,' Meg repeated, waving her hand in the direction of the front room. The shop had never had a name, other than maybe Walter Marsh's bakery. If currant buns were to be what they were known for in the town, Meg thought the new name was as good as any. She'd alighted on it during the night, when her restless brain had kept her from sleep.

'Now, repeat where you're going, who the delivery is for and where it's from,' Meg said, seeing Thomas's plate was empty. Satisfied he knew what he was doing, she handed him the package of currant buns, into which she had tucked a couple of biscuits as an afterthought. It wouldn't hurt to let Captain Clements see they could provide other things as well as Chelsea buns.

'Come straight back here when you've done it and I might have something for you,' she said. 'But if you go gallivanting all over town, I won't.' She ruffled his hair and sent him off through the front door, then called up the stairs, 'Eliza! Ma! Time to get up. I've got jobs for you today.'

She'd warned them both the previous evening – neither had

seemed enthusiastic. She would need to impress on them the importance of money coming into the house, not least for Thomas's clothes. Once the shop was clean, she'd go to the barracks and set up an account, and on the way back she would call to see Mr Wreakes about a place for Thomas at the Charity School. Then it only remained to find some employment for Samuel.

Meg bit her lip. It was hard to imagine what that might be. It would be unwise for him to seek a job in the brewery, the only other place in town, apart from the boatyard, that employed a good number of men. She could ask Joseph whether Samuel could help on his fishing boat, she supposed, but it hardly seemed fair when he'd probably take him on just to please her. It was a problem she needed to ponder further, but he couldn't be allowed to be a drain on their resources for much longer.

It was well into the afternoon before Meg found time to make her visit to the barracks, Thomas having long returned and received a shiny farthing for his work. Her mother and Eliza had done a good job in the shop, surprising Meg by working well together. With the windows cleaned, the buns, biscuits and cake displayed on their best blue-and-white china, she'd been delighted that they had attracted some passing trade.

The sun was dropping to the west as she walked towards the barracks, the pale blue of the sky promising a clear, cold night ahead. There'd be no meeting with the French boats tonight, Meg thought, not until the moon was on the wane. She'd be working at the Fountain later that evening: a chance to have a word with Michael Bailey about getting hold of some different goods – a length or two of chintz and a pair of embroidered slippers, perhaps.

The imposing gates of the barracks were before her, set into a brick wall at least twice her height. She'd passed that way many a time but never had cause to enter. Now she felt anxious, wondering how to make her presence known. Was there a bell pull, or should she just call? As she hesitated, a soldier stepped from the building and came up to the gate, looking her up and down. Meg was suddenly conscious of how shabby she must appear: she had been wearing an apron while she was baking but her skirt was still smudged and dusted with flour; the sleeves of her blouse, poking out from beneath her woollen shawl, were none too clean; her boots were worn and scuffed. She shook out the folds of her shawl to afford as much cover as possible and spoke up, hoping she sounded more confident than she felt.

'I'd like to set up an account with the barracks.'

'Would you now? What would that be for, then?' The soldier leered as he spoke.

A blush rose to Meg's cheeks. She knew perfectly well what he was insinuating and she wanted to put him in his place, but she couldn't risk being turned away. 'Captain Clements has ordered currant buns from my shop. He has received two orders and I need to be paid what's owed to me.'

'Currant buns, you say?' The man was sneering now, and called back over his shoulder to the building, where the lamps had been lit against the rapid onset of dusk. Meg heard laughter from within. Had she been misled? Had she lost the money for the buns she'd supplied? Her spirits plummeted. She'd imagined the barracks becoming a valued customer, but if she couldn't even get beyond the gates, how would that be achieved? How had Thomas managed that morning? He hadn't mentioned any difficulty.

The soldier was unlocking the gate now and beckoning her through – but Meg still felt anxious. The light was fading rapidly, the sun having fallen behind the large buildings, and the path ahead was gloomy.

'Well, are you coming in or not?' The soldier sounded impatient. She hesitated, not sure whether he could be trusted or whether it was better to turn around and leave.

Chapter Eight

'Is there a problem?'

Meg gave a start. A man had come up beside her, without her being aware of it. He was wrapped in a dark cloak, a hat pulled low on his brow. His voice marked him out as not from those parts. A cultured voice, she thought, even more so than Ralph Carter's.

The soldier clearly knew the man. His stance changed immediately: he pulled his shoulders back and used a politer tone than he'd afforded Meg, as he said, 'This woman is saying something about being paid for a delivery of buns. Currant buns, she says.' He couldn't help himself, the sneer had returned for his last words, and Meg heard another splutter of laughter from the guard room.

'Then she needs to see Warrant Officer Perkins. Send word at once. I'm here to pay my father a visit. I take it he's with the major?'

'Yes, sir.'

The soldier turned to Meg. 'You'd better wait in the guard room. I'll send word to Warrant Officer Perkins.'

The man had taken a few strides into the grounds of the barracks when he appeared to have second thoughts and turned. 'You might as well come with me. I'll be passing his office.'

'Thank you, sir.' Meg was relieved. She didn't want to spend another minute in the company of the soldier: she feared his insolent manner would return the minute her saviour was out of earshot.

The man glanced at her as they walked along. 'Have I seen you somewhere before?' he asked.

'I don't think so, sir. Unless you're in the habit of visiting the Fountain inn, which I think is unlikely.' Meg gave a nervous laugh, hoping he wouldn't think her foolish.

'You have a shop, you said? A bakery?'

'Yes, sir, in Prospect Street. Captain Clements has a fondness for Chelsea buns and heard we sold something similar. He's had near enough two dozen now and I'd like to set up an account.'

'As indeed you should.'

Meg thought the man sounded amused but her sideways glance revealed nothing – the brim of his hat obscured his expression.

'Well, here you are – you'll find the warrant officer inside.' They had come to a halt outside a panelled wooden door, with a lamp burning in the sconce beside it. It bathed Meg in light but cast her escort in shadow – she still had no idea what he looked like.

'Thank you for your help, sir,' Meg said, lifting the heavy brass knocker and letting it fall.

'Bartholomew Banks,' the man said, giving her a half bow. 'I'm sure we'll meet again.' He strode away without asking for her name, and Meg turned at the sound of the door opening. She explained her business to the young soldier who stood there and was ushered into a small room, warmed by a fire burning in the grate, where a man sat behind the largest desk she had ever seen. Documents lined the shelves on the walls and covered the surface of the desk, some in neat stacks tied with red ribbon. A lamp burnt at the man's elbow and several others were set around the room. Meg felt exposed by the brightness.

'What can I do for you?' the man asked. She supposed this must be Warrant Officer Perkins.

Meg explained her business once more.

'And how did you get in? Beyond the gate, I mean.' The

man frowned. 'I'd have expected a message. I'm a busy man, as you can see.'

'A gentleman escorted me. A Mr Bartholomew Banks. I had a bit of difficulty at the gate.'

'Bartholomew Banks, eh?' The man's eyebrows shot up. 'Well, let's see about getting this account set up and then you can be on your way.'

He pulled a ledger towards him, asked Meg the name of her business and her own name, and used a fine quill pen to scratch it onto a new page. She told him what had been supplied, and the cost, and he opened a drawer beside him and counted out some coins.

'Next time, you must send in an account with any goods that are delivered.'

Meg's expression must have given away her uncertainty, for he continued, 'Write down what has been supplied, and the cost of it. This account must be handed in to the guard room at the gate with the package.' Warrant Officer Perkins gave her a thoughtful look. 'You can write, can you?'

'Yes, sir.' Meg was indignant. 'I was schooled at the Charity.'

'Good, good.' Warrant Officer Perkins had returned to his papers. 'Ask the soldier on the door to escort you to the gate. Can't have a young woman wandering around here after dark.'

'Excuse me, sir, but how will I be paid in the future?'

'You must apply here every month.'

He waved her away and Meg knew she was dismissed. She already felt foolish – the procedures at the barracks were so much more formal than she had anticipated. She would have to get a book, she decided, to write down for herself what had been supplied to the barracks, and when payment had been received. She crossed her fingers as she followed the young soldier to the gate. She hoped there would be more orders to fulfil.

Meg decided to walk home past the Charity School to see whether the master, Mr Wreakes, was still there. Away from the high walls and tall buildings of the barracks it wasn't quite so dark and she felt safe enough back on the familiar streets. A lamp was burning inside the schoolroom on Lower Street and she found the master studying a book.

'Margaret Marsh!' he exclaimed, as soon as he noticed her. 'How are you? I've seen you out in the town since you left here, but never had chance to speak to you. I've often wondered about you.' His face clouded. 'I was very sorry when I heard about your father. And sorry to lose you from our classes. I'd hoped you might stay on as an assistant.'

His words raised a sudden wistfulness in Meg's breast. She hadn't known that Mr Wreakes had thought so highly of her, although she'd been one of the top pupils when she'd had to leave. How different might her life have been if she'd been able to stay on as an assistant? She batted the thought away: she was set on a different path now.

'I'm well, thank you, Mr Wreakes. I'm trying to build up my father's business – you'll remember he was a baker. My mother hasn't been well since my father died and the business has been neglected but I hope we've turned a corner now.'

She felt proud of herself as she spoke and Mr Wreakes looked impressed, she thought, as he nodded along to her words.

'I heard about your mother. A sad business,' he said.

There was a pause, and Meg looked around the schoolroom with its neat rows of benches, charts pinned to the wall, and a big window overlooking St George's churchyard. She remembered how much she had loved to gaze out there when she found the lesson dull, to watch the birds busy in the trees. Bright pupil or not, she'd received regular scoldings from the master for her wandering attention.

'I've come about my nephew, Thomas,' she said, remembering the reason for her visit. 'He's my brother's son and I'm worried that he's running wild during the day. I hope to employ him to deliver goods for the shop but he's seven years old and some proper learning wouldn't go amiss.'

Mr Wreakes frowned, then pulled a ledger on the desk towards him. He opened it and ran his finger down the first page. 'Ordinarily I would have to say no – school has started for the year and the classes are full. But one of the pupils in the morning class is moving away next week so I will have a place. There are others waiting, of course, but if Thomas is as able a student as you were, it would be a pleasure to have him here.'

Meg expressed her delight and thanked Mr Wreakes, all the while hoping that Thomas wouldn't prove a disappointment. She would have a stern word with him about his behaviour, but she smiled and nodded and promised to bring him along the following Monday at eight o'clock sharp.

She hurried home, feeling the day had gone well. She was tired, having been up early to bake, and she still had an evening's work ahead of her at the Fountain, but she felt a little burst of happiness. The aroma from the pie shop filled her nostrils and she fought against the urge to go in and buy pies for dinner for the second night in a row. There was no point in squandering pennies just yet: they would have to get by on whatever was already in the house that evening. Celebrations must wait until all her plans had come to fruition.

CHAPTER NINE

Returning from the Charity School, Meg had been pleased to find everyone at home, with mutton stew bubbling in a pot on the range. Mrs Marsh had had one of her rare bursts of energy and cooked the dinner. Meg declared it delicious as she hurriedly spooned it from a bowl.

'At least sit down,' her mother scolded.

'No time, Ma.' Meg glanced at the kitchen clock. 'I'm due at the Fountain.'

Mrs Marsh frowned. 'Mrs Dunn won't mind if you're a minute or two late.'

'I need to change, Ma. I can't serve behind the bar in the clothes I've worked in all day.' Meg set her bowl in the sink and turned to go upstairs, then remembered to ask about the shop. 'Was all well after I left?'

'Indeed it was.' Her mother looked proud. 'The currant buns and biscuits sold out and there are only a few slices of seed cake left.' She looked expectantly at Meg.

'I suppose I'd better bake again in the morning,' Meg said. She felt bone weary at the thought of another early start after a long evening at the Fountain. 'Well done,' she added hastily, remembering to sound encouraging. 'Where did all our new customers come from?'

'A soldier came from the barracks and took most of the buns

and biscuits, and some of our old customers dropped in and bought one or two things.'

'Did the soldier pay?' Meg asked, alert to a possible problem.

'No,' her mother replied, looking worried. 'I imagined you'd gone to the barracks to set up an account.'

'Well, it's not as straightforward as I thought. We have to send in a bill with every purchase.' Meg was irritated, then brightened. 'But don't worry – I'll just send two next time. The main thing is, they seem to be enjoying what we make.'

She kissed her mother's cheek then made for the stairs, only too aware that a few more minutes had ticked by. 'Perhaps you could bake something this evening,' she called over her shoulder.

'They seem to like your baking better than mine,' she heard her mother reply, as she reached the first landing. Thomas came out of the room he shared with his parents as she passed. She pinched his cheek, but didn't say anything about his schooling. She'd save it until she had more time, she decided, running up the last few stairs to her attic bedroom. She shivered as she pulled off her blouse and skirt, taking her last clean blouse from the press. Laundry would have to be added to her list for the next day. She struggled to do up the tiny buttons, her fingers trembling with the cold, and pulled on a skirt, tucking in the blouse as she ran down the stairs. It was a night for her father's cloak, she thought, taking it from the back of the kitchen door. Thicker than anything she owned, it covered her hair as well as her clothing, important on such a chilly winter's night.

She said a hasty goodbye to the family, now gathered around the kitchen table, then let herself out of the house and ran down the road. Her head was spinning with the next day's tasks as she pushed open the door of the inn. A warm fug and a buzz of conversation greeted her and she set a smile on her face as she went behind the bar to hang up her cloak.

'Sorry I'm late, Mrs Dunn,' she said, preparing to serve a

customer at once. She glanced at the clock as she did so. Fifteen minutes late – she'd make a point of working hard all evening. She couldn't afford to lose this job, at least not yet, and it was a good place to deal with her own private business, too. She caught sight of Michael Bailey by the fireplace – she'd need to speak to him about the arrival of the next lot of run goods before the evening was out. And Joseph was there, talking to his father, William. She'd tell him about her small successes with the shop, she thought. But not about Ralph Carter. That would be her secret for now.

Clearing glasses and tankards from empty tables gave her the chance to speak to Michael Bailey. 'Another clear night,' she said, glancing through the window at the moon, which hung high above the town. 'Will you be "out Downs" soon?' She spoke half in code, although there was little need in the Fountain. There were only locals present that evening and most were linked to smuggling in one way or another. 'Out Downs' referred to being in the protected waters that lay in the lee of the sand bar running across Castle Bay, an ever-present danger to the unwary.

'Tomorrow, I'm thinking,' he replied. 'Is there something special you're after?'

'Philippe already knows the sort of things I want. But if he could let me have some things on credit, I could pay him on the next run.' Meg kept her voice low as she listed the lengths of chintz and the embroidered slippers she had set her heart on.

Michael nodded. 'You're a better judge of such things than me but we can rely on Philippe, I think. You'll come next time?'

Meg was firm. 'I will. Tell him I hope to be wanting even more fine things then.'

Michael gave her a sharp look. 'Found a bit of business, have you?'

Meg shrugged. 'It's early days, but maybe. And don't worry – I'll make it worth your while.'

'I know you will. You're a good girl – honest.' Michael shook his head. 'More than I can say about some in here tonight. And you've an eye for what will sell – all that fancy cloth is wasted on us. Philippe knows he can't pull any tricks on you – not with you speaking his language.'

Meg saw Mrs Dunn glancing her way from the bar and began to move away. 'Don't forget the extras, will you?'

'I won't, Meg Marsh. And if Philippe won't do it, I'll pay for them myself,' Michael said comfortably.

Meg gave him her best smile. Michael had been a good friend of her father – they'd crewed the same galley for many a year. It didn't do, though, to be too obvious about conducting business under Mrs Dunn's nose. She saw what went on, but preferred not to know too much about it, in case the revenue men began asking questions.

Joseph was moving towards her but she shook her head slightly, to ward him off, then hurried back to the bar. He followed her anyway, plonking his empty tankard down in front of her.

'What must I do to talk to you?' he asked.

Meg smiled. She looked into his blue eyes, his dark brows pulled down into a frown. 'You just have to come up to the bar and spend money,' she said, as she served him his drink. Then she relented and, glancing over her shoulder to make sure the landlady was otherwise occupied, she said, 'I'm trying to keep on the right side of Mrs Dunn. I was late to work and then she spotted me with Michael Bailey. If you're still here when I've finished for the evening, we can talk then.'

Suddenly, she desperately wanted to share some of the details of what she had achieved with someone outside her family, someone who might say, 'Well done, Meg.' And in return, she might just be ready for another kiss.

Chapter Ten

By the time Meg had wiped down the bar and washed and dried the tankards, Joseph was yawning by the fire, now reduced to a few glowing embers.

Mrs Dunn had retreated to her parlour, telling Meg to call through when she had finished so that she could lock up. The landlady wouldn't have liked to see anyone waiting for Meg so she held a finger to her lips as she pushed Joseph out of the door in front of her, calling, 'Goodnight,' as she followed. The cold air made her gasp and she drew her father's cloak more tightly around her.

'Let's walk,' said Joseph, putting his arm through hers.

Meg glanced around, but it was late and most of the town was abed, with barely a light to be seen in any window. The moon, though, cast its hard white light and the stars glittered in the frosty sky. She and Joseph wandered a little way along Beach Street, then struck off across the shingle towards the sea. It looked black in the darkness, just a faint sparkle on the surface where the moonlight caught the gentle swell as the waves broke on the pebbles.

Meg realised that the stones weren't slipping and sliding with every step as they normally did. 'The shingle has frozen!' she exclaimed. This confirmation of the cold set her shivering all over again. They came to a halt by a boat – *Early Dawn*, the one belonging to Joseph and his father. Joseph drew her into his arms and she turned her face up to his, all at once eager for his warm lips on hers.

It was only the second time they had kissed and it was different this time – longer and deeper. Afterwards, he held her close and she told him about the shop: how they'd had unexpected business from the barracks and she'd had to go there to set up an account. She described the cleaning and the baking and her decision on a name: 'The Prospect Street Bun Shop'.

Joseph was quiet for a moment or two when she had finished, then said, 'You've done well, Meg. I hope your ma and your sister-in-law worked as hard. It can't have been easy for you, having to go to the barracks.'

Encouraged, Meg added, 'And on the way home, I went to the school and I've got a place for Thomas. Mr Wreakes said he can start on Monday, but I haven't told him yet.'

'And then you spent the evening working at the Fountain, and you'll be up before the sun to bake again, I suppose.'

'You'll be up before the sun to take the boat out,' Meg pointed out, suddenly defensive.

'That's different,' Joseph said.

'How is it different?' Meg's soft, yielding mood was ebbing away.

'It's my only job,' Joseph replied. 'But it's not just that. You've got others in your house who could do more to help.'

'Samuel, you mean.' Meg was deflated. He was right. 'I did think of asking whether you might take him on. But I didn't want to turn my problem into yours instead.'

Joseph didn't answer and Meg waited. Had she spoken out of turn?

Finally, he sighed and said, 'I'll think about it, Meg. I'd like to help you. But if he couldn't get up in time for the boatyard, how will he cope with an even earlier start? It's a hard life, you know. And my father and I, we barely make enough between us as it is.'

'I'm sorry, I shouldn't have mentioned it.' Meg was contrite. Her words hung momentarily as white clouds in the bitter air and, by unspoken agreement, they turned back up the beach, Meg rubbing her arms to encourage some warmth back into her body.

Once they reached the road, Joseph turned Meg to face him once more. 'I'm glad you did ask me, Meg. I want to help you. I want you to feel you can rely on me.' He leant forward to kiss her again, but this time Meg wasn't ready to yield to him as before. She was shivering violently and he pulled back, half laughing. 'I'll walk you home. We'd better hurry, before you turn to ice, like the pebbles.'

They hurried along as fast they could, slipping and sliding and taking it in turns to save each other from a tumble, until they stood outside Meg's door.

'Sleep well,' Joseph whispered, tilting her chin up towards him and kissing her lightly on the lips. Then he turned and went back the way they had come. As Meg opened the front door, she heard his feet skid and a curse rang out on the frosty air. She smiled to herself as she climbed the stairs but the sharp chill as she opened her bedroom door changed her mood at once. She paused only to unlace her boots before falling into bed fully clothed. She threw her father's cloak over the top of the covers and carried on shivering until, at last, warmth seeped into the nest she had made and she fell into a deep sleep.

Meg awoke the next day with the sickening realisation that she'd overslept. The sliver of grey light peeping through the gap in the curtains told her she had failed in her intention to start baking before dawn. She threw back the covers, a little surprised to find herself fully clothed, until memories of the previous evening returned. Had Joseph overslept, too? His father would have woken him, she thought, as she smoothed the creases in her skirt before going downstairs.

Her heart skipped a beat at the thought of Joseph – his warm arms around her, his lips on hers. Then she pushed away the thought. Tempting though it was, she must not rely on Joseph to care for her. She would find herself married with children by the time she was twenty if she did. Instead, she must hold on to her dreams of a shop in London, and creating a successful business for her family in Castle Bay. With determination, Meg threw herself into stoking the range and making ready to bake. She would not allow herself to be turned away from the plans she had made since she had met Ralph Carter. It wasn't fair on Joseph – it would be wrong to encourage him, to give him hope. She would have to let him go.

Chapter Eleven

Later that afternoon, with her mother and Eliza in charge of the shop, Meg went outside to get some air. The icy early-morning temperature in the kitchen had given way to an overly warm mix of spices and sugar and Meg felt she would stifle if she didn't get away from it. Stepping outside, she discovered that the temperature had risen by several degrees and the grey skies she'd glimpsed earlier that morning were now leaden and heavy with rain. The first drops were spattering on the road as she threw the cloak hood up and over her hair. The folds fell down across her brow, temporarily blindfolding her and causing her to stumble into someone who hadn't been in her path a moment before.

'Oh, excuse me,' she said, lifting the hood to find herself face to face with a tall, well-dressed young man.

'The girl from the bakery,' he said, seeming amused. He glanced back along the street. 'This is Prospect Street, so that leads me to believe your shop is somewhere along here.'

Meg was momentarily bewildered by his words, but she recognised the cultured tones in which they were uttered. It was Bartholomew Banks, whom she had encountered at the barracks only the day before. 'Thank you again for your help yesterday, sir. I don't think I would have got past the soldier at the gate without you. The shop's just here – can I offer you a Chelsea bun to take home with you?'

It was forward of her, Meg thought, but it would be foolish to pass up the chance to extend their business. The possible patronage of someone well-to-do couldn't be missed.

Bartholomew laughed. 'Thank you, but I'm well taken care of just now. I am on the way to dine at Throckings Hotel. I stable my horse here when I'm in town.' He gestured to the stable-yard he had just left.

Meg took in barely a word he was saying for she was busy studying his appearance. When he'd helped her the day before, he'd been shrouded in a cloak, his hat pulled low and hiding his face. Now she registered his height, the cut and fine quality of his breeches and jacket, the lustrous silk of his cravat and, above all, the careless tumble of his golden curls and the blue of his eyes. They were paler than Joseph's but in every other respect Bartholomew Banks was most decidedly a fine figure of a man. And he was as busy examining her as she was him.

'I don't believe we were properly introduced yesterday,' he said. 'I know you have a shop, and you are supplier of currant buns to Captain Clements.' He leant forward, so close that Meg, startled, drew back. She thought for a moment he meant to kiss her. Instead, he sniffed deeply. 'Hmm. I detect aromas of spice – cinnamon, I think. Am I right? And sugar. Delicious.'

Meg's embarrassment at the thought of baking smells clinging to her hair and clothing turned to mortification as she remembered she had slept in her clothes. She was relieved that her cloak covered the greater part of them.

'And quite the prettiest blush I've ever seen.'

Meg knew she should have excused herself and moved on, but she was rooted to the spot. It was left to Bartholomew to sigh and say, 'I suppose I must go and join my father and his party at Throckings, when I'd far rather spend my time talking to you. But, as we are walking in the same direction, I can enjoy your company for a few moments more.'

Obediently, Meg walked at his side for the few steps it took to reach the end of the street. The hotel lay opposite. She made ready to turn left and bid him farewell.

'Perhaps I'll call in for those currant buns later, after all,' Bartholomew said. He laid his hand on her arm to detain her, causing Meg's heart to beat so rapidly she felt giddy.

'Of course, sir. I'd be delighted. The shop is on the opposite side to the stables, halfway up the street.'

He smiled and let her go but she had taken scarcely five steps before he called after her, 'I still don't know your name, whereas you know mine. It hardly seems fair.'

She turned back, knowing she was blushing again. 'It's Margaret – Meg. Meg Marsh.'

'Well, Margaret Meg. I feel sure I will see you again.'

Meg turned away and hurried along Beach Street, her mind in a whirl. She wasn't sure she wanted him to come to the shop later, and to see how humble it was. She'd been proud of it until then, but now she imagined it seen through his eyes. It wouldn't do at all. But just in case, she must go home, change her clothes and try to look as presentable as she could. Her heart sank as she remembered she had put on her last clean blouse yesterday evening. If she changed into one of her only two good dresses, Ma and Eliza would want to know why. Deep in thought, she hardly heard her name called until it was actually bellowed.

'Meg!'

Her head snapped up and she followed the direction of the call, spotting Joseph and his father by the boat they had just hauled up from the sea. She felt immediately guilty at the direction of her thoughts, and at the reluctance she felt in stepping across the road to go down the shingle to speak to them.

'Was it a good catch?' she asked.

Both men shook their heads.

'Nothing much doing today,' Joseph said grimly. 'Barely worth the effort of going out.' He looked despondent, then made a visible effort. 'Where are you off to?'

'I've been baking all day. I just needed to get out for a breath of fresh air,' Meg said.

'You were deep in thought. Working out your profits?' he teased.

'Far more frivolous than that.' Meg gave him a weak smile.

Joseph was busy securing heavy ropes and thankfully wasn't paying much attention to her words. 'I'll see you later, at the Fountain,' he said. 'If you're working tonight, that is?'

'I'm not sure,' Meg replied. 'Mrs Dunn didn't say. I'd better get back before I get soaked,' she added, for the light rain showed signs of turning into a heavy and determined downpour.

She waved and hurried away. She would go home and make the best of herself, just in case Mr Banks did pay the shop a visit. Had he been more interested in her than she had the right to expect? She tried not to entertain the idea, but it was exciting. The world he lived in was so far removed from her own – why would he pay her any attention?

Joseph's mention of her working at the Fountain that evening threatened to crush her mood. She'd had the briefest glimpse of a different life, one in which the likes of Bartholomew Banks showed interest in her, and she wanted to hold on to that dream for as long as she could.

CHAPTER TWELVE

Meg arrived home with the hem of her skirt soaked and muddy, which gave her the perfect excuse to change into her second-best dress, a white sprigged print on dark-blue cotton. It felt odd to be wearing it to work in the shop. She told herself that when she had her London business she would wear a lovely dress every day.

Her mother and Eliza gazed at her in surprise when she entered. In addition to changing into a dress, she had taken time to tidy her hair, made frizzy by the rain but now tamed under a cap.

'I'll take over in here for a bit,' Meg said. 'Why don't you both go and rest?'

'Why are you dressed up?' her mother asked.

'We don't mind staying here,' Eliza said, at the same time. 'I'm sure you could do with a sit-down. You've been so busy with all the baking.'

'Perhaps you could prepare some dinner,' Meg tried, hoping to get the shop to herself in case Bartholomew Banks did pay a visit.

'I'll do it,' her mother said. 'Mrs Dunn sent word that she'll need you in the Fountain tonight so you'll have to eat before you go. Eliza can stay here with you.' She paused, frowning. 'Have you dressed up to work at the Fountain?'

'No, Ma.' Meg was exasperated. 'I got wet when I was out and I haven't got another clean blouse or skirt. In any case, I thought it might help the business if we all looked a bit smarter when we work in the shop.'

'Folks round here will get it into their heads we're making too much money if we do that,' her mother retorted. 'Don't go putting on airs and graces just because we've got a bit of business from the barracks. They're mostly a rough lot.'

Meg wanted to protest that she had met a very nice gentleman there, but thought better of it. 'Well, it doesn't alter the fact I've got nothing else to wear.'

She turned away and began adjusting the position of the plates of cakes in the window. Her mother tutted and went off to the kitchen, but Eliza stayed. Meg knew she should be pleased that her mother had regained some of her old spark, but she hoped it wouldn't create difficulties with her plans. As for Eliza, Meg was surprised that she had so fully embraced working in the shop. Perhaps she was glad to be spared keeping Samuel company at the inn. She rather suspected she had been doing it in an effort to stop him drinking too much.

'Have you been busy?' Meg asked. She surveyed the window and the table that served as a makeshift counter.

'Quieter than yesterday,' Eliza replied.

The persistent rain made it unlikely they would have much custom now. Meg knew she should suggest they shut up shop. But what if Bartholomew Banks kept his word and came by? How long did a gentleman take to dine? Over an hour had passed since she'd seen him: she suspected it took longer than that. She decided they would remain open for another half an hour: she could talk to Eliza about Samuel and tell her about Thomas's school place.

'Where is Thomas?' she asked. 'And Samuel?'

Eliza shrugged. 'You know what those two are like. They're always out doing something. In Samuel's case, I suspect that involves making foolish plans in the Ship.'

Meg frowned. She peered out of the window, where the rain clouds had made it prematurely dark. They should light the candles – it wasn't worth lighting the lamp if they were going to close the shop. 'Thomas shouldn't be out roaming the streets. I called in to see Mr Wreakes at the Charity School. He has a place for Thomas, starting on Monday,' she said. 'I think it will do him good to have some learning. And if the business grows, he can run errands for us in the afternoon, when school is over.'

Eliza looked doubtful. 'Do we have to pay?'

'Not for his schooling,' Meg said. 'But he's outgrown all his clothes. Can you take him to Mrs Voss tomorrow to see whether she has something to fit him?'

Eliza shrugged. 'She won't let us have anything on credit and I've no money to pay her.'

'It can come out of the takings,' Meg said. 'Just for now. Once we're making some money, you'll have some earnings.'

She wondered privately when that day would come. Her earnings from the Fountain helped to run the shop. Unless they sold everything she'd made by the end of the following day, they would make a loss. They'd have to live off stale currant buns for the week ahead.

'We'll never get Thomas to school,' Eliza said.

'I haven't mentioned it to him,' Meg said. 'I don't think you should either, or he'll be running off somewhere on Monday morning.'

Eliza didn't seem very enthusiastic about the school plan and Meg supposed she should have consulted her before she'd approached Mr Wreakes, but she was single-minded in her determination to improve the family's lot. She was about to raise the subject of work for Samuel when the jangling doorbell announced a customer. Meg's heart began to pound at the sound of heavy footsteps in the hall. She had barely a second to compose herself before Bartholomew Banks was standing in the doorway, stooping a little because of his height. He stepped forward, his gaze sweeping the two women before him.

'You *are* still open, then,' he said. 'I wasn't sure – it looked rather gloomy from outside.'

'Yes, we are,' Meg said, thrusting the lamp into Eliza's hands. 'We were just about to light the lamp. How was your dinner?' she asked, as Eliza hurried away to the kitchen.

'A very dull affair,' Bartholomew said. 'I was pleased to make my escape before dessert – there was too much talk of politics for my taste. But I thought I could come here in search of something sweet.'

Eliza arrived back with the lamp at that moment, closely followed by Mrs Marsh.

'Quite an array of beauties,' Bartholomew said, bestowing smiles on the new arrivals. 'I can see you all clearly now we have some light. You must be Mrs Marsh.' He inclined a half-bow in the direction of Meg's mother. 'I can see the likeness. Although I would swear I could take you for sisters. And you are . . . ?' He looked enquiringly at Eliza, who almost dropped the lamp in her confusion.

Meg took it from her and set it in the window. 'Eliza Marsh, my sister-in-law.'

'Ah, so you have a brother, too. Is he hereabouts?' Bartholomew looked around, as though expecting the imminent appearance of another family member.

'No, he's in the – he's out this afternoon.' There was a pause. Then Meg remembered her manners. 'This is Mr Bartholomew Banks. He was kind enough to help me at the barracks yesterday, and I met him again by chance this afternoon.'

'I make use of the stables at the end of Prospect Street,' Bartholomew explained easily. 'But I had no idea that such a charming establishment as this lay further along it.'

'We've only recently opened properly,' Meg said. She was aware of the expressions on her mother and Eliza's faces: the former tight-lipped, the latter entranced.

'Can I interest you in the currant buns – the favourites of Captain Clements?' she asked. 'Or we have biscuits, and seed cake.'

Bartholomew drew closer as she stepped towards the window to point out the cakes on display.

'Well, I declare I'm unfamiliar with any of them so I had better try them all,' he said.

'Thank you, sir,' Meg said. 'I trust you will enjoy them so much that you return for more.'

'Oh, I'm sure I will,' Bartholomew said. The smile he gave her made a thrill run through her.

Meg sensed her mother was about to speak but before she did, Bartholomew added smoothly, 'After all, my stables are so close and I'm there quite regularly.'

Meg laid paper on the table, ready to wrap his purchases. 'How many would you like?'

'A dozen of each.' Bartholomew pointed to the buns and biscuits. 'And a cake.'

'A whole cake?' Meg could hardly contain her surprise.

Bartholomew shrugged. 'Why not?' He winked. 'I did say I had to leave before dessert.'

Meg made haste to wrap everything – it was the perfect way to conclude their business for the day. It would mean they could pay for Thomas's clothes and still have money to buy the ingredients needed for the following week. Then she was struck by a thought: would he expect to pay on account, like the barracks?

Even as she wondered how to raise the question, Bartholomew was pulling a leather pouch from his jacket pocket. 'How much do I owe you?' he asked.

Meg, who quickly added a little extra, expected him to raise an eyebrow at the price she had quoted, but he was unmoved.

'It's lucky the rain has eased,' he said, glancing out of the window, 'for this package must sit before me on my horse, all the way home.'

'Have you far to go?' Meg asked. She wondered whether she should try to find Thomas and offer to send him along later with the purchases.

'A mile or two,' Bartholomew said. 'Hawksdown Castle.'

He nodded to Mrs Marsh and Eliza, smiled at Meg and departed, leaving Meg to face the two women, who looked ready to spill out their questions before the door had even closed.

CHAPTER THIRTEEN

'Oh, Meg,' said Eliza. Even by lamplight it was apparent that her cheeks were flushed. 'He's charming! And he's taken with you. I can tell.'

'Rather too taken,' Mrs Marsh said tartly. 'You'd do well to watch your step with that young man. He's a sight too forward for my liking.'

'What do you mean, Ma?' Meg frowned.

'All that nonsense about an array of beauties.' Her mother snorted to show her contempt. 'He'll not get round me that way. Don't you let him turn your head with his flattery.'

'Oh, Ma,' Meg was exasperated. 'He's just being polite – charming, as Eliza said. He comes from a different world. I dare say people like him talk in that way all the time.'

'A different world is right,' Mrs Marsh replied. 'A world you don't belong to, so don't go getting ideas above yourself. If he's from the castle, he's something to do with the Lord Warden. His son, maybe. Joseph Huggett is the right sort of man for you, Meg. Steady, with a good head on his shoulders. I've seen for myself how he looks at you. It won't be long before he asks for you, I'm sure of it. Don't go getting foolish notions in the meantime.'

Mrs Marsh retired to the kitchen, leaving Meg feeling ruffled.

Eliza gave her no time to dwell on it, though. 'Bartholomew – I don't believe I've come across that name before. He's very handsome,

Meg. Do you think he'll come back?' She paused a moment. 'Oh, I know he'll come back. I could see the way he was watching you.' She was made girlish by her excitement, as if she herself had been the object of Bartholomew's attentions rather than Meg.

'Well, I hope it will be good for business if he does,' Meg said, wishing to change the subject. Her mind was running on. She would have to find new recipes: three varieties of cake and biscuit simply wouldn't be enough. Perhaps her mother could be persuaded to bake, after all – she could surely suggest some alternatives.

She closed the shop for the day and realised that, once more, she had time only for a hasty dinner before she must leave for work at the Fountain. Mrs Marsh had roasted a scrawny fowl that their neighbour had given them in exchange for the regular donations of pig scraps. Meg cut herself a slice and ate it with bread and pickles, to keep her mother happy. It was an effort to force it down – the encounter with Bartholomew had filled her with nervous excitement and stopped her appetite.

Meg's gown earned her a comment or two in the Fountain.

'Have you come to the wrong place?' a fisherman asked, looking her up and down. 'Did you think you were working next door tonight? At Throckings?' His fellow fishermen laughed obligingly, although Joseph threw Meg a sympathetic glance.

Mrs Dunn gave the man short shrift. 'It's a shame you didn't think to change your own clothes for something more suitable. You've got such a stink of fish about you that the cats are queuing up outside.'

Meg was more provoked than wounded by the fisherman's words. She had never been inside Throckings Hotel – and was sure he hadn't either – but she didn't imagine they would be welcome. It was the place where visitors from out of town stayed, and where the well-to-do townsfolk supped and dined. It irked her that Bartholomew was quite at home there, yet she would likely be denied entry.

When Joseph came to the bar for a refill of his tankard, her mood hadn't much improved.

'Your gown suits you,' Joseph said. 'It makes your eyes more – vivid, somehow.' Colour rose to his cheeks as he spoke.

Meg knew he wasn't much given to compliments but she couldn't stop her tongue. 'I don't know why the men in here think they can make free with their comments about what I choose to wear. I don't offer the same insult to them.'

She made a point of looking Joseph up and down as she spoke, and slammed his refilled tankard down in front of him so that the ale slopped over the side. It was unfair: his intentions were of the best and, unlike his fellow fishermen, he had at least washed since he'd brought his boat in. She noticed he was wearing a different shirt from the previous day.

Joseph paused only to drop a few coins onto the bar, before picking up his ale and walking away without a word. He went to join a group in the far corner of the inn and Meg busied herself behind the bar, studiously avoiding looking in his direction. She supposed she must apologise later for her behaviour but, since Bartholomew's surprise visit to the shop, she felt irritated, as though everyone was bent on annoying her.

Her thoughts were diverted by the arrival of Michael Bailey at the bar. She reached for a tankard to serve him but he shook his head. 'I won't be staying. I just came to tell you that the weather is on our side tonight.' He gave her a small nod, then turned to survey the room, before walking around, tapping a man here and there on the shoulder and murmuring a few words to them. One by one, the men he had approached brought their empty tankards back to the bar and left, hats pulled low over faces and collars turned up against the squally rain that had returned.

Meg sensed an air of tension among the remaining customers of the inn. The drinking slowed. Other men were waiting for a signal that would be a while yet in coming, but would tell them that they were needed on the beach, or at the entrance to cellars located along the narrow alleys leading away from the seafront. Once the goods that had been shipped from France had landed, they would have to be conducted away quickly and silently under cover of darkness, without alerting the revenue men.

Only one group of men carried on as before: the fishermen, with Joseph Huggett in their midst. It wasn't until much later, when the few customers remaining were mainly elderly men, too frail to be of use in unloading tubs of brandy or chests of tea, Meg saw Joseph had gone too, without a word. He wouldn't be taking part in the unloading or distribution of goods, but he would be planning to take his fishing boat out early in the morning. She was contrite – it was stupid to quarrel with him. It was her mother's fault, she thought, as she counted the coins from the night's takings into piles, while Mrs Dunn chivvied the remaining drinkers to their homes. If Ma hadn't gone on about Joseph Huggett being the right man for her, she might have acted more favourably towards him. As it was, she knew her own character. If she was told to do something, like as not she would take it upon herself to do the exact opposite.

With the takings bagged and given to Mrs Dunn, she let herself out of the inn and onto Beach Street. She half thought Joseph might be waiting for her there, tucked away in the shadows, but the street was empty.

No matter, she thought, as she hurried the short distance home. She had plenty of other things to occupy her mind, and by the time she reached the front door, all thoughts of Joseph had slipped from her mind.

Chapter Fourteen

When Meg awoke the next morning, she felt excited, without knowing why. Then she remembered the boat that had come in the previous evening. She would go and see Michael Bailey to discover what he had for her.

It was an effort to bake the buns and biscuits to restock the shelves but it had to be done, and without making it apparent that she was in a hurry to be away. It was not long after breakfast time when she was able to lay aside her apron, wash her hands and slip out of the back door.

She hurried from the house before her mother or Eliza could waylay her, and walked the short distance to Michael Bailey's shop in Middle Street. He, too, was the owner of a bakery, which gave him the perfect excuse for lights burning in the early hours, and for having frequent visitors throughout the day. Even so, from habit Meg checked the street for signs of revenue men before entering. The February weather had kept most people indoors – in the summer, women would have been chatting outside their open doors while children played along the street. Today, there was no sign of anyone, unfamiliar or otherwise, so she slipped inside the shop and nodded to Michael's son. He had taken over much of the bakery business, leaving his father free to pursue other interests.

'Is your father here?' she asked.

'In the back,' the young man replied, and Meg went through

to the kitchen where Michael was sitting by the range, smoking a pipe and keeping an eye on his grandson as he crawled around the none-too-clean kitchen floor.

'I'm glad to see you, Meg.' Michael pushed himself out of the wooden chair. 'I hope you'll be pleased with what Philippe has sent.' He reached up and pressed a section of the wood panelling beside the dresser. It opened a crack and Michael pulled it back to reveal a narrow cupboard. He extracted a package and handed it over.

Meg felt a rush of excitement and wanted to tear off the wrapping straight away.

'How much do I owe you?' she asked Michael. The sum he named made her bite her lip. It would be covered by the money Ralph Carter had given her, but if she spent it all, she'd have nothing left to buy more. And she would have to wait before she received any further payment from London.

She hesitated, then counted out the coins onto the table.

'Pay me half,' Michael said. 'You can treat the rest as a loan, and give me something each week. It shouldn't take you long to earn the money back.' He paused. 'I see you've opened the bakery again.'

Meg wondered whether he thought the Marsh family meant to offer him competition and hastened to reassure him. 'We're selling cakes, not bread. We don't plan to do so again. My father made the loaves and there are already plenty of good bakers in town, like your son.' She hoped a bit of flattery would help.

Michael nodded and opened the back door for her. 'Go out this way,' he said. 'Fewer prying eyes.'

Meg thanked him and stepped into the yard, leaving behind the warmth of the kitchen and its aroma of freshly baked bread. She moved quickly along the alleyways, coming out on Beach Street for a short stretch before taking the alley that led to the back of her house.

She clicked the latch on the door and stepped in, to find her mother in the kitchen.

'What have you got there, Meg?' Mrs Marsh frowned.

Over the last year, Meg had successfully evaded her mother whenever she had involved herself with run goods. Throughout this period, Mrs Marsh had taken to her bed early in the evening, and seemed disinclined to ask questions if she suspected anything. Meg knew she wouldn't approve of any involvement in what she regarded as a risky business, blaming it for the premature death of her husband. Now that she was revitalised, though, Meg couldn't rely on her continued disinterest.

'It's just a package for Mrs Dunn,' Meg said. 'She asked me to pick up a few bits for her from Mrs Voss. She's short-handed today and can't get to the draper's herself.' The lies tripped off her tongue.

Mrs Marsh looked ready to question her further, but the shop bell jangled and a moment later Eliza called for her.

Meg waited until she could hear her mother's voice in conversation, then slipped up the stairs. Closing her bedroom door behind her, she tore off the wrapping and let the contents of the package tumble onto the bed. A length of that much-coveted hand-painted cream silk, decorated with unfamiliar bright red blooms twining among green foliage. Two pairs of white kid gloves, soft as butter. A fringed paisley shawl, three pairs of satin slippers embroidered with gold thread and several lengths of plain muslin. It was all very fine and of high quality; previously the muslin alone would have been enough to delight Meg, but the beauty of the other items outshone it.

Even as she rejoiced in what Philippe had sent, Meg wondered whether these things, along with the few pieces she already had, would be enough to please Ralph Carter when he received her first delivery. She pulled the other items from their hiding places – behind wall panelling and under floorboards – and looked at everything collected on her bed. She would have liked to press the lengths of fabric, but feared they were too delicate to subject to the heavy flat iron they heated on the range. And, of course, she couldn't risk her mother catching her with such things. She smoothed the fabric lengths as best she could, then folded each piece, making a neat pile, coiling the lace and silk ribbons on top.

Now they sat on her bed, a kaleidoscope of colour to brighten a dull day. She must make a note of the purchases in her diary, before wrapping her first package for London, using paper taken from the shop for the purpose, and securing it with string. As Meg regarded the pile, doubt crept in – would Mr Carter have expected more? Would he be annoyed when he received her account, for she would be charging him more than the money he had given her. Then she scolded herself. This was just a trial. If he liked what he saw, their business would continue.

CHAPTER FIFTEEN

✥

The shop was open and trade was slow but steady by the time Meg left the house on Saturday morning. She had to wear her second-best dress again, but she'd found time to wash her skirts and blouses, scrubbing them with hard soap at the scullery sink. The water had been barely warm enough – she'd been too impatient to allow the big pot to come to a boil on the range. Her clothes now hung over a line strung across the garden, flapping and snapping in the stiff breeze, and her hands were reddened by the harsh soap, and the icy water she'd used for rinsing.

When she had her London shop, Meg thought, her clothes would be made from the kind of fabrics inside Ralph Carter's package, now clutched beneath her cloak. Someone else would launder and mend them, and her hands would be soft and white – just like those of Mrs Wallace, who was a patron of the Charity School.

Such thoughts carried her the short distance to South Street, where she tried to find a spot to shelter from the wind, which whipped straight up the road from the sea. Huddled behind the high wall of the grandest house in the road, the one that belonged to Mrs Wallace, Meg began to wonder how she would know which carriage to approach with her package. Two were waiting at the roadside already, their coachmen in conversation. She decided it couldn't be them, for if a carriage had just arrived from London, the horses would be tended in the yard at the Castle Bay Inn and the men would be inside, taking refreshments by the fire.

The brisk clip-clop of hoofs announced an arrival from the Dover turnpike. It swept around the corner and the coachman reined in the horses, drawing them to a halt outside the inn. The carriage drew Meg's eyes – a painted crest adorned the doors and she could see that the horses, although clearly in a sweat from their journey, were particularly fine.

She waited to see who would step down, but no one did and the coachman remained in his seat. Seeing him glance over the road at her, she stepped across and called up to him, 'Would this be Mr Ralph Carter's carriage?'

'It is not his carriage.' The coachman couldn't disguise his amusement. 'But I am expecting to carry a package for him. Would you be Miss Marsh?'

Meg drew herself upright at his words. 'I am. And this is what you are expecting.'

She withdrew the package from the folds of her cloak and he extended a gloved hand to take it. As she reached upwards, the horses moved impatiently and the carriage wheels advanced a little, causing her to stumble back in fright.

'Tsk, tsk.' The coachman shook the reins and scolded the horses. 'Be patient – you'll get your rub-down soon enough.' Then he took the parcel, which Meg held up to him in a now trembling hand.

'This is all?' There was no judgement in his voice but worry surged in Meg's breast once more.

'Yes, for now. I hope next time there will be more.'

The coachman nodded, then removed a glove and reached inside his greatcoat. He extracted a folded piece of paper, with a red wax seal. 'This is for you, Miss Marsh,' he said, handing it down to her. Then he placed the package on the seat beside him, shook the reins and encouraged the horses to turn into the stable-yard at the inn.

Meg clutched the letter within the folds of her cloak and turned for home. She had taken only a few steps before the sight of Bartholomew astride a chestnut mare, beside the very wall where she had so recently taken shelter, brought her to a halt.

'If it isn't Meg Marsh,' Bartholomew said. 'Undertaking a bit of business with one of the London carriages, I see.' His eyebrows were raised but a smile played around his lips. 'Has word of your currant buns spread to the capital?'

Meg coloured at his teasing. She bit back the retort she was tempted to offer in return. After all, if he was the son of the Lord Warden – the man who was the scourge of the smugglers in the town – she didn't want him suspecting anything of the trade she had just conducted. So she smiled and said, 'Have you come into town to buy cakes, Mr Banks?'

'Bartholomew, please,' he replied. 'I was just on my way to the stables and I was intrigued to see you here, with a package for Mr Ralph Carter, if I'm not mistaken?'

Meg's astonishment must have been clearly written on her face for Bartholomew laughed.

'Mr Carter is well known to the ladies who visit Hawksdown Castle. While their husbands closet themselves with my father in his study, making earnest plans for their political futures, the good ladies seek out whatever can be found by way of silk and lace and have it sent up to town to be collected from the obliging Mr Carter.'

Meg was puzzled. 'Your father – isn't he the Lord Warden? Does he know about this?'

'He doesn't know half of what goes on right under his nose.' Bartholomew smiled. 'I dare say he has no idea how the household comes by the fine French brandy he takes after dinner each evening.'

He turned his horse and began to walk it towards Prospect

Street, keeping Meg company. 'If you have a supplier of all those fancy things that the ladies find so appealing, I could find you a ready market for them among the visitors to the castle.'

Meg didn't trust herself to speak and could only gaze up at him. It was such an unexpected turn of events. Could she trust him?

'Don't worry. I wouldn't say a word to my father.' Bartholomew gave a grim smile. 'It would give me a lot of pleasure to flout his authority. And it might turn out to your advantage. No middleman taking his cut of your earnings.'

With that, Bartholomew tipped his hat to Meg, shook the reins and his horse trotted away down the street, leaving her staring after him while a great many thoughts jostled for prominence in her mind.

CHAPTER SIXTEEN

Meg let herself back into the house with a brief greeting to her mother in the shop, then took herself upstairs before anyone needed her.

In her room she took the letter from the folds of her cloak, hesitating a moment before breaking the wax seal. She scanned the words on the single sheet of paper, then smiled in relief. Ralph Carter had listed the items his customers were looking for, promising full remuneration by return for anything she was able to send him in her next package.

Meg's smile turned to a frown as she realised her outlay on goods would always be in advance of her payment for them. She wasn't sure she could afford to trade in this way. How was she to finance these early requests? Her profits would grow with each delivery, but she already owed money to Michael Bailey and the little she had set aside wouldn't buy much more. Ralph Carter clearly had no idea what it meant to live from hand to mouth; she wished she could speak to him again.

Her thoughts turned to Bartholomew's astonishing suggestion. Could she earn a quicker return by trading with the guests at the castle? Would she do better to abandon Mr Carter and keep her trade local instead? It was a tempting prospect, but her instincts told her the risks of doing such business in the Lord Warden's own residence were too great. It was something to consider for the future, perhaps, but for now she must concentrate on making the best of what she had. And by keeping a link with London through Ralph Carter, she could work towards her idea of establishing her own business there in the years ahead.

She would have to hope that the weather proved favourable enough for more French trade to take place soon, so that she could send another package to London. Ideally, she needed to speak to Philippe herself to describe the sort of things she would be looking to buy in the future. Above all, though, she must find a way to fund her purchases while she waited for payment to come from London.

Meg knew there would be questions if she stayed in her room any longer, so she went downstairs to find Eliza examining the clothes she had bought from Mrs Voss. Choosing not to take Thomas with her in case he learnt of the school plan, she had erred on the generous side with what she had bought.

'Don't you think it might all be a bit big?' Meg asked, surveying the jacket and trousers, which looked as though they would fit a small man rather than a boy.

'We can roll up the sleeves and the hems.' Eliza was confident. 'And hold up the trousers with string if need be.'

Meg was unconvinced, but the need for her to do some baking, and for Eliza to take her turn in the shop, meant the alterations had to be set aside until the following day.

Attending church the next morning offered a break from routine. Mrs Marsh was disposed to linger after the service, to talk to Mrs Millgate, but Meg urged her homewards.

'Thomas must try on his new clothes and it will take both Eliza and me to manage him. Can you get dinner under way, Ma? I'll help as soon as any alterations have been done.'

'New clothes? Whatever for?' Meg and Eliza had kept the news of Thomas's schooling from Mrs Marsh and Samuel, too, in a determined effort to keep Thomas in ignorance.

'Look at him, Ma. He's outgrown everything he owns.'

They both contemplated Thomas, walking ahead of them between Eliza and Samuel, his jacket sleeves too short by a hand span, his trouser hems ragged and frayed.

'It doesn't reflect well on us, Ma,' Meg continued, as her mother grumbled. 'It looks as though we can't afford to look after him properly.'

Mrs Marsh bridled at the idea, and no more was said on the walk home from St George's.

By way of a penny bribe, Eliza persuaded Thomas into the clothes she had purchased. As Meg had guessed, the jacket, trousers and shirts were all too large. There was little point in cutting them down, as Thomas would eventually grow into them. The sleeves of the jacket could be rolled, the trousers held up with the thickest string they could find. The shirts were more of a problem – the sleeves wouldn't stay rolled up in the jacket sleeves. Eliza suggested a tuck of excess fabric just above the elbow of each. Thomas, wriggling and complaining that the jacket and trousers itched, fidgeted from one foot to the other throughout the fitting. He was finally released while Meg and Eliza took their stitching to the kitchen.

'Where is Samuel?' Meg asked, realising she hadn't seen him since church that morning.

'He'll have gone out somewhere.' Eliza was vague, hunting in her workbox for a spare button to sew on one of the shirts.

'Gone where?' Meg couldn't think what would call him away from the house on a Sunday.

Eliza shrugged. 'I don't know. He'll be back to eat.'

Thomas, too, had vanished. At least he would have schooling to curb his wandering, Meg thought. Samuel was a different matter. It was high time he contributed to the household instead of being a drain on it. She had to grit her teeth to control a sudden rush of irritation. She stitched doggedly at the sleeve tuck until the thread knotted and broke as she yanked it through, whereupon she flung the shirt to the floor in a fit of temper.

Her mother and Eliza regarded her with surprise.

'I've always hated sewing,' Meg said, by way of explanation. It was true enough: she'd shown no skill in that area, either at home or at school. The sampler she'd had to stitch in class, to exhibit her skill to potential employers, had been dotted with pinpricks of blood and adorned with wavering lines of uneven stitches. She'd never wanted to be a servant – Meg was headstrong, like her father, and she'd known from an early age that it would never suit. She was lucky that Mr Wreakes had recognised it, too, and encouraged her to develop her reading, writing and mathematical skills.

She sighed and picked up the shirt again, rethreading the needle and stitching on with determination. Eliza had finished two shirts in the time it took Meg to complete one sleeve. Meg, aware that she was being watched, became even clumsier.

'Let me finish it,' Eliza said, holding out her hand. 'Your skill lies in baking. And organising us all.' She smiled at Meg. 'You've inherited your father's talents.'

Meg was happy to relinquish the work and started to lay the table, wondering whether Samuel and Thomas would return in time. It was as though they had smelt the food – mutton stew again – for they arrived separately, but within five minutes of each other.

Meg, busy urging them to wash their hands and sit down to eat before the food grew cold, missed the opportunity to question them about their absence. Instead, half listening to the happy family chatter around the table, she sat back and watched her brother. She and Samuel had inherited their hair colouring from their mother, and their brown eyes from their father. But the similarity stopped there. What went on inside Samuel's head? Meg couldn't begin to guess. He seemed to have no ambition and wasn't at all embarrassed by what she viewed as his fecklessness. She suspected that telling him he must get work would simply make him resist her. He was like her in that respect, she supposed – stubborn. He wouldn't respond to being told what to do and an appeal to his better nature would likely have no effect.

'You're quiet, Meg.' Samuel was regarding her as though he knew exactly what she had been thinking.

'Just planning tomorrow's baking,' she said, then turned her attention to Thomas, suggesting she might read him a story after they had cleared the dishes. He would not be happy with her tomorrow when he learnt he was to go to school. All the more reason to make sure he enjoyed his Sunday afternoon.

CHAPTER SEVENTEEN

❧

'I don't see why I have to go.' Thomas's bottom lip, stuck out in a sulk, trembled.

'Because you will learn to read and write, and both will be important to you when you grow up,' Meg said. She had a firm grip on Thomas's wrist and was half pulling him towards the Charity School. She had insisted she should take him rather than Eliza, whom she suspected would simply give in to his pleas and let him go before they got there.

'I don't want to read and write.'

Meg tried a different approach. 'You'll meet lots of other children of your age. I went to the Charity School and it was fun. Well,' she reconsidered, 'not fun exactly but I learnt such a lot.' They were almost there now – she just had to distract him with talk for a few more steps.

'I don't want to meet other children.'

'Thomas, you can't be running around town, doing who knows what and getting into all sorts of trouble.' Meg was exasperated. 'I'm forever getting you out of bother with shopkeepers. You're only seven. I don't like to think of the sort of trouble you'll be in when you're older.'

'I'm eight,' Thomas said.

'Are you?' Meg was surprised. She stopped and faced him.

They'd reached the school entrance now, although she didn't think Thomas had noticed. 'Well, all the more reason to be in school.'

She wiped a tear from his cheek, bent down to kiss the top of his head and pulled a biscuit from the pocket of her apron. They'd left the house in such a hurry that she was still wearing it, her cloak thrown over the top.

'Here you are. Still warm from the oven. Eat it mid-morning, when you get a break.'

She rapped on the knocker of the school door and it was opened by a young girl wearing a plain brown dress, a white cotton cap over her hair.

'Thomas Marsh,' Meg said. 'A new pupil for Mr Wreakes.'

The girl smiled, reached out her hand and drew Thomas inside, shutting the door behind him. Meg faced the dark wood, the curved black iron door knocker blurring in her vision as she blinked back tears. She hoped Thomas would settle.

Then, squaring her shoulders, she turned for home. That was one problem dealt with. Two more still to be resolved: Samuel's lack of work, and the money she needed to supply more run goods to Ralph Carter. Deep in thought as she walked along Lower Street, she paid no heed to the sound of a horse's hoofs. It wasn't unusual: carts and men on horseback passed up and down the street throughout the day. She realised that the horse – a chestnut mare – was keeping pace with her at the same moment as, looking up, she saw the rider was Bartholomew Banks. Had the man been so much around town before and she had simply failed to notice him?

'Where are you going at this early hour?' Bartholomew asked.

'I've just delivered Thomas, my nephew, to school,' Meg said. 'His first day,' she added.

Bartholomew nodded approvingly. 'An excellent idea. Education: the first step on the road to better things.'

'I hope so,' Meg said. She doubted Bartholomew had any idea of the sort of education offered by the Charity School but, still, she was happy to keep talking to him. The encounter had set her heart beating fast. 'Where are you bound this morning?' she asked.

'The barracks,' Bartholomew replied. 'I've just been to the timber yard to ask whether they can recommend a carpenter, but they said all their men are working at the barracks. I'm on my way there to see whether one can be spared.'

'Is that not a task for someone already employed at the castle?' Meg asked. She'd imagined acquiring labourers to be beyond the concern of a person such as Bartholomew.

'It's for a little venture of my own,' Bartholomew said. 'I don't wish to bother my father or any of his workers with it. Just some boxes I wish to have made. Nothing fancy, just for packing items.'

'I may know of someone,' Meg said, struck by a thought. Samuel had been employed at the boatyard, after all, and she had seen him undertake various basic repairs around the house and yard. He was surely capable of nailing a few planks together to make a box.

'Well, Meg Marsh, could this be my lucky day? I not only keep company with the prettiest girl in town, but she tells me she has the solution to my problem. Clearly I need to be up and abroad at this early hour more often.'

'It's eight thirty, sir,' Meg protested, to hide her blushes. 'Hardly early.' Prettiest girl in town – the words ran through her head. No one, not even Joseph, had ever referred to her as such. 'Where shall I send the – carpenter?'

'Let him meet me at the stables at noon to see whether he will suit,' Bartholomew said. 'I have business about town this morning and will leave my horse there.' He encouraged the horse to walk on at smarter pace, calling over his shoulder, 'And, remember, it's Bartholomew, not sir, now that we are better acquainted.'

Meg hurried home, bursting into the kitchen and startling her mother and Eliza. 'Where's Samuel?' she demanded.

'Still abed.' Eliza was alarmed. 'Has something happened to Thomas?'

'Thomas? No.' Meg was puzzled, having half forgotten why she'd been out. 'No, he's at school. But I have word of a job for Samuel.'

Eliza was wary. 'What sort of job?'

Meg's excitement turned to anger in an instant. 'It hardly matters what sort of job. He hasn't earned a farthing in weeks, yet he's happy enough to sit and eat at this table. I don't care how he thinks he should fill his days. You and I and Ma are all working hard. He must, too.'

Mrs Marsh stood up from the table. 'I'll get back to the shop,' she said, and left swiftly.

'Will you tell him, or shall I?' Meg was calmer now, her anger spent.

'I will.' Eliza stood up from the table. 'What work is it?'

'Carpentry, working for Bartholomew Banks at Hawksdown Castle. To make boxes – nothing fancy, but it might lead to more work.' Bartholomew hadn't said as much but surely, if Samuel did a good job, it was a possibility, Meg thought. 'He'll see him at noon at the stables at the top of the road.'

Eliza nodded and left, while Meg busied herself with more baking. By eleven o'clock, with no sign of Eliza and Samuel, she was feeling anxious. She took over from her mother in the shop, to give her a short break, telling herself that when she went back into the kitchen her brother would be there. He wasn't, and by a quarter to twelve, just as Meg had decided she would have to go to the stables and explain she hadn't been able to locate the carpenter, Samuel and Eliza came into the kitchen. Samuel was wearing a clean shirt and it looked as though Eliza had brushed his jacket. Meg's spirits rose.

Samuel didn't ask Meg for any more information – he just kissed Eliza's cheek and let himself out of the back door. At twelve thirty, as Meg was lacing on her boots to collect Thomas from school, Samuel reappeared.

'Well?' Eliza asked.

He nodded. 'I start tomorrow, ten o'clock at the castle.'

'Ten?' Meg was surprised.

Samuel grinned. 'Your Mr Banks doesn't like to start too early. Suits me. Since I'm to work under his instruction, he said to be there by ten. After that, I can do the hours to suit myself as long as the work gets done.'

'Very good,' Meg said, smiling at him as she left. Once outside, she frowned. Such a late start would suit Samuel's lazy disposition only too well. Bartholomew would need to keep him in line.

Back at the Charity School she stood in the schoolroom doorway, watching Thomas at the centre of a small, animated group, before she stepped forward to collect him.

'How was school?' she asked, as they walked home.

'It's all right, I suppose.' Thomas was guarded.

'And what did you learn today?'

Thomas considered. 'Nothing,' he said.

Meg hid a smile. 'Nothing?' she exclaimed, in mock consternation. 'That's no good. Perhaps you shouldn't go back tomorrow.'

Thomas didn't reply but he didn't rush off in the afternoon, as she'd expected him to. Instead, he spent time with his parents in their room: Meg heard the murmur of voices as she passed the door.

The next morning, braced for a tussle, she was astonished when he came into the kitchen a good half an hour before they needed to leave. 'Could I take two biscuits today?' he asked, eyeing them cooling on a rack. 'I want to give one to a friend.'

Chapter Eighteen

❧

As the week went on, the weather changed. The chilly, dreary February days were consumed by a banshee wind, which growled and shrieked around the rooftops. It whipped the sea into a seething cauldron of brown waves, and blew Meg sideways when she crossed Beach Street of an evening to work at the Fountain.

The wooden planking of the building creaked and groaned and, on occasion, shook so hard that Meg took fright. Were they to be uprooted and carried away on the wind, glasses and tankards tumbling from the shelves, customers flung from their stools, the coals pouring from the grate?

Mrs Dunn was unconcerned. 'This building has withstood a fair few storms in its past. I dare say it'll see this one through. It'll blow itself out.'

But it didn't. Instead, it blew snow in. Meg's skin felt scoured and flayed when she ventured out into the street, and the chill seeped through the worn soles of her leather boots. She stayed at home as much as she could, as did their shop customers. It was hardly worthwhile baking of a morning.

Samuel made his way home from Hawksdown Castle the first evening, his jacket encrusted with snow, face and fingers bright red. 'I'm not going to make the journey twice a day in this,' he said, once he had thawed out enough to speak.

Meg was anxious. 'If you don't turn up, Bartholomew – Mr Banks – will wonder where you are. You'll lose the job.'

Samuel was unmoved. 'He's not paying me enough to freeze half to death on the journey.'

'Stay the night there,' Meg urged. 'You said you're working in the old stables. Get some straw, make a bed. Take a blanket and some clothes with you tomorrow and just wait until it eases. I'm sure the kitchens there will spare you some food.'

She expected Samuel and Eliza to resist but to her surprise, although Samuel grumbled again the next morning, he set off with his blanket rolled and tied tightly with string, anything else he needed snug inside. Meg saw it wasn't snowing and was thankful – he would remain dry on his journey at least. The wind, though, was icy and the snow had crusted hard underfoot. It was to remain that way for a full week.

With Saturday fast approaching, Meg wondered about Ralph Carter. She had little to send him, for the weather had made it impossible for the boats to go out. The coach might not even get through, of course, but Meg didn't know whether the weather was as harsh in London. Mr Carter might have no idea of the conditions they were enduring and be angry when he received so little.

Meg still had the kid gloves and the shawl hidden away. She'd kept them back on a whim and now she was glad. They were of very good quality and, she hoped, would be enough to keep Ralph Carter sweet. Perhaps the weather would change enough in the coming week to allow the French trade to re-commence.

She still hadn't solved the problem of money. She had half a mind to insist Samuel gave all his wages to the household, to make up for his months without work. But even that wouldn't go far, with the loan from Michael Bailey to be paid off and a substantial purchase from Philippe essential. She had racked her brains, trying to think where she could get money from. The glimmer of an idea had come to her and, although she tried to push it away, the thought remained as a persistent voice in her head. *You know someone wealthy enough to lend you the money*, it said. *Ask him.*

By the time Saturday came, Meg had reached a decision. She would relinquish the gloves and shawl to Ralph Carter's carriage, with the promise of more goods of that nature to come, once the easterly wind eased. The shop had brought in virtually no money all week due to the weather and Samuel still hadn't come home with his wages. The Fountain had been quiet, too, so she hadn't worked her usual number of hours. The expected payment from Ralph Carter would be enough to feed the family and run the business for a week, but not sufficient to buy all the goods she needed to sell. She owed money to Michael Bailey, as well. It made her head ache when she tried to work out how to juggle it all.

Meg woke on Sunday morning to clear blue skies and an unusual silence. It took her a moment to realise that the wind wasn't troubling the chimney as it had all week, sending unwelcome puffs and eddies of smoke into the fireplaces of the house. Her first thought was that the boats could set out at last, perhaps that very night. Her second was to wonder when Samuel would come home.

She had her answer when they got back from church. Samuel was sitting in the kitchen, feet up on the range, looking pleased with himself. Eliza gave a cry of delight and rushed over to give him a hug. Thomas went to stand beside his father – he, too, seemed happy to see him.

'How are you enjoying school?' his father asked.

'It's all right,' Thomas said, but he couldn't help a grin spreading across his face. 'I can write my name now.'

'Show me,' Samuel said, but they had no slate or chalk to hand, so Thomas wrote it on a steamed-up windowpane.

Meg saw a small pile of coins on the table in front of Samuel. He noticed her looking and pushed the pile towards her. 'For the housekeeping pot,' he said. 'I've finished the work and Bartholomew was happy with it.'

So it's Bartholomew and not Mr Banks, Meg thought, just as Samuel dropped a drawstring purse onto the table.

'This is for you. Bartholomew thought you might have need of it.'

Meg was baffled. What was he talking about? Her mother, after patting her son on the shoulder, saying, 'Welcome back,' had moved to the kitchen sink to prepare vegetables. She stiffened and swung round at Samuel's words.

'I don't understand,' Meg said.

'It's a loan,' Samuel said. 'Apparently you have some trade afoot with a Mr Ralph Carter, in London. Bartholomew seems to know about it and he thought I did, too.' Samuel threw Meg an accusing look. 'He has it in mind that you are going to supply some of the visitors to the castle and wanted you to have this. To help you do so,' he added, as Meg still looked puzzled.

Mrs Marsh had her hands on her hips. 'Trade with London? Is this something to do with run goods, Meg Marsh?'

Meg faced her mother. Her hope of keeping her enterprise secret drained away as she saw the anger written across her mother's features.

'Yes, Ma. Fabrics – beautiful fabrics from France that wealthy ladies want, along with lace, slippers, shawls and the like.'

'And have you got those things in this house?' Mrs Marsh did not look as though she was asking because she was eager to see them.

'Yes,' Meg admitted, adding hastily, 'although nothing at the moment. There's little risk and it's a ready market.'

'And what about when the revenue men come calling?' Mrs Marsh demanded.

'When has that ever happened?' Meg countered. 'I keep everything well hidden, and in any case it's only here for a short time.'

'You don't know what you're getting yourself into, Meg,' her mother warned. 'People need to be paid for their silence, and there's others who will be jealous if you do well. And I don't like you getting involved with Bartholomew Banks – I don't trust him.'

Meg shook her head. 'I had no intention of involving him but there's no denying the money will be useful. I can't afford to buy the goods I need without it.'

Her words weren't strictly true: she had considered asking him, and now it was as if Bartholomew had read her mind. The chink the purse had made when Samuel dropped it onto the table told her it held a substantial number of coins.

Mrs Marsh pursed her lips. 'We'll talk about it later,' she said, turning back to the sink.

'Yes, Ma.' Meg was eager to change the subject. She turned to her brother. 'If you've finished that work, Samuel, will Barth—Mr Banks need you for anything else?'

'He said to come back tomorrow and he'll have something for me.'

'More boxes?' Meg asked, wondering what he could possibly need them for.

Samuel shrugged. 'I don't know. He seemed happy enough with what I've done. It wasn't a straightforward job – making them with false bottoms wasn't easy.'

He clapped a hand over his mouth. 'I shouldn't have mentioned that. He said he relied on me not to tell a soul.'

'I won't breathe a word,' Eliza said.

Meg saw her mother's grim expression as she fetched a pot for the peeled potatoes. Boxes with false bases could mean only one thing, Meg thought. Smuggled goods. Was Bartholomew aware of Samuel's weakness for ale, and the amount of time he spent in the inn? Could he be trusted with such a secret?

Chapter Nineteen

When Meg took the purse up to the privacy of her room that evening and counted the coins, she was astonished to discover they amounted to twenty guineas.

Samuel had told her privately that Bartholomew felt it wrong to give the money directly to her, in case she had thought it inappropriate. 'He considered that handing it to me, your brother, and asking me to make it plain that it was a loan for your business was the right thing to do.'

Samuel had clearly felt flattered at being entrusted in this way, but Meg experienced a flutter of unease as she looked at the pile of coins. What if it was a trap? Could the son of the Lord Warden really be trusted?

The glint of gold in the candlelight banished her fears. Meg's imagination was already showing her what she might buy with such riches. How pleased Mr Carter would be with his next delivery! Then she checked herself. She could not send everything she bought to London. Bartholomew would expect his loan to fund goods for the visitors to the castle. A way must be found to make safe that new risky trade.

As Meg drifted into sleep that night her thoughts had strayed again to Bartholomew. He'd mentioned that it gave him pleasure to defy his father, but did he expect a cut of the profits? She supposed he must, for what other reason could he possibly have to make such a generous offer? If any other thoughts occurred to trouble Meg, they were soon lost to the sleep that quickly overwhelmed her.

Word came to Meg on Monday morning that the boats would be going out that night. Her messenger, Michael Bailey's delivery boy, said he needed to take an answer back with him: would she join them? Meg hesitated for a second or two then nodded. 'I'll take an oar.'

The good weather had remained: it was still February, but the morning had brought a foretaste of spring. The sea was calm, the sun shone and it even felt as though it had some warmth to offer. Meg continued walking Thomas to school, cautious in case he got it into his head to play truant. He had, though, defied expectations and shown every sign of enjoying being there, even throughout the bitter weather of the previous week. As she walked home, the early sun on her face, Meg had felt her spirits lift. The news of the night's planned activity raised them further.

In the past, she had acted as watch for the Silver Street gang on more than one occasion, huddled in her cloak on the beach, watching for the faint lantern signal that told her the boats were returning and hands must be fetched from the inn to help them unload.

She'd had the chance four or five times to take an oar, when one of the regular crew fell ill. Michael Bailey knew that Meg was a strong rower, and fearless. From an early age, she had been out in boats with her father, who favoured her as a companion over her brother. Meg suspected Samuel was frightened of the water.

It didn't worry her, being out at night on the dark sea. In fact, she relished it. The team of four rowers, with an oar each, worked as one without a word spoken. The only sound was the wind, the creak of the rowlocks, the slap of the waves against the sides of the boat and focused, rhythmic breathing. They met with the French ships three or four miles offshore, transactions conducted quickly before barrels and packages were passed along the boat and stowed between the planks that served as bench seats. The urge to cram in just a little bit more had to be resisted by whoever was in charge that night. The risk of the boat sitting too low in the water and the wind direction changing was too great. If a wave caught them unawares the boat would sink. It had happened only once to a Castle Bay galley but the memory lingered on in those who rowed out on those dark nights. That, and the threat of discovery by the revenue men, was always on everyone's minds as they pulled back for shore after making their assignation.

It was the memory of her mother's anger the previous day that had caused Meg to hesitate before accepting Michael Bailey's offer to take an oar. Yet she knew she could slip away easily enough – she would just say she was working at the Fountain, as usual, and her mother would be none the wiser. She was always asleep before Meg came home and tonight would be no exception.

As for risks from the revenue men – these had faded with time. If they were spotted, they would have to pay half their income from the run goods to buy the revenue men's silence. Above all, though, her decision to take an oar had been influenced by the thought that if she didn't go, someone else would make a hasty decision about Philippe's goods. She needed to have the conversation with him herself: it was too important for her future trade with Ralph Carter.

Even as she had shut the door on Michael Bailey's messenger, thankful her mother hadn't been aware of his visit, she was feeling a thrill of anticipation about the night ahead. The money from Bartholomew had given an added fillip – she had never had such a wealth of funds at her disposal. Bartholomew had been truly generous.

Chapter Twenty

After the message regarding the planned run that night, Meg had found herself wishing that the clouds would roll in. It was not until darkness began to fall that her wish was granted: the wind changed direction and the clear skies gave way to a blanket of cloud. If the moon made an appearance that night, it was likely to be brief. She found it hard to contain her excitement at what lay ahead.

It turned out to be more of an adventure than Meg had expected. Rowing out onto the dark seas was uneventful, but she endured a heart-stopping moment when a gust of wind caught her skirts as she clambered up the rope ladder to board the creaking French ship. She was flung momentarily at right angles to the vessel, too terrified to look down, imagining only too well the plunge into the cold dark depths below. She saw herself dragged beneath the waves in an instant, her cloak and clothing waterlogged, before her rowing companions could grasp her beseeching hands.

Her legs were shaking by the time she was helped on board and she was glad of the need to exchange only silent nods with the French crew before they directed her below. Here, an oil lamp hanging from the low beam cast its glow over the two trunks already open on the floor. One was stuffed with fabric, the other with shawls, lace, slippers and ribbons, some of which were spilling over the sides. Meg murmured a greeting to Philippe, registering other items piled on a wooden table to the side, before falling on her knees before the trunks.

Conscious of the limited time, she passed her hands rapidly over the folded fabrics, pulling out colours and designs that appealed to her before reconsidering. Had she chosen fabrics too dull for the ladies of fashion in London? She exchanged some of the sprigged cottons for bright, plain silk before turning her attention to the other trunk. She chose swiftly, trying to suppress a worry that she had no idea of what was in fashion. She could work only by instinct, as well as paying attention to Philippe's murmured suggestions. Once he saw that she was planning to buy more than her usual restricted amount, he began laying out lace, showing her the intricate designs, and shaking out shawls beneath the lamplight so that the subtle beauty of the embroidery was shown to its best advantage.

Meg, smiling, eventually had to call a halt. She pointed to the pile of goods she had amassed and asked, '*Combien?* How much?' Although Philippe spoke a little English, she liked to speak in French as a courtesy, including a translation to make sure she had used the right words.

Philippe worked rapidly through the pile, writing down a figure for each piece, then showing her the total. Meg bit her lip and shook her head. It was too much. She took the paper from him, scanning it to see which pieces were the most expensive. One was a shawl, which she was particularly keen to take. She began laying pieces aside in an attempt to reduce the total, but Philippe stopped her, shaking his head.

'*Non, non,*' he said.

'*Mais, c'est trop cher,*' Meg said, pointing to the paper. 'Too much. I can't pay that much. *Je n'ai pas beaucoup d'argent.*' She hoped her mix of French and English was making the point.

Philippe took the piece of paper back, crossed through the

figure and wrote another. The reduction was enough to bring it closer to the money Meg had with her. She hesitated, deliberating. 'Without – *sans* – this.' She held up a lace collar with a diamond-pointed edging.

Philippe nodded, then swiftly wrapped the goods into two packages for Meg, while she tipped the contents of her purse onto the table. She knew it was still a little short – what would Philippe say?

He counted the coins into piles, then wrote the figure still out-standing at the bottom of the paper. '*À la prochaine fois*,' he said.

'Next time?' Meg asked, and he nodded. They shook hands and Meg turned to go with her packages but Philippe held out the lace collar.

'*Pour vous*,' he said.

'For me?' Meg was astonished. It lay across her palm, almost weightless, the fineness of the thread and the delicate intricacy of the work unlike anything she had seen before. Tears started to her eyes.

Philippe took it back from her and for a moment she was bewildered. Had he changed his mind? But he was wrapping it into a separate package. Then he ushered her up the open wooden stair, back onto the deck of the ship. Meg peered over the side, worried that her transaction had taken too long and the men would be growing restless. They were still busy stowing goods, so she called softly down to get their attention. Once she had dropped her parcels into their hands, she took a deep breath and readied herself to descend. A couple of the French sailors sprang to her side, one seizing her waist as she climbed over the wooden rail, the other holding his hands over hers as she gripped the top of the ladder and steadied herself. Then she descended into the darkness, feeling her way one foot at a time. Her cloak and skirts flapped in the wind but she made it safely to the galley. Here she was once more seized with a fit of trembling, but she gritted her teeth, took up her position at the oars and prepared for the signal to return.

Within five minutes, she and the men had their heads down and were rowing hard. Meg concentrated on each pull of the oars, only glancing up occasionally to see that the ship they had left behind was growing smaller and more indistinct – the only way she had of telling that they were drawing closer to land. There the goods would be rapidly dispersed. The barrels would be sent in different directions so that if they were intercepted not all would be lost. The dry goods – tea, coffee, salt and the like – would be received in different hands, while Meg would take responsibility for her own packages. Once everything had been safely stowed away, all would meet back at the Fountain for a drink to celebrate their success. The whole procedure, if all went well, would take less than an hour.

CHAPTER TWENTY-ONE

Meg had begun to feel a burning ache in her shoulders and arms when Christian, Michael Bailey's trusted deputy who was acting as spotter, hissed a sharp instruction to stop rowing. They must be very close to shore, she thought. She could smell wood smoke on the wind. And could she hear voices?

'We'll have to land closer to North End,' Christian said, in a low voice. 'Something's up on the beach.'

Meg risked a glance over her shoulder. More than one boat from Castle Bay had ventured out to meet with the French that night and now a galley that had made land earlier was lit by the flaming glare of burning torches, the men caught in the act of unloading their wares.

'Alter course and pull!' Christian's voice was urgent.

Meg calculated their risk. The revenue men would likely concentrate on their current prize, so they should be safe further along the beach. The problem then lay in transferring their wares to a place of safety from this new, more distant, spot. The beach sloped gently to the sea at North End, so that was in their favour, and the men's knowledge of the warren of alleys to negotiate in the dark gave them an advantage, too. Even so, Meg's heart was thumping uncomfortably by the time Christian gave the order to 'Ease off the oars – now!' and the boat's bow slid up onto the shingle with a crunch.

The men were overboard in a moment, hauling the galley up beyond the high-water mark even as others began swiftly to unload. There was no sign of those who normally came to help spirit away the barrels and packages and Meg's heart sank. Had they been apprehended by the revenue men? Or had the watcher on the beach failed to notice them changing course for their new destination?

She set to with the men, unloading what she could and placing it beside the other boats beached there, the piles of goods quickly merging into the shadows. As the boat's load lessened, some of the men made a start on removing things from the beach. Meg knew they couldn't complete the job on their own. All were tired after the rowing and although spirits such as brandy were transported in the smaller barrels known as tubs, they were still a burden for weary arms and sore backs.

As she retrieved her own packages, resolving to go up into town and get help for the men, she saw dark figures detach themselves from the shadows further along the beach. One by one, the men around her noticed, too, until all were motionless, watching. Were they revenue men? Or was help on its way at last?

As she stood, hardly daring to breathe, moments seemed to stretch in time. Meg was half expecting the flash of a pistol in the dark, until the indistinct figures resolved themselves into more familiar silhouettes. There were no revenue men's caps on their heads: instead she recognised the height and bulky shapes of the usual band of regulars from the Fountain.

The new arrivals didn't waste time discussing the forced change of plan but simply took up their usual roles – some transporting the tubs of brandy, others filling their pockets with packets of salt or bags of tea and coffee. Meg thought it best to leave them to it. Staying in the lee of the boats, she made her way up the beach until she gained the road. Then she went straight ahead, up into town, calculating how to make her way home.

She would walk along Lower Street, she decided. It was by far the longest route, but she was keen to stay as far from the beach, and the revenue men, as possible. It would be wise to keep clear of Middle Street, too, while the transfer of goods from the boat was taking place. She walked quickly, head down, cloak pulled over her hair, packages clutched tightly within its folds. The street was deserted, the shops shuttered – all good, law-abiding folk were in bed.

Meg held her nerve for as long as she could until, hearing the beat of horse's hoofs, she slipped into Chapel Street, opposite St George's church. She was only one street away from home and within sight of an alley where she thought to hide, but the rider had turned his horse and was following her. She was running excuses through her mind for being out so late – a sick mother, or nephew, and the need to seek help from a relative – when the rider spoke.

'Well, Meg, a good disguise but I know it's you. There's not many around here who go out wrapped in such a cloak.'

Startled, Meg spun around. Bartholomew, his face in deep shadow under his hat, was looking down at her from his mount.

'What are you up to, out and about at this time?' he continued.

Meg hesitated. Should she admit to this evening's activities? After all, Bartholomew had financed them and she hadn't yet thanked him for the generous loan. But something held her back. What was he doing in this part of town? She would have expected to see him near the stables, or at Throckings Hotel, but what business could he have around here at night? She still had concerns about his relationship with the Lord Warden – could Bartholomew have anything to do with the presence of the revenue men that night?

'A sick relative,' she said, decision made. 'I was called out to help.'

'And this person is better now, I trust?'

She still couldn't see Bartholomew's face.

'Perhaps you took them some of your fine currant buns?'

Meg laughed, hoping it sounded natural and not forced. 'Yes, a little better. You must excuse me, though. My mother will be waiting up, worried, until I return.'

'Then I will escort you to your door,' Bartholomew said. 'It's no time for you to be out alone.'

The horse's hoofs echoed on the cobbles as they proceeded, and Meg was glad they didn't have far to go. She had no wish to draw attention to herself, although she supposed being in the company of the Lord Warden's son would keep her free of harassment by the revenue men. They had no further conversation in the time it took to reach her door. Bartholomew removed his hat and swept a bow from his mount before proceeding on his way.

'Until the next time,' he said softly, over his shoulder.

Meg, watching him go, realised she had still failed to thank him for the loan.

'Until the next time,' she said to herself, opening the door quietly and slipping into the hall. She closed it quietly and leant against it, waiting and listening. All was silent, so she took herself upstairs to bed. Opening the packages and revisiting what she had purchased would have to wait until the morning. For now, Meg was bone weary and sleep was all she desired.

Chapter Twenty-Two

Meg discovered before too long that her chance meeting with Bartholomew was to have unforeseen consequences. The following day passed well enough – at breakfast it was clear her mother had no suspicion she had been out so late the night before. Meg slipped back to her room afterwards to unwrap the packages and admire the goods once more. After some hesitation, she added the fine lace collar, Philippe's gift, to the pile before rewrapping and concealing everything. When would she ever have need of something so beautiful? She listed the new purchases in her diary, then stowed it safely with the packages, too. She would need to decide what to send to London in the next delivery, and to pen another note asking Ralph Carter whether there were any further requests from his customers, but that could wait.

By the time she entered the Fountain that evening she was feeling not only the effects of her late night but also of her busy day of baking and helping in the shop. She was impatient, though, to see the men involved in the previous night's enterprise and to check that everyone had got away safely.

It was a little while before Meg grasped something was amiss. She had hung up her cloak, wiped down the bar and washed up some used tankards and glasses before she noticed that customers waiting for service were clustered at the other end of the bar, in front of Mrs Dunn. That in itself didn't seem particularly unusual, until she saw that the drinkers in the room were gathered in little huddles, mostly with their backs to her. One or two glanced at her from time to time, then looked quickly away.

Was there some bad news that they were all afraid to share with her? Meg wondered. When it became apparent that no one was going to approach her to request a drink, she ventured out into the room. Collecting empty tankards as she went, she came to a halt in front of a group of the men who had been on the boat with her the previous night.

'Did everyone get home safely? And everything safely retrieved?' she asked.

'Aye, no thanks to you, Meg Marsh,' said Christian.

'What do you mean?' Meg was taken aback. Did they think she had left the beach too hastily? Had they expected her to stay and help shift the goods?

'You were seen,' Christian said. The other men were glowering at Meg, who was still puzzled.

'Seen?' she repeated.

'Walking home with the son of the Lord Warden.' Now Christian was glaring at her. 'Did you tip him off about what we were doing? Was that why the revenue men were waiting on the beach?'

'Me? Tip him off? Why ever would I do such a thing?' Meg was baffled.

'Money,' Christian said.

Meg felt her face grow hot. 'How can you suggest I would betray you? It makes no sense. I need to make money from the goods we got, just as you do. Why would I risk jeopardising that?'

'Michael Bailey said you were short – needed to borrow from him to pay for the last run. And yet last night you weren't holding back. Spent quite a bit, judging by the size of the packages you had. Where did that money come from?'

Meg had a sudden sickening realisation of how it would look if it became known that she had, in fact, taken money from Bartholomew Banks. The men would never believe it was a loan to buy goods to be sold at Hawksdown Castle. They'd think she'd sold them out – risked having them arrested at worst and confiscation of their goods at best – for the sake of a few guineas and a blind eye turned to her own dealings.

'I'm trading with London,' she said, 'with a man who came in here a few weeks ago. You all refused to have anything to do with him but it turns out he has a market for my fabrics and the like. There's a profit to be made among the ladies of fashion in town. So that's where my money is coming from.'

There were murmurings but Meg hoped she'd said enough to convince them. She gave them a defiant look and swept past, head up, continuing to collect tankards, returning any glares with a hard look.

Twenty or so minutes later, Christian came up to the bar. 'Meg, I'm sorry if I upset you. But you being seen with Bartholomew Banks on the same night we barely managed to escape a raid seemed like too much of a coincidence.'

'He just chanced upon me as I walked home,' Meg said.

'You were seen talking together,' Christian persisted.

Meg let out a sigh. 'He stables his horse at the end of my street when he's in town. He came into the shop and bought some cakes. That's all. Last night, he was worried to see me out so late, alone.'

Christian still looked sceptical but he held out his tankard for Meg to refill. She took his coins without comment, hoping her face didn't betray her feelings. Were her suspicions about Bartholomew justified? Then she was struck by a reassuring thought. She hadn't told Bartholomew of the proposed run, so she didn't see where he could have got such knowledge. It was hardly likely he could have informed on them. It was best that no one knew of Bartholomew's loan to her, though. She must impress on Samuel that it had to remain secret.

Gradually, others followed Christian's example and came up to Meg to be served, and she heard tales of how they had all suffered hazardous journeys to stow the goods brought ashore at North End. She suspected the stories had been embellished to add drama, but she played along, congratulating them on their bravery and lucky escapes.

Joseph came in with his father, close to ten o'clock. As soon as she saw him, Meg realised she had barely thought of him over the last week or so.

'Are you keeping well?' he asked rather pointedly, as she served him. His father, surprised by his cool tone, gave him a sharp look.

'Very well, thank you,' she said, giving Joseph a smile – not her best one – and accompanying it with a look that she hoped told him she knew the game he was playing.

He nodded to her and moved away with his ale. Meg resolved to speak to him later – was it only two weeks since they'd exchanged kisses on the beach? Then she remembered her resolution: to concentrate on her business alone. It wasn't fair to raise false hopes in Joseph's heart.

Lost in such thoughts, she was straightening glasses on the shelf behind the bar when she heard Samuel's voice: 'I've brought you a visitor, Meg.'

A wave of silence rolled across the room as the drinkers nudged each other into awareness of the new customer: Bartholomew Banks, the Lord Warden's son.

CHAPTER TWENTY-THREE

Meg stifled a gasp. What on earth was Samuel thinking? She felt, without looking, that Joseph was staring at her. Try as she might, she couldn't stop the colour rushing to her face.

'Samuel,' she hissed, 'are you mad?'

'Bartholomew had a wish to see the inside of the Fountain and I said I'd bring him along.' Samuel smiled around the room. Meg wasn't sure whether he was oblivious to the atmosphere or revelling in it.

Meg addressed Bartholomew. 'Mr Banks, my brother has misled you. You won't be welcomed by the regulars here. You are the Lord Warden's son and they will assume you to be an informer. I think you'd be wise to leave.'

Meg, even with her eyes fixed on Samuel and Bartholomew, was aware that Mrs Dunn was bearing down on them.

'They have nothing to fear from me,' Bartholomew said. Now he, too, was smiling around the room. 'I'd like to meet some of the fellows here. I'm more than happy to let them know how things sit with my father and me.'

Meg, even in her agitation, noticed how Bartholomew stood out in the room. He was a head taller than every other man there and he carried himself with a confident air. His clothes might be simply cut and restrained in colour but there was no hiding the superior cloth and the quality of the workmanship, in contrast to everyone else in the room. Then Mrs Dunn was upon them.

'I'm afraid I'll have to ask you two gentlemen to leave,' she said. 'You're upsetting the customers. Samuel, you know better than this.' She was unsmiling, and for the first time Meg saw uncertainty on Samuel's face.

Bartholomew turned to Mrs Dunn and gave her the full benefit of his charm. 'I do apologise – this is entirely my fault. Samuel has been working with me and I bothered him until he agreed to bring me along. I've passed your establishment many times and wanted to step inside, but feared the reception. Samuel convinced me it was a friendly and welcoming place, full of a great many characters with tales to tell. But I have no wish for unpleasantness. I will depart at once, with apologies for any distress caused to your good self and your customers.'

Bartholomew bowed to Mrs Dunn, without a hint of irony. By the end of his speech the landlady appeared somewhat mollified. Meg couldn't take her eyes off him – his handsome profile and grave yet dancing blue eyes, lips that matched every emotion expressed: hopeful, disappointed, solemn. As the shock of his appearance in the Fountain faded, Meg felt a little thrill of excitement.

'Well.' Mrs Dunn, unused to such fine manners, took a moment or two to collect herself. 'Meg can serve you but I'll thank you to keep to yourselves while you drink.' She turned away, ready to move off down the bar, then something else occurred to her. 'I hope you've not come here to gawp at us and take back tales to entertain your fancy friends. My customers work hard and deserve some respect. I'll not have them turned into a spectacle.' With that, she swept away.

'Understood.' Bartholomew addressed Meg and gave her a wink. 'Samuel, what will you have?'

Samuel had looked uncomfortable throughout the exchange as it dawned on him that he'd made an error of judgement. 'The usual, Meg,' he muttered.

'Then I'll have the same,' Bartholomew said. He didn't appear in the least put out by Mrs Dunn's reaction, Meg noticed. He had neither smiled nor protested, simply nodding gravely at her words. 'We'll tuck ourselves away here at the end of the bar and we won't disturb anyone,' he added.

Meg served them their drinks and turned away. Her heart was beating uncomfortably fast but she was determined to act as though nothing untoward had happened. She hoped none of the men believed she had played a part in Bartholomew's appearance. The timing could hardly have been worse.

A gentle murmur of conversation had resumed but she saw glances cast in the direction of her brother and his companion. Bartholomew kept his back to the room but appeared to be in no hurry to drink up. A succession of men came to be served and stood close to him, but he paid no heed and Meg was relieved he didn't offer to stand drinks for any of them. Such an attempt to ingratiate himself could only cause trouble.

Joseph's eyes were still on her from the other side of the room, which added to her discomfort. She could only hope that well within the half-hour the unwelcome pair would finish their drinks and leave. Just as that time drew close, Christian came up to the bar. She served him without needing to ask what he'd have and turned to chalk it up to his account. As she did so, to her horror he addressed Bartholomew.

'Not partial to the ale here, then?' he asked, pointing to Bartholomew's almost empty tankard.

'On the contrary, I could develop quite a taste for it,' Bartholomew said, smiling. He drained the last drop and stood up. 'But I must be on my way.'

Christian rested his hand on Bartholomew's arm. 'Why don't you stay and have another? On me,' he said.

Was Christian going to pick a fight with Bartholomew? Meg glanced anxiously at Mrs Dunn, but she was occupied at the other end of the bar. She would have to intervene herself. She moved across and picked up the empty tankards.

'Now, Christian, you heard Mrs Dunn.' She gave him a challenging look. 'One drink, she said. Mr Banks and my brother are about to leave.'

'Well, I'd like to have a talk with them first,' Christian said. 'No trouble, I promise you. Let's say I'm curious. Chalk up two more to me.'

Meg hesitated. Mrs Dunn was still unaware of what was going on.

'I'll square it with her, if need be.' Christian nodded to Meg. 'But if there's no trouble, she's got nothing to complain about. Get on with it quick, like, and she'll never know.'

Meg shook her head but did as she was bade. Christian wasn't usually the fighting kind but he'd been angry with her over Bartholomew earlier in the evening. She was certain he intended to question the Lord Warden's son to discover whether he'd played any part in last night's beach raid. With a lurch of her heart she remembered Christian's suspicions about where she'd found the money to make her purchases. Was there any danger that Bartholomew would mention the loan he had made to her?

She thought it more likely Christian had suspected her of taking money from the revenue men, rather than Bartholomew, but her sense of guilt made her eager to distance herself from the little huddle of three men at the end of the bar. Meg set off once more around the room, collecting glasses and stopping to exchange a word here and there. One or two of the customers asked her what Samuel was up to but she could only shrug.

'I really couldn't say,' was the best she could offer, which was the truth.

She'd intended to have a word with Joseph, but when she reached the corner where she had last seen him, he had gone.

'I didn't notice Joseph leave,' she said to his father. 'I wanted to speak to him.'

'Aye, well, he saw you only had eyes for your brother's new friend,' William Huggett said, and turned his back on Meg, leaving her standing, shocked.

CHAPTER TWENTY-FOUR

The rest of the evening passed without incident. Samuel and Bartholomew left after they had finished their drinks and Christian went back to join his fellow Silver Street gang members, winking at Meg as he passed. By the time she returned home, the house was in darkness, as usual. She was determined to have a word with Samuel in the morning, but there was no sign of him before she took Thomas to school, and he'd left by the time she returned.

Meg couldn't raise the topic with Eliza, for fear of her mother picking up on the conversation, so she tried to put aside her worries while she concentrated on the day. Another order had come in from the barracks so Meg had Captain Clements's Chelsea buns baked and cooling on a rack by the time Thomas returned from school. He could have the job of delivering them that afternoon.

March had brought with it a further hint of spring and additional customers for the shop. Many were observing Lenten customs so Meg experimented with recipes where she could leave out butter and eggs. Jam tarts, made with a very plain pastry, seemed to find favour, especially with small children.

By Friday of that week, Meg had all but forgotten about quizzing Samuel regarding his reasons for taking Bartholomew to the Fountain. She'd barely seen her brother – he was being kept busy at Hawksdown Castle, which could only be a good thing, in Meg's view. Neither Joseph nor Bartholomew had been in evidence at the Fountain on the nights that Meg worked, although Joseph had just sent an unexpected gift of fish for the family. Meg knew the value of this – it was money that would otherwise have been in his pocket if he had sold it on the open market – and she was grateful. She hoped he would be at the inn when she worked there on Saturday, so she could thank him and, hopefully, put an end to any bad feeling between them.

Saturday brought with it the need to put together another delivery for Ralph Carter. She had divided her purchases from Monday night's trip, packing a third of them for the London carriage, keeping a third for the following week, with another third in reserve in case Bartholomew demanded evidence of what she had done with his loan. Meg still hadn't mentioned it to him. It was something she urgently needed to address.

Only then did it dawn on her. Samuel could carry a note of thanks to the castle when he went to work. Meg was angry with herself for not considering it before. She would write the note on Sunday and ask Samuel to deliver it on Monday.

The carriage for London was already waiting in its usual spot when Meg arrived in South Street and the transfer of goods was easily made. Meg took home the envelope she received in return, going straight to her room, eager to discover what Mr Carter had to say. He had been disappointed by the few things in the last delivery, she read, leaving her to hope that the new one would satisfy him. Once again, he had supplied a list of popular items requested by his customers. Meg noted with pleasure that he would have some of these by the end of the day as they were in her latest package. Some she had never seen among Philippe's stock, but she would ask him whether they could be found.

Meg was already keen to make another trip. She hoped Michael Bailey would be in the Fountain that night so she could discover when the next was planned. The full moon and clear skies made it unlikely that it was imminent, but Ralph Carter's note had made her impatient.

Meg looked for Joseph when she arrived that evening at the Fountain, even though she knew it was too early. He rarely came in before eight o'clock – Meg suspected it was to stop his father drinking too much before their early starts. She wanted to speak to him about the gift of fish – a rare treat in a household still struggling despite the upturn in their fortunes. Meg ploughed the shop takings back into buying baking ingredients and used her income from the Fountain, along with Samuel's contribution, to buy food and keep the household running. Whatever she earned from the trade with Mr Carter she set aside to finance more purchases, pay off her debt to Michael Bailey and, of course, to help pay back Bartholomew's loan. They should have felt wealthier, for they were all working harder, but as yet they hadn't felt the effects. Joseph's fish had been very welcome, enjoyed by all, and provoking comment from Mrs Marsh.

'If you listened to me, Meg, you could be enjoying such a dish every day.'

Meg had rolled her eyes but refused to be drawn. She intended to thank Joseph, though. When had she last spoken to him properly? When she had last worked at the Fountain, he had left without a word. And, if his father was to be believed, he thought she had been paying attention to Bartholomew. Yet despite that, he had still made a point of dropping off the fish – handing it to her mother with just a tip of his cap, by all accounts. Once more, she reminded herself she had no interest in forming a relationship with Joseph. But she did want to remain friends.

As the evening wore on and the bar became busier, there was still no sign of him. Meg was shelving glasses when a distinctive voice behind her made her start. Her hand knocked a glass and she had to move swiftly to prevent it tumbling and smashing on the flagged floor.

'I'll have a tankard of your best ale when you're ready, Meg Marsh.'

She knew it was Bartholomew without turning around. A light, teasing tone, but more cultured than the voices usually heard in the Fountain. This time, there was no cessation of conversation around the bar. The odd person glanced up, but most paid him no heed. And this time, he wasn't in the company of Samuel, but of Christian.

Meg, taken aback, reached for two tankards, checking first with Christian, who nodded assent.

'So, the Fountain is your new favourite drinking place, is it?' she asked Bartholomew. 'You've forsaken Throckings Hotel for the likes of us?'

'Your establishment has far prettier serving maids,' Bartholomew said.

Meg saw a frown crease Christian's brow. He had known her father well and had a protective attitude towards Meg.

'Mrs Dunn attracts a great many compliments,' Meg said smoothly, smiling and making light of it. She set down the tankard in front of Bartholomew so that the ale sloshed and foamed over the side. She was more careful as she served Christian.

The two men withdrew to a table in the corner, leaving Meg to her curiosity. What had brought Bartholomew to the Fountain again? And why had he merited barely a glance from the regulars? Had something happened in the evenings since she had last worked behind the bar?

Chapter Twenty-Five

Meg wasn't sure who had sown the seeds for Bartholomew to become involved with the Silver Street gang, but it seemed his first appearance at the Fountain had been enough to set ideas in motion. Bartholomew's willingness to provide a new conduit for run goods and Christian's recognition of how useful this could be had become apparent in their brief initial encounter. Christian took some delight in imagining conducting such a line of business right under the nose of the very man dedicated to cracking down on it, which chimed very well with Bartholomew's sentiments. A combined enterprise had been born during one or two evenings spent drinking at the Fountain, which Meg hadn't witnessed as she wasn't working. Christian had spread the word that Bartholomew could be both useful and trusted, and now his presence merited barely a second glance.

Meg learnt all this from a Silver Street gang member, who was cautious but excited as to what the relationship could offer. 'He's had boxes made to send produce from the Hawksdown Castle gardens to London once spring comes. And they've all got false bottoms, which can be packed with rum or tea or whatever we have. They'll travel up to the city with as good as the Lord Warden's blessing.'

The man, overcome with merriment at the thought, slapped his leg and almost choked on his ale.

Meg, not sure what to make of it, smiled and shook her head. Did none of the men think to question Bartholomew's motives?

Was there the faintest chance that they were walking into a trap? She glanced at Bartholomew, to find his eyes upon her. Their gaze locked for a second – enough to cause her colour to rise. She turned away at once and found herself thinking that if she'd known he would be there that evening she'd have dressed with more care.

The evening was busy – it was as though the signs of spring had raised everyone's spirits as the cold, hard winter began to recede and the townsfolk could look forward to better times. Everything was simpler in the warmer months for a place so closely allied to the sea and affected by its moods. Smuggling and fishing might be year-round occupations but there was no denying they were preferred when the conditions were easier.

Meg was weary by the time she wiped down the bar for a final time, took a last look around and called goodnight to Mrs Dunn. The hint of spring had not extended to the night – it was cold and clear, and Meg shivered as she turned for home.

A figure detached itself from the shadows nearby and Meg's heart leapt. Joseph hadn't been in all evening and the feeling that something was wrong had been at the back of her mind. Now was her chance to find out.

'I wasn't expecting to see you,' she said.

'I didn't like the idea of you walking home alone,' came the reply. It wasn't the voice Meg was expecting and she stopped, taken aback.

'I have to walk your way to the stables so it was no hardship to wait and escort you. I really don't like the idea of you out alone at this time of night.'

'I'm used to it,' Meg protested, heart thumping. She glanced around, half expecting to find Joseph lurking, too. She didn't like to think how he might react if he was.

'You're shivering,' Bartholomew said. He reached out and drew her to his side.

Meg half stumbled as she tried to match her pace to his, not liking to protest at his assumed intimacy. She barely noticed that they weren't following the route that would have taken them directly to the stables. Instead, Bartholomew guided her down an adjacent street and she had to force herself to pay attention to his words, not just his proximity.

'So, my pretty Meg, where's this beau of yours, the one who was glaring at me all evening when you last worked at the Fountain? He didn't come in tonight. Have you quarrelled?'

Meg was uncomfortable with this line of questioning. And she also had one or two questions of her own to pose. She said hastily, 'He's not my beau. I don't know where he was tonight or why he didn't come in. It's not my concern.'

Bartholomew laughed softly. 'Ah, you don't know how happy it makes me to hear that.' He stopped and moved in front of her, taking her by the shoulders. 'I'm going to do something I've wanted to do since I first set eyes on you.'

Startled, Meg would have stepped back, had it not been for his grip on her. The next instant, his mouth was on hers: warm and pliant, the lips soft and gentle. She responded without thinking and, after a moment or two, she didn't want the kiss to end. When it did, he smiled at her and resumed their walk as though nothing had happened, steering her around a corner so they were now walking back towards the stables.

Meg forced herself to focus on the questions she wished to ask, even though an astonished refrain – 'The Lord Warden's son just kissed me' – was running through her brain.

'Bartholomew,' she stumbled over the name but couldn't call him Mr Banks after what had just happened, 'why do you want to involve yourself with Christian? You aren't going to expose us to your father, are you?'

They'd reached the entrance to the stables and Bartholomew

put his finger to his lips. The stable lad on duty in the doorway was asleep and snoring, legs spread in front of him and an empty ale jug at his side. Bartholomew stepped over his legs and pulled Meg after him. Then, standing in the warmth of the stable, the horses shifting in their stalls, he drew her close and whispered in her ear, 'I mean none of you any harm, and that applies most especially to you, Meg.'

As he spoke, his hands had found his way inside her cloak and he held her around the waist. His touch raised a warm thrill that ran right through her.

'I owe you gratitude – for the money you gave to Samuel for me. I haven't had a chance to thank you.' She murmured the words, fearful of waking the stable lad, so that Bartholomew had to lean forward, laying his cheek against hers, to hear.

'The ladies will be coming to visit the castle now that spring draws near. They can't abide the place in the winter – too many draughts.' Bartholomew gave a low chuckle. 'I hope you will use the money to purchase goods to show them: silks, velvets, lace. The sort of things I'd like to see you wear.'

He stroked her cheek and his fingers traced a line along her jawbone and around the back of her neck, catching in her hair. There was a moment when all of Meg's reason told her to stop this, to leave at once. But the strangeness of the sensations overwhelming her, and her wish for them both to cease and continue kept her anchored there. The horses shifted around them and the smell of them, and the stable, mingled with the warm scent of Bartholomew – a faint trace of soap on his cheek, the scent of leather from the gloves he'd removed and laid aside, the ale on his breath.

At last Meg pulled away, breaking the spell that bound her. 'I have to go,' she said. She feared the stable lad would wake and she would be caught, compromised and shamed.

'I wish . . .' Bartholomew began, then stopped. 'I wish it wasn't so.' He took her hand and kissed it. Then she turned and left as silently as she had entered, slipping out into the empty street. She hurried the short distance to her door, her heart hammering and her teeth chattering in fear and a kind of joy. She would have a great deal to share with the pages of her diary that night.

CHAPTER TWENTY-SIX

When Meg awoke the following morning, after a restless, excited night, she told herself that the events of the previous evening must never happen again. It was wrong, and Bartholomew had no doubt taken too much ale to act as he did. Then his last words came back to her, how he'd said, 'I wish it wasn't so,' when she'd told him she must leave. No matter how she tried to suppress it, her imagination ran on. She remembered how Bartholomew had expressed a wish to see her dressed in silks and velvet and, on her walk home after taking Thomas to school, she fell into a daydream. She saw herself drifting around Hawksdown Castle wearing a dress made of the fine cream silk she had hidden carefully in her bedroom. Since she had never set foot inside it, or any other castle, all she knew of it was the forbidding stone blocks of the thick outer walls. Yet she felt sure a castle would be the sort of place you could wear cream silk without ruining it the instant you crossed the floor.

Such daydreams sustained her through the routine of her days, for now she found herself eager to get to work at the Fountain in the evenings, to see whether Bartholomew would be there. When he wasn't, Meg made an effort to appear her normal cheery self and to stop her eyes being drawn to the door every time it opened. Joseph, however, was often present, which only served to remind Meg she had never longed to see him in the same way. She took care to be civil, and had remembered to thank him for the fish, although she was brisk in her manner. He never waited for her again at the back of the Fountain after it had shut for the evening, although Bartholomew did. He was sometimes there even when he hadn't paid a visit to the inn that evening. Meg's disappointment was bitter on the nights when she found the street empty.

On the occasions when they met, they trod the same path to the stable door without question. Meg began to suspect Bartholomew of plying the stable lad with drink for he was always in the same comatose state. She felt sure his wages wouldn't run to such a quantity of ale each night.

She and Bartholomew rarely wasted time with conversation when they met. Instead, leaning against the straw heaped in the corner, Meg surrendered herself to the sensations Bartholomew could conjure with his mouth on hers and his hands on her body. Each evening their embrace was a little more prolonged, their kisses more feverish. Meg, longing for privacy, resented the stable lad yet it was only his presence that saved her. Occasionally, his snores and mumblings caused them to dissolve into laughter and break apart.

'I want you to come to the castle,' Bartholomew said one evening, as she was about to leave.

'Soon,' Meg promised. 'We have another run planned in the next few days and then I will have plenty of beautiful things to please the ladies there.'

'No.' Bartholomew shook his head. 'I mean, so we can spend some time with each other. Somewhere better than this.'

Their conversation was conducted in a whisper, as always, while the lad snored in the background. Meg considered: the idea both intrigued and terrified her.

'You could come to my room.' Bartholomew warmed to the idea. 'It would be easy enough to manage. There's a staircase close by that leads up from the garden.'

Meg tried to imagine this, and failed. Somehow, their relationship belonged to that place, the stable, and the secret hideaway they had created for themselves there. Bartholomew might suggest meeting her at the castle but she knew it would never be with a view to introducing her to his parents.

That night, as she lay in her bed, she wasn't lulled to sleep by blissful memories of their time together. Instead, wide awake and staring at the ceiling, she saw their relationship as others might see it. They would be deeply shocked, she knew, and, much as she liked to imagine herself in company on Bartholomew's arm – still wearing that beautiful cream silk dress – she knew she was fooling herself. It could never be.

She slept badly, but forced herself to get up early to bake for the shop. They had achieved a modest success and she couldn't afford to let down the regular customers. Meg resolved, not for the first time, to give up all thoughts of relationships and focus instead on making enough money to set herself up with a shop in the city. Even so, the arrival of Michael Bailey's messenger with the news that the boats would be going out that night was unwelcome. Meg was tired – the thought of having to row such a distance, then clamber aboard the French ship to make important choices of goods before embarking on the return trip was just too much. She burst into tears.

Eliza, coming into the kitchen to see whether the latest batch of currant buns had cooled enough to sell, found her sister-in-law sobbing. Meg's face was buried in her arms, which rested among the mess of flour and dough scraps on the table. Two trays of currant buns sat on the side, still waiting to go into the oven.

'Why, Meg, what is it? What's happened?' Eliza was concerned. She closed the door between the kitchen and the hall, hesitating a moment, then quickly putting the trays of buns into the oven. She hurried to sit beside Meg and put an arm round her shoulders. 'Tell me about it.'

Meg, in between bursts of hiccuping sobs, spilt out a jumble of worries from which Eliza was able to pick out the bare bones of the problem.

'I'm going to clear up this table,' she told Meg firmly. 'Then I'm going to make you some soup and bring it up to you in your bed. I'll be very pleased if it goes to waste because you're fast asleep.'

She helped Meg to her feet, dusted off the flour and untied her apron. 'And, Meg,' she said, 'you can't manage everything on your own. You need someone to look out for you. Don't discount Bartholomew – he might be the son of the Lord Warden but he's the youngest. He won't inherit and it's up to him to make his way in the world. Samuel told me how it is. Play your cards right, and who's to say he isn't yours? Now, off to bed.'

And she gave Meg, already half asleep on her feet, a gentle push towards the door.

Chapter Twenty-Seven

Meg, worn out by her burst of emotion, slept long and deeply, waking to find a stone-cold bowl of soup on the floor beside her bed. She would take it downstairs and reheat it, but first she indulged herself in daydreams, smiling at the memory of Eliza's words. Had she been wrong to imagine Bartholomew was so far beyond her? Maybe there was some truth in what Eliza had said about his prospects as the youngest son. It went some way to explaining why he was happy – if not keen – to be involved in smuggling. Perhaps he felt he could be someone in that world when he could never be important in his own family.

Refreshed by her sleep, Meg was now looking forward to that night's trip. She pulled out the packages of run goods hidden around the room, under floorboards and behind panelling, and examined the contents to remind herself of what she already had. She had committed Ralph Carter's list of requirements to memory and she would also be purchasing items with the ladies of Hawskdown Castle in mind. Bartholomew would surely be impatient to set up a meeting before too long.

That evening, Meg joined the Silver Street gang on the beach. The others had met first in the Fountain but Meg never joined them there before a trip. She didn't want to make it obvious to Mrs Dunn what she was up to although she was sure the landlady suspected. She wouldn't have approved, even though she was happy to turn a blind eye to the comings and goings of the smugglers. While it was acceptable for women to be involved in any of the shore roles, such as handling and concealing goods, she would have considered going to sea far too risky.

Everyone who had gathered on the beach near the galley was dressed in dark clothing, hats pulled low and faces covered, apart from the eyes. Even so, Meg knew everyone by their stature and stance. One figure, standing slightly apart, caused her to wrinkle her brows in a frown. Surely it was Bartholomew. Had Michael Bailey taken leave of his senses and added him to the crew for that night?

Christian was walking around, checking that everyone was there, as they quietly took up their usual positions on either side of the beached boat. Bartholomew still stood to one side and he hadn't acknowledged her. As Christian passed, Meg seized his arm. 'Is that Bartholomew? Is he coming with us tonight?' she asked, in low tones.

'He's tonight's watcher on the beach,' Christian replied, then moved on with no further explanation.

There was no time for Meg to speak to Bartholomew for a flurry of activity followed the signal to put the boat into the water. By the time the oars had settled into a rhythm and Meg was able to glance back, they were too far distant from the shore to see his figure. She was seized by misgivings. Did Bartholomew know what was he doing? Who had agreed that he could stand in for old Tom, who had years of experience in watching? Then her worries were forgotten as a gusty squall hit the boat and the crew struggled to hold their course in the resulting choppy waters. Meg, usually exhilarated by such challenges, found herself unexpect-edly anxious. The money for her purchases was safely stowed in her pocket, beneath her skirts, but if anything happened to her it would go with her to the bottom of the sea. And what use would it be to her family there? An image of them all rose unbidden in her mind – her mother at the kitchen range, Eliza, Thomas and Samuel seated around the table, all weeping.

She shook her head and spoke crossly to herself. 'Stop it,' she said, causing Christian, keeping watch, to glance back at her. She shook her head again, this time apologetically. What was wrong with her this evening?

She focused on counting the strokes in an attempt to still her mind. Castle Bay was far distant now – just the odd pinprick of light visible every now and then as they crested a wave. It was still gusty, but they had become used to the conditions and settled into them. Meg, lulled by the rhythm of rowing, was surprised when Christian called a low warning that they had arrived among the boats they sought. They eased off the oars and allowed the galley to drift alongside the largest of the anchored boats, the one where she would find Philippe. She remembered the heart-stopping clamber aboard last time and had to nerve herself to grab at the rope ladder as they bumped alongside. She hauled herself up and onto it, almost losing her grip in the stinging rain as another squally gust struck. Skirt and cloak flapping, she climbed as fast as the conditions allowed, greatly relieved when strong arms grasped her and pulled her aboard.

She descended into the hold on shaky legs, her distress quickly forgotten when she saw what Philippe had spread out in anticipation of her arrival. He'd lit more lamps this time, which enhanced the rich array of goods, their sumptuous colours and textures in stark contrast to the austere whitewashed planking of the hold. Meg barely paused to offer a greeting to Philippe before starting to pile up her purchases. He had done well, sourcing delicate lacework, coils of ribbon, kid gloves and folded silks and velvets that could only have come from the East Indies merchants. Traces of perfume clung to some of the fabrics. Meg imagined them packed into the hold of a great ship, with a cargo of spices.

Her final pile of goods was nearly twice as large as before, and although Meg had more money with her, she still owed a debt to Philippe. He was busy totting up his figures when she heard her name called. Had she spent longer than she'd thought down there, absorbed in choosing her purchases? Was it already time to return or had something gone wrong? She glanced anxiously at Philippe but he was double-checking his addition and was not to be rushed.

'*Un moment* – a moment,' she said to him and hurried up the open wooden stairs onto the deck. She looked over the side to see anxious faces peering up at her.

'Signal from the shore, Meg,' Christian called. 'We need to go.'

Meg looked over in the direction of the distant shore but could see nothing. Christian, however, had the advantage of the spyglass he held in his hand.

'I'm coming,' Meg said, but instead of making ready to climb over the side she hurried back down into the hold, almost stumbling on the last few steps in her haste.

'*Nous partons. Maintenant!* We're leaving, Philippe.'

Philippe showed her the figure he had written down. Once more, it was too much. Meg fought down rising panic. She didn't have time to bargain, or to choose what to leave behind. And she certainly didn't want to leave everything, but she could hear the calls growing angrier.

She put all her money on the table and looked at Philippe. Then she took five things off the top of the pile and looked at him again.

He flapped his hands at her. 'Next time. *Allez!* Go!'

He swept everything she had chosen into one pile and deftly wrapped it, securing it with string. It would be hard to stow such a large parcel on the boat but there was no time to explain. Instead, heart thumping with agitation, she murmured, '*Merci*, Philippe,' and scrambled up the stairs.

Afraid they had left without her, she peered over the side. The galley was still there, the men hunched over the oars. She called to alert them to her descent, tipping the package overboard. Then she descended in a flurry of flapping clothes, hands and feet slipping on the wet wooden rungs. Her fear of falling was tempered by her fear of the men's wrath.

'I'm sorry,' she gasped, breathless, seizing the oars the minute she had gained her seat. Her words were greeted with grim silence.

'What's happened? Onshore, I mean,' Meg pressed on.

'We don't know. The signals have stopped coming.'

The air was heavy with accusation, Meg felt. Was it aimed at her, for holding them up? Or at Bartholomew, whose inexperience would be blamed for putting them at risk?

Meg rested the package on her feet in an attempt to keep it out of the water that always accumulated at the bottom of the galley. She set her mind to maintaining the stroke as they rowed. Christian kept anxious watch, periodically scanning the shore with his spyglass. No one spoke, all preoccupied with what might await them there.

Chapter Twenty-Eight

An exclamation from Christian caused the rowers to falter in their stroke as they neared the shore. Their backs to the direction of travel, they didn't know what he'd seen.

'We're getting the all-clear,' he said. There was relief in his voice but the crew couldn't cheer his words. There was too much risk of discovery so close to the town. Instead, they turned their energies to making land as quickly and quietly as possible. Figures they recognised – regulars from the Fountain – detached themselves from the shadows to lend a hand in hauling the boat up the steeply shelving beach. Then everyone set to, spiriting away the barrels and packages as quickly as possible. Meg saw Christian glance up at the sky. The squally gusts were threatening to disperse the blanket of cloud, making it even more urgent to complete the unloading.

Bartholomew was once again standing to the side, watching. She supposed he was unsure of what to do. Everyone else knew their role and not a word was spoken. She was about to slip away, keen to get home and hide the contents of her package, when he caught her arm. 'Come to the Fountain, Meg. I want to tell you what happened.'

Meg hesitated. She wanted to go home but also to hear what had taken place. She suspected the Silver Street gang would be ready to wash away some of the night's tensions with a quantity of ale.

'I can't be found with this,' she murmured, clutching the package to her. 'I'll take it home and then I'll come to join you.'

She sensed Bartholomew was torn between accompanying her and staying with the smugglers. He would be proud of whatever he had accomplished for them that night.

'You stay. I'll be quicker on my own. And quite safe – I know all the back alleys. I'll see you at the Fountain.'

On impulse, she stood on tiptoe and brushed his cheek with her lips. It was the first public acknowledgement she had made of what there was between them. As she turned to leave, she saw a pair of eyes fixed on her, just visible in a pale face mostly obscured by a scarf. Even that small glimpse was enough to tell her it was Joseph. He never got involved with the smugglers for fear of falling under suspicion and risking his boat and his livelihood. What had happened to bring him there that evening?

Caught out, she felt a flash of shame. She put her head down and made her way up the beach, forcing herself to stay alert for revenue men on the journey home. And this time it was a short journey for the boat had come in at its rightful spot, directly opposite the junction of Silver Street and Beach Street. The quickest way home would be to walk along Beach Street but it was too risky: the bulky package couldn't be hidden beneath her cloak. So Meg wove her way through the warren of alleys, wrinkling her nose at the unpleasant smells that lingered there – rotting fish, stagnant water and worse – doubling the length of her journey.

She reached home without incident, slipping into the house from the backyard. She stood in the kitchen, listening. Was her mother stirring in the room above? She made her way upstairs as quietly as she could, holding her breath and avoiding the treads that creaked. As she passed her mother's door she heard her shift in the bed and call out. Meg paused, heart hammering. Then her mother began muttering and Meg knew she was caught in the throes of a dream. Samuel and Eliza were much less likely to stir, as was Thomas, and Meg reached her room on the top floor with a sigh of relief. She would have to negotiate the stairs again to join the others in the Fountain, but it was important to stow everything carefully away. Impatience made her disinclined to examine her purchases, but she felt happy with everything she had bought by the time she had found a home for it all.

Her hiding places were full and could take no more. It was time to have the discussion with Bartholomew about selling to the ladies at Hawksdown Castle. Delaying no longer, she crept back down the stairs and let herself out of the front door. Prospect Street was silent, but as she rounded the corner onto Beach Street she could already hear sounds of merriment coming from the Fountain.

The inn was full, all the customers up on their feet, the animated talk fuelled by slopping tankards of ale. Bartholomew was surrounded by a crowd – some from the boat, some from the beach. Meg gave a wry smile. He was no doubt explaining what had happened on the shore to cause Christian such concern. She would have to wait a while before she could discover for herself. She could see Mrs Dunn was overwhelmed at the bar, the young pot-washer she had drafted in to help unable to cope and almost in tears.

Meg, thinking to offer her services, pushed through the crowd to reach the narrow passage that gave entrance to the bar. She noticed Joseph – he was standing against the wall, tankard in hand, observing. His eyes caught hers and a smile rose to her lips but he turned away, expressionless. She was stung by his reaction but the crowd around the bar was building so she hung up her cloak and set to work, Mrs Dunn offering her a smile of gratitude. Meg knew she wouldn't ask where she had been that evening, or enquire of any of her customers. It was useful to be able to claim ignorance should the need arise.

Once Meg had satisfied the apparently raging thirst of the men, she was impatient to know what had happened that evening. She feared that by the time she heard the story it would have been embellished too many times in the retelling to bear any resemblance to the truth. Then Michael Bailey was standing before her at the bar. Mrs Dunn, seeing the waiting customers all dealt with, had retreated to her parlour leaving Meg and the pot-washer in charge.

'The same again,' Michael said. 'And one for yourself. I hear you had quite a night of it.'

Meg hesitated. She rarely drank while working, but there was wildness in the air that night and she was excited by her purchases from Philippe's treasure trove. 'Why not?' she said, and poured herself a measure of gin, not having much fondness for ale.

The fiery liquid made her cough, bringing tears to her eyes and a smile to Michael Bailey's face. He never went out in the boats, declaring himself too old to be useful on the oars, but he had proved skilful at coordinating the trips, and the onward journeys of the run goods. Naturally, he took a little of the profits for his trouble.

'So, Meg, we must talk about money.'

Meg glanced around to make sure the pot-washer was too far away to overhear them. 'I will be able to pay the outstanding debt,' she said, 'after Saturday, all being well.'

Michael Bailey nodded. 'And then we can talk about what you owe for running a sideline. If you're going to take up a place in the boat but not sell on your goods through me, there's a price to be paid.'

Meg knew it, of course, but her heart sank all the same. In her wish to get herself established she'd ploughed all her profit into buying more goods and she hadn't put anything aside to keep the Silver Street gang sweet. 'After Saturday,' she promised. 'You can trust me, Michael.'

He looked unusually stern. 'I hope so, Meg. And I'm hoping that man yonder,' he inclined his head towards Bartholomew, still holding forth to a small huddle, 'is as trustworthy as he says he is ... since he seems to have come to us through you and your family.'

He took up his ale, nodded and moved away. Meg looked at Bartholomew and bit her lip. She still didn't know what had happened that evening but somehow it had caused disquiet to Michael Bailey, although not, it seemed, to the rest of the men. Her earlier satisfaction with the goods she had bought began to fade, replaced by anxiety over meeting all the demands she faced.

Chapter Twenty-Nine

An hour later, and the bar was considerably quieter. Most men had gone to their beds and Meg yawned, realising all at once how weary she was. She still hadn't had a chance to speak to Bartholomew, although every other member of the Silver Street gang and most of the inn's other customers certainly had. He'd been bought a quantity of ale as a result. Joseph had left: he'd avoided Meg's glances and departed without buying another drink so she hadn't spoken to him.

Impatient to go home, she made a point of clearing tables and wiping them, pushing chairs and stools back into position, yawning again as she did so. Next, she would go around turning down the lamps, hoping that would send the last few stragglers on their way.

Then Bartholomew was standing before her. 'Shall we go?' he asked.

'Not tonight, Bartholomew,' Meg said. 'I'm so tired. I need my bed.'

'Now that sounds appealing,' Bartholomew said. He looked at her, head to one side and a smile playing on his lips.

'Get on with you,' she said, laughing in spite of herself.

'But I want to talk,' Bartholomew said. 'I haven't told the most important person in here what happened tonight.'

Meg had been curious earlier but the impulse to know had faded

127

as her weariness grew. 'I'm sure I'll hear all about it,' she said. 'It'll be the talk of the town tomorrow, no doubt.'

'But I want you to hear it from me,' Bartholomew persisted.

While they had been talking, the room had emptied and they were alone at the bar.

'Tell me now,' Meg suggested.

Bartholomew shook his head. 'In our special place. I'll see you there in ten minutes.' He blew her a kiss and was gone.

Meg sighed and began to tidy away the last few glasses and tankards. Yet, despite her exhaustion, she was pleased by Bartholomew's persistence. And it wasn't lost on her that he'd described her as the most important person there.

When Meg woke the next morning, sun was already pouring through the flimsy curtains. She smiled and stretched, before a thought struck her. She'd overslept: had someone else made sure that Thomas got to school? And another, darker, thought lurked at the back of her mind, one she couldn't place. What was it?

It came back to her in a rush – memories that made her gasp and put her hands over her face, as if the act of hiding could banish what had happened. After she had left the Fountain, she'd gone to find Bartholomew in the dimly lit stable, noting with surprise that the boy wasn't there. Bartholomew had drawn her into the darkness and told her of his exploits that night: how the revenue men had appeared on the beach where he was waiting and how he'd told them he'd heard a rumour that boats had gone out and were due to make land out of town, on the deserted stretch of beach towards Hawksdown Castle.

He hadn't told them who he was but, as he said, 'I put on my most cultured voice and addressed the leader as "my good man". And I suggested that the Lord Warden would reward them most handsomely for their efforts.' He chuckled. 'They took off up the beach, cursing, but once they were out of sight I signalled to your boat, warning you to hold back until I was sure they were gone. The fools didn't think to question what I was doing there, or why I had a lantern I was clearly trying to hide from them.'

All the while, Bartholomew had been interspersing his words with kisses to her cheek and neck, his hands roaming across her body. She'd wanted to protest but she was so tired it was easier to allow it, responding half-heartedly before being caught up in Bartholomew's mood of excitement. Was it the gin she had drunk, her tiredness, his obvious delight in the role he had played that lulled her into allowing him a far greater liberty than ever before? She remembered that Eliza's words had come back to her – that he could be hers if she wanted him – and at that moment she had indeed wanted him.

Now she was filled with shame. What had she done? She knew it was wrong and that she had taken the most terrible risk. If only the stable boy had been there. If only they hadn't been entirely alone. She could only hope and pray her foolishness wouldn't have consequences. And now, somehow, she must get up and face the day, make excuses for oversleeping and all the while carry the burden of this secret. Nothing would ever be the same again, she was sure.

She felt changed utterly, yet as the day progressed no one seemed to notice anything unusual. It was a Thursday much like any other Thursday and, although she was behind in her household duties and in the baking to be done for the shop, there was little else to cause her concern. Apart from a sudden memory every so often that caused her heart to race and her cheeks to burn: Bartholomew's hands on her; her skirts raised; the press of his body; her wish for it both to stop and go on; the awkwardness of parting.

Meg didn't want to work at the Fountain that night – she sent word to Mrs Dunn that she was sick and wouldn't come in until the following week. She couldn't face seeing Bartholomew, if he was there, although she knew she should speak to him, and urgently. But she couldn't spend an evening serving drinks, watching him and wondering, all the while acting as though nothing had happened between them. And if Joseph should happen to be there, she felt sure her guilt would be plain for him to see. For now, she needed a day or two to think about what had happened and what her next steps should be.

She went early to bed, intent on looking at the figures in her diary. Her original debt to Michael Bailey would be paid off by this Saturday's receipt from Ralph Carter, leaving a little extra to pay as a sweetener. After that, she would be reliant on the next payment from London, which she would need to make more purchases. If she was to put money aside to pay off Bartholomew's loan, she must either send a larger quantity of goods to London or speak to him, as she had intended, about the market among the ladies who visited Hawksdown Castle. But how to do this when her soul shrank for shame from dealing with him? She could hardly bear to share what had happened with the pages of her diary, before blowing out the candle, but who else could she tell? It must be done, as a warning to herself never to behave in such a way again.

CHAPTER THIRTY

On Saturday, Meg's spirits lifted a little as she put the goods together for Ralph Carter's package. In her haste to leave Philippe during Wednesday's trip, she had forgotten to mention the specific requests. She hoped, though, she had fulfilled most of Mr Carter's wishes. She couldn't help admiring the items as she packed them: stroking and smoothing the fabrics, setting slippers atop shawls so they would be the first things visible when the paper was torn off.

Yet as she made her way to South Street on a brisk March morning, the brightness of the sun deceptive as the wind still held a chill, the gloom that had bedevilled her returned. How could she go forward from here? What she had done could not be undone but how she longed for someone to confide in.

With the package safely lodged with the carriage driver, and Ralph Carter's payment received, she was making her way home again, deep in her thoughts, when a familiar voice broke in on them.

'Meg! I was hoping to see you. You didn't come to the Fountain and I was worried. I was going to come to the shop . . .'

It was Bartholomew, on foot, which was unusual. His words tailed off and the anxious frown that creased his brow made Meg question her worries.

'Meg, I should never have acted so. I'd taken too much drink and got carried away. You must think I'd behaved selfishly, without a thought for you.'

Bartholomew's words were tumbling out and Meg saw that they were attracting curious looks as people passed by on their way to the Saturday market. She guided him away from the centre of town towards Beach Street, where it would be quieter. As she walked and listened, her relief grew. She had believed herself cruelly used but Bartholomew's clumsy apology offered her hope.

He needed to hear her troubled thoughts, she decided, and spoke out boldly. 'It's true I was upset,' she said. 'I feared you would think badly of me. I've never done such a thing before – I thought to save myself for my wedding night.' She was despondent again, as her own words struck home.

Bartholomew seized her hand and clasped it in his own, taking it to his lips. 'Then I hope you will consider it *our* wedding night. I'm going to speak to my father. What objection can there be? He has his heir in my older brother. And when he meets you, he will understand.' Bartholomew, full of delight at his plan, was now beaming.

Meg could scarcely believe her ears. If she understood him correctly, he was suggesting marriage. In the midst of her astonishment at his words, she tried to suppress a niggle of doubt. Bartholomew, she had come to realise, threw himself wholeheartedly into things without too much thought for the outcome – in fact, the riskier the better.

'I shall go to him now.' Bartholomew was pacing backwards and forwards on the beach. 'I hope he will see I'm not as feckless as he believes.' He stopped, and looked at Meg, struck by a thought. 'If you wish it, of course?'

'Of course I do.' Meg chased away her doubts, even as her spirit quailed at the thought of meeting Bartholomew's father. 'I never thought to be so happy.' Her daydreams of a London shop suddenly seemed of little consequence, compared to such a marriage.

'Then I am on my way,' Bartholomew said. 'I'll fetch my horse from the stable and ride straight home.'

'Can I tell anyone?' Meg wasn't sure whether she could contain the news.

Bartholomew considered. 'No. Wait until I am able to put a ring on your finger to show everyone you are mine.' He cupped Meg's face in his hands and pulled her close, planting a soft kiss on her lips. 'I'm glad I'm forgiven, Meg. I promise never to cause you such unhappiness again.'

And with these words he strode away, coat tails flapping in the wind. Meg watched him go, filled with wonder. How could her fortunes have turned around so completely in the space of less than an hour? She stood on a little longer, turning to gaze out to sea, her fingers pressed to her cheek where she was sure some warmth from his lips still lingered.

She tried out her name intertwined with his. Meg Banks – or would Margaret Banks be a better fit? Bartholomew and Margaret Banks. Whatever would her father have made of it? His daughter to be married to the son of the Lord Warden.

In the midst of her excitement, she remembered her promise to pay the debt owed to Michael Bailey: she would go now before returning home. She hoped the walk would allow her thoughts to settle but instead they skittered here and there as she went along. Meg was so distracted that she was almost upon Joseph before she noticed. He was walking towards her, arms filled with a pile of nets and his cap pulled low against the sun. Hoping he hadn't seen her, she made an abrupt turn into the nearest street. What could she have said to him, her head and heart full of what had just happened with Bartholomew? Now even more unsettled, she found herself in front of Michael Bailey's shop, where his son was putting up the shutters, their bread all sold.

'He's in the back,' the son said.

She smiled her thanks and went through.

'Ah, Meg. Have you something for me?' Michael was sitting in his usual chair by the window in the back kitchen.

Meg nodded and began to count out the coins. When she had finished, Michael looked at her expectantly.

'A little extra for interest, I think, to discharge the debt?'

Meg sighed and added another coin to the pile. She'd thought his fondness for her father might have counted for something but Michael Bailey's shrewdness had earned him his position among the smugglers.

'Now, Meg, what are we to do about your London business? It must be going well for I hear you held up the boat for quite some time the other night while you made your choice. And then you appeared with a very large package of goods. Since I've no way of knowing your profits, what do you say to a fee for your seat in the boat? A half-guinea, say?'

Meg gasped. It was way beyond what she'd expected. 'I help to row,' she protested, trying to keep her temper. 'And not all those goods are destined for London. Some will go to visitors to Hawksdown Castle, but it could be a while before I'm able to arrange that, and get the money in return.'

As soon as she saw Michael Bailey's expression she wished her words unsaid. She'd hoped to make him understand that since the goods wouldn't be sold for some time she didn't have the money to pay such a debt. Now she saw that she had offered him the perfect excuse to extract more money from her. He doubtless thought the well-born ladies at the castle would pay her well.

She spoke up before he could. 'I don't know what my father would have made of your terms, but I find them too harsh. I can afford this for my place.' She slapped two more coins onto the table. 'If it's not enough, I'll find another boat happy to have my help for the next trip.'

Michael regarded her coolly. 'Don't go getting above yourself, Meg. There's plenty of men waiting for the chance of an oar with the Silver Street gang.'

Meg shook her head, turned on her heel and left, pushing past Michael Bailey's son in her haste to be gone. As she walked home, cheeks pink with indignation, a welcome thought occurred to her. As the wife of the Lord Warden's son, she would no longer need to make such trips, or negotiate with the likes of Michael Bailey.

CHAPTER THIRTY-ONE

Meg attended church on Sunday as usual and tried to behave as naturally as possible throughout the day, all the while hugging her secret to herself. Her mother, after sending several curious glances her way at the dinner table, eventually asked, 'Meg, is everything well?'

Meg thought she had probably overdone her protests that nothing was amiss when she saw Eliza casting odd looks in her direction, too. And when Meg volunteered to stay behind to do the washing-up, after Mrs Marsh decided they should take advantage of the good weather and go for a walk, Eliza said she would help her. She had dried barely two plates before she asked, 'What is it, Meg? I can't decide whether you are nervous or excited but I feel you aren't yourself.'

Meg hesitated, unwilling to break her word to Bartholomew, but felt she would burst if she didn't share her news with someone. 'Bartholomew has asked me to be his wife,' she said, then added hastily, 'but it's a secret. You can tell no one – not even Samuel – until Bartholomew has spoken to his father.'

Eliza seized Meg around the waist and danced her around the room, sending water flying.

'Stop! Stop!' Meg was laughing.

'Such exciting news! When will the wedding take place?'

'I don't know yet,' Meg said. 'It was all very sudden. Nothing can be decided until he has his father's blessing.'

They passed the rest of the time washing and drying dishes in happy imaginings of where Meg might live and how she would fill her days when she was Mrs Banks. Only the return of Mrs Marsh, Samuel and Thomas, all a little windswept after their walk, put paid to further discussion.

'I declare the pair of you must have been gossiping rather than clearing up,' Mrs Marsh said, finding the kitchen still not put to rights. Meg gave Eliza a warning look and turned her attention to Thomas, asking him about their walk. With such joyous prospects on the horizon, she was filled with love for her family.

During the week that followed, Meg waited with increasing impatience for word from Bartholomew. She didn't imagine he would come into the shop but she expected him to make an appearance at the Fountain. There was no sign of him on Monday or Tuesday evening so on Wednesday morning she decided to make a casual enquiry of Samuel.

'Are you still doing work for Bartholomew?' she asked, as she prepared to take Thomas to school. Samuel appeared to be in a hurry, cutting a piece of bread, smearing it with butter, then cramming it into his mouth without even sitting down.

'He's gone away,' Samuel said, his words somewhat indistinct as he chewed. 'I'm working for the head gardener now. He keeps earlier hours than Bartholomew and I'm late.' He was out of the door before she could ask where Bartholomew had gone.

That night, she waited impatiently for Samuel's return for there was no one else she could ask about Bartholomew's absence. Her brother, though, was grumpy and uncommunicative after a day spent working for a harder taskmaster than the Lord Warden's son.

'I've no idea where he is,' he said. 'But if he doesn't come back soon, I'm leaving. I'll not work for such a miserable man.'

Ordinarily Meg would have insisted Samuel must stay on at the castle, for they needed every penny he could earn, but she was too preoccupied to worry about his threat. Instead, a growing anxiety filled her mind. Where was Bartholomew? She tried to tell herself that, after all, only a few days had passed since their conversation. Perhaps the trip had been planned all along. Try as she might, though, she couldn't quell a growing sense of unease.

It was Friday afternoon before she received word, in the form of a letter delivered to the shop. Meg was thankful to be working with Eliza rather than her mother; it meant she didn't have to wait before she could break the seal and open the folded paper.

It was the first time she had ever seen Bartholomew's hand. It was an elegant script, but there were disappointingly few words. His father had sent him to London on business, he wrote, and he was sorry he had had to leave without notice but he hoped to return before too long. Meg read it twice, then turned the paper over to check, but there was no return address.

'Well?' Eliza demanded.

'He's been sent to London by his father,' Meg said flatly. There was no word of how the Lord Warden had responded to Bartholomew's wish to marry Meg. What was she to make of it?

'And?' Eliza was impatient to know more.

Meg shrugged. 'Nothing. No address, nothing other than that he's away and hopes to be back soon.' Disappointment made her voice tremble. She could see Eliza was searching for something reassuring to say.

'Well, at least he has written,' was all she could manage. Then, after thinking on it for a minute or two, 'I expect he will write more fully when he can. I'm sure he just wanted to send you word to explain his absence.'

'I suppose so.' Meg tried hard to be cheered by Eliza's words. Bartholomew had at least wanted to reassure her. Perhaps that was a good sign. She tucked his note into her chemise, next to her heart. She would keep it safe – the first words he had ever written to her.

She was to return to the note again and again over the coming days and weeks, hunting for clues. It was to be the middle of the following month before she heard from him again.

My dear Meg,

My father has found reasons to keep me busy in town, so preventing my return to you, but I hope to manage it before long. The business is too dull to describe – many times I have thought enviously of you at work in the Fountain or walking along the shore and wished myself at your side.

I have been kept moderately entertained by the daughter of my father's friend, Miss Eustacia Blythe. She has been kind enough to let me join her on some delightful promenades in the parks here, which look at their best in this sunny May weather. I have also reacquainted myself with some friends from my school days and they have provided evening diversions of a different kind.

I trust this letter finds you well – hold me in your heart,

Bartholomew

The letter was shaking in Meg's hand by the time she reached the end of it. It had started well enough, but she didn't like the sound of Miss Eustacia Blythe or the 'diversions' offered by his friends. It crossed her mind that perhaps Bartholomew's father had sent him to town to rid him of the notion of marrying her – if he had even got as far as expressing that wish, of course.

As before, there was no return address and no possibility of sharing her anxieties with Bartholomew. In addition, another worry was pressing on her mind. She didn't know whether it was too early to be sure, and she had no one she could trust with the question, but she feared she might be with child. If her suspicion was correct, and if Bartholomew proved untrue, she was in a very great deal of trouble.

CHAPTER THIRTY-TWO

Meg missed Bartholomew terribly and attempted to find reasons to justify why he had stayed in town. Every so often, Eliza asked whether she had heard from him, then stopped when she could see it distressed her. Meg began to go over all her encounters with Bartholomew. Had he been toying with her, and with the Silver Street gang, all this time? Was he just bored and casting around for something that would upset his father?

She tried to counterbalance this notion with Bartholomew's loving words, with the concern he had shown for her, with his marriage proposal. But with each day that passed her faith in him dwindled and her frustration at being unable to reach him grew. She considered going to Hawksdown Castle and asking to speak to his father but her courage failed her. She'd asked Samuel to describe the Lord Warden to her. He'd had no dealings with him, of course, but he wasn't well spoken of in the household. 'He has a temper on him, by all accounts,' Samuel said. 'Bartholomew told me he was very strict and he could never do anything right in his father's eyes.'

It was a shock to Meg to hear how little Bartholomew's father favoured him. She felt her dreams drifting away, like the morning fog that rolled in early off the sea, creeping up Prospect Street until the heat of the sun drove it off. She began to fear she must make her own plans for the future, but she stubbornly clung to her hopes a little longer.

In the meantime, the goods she had put aside for the ladies at Hawksdown Castle would have to be used to supply Ralph Carter instead: she had no money to buy her place in the boat to make another trip to see Philippe. She was forced to ignore any requests that Mr Carter made and simply send him what she had hidden away. When his notes became tetchier in tone, she wrote back to say her supplier didn't have such things but had promised to look out for them.

Then, as her stocks dwindled, she started to send the packages fortnightly rather than weekly, with the excuse that the weather had been unsuitable to make a trip, or the summer nights were too bright to risk it. Mostly, this wasn't true. The boat still went out but Michael Bailey didn't offer her a place. And there had been a noticeable coolness in the attitude of the Silver Street gang members towards her ever since Bartholomew had absented himself.

One evening in the Fountain Christian asked her whether she knew of his whereabouts. She could only answer that she'd heard his father had sent him to town on business.

'What about the goods he promised to send up to London for us, in those boxes he was so proud of?' Christian had a sour expression on his face. 'I should have known better than to trust the likes of him. All that nonsense about saving us from the revenue men the night he kept watch? I don't believe a word of it. I heard that the revenue men were at work up the coast at Kingsdown that night.'

He took his ale and stalked off, leaving Meg unsettled. Was Bartholomew a liar? Had he made up such a story to cast himself in a good light? Worse, had she been completely taken in by him?

Joseph was still a regular at the Fountain and Meg took care to be civil but not over-friendly towards him. She knew she couldn't play with his affections after what had happened, but deep inside she wished she had listened to her mother's words. Joseph, though, had been seen keeping company around the town with Kitty Nash, the daughter of the pie-maker. She was attractive and flirtatious, and Meg had to give herself a stern talking-to when she saw how Joseph looked at Kitty when the pair were together in the street. He was a good, steady man who deserved happiness, and she couldn't allow regret to add to her worries. She did, though, wear the little shell he had given her, keeping it hidden beneath her clothing. His eyes no longer sought it out, she noticed sadly, when she served him his ale. She scolded herself for even having the thought.

As June came in, Meg could scarcely believe her foolish happiness back in April. While all around her rejoiced at the warmer weather and longer days, she shrank from what lay ahead. She hadn't dared to tell Eliza about the baby, even though she was now sure of it. Although she wouldn't need to hide the changes to her figure for a little while yet, she must face the fact she was about to bring shame on her family. Her mother, once she had recovered from her fury, would help her, she was sure. The baby would be brought up as a brother or sister for Thomas, but Meg's future was less assured. Who would want her now, unwed and shamed? Any dreams of opening a shop in London were dashed.

Into this maelstrom of emotions, another letter arrived from Bartholomew. Meg no longer felt any hope when she saw his writing and the unmistakable crest on the seal. She put it aside it to open that night in her room, shrugging off Eliza's curiosity. Nearly ten weeks had passed since his departure and Meg was under no illusions now about his promise to her. Even so, she wasn't prepared for what she read.

My dear Meg,

I hope this letter finds you in good health? I understand this may come as a shock to you but I must inform you, before you hear it from other sources, that I am to be married within the month. Eustacia has done me the honour of agreeing to be my wife. My father is, of course, delighted at the union between two such great families.

You must have realised by now that I couldn't fulfil my rash promise to you. My father wouldn't entertain the idea, and the longer I have spent in London, the more I have come to see how foolish I had become, involving myself with romantic notions of smuggling. And yet I haven't entirely cast off all such ideas – when I return to Hawskdown Castle at the end of the summer I feel sure I can help you by finding you good business among the ladies there. I have already promised Eustacia a fine shawl and perhaps some velvet for the winter. So I will send for you but, in the meantime, I hope you will accept my loan as a gift that might in some way repay you for any disappointment.

Your faithful servant,
Bartholomew Banks

CHAPTER THIRTY-THREE

Alone in her room at the top of the house, Meg let the letter fall to the floor. She had told herself enough times not to hope for anything from Bartholomew but she supposed a little flicker of hope had still burnt. Now it was extinguished. And she would have to bear the mortification of seeing him in town with his new bride, while she carried his child in her belly. She covered her face with her hands. There would be talk in the Fountain – there had already been gossip and teasing about her being sweet on Bartholomew. As his absence had become prolonged, it had faded, but how long until there was no disguising the fact she was with child? She feared it would be doubly shameful when speculation about the father linked her name with that of a newly married man.

Meg picked up the letter and read it again. How could he suggest that she would still provide goods so he could impress his wife and other ladies at the castle? Did he expect her to behave as though nothing had happened, now that he had cast her off without a thought? No doubt he thought he was being generous with his attempt to buy her silence by waiving repayment of his loan. The idea brought a rush of colour to her cheeks and a determination to pay back every last farthing. She could have no further dealings with this man, she resolved.

And how dare he ask after her health? He had no idea of how she had suffered during the long nights when she had fretted and worried over his mysterious absence, and the silence that followed it. Or of the creeping fear when she realised she was carrying his child: the nausea that had to be hidden from the family, the tiredness that overwhelmed her at the end of the day, the terror that someone would comment on her pallor or her gradually changing shape. Over the last few weeks, she had held herself aloof from everyone, overwhelmed by the burden of the secret she carried. And he knew none of this, of course, because he had never supplied her with his address.

Briefly, she contemplated how it all might be different if she was able to tell him about the baby. Would he call off his marriage and take her for his bride instead? She wasn't even sure she would want that now. What sort of marriage could they make under those circumstances? Him filled with resentment at the loss of his prospects, and her – now that she knew the sort of man he was – unable to trust his word or deed. It would be a miserable existence for them both.

Meg cast her mind back to how she had once felt about Bartholomew. She barely recognised herself: her optimism and hope for the future had been dashed. Would there, though, be any benefit in him knowing about the child? She was filled with indecision. Although she shrank from any thought of involvement with Bartholomew, a part of her could see there might be something to be gained for the child's future. As she contemplated this, a chilling thought struck her. If Bartholomew, living in the area with the wretched Eustacia, should discover about the baby, would he see it as a threat? He would be concerned, no doubt, that his wife shouldn't hear of what he would doubtless shrug off as an indiscretion.

Her pride wanted no involvement with him so it was far better he didn't know, she decided. The identity of the father must remain a secret, even though it would make her life more difficult. And now that it was clear Bartholomew was lost to her, she would have to tell her family about the baby to come and weather the storm of her mother's anger. Eliza would guess who the father was, of course, but she would have to be sworn to secrecy.

The following morning, Eliza was already waiting in the kitchen when Meg came downstairs. 'Well?' she demanded, without any preamble.

Meg had no excuse prepared. 'He's getting married,' she said, her voice breaking despite her determination to be strong.

'Married?' Eliza's eyes widened, her eyebrows raised. 'Who? Not you?'

Meg let out a cross between a snort and a sob. 'No, not to me. He hopes I'll understand.'

Wordlessly, Eliza came around the table and hugged her sister-in-law. Then she held her at arms' length and Meg guessed she was about to offer something helpful, but 'Oh, Meg,' was all she could raise.

Meg thought there was no point in delaying yet more bad news. 'And I'm having his baby.'

Eliza opened her mouth to speak but she couldn't find the words. Both women sat down at the table.

'Does he know?' Eliza asked at last.

'No, and I don't want him to.' Meg was fierce.

Eliza looked worried. 'What will your mother say?'

Meg shrugged. 'I think we can guess. But she'll come around to the idea eventually. And Thomas might enjoy having a baby in the house.' Her words sounded forlorn, but it was an idea Meg clung to.

'I'm sure he will.' Eliza nodded slowly. 'And Samuel? What will you say? He's going to be furious, and he's still working up at the castle.'

Meg was firm. 'He's not to know. At least, he's not to know

about Bartholomew. I'll have to say—' She stopped. What would she say?

'Meg, he'll guess. There was gossip about you and Bartholomew, you know. And if you say it wasn't him, folk will think it was Joseph.'

'I don't want Joseph dragged into this.' Meg buried her head in her hands in despair. 'What must you think of me?'

Eliza didn't speak and when Meg eventually looked up it was to find her sister-in-law gazing into the distance.

'How long can you keep it a secret, do you think?' Eliza asked. She glanced involuntarily at Meg's stomach.

'Why?' Meg was puzzled.

'Maybe we could pretend that the baby is mine. He or she could be brought up in the family, by us all.' Eliza's enthusiasm grew as she elaborated on the idea. 'Only you, me, Samuel and your mother know. And maybe Thomas.' Eliza looked doubtful, then brightened again. 'It would mean your reputation was . . .' she hesitated '. . . safe. And I always wanted another baby but it wasn't to be.'

They sat on in silence. Meg, stunned, reflected on the idea. It could work, she thought, provided she could disguise the changes to her figure, most of which would happen in the autumn as the weather changed. Eliza would need to wear padding and the midwife would have to be paid to keep silent, of course. But might it be the best answer for them all, under the circumstances?

CHAPTER THIRTY-FOUR

'Will you do it?'

Meg could hear the hunger in her sister-in-law's voice. She tried to marshal her thoughts. Eliza wanted a baby. Meg didn't. Surely it was the perfect solution. She couldn't think of a good reason not to agree to the plan. Even if she discovered some sort of bond once the baby was born, she'd still see it. Every day, provided she stayed in the area.

She shrugged and nodded. 'Yes,' she said.

Eliza took charge, then, sending Thomas to school with Meg as usual. Once Meg had returned, Eliza asked Mrs Marsh to come into the kitchen.

'Meg has something to tell you,' she said.

Mrs Marsh wore a puzzled frown as her daughter, haltingly, began her tale. She could barely contain her rage by the time Meg had finished.

'Whatever were you thinking?' she demanded. 'What persuaded you that the Lord Warden's son would look twice at you after he'd taken his pleasure?' She accompanied her words with a look of such scorn that Meg's heart all but withered in her breast.

'It wasn't like that, Ma,' she protested. Indeed, despite all that had happened, Meg thought Bartholomew had been genuine in his offer of marriage. It was his father who had put paid to the idea, she was sure. Bartholomew was weak and easily influenced, she

148

realised now. But if she couldn't believe his feelings for her were genuine at the time she didn't think she could live with herself.

'Well, you've learnt the lesson that many girls before you have learnt and many will after.' Mrs Marsh was grim-faced. 'Whatever would your father have said?' She paused. 'But, then, it would never have happened if he was still with us. I blame myself.'

'No, Ma,' Meg protested. Would it have been different if her father was still alive? She thought not. She feared she would still have found a way to behave as she had done.

'So secretive, Meg.' Mrs Marsh hadn't finished. 'All this going on behind my back. Are you set upon bringing shame on the family? What else is there I don't know about?' A thought came to her. 'We never did talk further about the run goods.' She glared at her daughter.

Meg thought guiltily of the little stock of fine fabrics and fripperies hidden upstairs. Then she comforted herself with the thought that the money they would earn would be important in the future.

Eliza tried to divert Mrs Marsh by explaining her plan for the forthcoming baby, which only earned her the sharp edge of her mother-in-law's tongue. 'You think to distract from Meg's shame by wearing padding? What will Samuel have to say about it? And Thomas? We'll have the whole town talking about us. How can I hold up my head in church?'

'Meg is young and fit and she may not show very much,' Eliza soothed. 'And if she does, she'll have to hide away and we'll say she is sick.' Mrs Marsh didn't respond so Eliza continued, 'Whatever happens, we'll keep the baby here in the family. Why not spare Meg from gossiping tongues and let everyone believe the baby is mine?' She looked appealingly at her mother-in-law.

'You haven't heard the last of this from me, Meg.' Mrs Marsh got up from the table. Her movements were those of a woman much older. 'I won't be working in the shop today. I'm going back to bed to think about it.' She paused at the door. 'Not a word of this to anyone, do you hear?'

Eliza and Meg listened in silence to her slow, heavy progress up the stairs. With a sinking heart, Meg wondered whether the shock would drive her back to the state she had been in for so long after her husband's death.

'That didn't go too badly.' Eliza was cheerful.

Meg stared at her, incredulous.

'No, really.' Eliza tried to reassure her. 'It was a shock, but she'll come around when she's thought about it. She'll see it's best for everyone, I'm sure.' She got to her feet. 'I'm going to open the shop. Can you do some baking? We don't have much left to sell.'

Meg supposed she must. In truth, though, the smell of the baking, previously so appealing, had begun to turn her stomach. She had learnt to go out and stand in the yard, taking a few deep breaths of fresh air to help fight the sensation. She was weary: her troubled night and the emotion of unburdening herself to Eliza and her mother had taken its toll. As she stirred the mixture for the currant buns, her eyelids drooped. She yawned and would have given anything to lay her head on the table and sleep. The temptation grew even stronger once the trays of buns were baking but she forced herself to wait until they were out of the oven and cooling on a rack. Then she crept up the stairs, laid her head on the pillow and was fast asleep in an instant.

When she woke an hour later she was puzzled. What was she doing in her bed, fully clothed in the daytime? Then the memory of what had passed that morning returned to her and she closed her eyes briefly in shame and distress at her mother's reaction. Eliza's plan was for the best, she told herself. The child would have a better future brought up as a brother or sister for Thomas rather than as the bastard child of an unwed mother. And it seemed to have given Eliza a new sense of purpose. Yet she couldn't shake off the unsettling sensation that the baby didn't belong to her any more, that since this morning it had somehow become Eliza's. Meg was just the vessel carrying it for a while.

Her thoughts turned to money. It was important to ensure there was enough for the family in the coming months. They had three sources of income: the shop, Samuel's work, and her trade in run goods. The shop was ticking along nicely but, considering it took Meg, Eliza and Mrs Marsh to provide for it and run it, it was barely profitable. Samuel's job wasn't secure and the run goods hadn't provided much of an income. Until now she had kept most of her earnings from Ralph Carter to fund the purchase of more goods. And the price Michael Bailey wanted to charge for her place in the boat was still a stumbling block.

An idea had taken root in her mind, but Meg tried hard to push it away. Pride had made her determined to pay back Bartholomew's loan, but what if she didn't – at least for a while? There was no denying the money would be very useful, and what remained of it would allow her to buy more goods. If she sold these direct to the ladies at Hawksdown Castle, as Bartholomew had suggested, she would no doubt get a good price without a middleman such as Ralph Carter taking his cut. She had vowed to have nothing to do with Bartholomew when he returned, let alone entertain his idea. Now she was not so sure. Could she turn down the chance of making enough money to provide security for the family, and her baby, in the coming months?

Chapter Thirty-Five

As summer progressed, Meg stuck grimly to her resolve that it was her duty to be responsible for the security of the family income and to provide for the baby while she could. She supposed Eliza's plan was a good one: in any case they seemed set on following it, although Samuel and Thomas were still in ignorance. Mrs Marsh remained tight-lipped and this saddened Meg. She didn't like to feel she was such a disappointment to her mother. There was nothing for it, though, but to try to earn back her good opinion by keeping her head down and working hard.

She continued to help out at the Fountain when asked, thankful that as yet there was little change in her figure. And, after nausea prevented Meg from baking on more than one occasion, Eliza stepped in. Her sister-in-law proved that she was a more than capable baker in her own right so Meg took care to ask her more frequently, wondering whether she had been guilty of assuming Eliza to be lazy and incapable when she simply hadn't given her the chance.

Her trade in run goods weighed heavily on her. She knew it upset her mother, but Meg saw it as the best way to make money for the family. And, with her marriage hopes dashed, she'd gone back to the idea of having her own shop one day. Eliza's plan to bring up the baby as her own within the family meant that wasn't as impossible as it had once seemed, although the shop could no longer be in London, of course. Yet, her store of goods was dwindling. She had kept Ralph Carter reasonably well supplied, but the peevish notes he sent after she'd needed to skip the odd week discouraged her from negotiating the prices upwards, as she had once hoped. He kept requesting items, though, so she felt sure that Philippe supplied better goods than he was able to buy elsewhere.

Since her disagreement with Michael Bailey, she hadn't taken an oar in the galley again. She had been able to request goods from Philippe, going through Michael with Christian acting as go-between, but she longed to be able to see the wares and make her own choices. She couldn't expect Christian to bargain on her behalf, either, so she feared she was paying above the odds. Even if Michael relented over charging her for her place in the galley, it would be too late. She wouldn't want to risk the exertion of rowing and clambering aboard the French vessel, not in the condition she was so successfully keeping secret.

Such thoughts came to her throughout her days, causing heavy sighs and a furrowed brow, so that Eliza would ask anxiously, 'Are you feeling unwell, Meg?'

Meg, unconscious of her actions, would adjust her expression, saying, 'No, no, Eliza. I'm perfectly well.'

She hadn't realised how habitual her worry had become until the day when she was returning from the barracks, having had cause to visit Warrant Officer Perkins again to request settlement of their outstanding account. She had been careful to visit during daylight hours and this time hadn't experienced any unpleasantness from the soldier on the gate. She was walking away, head down and deep in thought, when she became aware of someone calling after her. She turned without thinking, her heart giving a great lurch when she saw Bartholomew.

She had supposed the day would come when he would reappear in town but, as the weeks passed, she had stopped expecting it. Now, in late August, here he was. She supposed she must be staring for she fancied he blushed, but perhaps it was the heat. He looked much the same, although he was dressed even more smartly than usual in a pale frock coat and breeches. She tried not to think about her shabby skirt and second-hand blouse, purchased from Mrs Voss and chosen because they were too big for her frame and would hopefully disguise any future changes in her figure.

'I didn't know whether to speak,' Bartholomew said. Meg thought he looked as though he now regretted doing so. 'You were so deep in thought when you walked by me, with such a frown—' He broke off. 'I do hope you haven't suffered mistreatment at their hands again?' He indicated the barracks.

Meg shook her head. 'No, no, not there.'

There was an awkward pause. Had the thinly veiled barb struck home? Bartholomew didn't press her further and Meg made to turn away.

'Wait – how are you, Meg?' There was a note of eagerness in his voice, as if he wished to detain her.

Meg shrugged. 'Well enough.'

Bartholomew's glance passed over her from head to toe and it was a struggle to hold herself proud.

He nodded. 'You look well. But I feel something is troubling you.'

Meg almost laughed. How to answer? she wondered, with some bitterness.

'I was thinking …' Bartholomew began, then paused. He seemed uncertain whether to continue and Meg was ready to turn away again. Then he continued in a rush, 'My father is having a party in two weeks' time.' For a moment Meg, startled, thought he meant to invite her. Then he continued, 'There will be many guests from London, with their ladies, of course. It might be a good time for you to bring goods to the castle.'

154

Meg couldn't fathom his look: there appeared to be a hint of eagerness, quickly masked and replaced by mild enquiry, as though he'd asked her about the weather.

She bit her lip. She would dearly have liked to refuse, and to give him a piece of her mind while she did so, but she was held back by the thought of the money to be made and what it might mean to the family. And to the baby.

She must have hesitated too long for Bartholomew added, 'I thought you must have amassed quite a selection of goods to show, from the money I lent you.'

She shot him such a look that he hastened to correct himself. 'The money I gave you, I mean.'

'Name the time and place,' she said. She wanted to be as businesslike as possible. 'I can bring samples of what I have, take orders, and arrange for the goods to be delivered the following day.'

There was little point in taking everything she had all the way to the castle, she reasoned, when Bartholomew would probably have her display it in secret in a barn. Better to have samples to tempt the ladies, or their maids, and to encourage them to compete against each other. Thomas could act as delivery boy the next day.

'The second Friday in September,' Bartholomew said. 'Come to the castle garden, by the side gate in the wall as you leave the sea path. I'll meet you there at nine.'

Meg nodded and began to walk away, deep in thought once more but with the frown erased from her brow. She resented his reference to the money, but the arrangement he suggested could be the answer to some of her worries. A memory came to her and she turned back to Bartholomew.

'I'll bring the shawl,' she called after him.

Bartholomew, who had remained on the same spot, watching her depart, appeared puzzled. 'Shawl?' he asked.

'For your wife. You said you had promised her one.' Meg was sure those were his words.

'Oh, yes, the shawl. Yes, do that.' Bartholomew smiled, but not at Meg. It was a peculiar smile, she thought, as though at a private jest. She wondered at it, then shook off the uneasiness it had prompted in her.

She walked home, feeling the sun on her back and noticing the sparkle of the sea, glimpsed at the end of the streets she passed along. It was as if her senses had come back into focus after a long spell of living in a muted world. She had survived her first encounter with Bartholomew, managing to be civil and hold her tongue, despite all she wished to say. Above all, though, after the initial shock of seeing him, he had left her unmoved. She was no longer in thrall to Bartholomew Banks: he had shown her only too clearly what kind of man he was.

CHAPTER THIRTY-SIX

M eg didn't mention her encounter with Bartholomew to Eliza, or the arrangement they had reached. She suspected Eliza would say her plan to sell to the ladies at Hawksdown Castle wasn't worth the risk, when her regular trade with Ralph Carter involved little more than a trip to South Street on a Saturday to deliver a parcel to his carriage. Meg, though, had been provoked by Bartholomew's mention of the loan, especially after he had sought to ease his conscience by suggesting she should keep the money. His uncalled-for reminder had given her a jolt. She was determined to show him she was still successfully conducting her business, even if he never gave her a second thought now he was married.

And, in truth, Meg relished the excitement of undertaking a secret adventure. She missed being an occasional crew member of the smugglers' galley: the exhilaration of rowing out to the French boats and back, with the danger of discovery ever present. Her trip to Hawksdown Castle would be undertaken alone, with none of the silent camaraderie of a smuggling voyage, but the anticipation of it gave her the thrill she had been missing.

On the evening of the party at the castle, Meg stepped out into the darkness, quietly drawing the door closed behind her. She'd left her mother dozing by the kitchen range – when she woke she would believe her daughter already abed and she would make her own way upstairs without thinking to check. Now Meg hesitated in the road. It was cloudy, which suited her purpose well, but a ferocious wind howled off the sea and she feared it would blow out her lantern on the lonely walk to Hawksdown Castle.

A movement in the street caught her eye and she turned sharply, but there was nothing to be seen. A cat, perhaps, or – more likely – a rat. She pulled her father's cloak tightly around her to hide the package she carried. She knew well enough how to keep herself hidden when she was out after dark, so she threw the hood of her cloak over her hair and set off, choosing to slip in and out of the alleyways, rather than follow the more direct route out of town.

Her heart beat faster as she thought of what lay ahead. It would be only the second time she had seen Bartholomew since he'd offered to marry her. And now he was married to another woman, no doubt residing in comfort in Hawksdown Castle, while she would be reduced to furtive dealings in the castle gardens. She'd once thought Bartholomew the man for her. Now she could see him for the weak fool he was, tied to his father's wishes. And yet, if she conjured up the memories of their trysts in the stable, she could still feel the thrill of them. Had it been so wrong to find him attractive? His devil-may-care attitude and his flouting of his father's rules behind the Lord Warden's back had appealed to her every bit as much as his blue eyes and blond hair, curling over his collar. He'd tilted her chin up towards him as they'd kissed in the shadows and promised her riches, 'the like of which you've never seen', from her smuggled goods. Tonight would show whether there was any truth in those promises, or whether they were empty words, like all his others.

She imagined the castle full of ladies from London, eager to buy. She'd chosen the goods carefully: her package held samples of fine French lace, a pair of kid gloves, lengths of muslin and silk, as well as the embroidered shawl for Bartholomew's wife. As she left the town behind, stepping out onto the path along the coast, she was caught and buffeted by the wind. There was no shelter from the elements here and her lantern flickered and died almost as soon as the last lights of Castle Bay faded from view. Meg sighed and set the lantern down a little way from the edge of the path, casting about for a landmark to recognise the spot. It was pointless carrying it further – she would collect it on her return. She set her face into the wind and hurried on.

She thought she was in good time but there was no point in dawdling. There was little between her and her destination – a few grander houses, set back from the seafront, then a little cluster of fishermen's cottages, feeble light filtering through one or two tightly closed shutters. After that, just open space with not another soul to be seen.

Meg pressed on until the walls of the castle rose before her. In the darkness she could just pick out the gate that led to the garden, left slightly ajar for her. She stepped through it cautiously, pausing as the gravel path crunched beneath her feet. It was quieter here, the bulky castle walls keeping out the constant roar of the wind, and she moved onto the grass, advancing across it towards the moat, her senses on high alert.

Even so, she wasn't ready for the hands that grasped her, pulling her arms roughly behind her back. The leather glove clamped across her mouth stank of horse sweat and the voice in her ear was a harsh whisper. 'Don't make a sound or this knife will part your pretty flesh.' The clouds lifted for a moment to reveal a blade, glinting in the cold moonlight.

PART TWO

CARRIE: 1913

CHAPTER ONE

Carrie Marsh collected up the slates from the tables and stacked them in neat piles. She loved her work, but was she a good teacher? The children sat and listened obediently but she could hardly fail to notice that they left the schoolroom in a joyous rush at the end of the day. Mrs Chambers, the principal of the two-room school, seemed happy enough with her although Carrie suspected that, to save money, she had chosen to overlook her lack of a formal qualification.

Carrie straightened the leather belt that circled her slender waist, pulled down the cuffs of her blouse and smoothed her skirt before stepping through the school's heavy oak door, turning to lock it behind her with the iron key that was as large as her hand. She would leave this with the caretaker in his cottage around the corner, as she did every school night, then retrieve her bicycle from his yard. She would pedal the uphill mile home and make her mother something to eat, befitting what she saw as her invalid status. This would be a piece of lightly steamed fish, three potatoes of equal size and a small carrot stored from their summer harvest. After that, Carrie would be free to take another iron key – the one that hung beside their back door, left by there by the gardener who once lived in the cottage – and slip it into her pocket for the short walk up the path to unlock a creaky iron gate. Checking to make sure she was unobserved, she would slip through it, grip the rusting handrail and hurry down the steps hewn into the side of the old chalk quarry: steps that would take her down into the Glen, the secret garden where Oscar waited for her.

At the thought of Oscar, colour rose to Carrie's cheeks. She forced herself to focus on the journey ahead, reaching up to pin her dark brown hair firmly in place. It was a blustery October afternoon and it would take little for her hair, unruly at the best of times, to break free and whip itself into knotted tangles. She didn't relish the thought of cycling home, buffeted by the wind that would cause her ankle-length skirt to flap and make her unsteady. It was the sort of weather that would certainly make her mother question why she would want to leave the house again.

She had met Oscar through her friendship with his sister, Ada. Their family, the Hadleys, lived in Hawksdown Lodge, a substantial house overlooking the sea, set in a walled garden a little way from the school along Grove Lane. They moved in very different circles from Carrie and she wouldn't have been introduced to them in the ordinary way of things, if Mrs Hadley hadn't invited the schoolchildren to a tea party that summer in the grounds.

Mrs Hadley, whose husband, Charles, was a banker and a patron of the school, had initially presided over the proceedings but, as the children's spirits rose and the volume increased, she murmured an excuse and drifted away into the house, leaving her daughter, Ada, to deputise for her. Ada seemed to relish the challenge. Surveying the tea tables on the lawn, dotted with puddles of spilt lemon cordial and piled with more sandwiches and cakes than the over-excited children could ever hope to eat, she suggested some rounds of games.

'Let's have three teams,' she said. 'And I think I can find a prize at the end for the best one.'

Mrs Chambers, who taught the other class in the school as well as being the principal, had anticipated a relaxing afternoon of tea-drinking and admiring the garden and was not best pleased at being called upon to exert herself. Luckily the children, despite their excitement at being out of school for the afternoon, proved remarkably biddable. Or perhaps Ada had a way with them, Carrie had reflected, before throwing herself into helping organise the running races and games with tennis balls, of which the family seemed to have a plentiful supply.

An hour later, the activities concluded, the children returned to the sandwiches and cake, oblivious to the fact that the former were now dry and curling. 'I'll go and find something for a prize,' Ada said.

'Then we really must get the children back,' Mrs Chambers said. She'd noticed that some, clutching cake, were vanishing down the winding paths that led through the garden. She clapped her hands to summon them but they pretended not to hear.

'I won't be long,' Ada said. She turned to Carrie. 'I wonder, Miss Marsh, whether you would accompany me? I would value your advice. I don't want to choose something unsuitable for a prize.'

She led the way into the house through the French windows from the garden. Carrie followed, trying not to stare as they passed through light-filled rooms, hung with heavy silk curtains at either side of floor-to-ceiling windows overlooking the sea. Thick rugs on the polished floors muffled their footsteps.

Two men lounged on chairs in a hallway so large that Carrie at first mistook it for another room.

'Have they gone yet? Oscar and I want a game of tennis.' The speaker was a dark-haired young man, idly spinning a tennis racket on the floor. It fell with a clatter as he noticed Carrie.

'This is Miss Marsh, one of the teachers,' Ada said. She turned to Carrie. 'My brothers, Oscar and Jeremy. Please excuse Jeremy's manners.' He had the grace to blush and Carrie saw that he was her age or perhaps a little younger.

Oscar glanced up as she passed, and she gained the impression of curly dark hair and dark eyes in a very handsome face, before Ada led the way upstairs.

'I thought a book,' Ada said, over her shoulder, as they climbed the stairs. Carrie, studying the portraits lining the walls, was momentarily confused.

'A book? Oh, yes, for the prize. Anything would be lovely. It's very generous of you.' She wanted to enquire whether the paintings were all of Ada's relatives – there was certainly a resemblance in the eye and hair colour – but instead asked, 'Have you ever taught children? You seem to have quite a way with them.'

'Goodness, no.' They were standing in a bedroom overlooking the garden. Carrie tried to ignore the childish shrieks drifting in through the open window. 'Although Mother has suggested I should offer to help at the school. She thinks I need to do something useful to fill my days.' She was running her fingers along the spines of books on a shelf as she spoke.

'We'd be very happy to have you,' Carrie said. She would like to get to know Ada better, she decided: a young woman of a similar age but from such a different background.

Ada pulled out three volumes and held them out for Carrie's inspection. *The Railway Children*, *The Phoenix and the Carpet* and *The Secret Garden*, each with a cover more enticing than the one before. The little girl in a red coat and hat, reaching out to open the hidden gate in *The Secret Garden*, caught her eye, but before she could volunteer her thoughts, Ada said, 'Actually, why not take all three? A prize for each team. They can't take them home, of course, but you could keep them in the library.'

Carrie hardly liked to say that the two-room school had no library, although Ada would discover that soon enough if she came to help. Instead, she enthused, 'They are lovely and the children will be delighted. We will read them aloud to the class and keep them away from harm. But are you sure you can spare them?'

'I haven't read them in a long while,' Ada said. 'Now, I think we'd better get back to Mrs Chambers and help her retrieve the children from the shrubbery.' She laughed and led the way, while Carrie took one last look around the bedroom, evidence of comfort everywhere, from the bed with its blue satin eiderdown to the velvet-upholstered chair in the window.

Oscar and Jeremy were in exactly the same spot as they passed through the hall. Jeremy ignored them but Oscar glanced up again. Carrie was immediately conscious that her hair was escaping from its pins after their earlier games, and her blouse was a good deal more creased than when she had left home that morning.

The sound of Mrs Chambers trying to call the children to order hurried her on. Remarkably, all forty children seemed to be gathered on the lawn below the terrace. Ada was the first to spot the reason.

'Who let out Jasper and Juno?' she asked, as if to herself. Carrie followed her gaze and spotted two large hounds coursing backwards and forwards over the lawns, tails wagging and noses to the ground. 'It must have been Jeremy.' Ada answered her own question.

'Well, it looks as though it worked.' Carrie was amused. 'They've rounded up the children nicely. And now we must leave you in peace.'

She turned to the children. 'Miss Hadley has been very kind indeed. She has given a prize of a book for each team.' She turned to Ada with a smile. 'And I hope, if you ask her politely, she might be persuaded to come and read them to you.'

The chorus of 'Please, miss,' was quelled by Mrs Chambers, who asked them to show their appreciation for the afternoon by applauding, which the children duly did. Mrs Hadley had

167

reappeared on the terrace, smiling graciously as the children formed ragged lines and departed on the short journey back to school.

Ada accompanied them to the garden gate. 'I will come,' she said to Carrie, as she waved them off. 'I can't possibly let the children down.'

And in this way the friendship between Carrie and Ada began.

CHAPTER TWO

The following day at school, Mrs Chambers asked the children to write letters to Mrs Hadley and her daughter, thanking them for their kindness in holding the tea party. Carrie supervised her class as they laboriously copied down the words from the blackboard: *Thank you for having our school to tea. We had a lovely time and enjoyed the sandwiches, cake and games. We love our new books and we are looking forward to hearing the stories.*

They could decorate the edges of the paper in any way they liked. Carrie handed out the coloured pencils that were only ever used on special occasions and watched as the children drew sandwiches and cakes, which bore little resemblance to those served on the day. Some of the girls added butterflies and flowers and one or two of the boys attempted to draw the dogs, Jasper and Juno. Carrie put all the letters into a card folder, along with those from Mrs Chambers's class. She added a note herself, addressed to Ada:

Dear Miss Hadley,

The children would be delighted if you could read to them. I've told them we will wait to start The Secret Garden *until you are able to come in. I hope that isn't too presumptuous. I wondered whether 2.30 p.m. on Wednesday would be convenient.*

Yours sincerely,

Carrie Marsh

She tied a piece of ribbon, brought from home, into a bow around the folder and took it to Hawksdown Lodge, wheeling her bicycle to the garden gate and leaving it there while she made the delivery. When the school had visited they had been met on the terrace, but she decided it would be more appropriate to go to the front door, even though it meant walking across the lawn in clear view of the house.

Before Carrie had progressed very far, a voice called, 'Can I help you?'

She turned to see Oscar on the terrace, rising from a wicker chair half hidden behind a potted palm, folding a newspaper under his arm. Carrie went towards him, holding the folder before her, like an offering. 'I'm Carrie Marsh from the school. We visited the other day for tea. The children have written thank-you letters and I wonder whether you'd be so good as to give them to your mother.'

Oscar inclined his head. 'Put them on the table and I'll make sure she sees them.'

Carrie did as she was bade, trying not to appear put out by his rudeness. Would it have hurt him to take them from her? He was treating her as though she was a servant.

She nodded to him, unsmiling, and marched back to the garden gate. She hoped he was watching her and would notice how cross she was. But when she closed the gate behind her and glanced back, he was sitting in his chair hidden behind the newspaper once more.

Thankfully, Ada proved to be friendlier than her brother. She sent a note to Carrie, confirming she would be delighted to read to the class, and she was as good as her word, arriving promptly at two thirty on Wednesday. Mrs Chambers had declared it would be unfair for Carrie's class alone to benefit, so her pupils were crammed into the classroom, too. Children were sitting cross-legged on the floor at the front and squeezed two to a chair behind the tables.

Carrie hoped Ada wouldn't find it overwhelming. The children had become noisy with excitement and the room was hot and stuffy with so many extra bodies. Carrie feared that it smelt stale: not all the children had facilities to wash regularly and although she had grown used to it, it might come as a shock to Ada. She'd taken the precaution of bringing in flowers, which bloomed unloved in the Glen, and setting them in a large jar on the teacher's desk. Their scent would hopefully overpower anything unpleasant.

Ada's visit was a great success. She was a natural storyteller, reading with a good deal of drama, and the children listened, spellbound, until discomfort led to an outbreak of wriggling and squirming just after three o'clock. Carrie stepped in and suggested it was time to thank Miss Hadley for her visit. After the chorus of thanks she left the children to tidy up the classroom under Mrs Chambers's supervision, while she saw Ada out.

Ada lingered on the school steps and said, 'I really enjoyed myself. Can I come again?'

Carrie had no hesitation in saying, 'Yes.'

After a couple more visits to the school, Ada asked Carrie to join her for tea on the coming Saturday. 'The boys have invited friends over for tennis and I'd like to have a friend for company, too,' she said. Misreading Carrie's astonishment at being deemed a friend she added hastily, 'I don't expect you to play tennis.'

Carrie laughed. 'I've never played tennis, but tea would be lovely. I'd be delighted.'

'When the boys get bored, we can take a turn,' Ada said.

Carrie thought she wouldn't like her first attempt at tennis to take place under the unfriendly eyes of Oscar and Jeremy, but she held her counsel. Instead, she promised to join Ada on Saturday at three o'clock, provided the weather was fine.

She arrived promptly, under sunny skies and bearing a bunch of flowers, again picked from the Glen.

'These are beautiful,' Ada exclaimed. 'Much nicer than anything we grow here.'

Carrie's gaze swept the garden, the borders in full bloom, and she immediately felt embarrassed. 'You must forgive me – what was I thinking? You have so many lovely flowers here. You hardly need more.'

'Not at all,' Ada protested. 'I will put these in a vase in my bedroom.' She clutched them to her as though she feared Carrie would snatch them back.

'They're from the Glen,' Carrie said, to cover her embarrassment. She went on to explain about having access to the secret garden at Hawksdown Castle. 'The Glen is overgrown and neglected now but it must have been loved at one time, judging by the flowers that still bloom there.'

Oscar and Jeremy came sauntering past as Carrie explained this to Ada. She caught Oscar's arm and demanded he sniff the flowers.

'Have you ever smelt anything so divine as these roses?' she asked. 'We don't have anything like that here.'

'I can show you the secret garden, if you like,' Carrie offered. 'I have a key.'

Oscar appeared interested. 'A secret garden?' he asked.

Carrie nodded and would have replied but Ada interrupted, 'Why don't we have a picnic there next weekend?'

Much as Carrie would have liked to say yes, she knew the Glen wouldn't be suitable. The paths were so overgrown it was hard to reach the bottom, and even if they could find a clear spot to spread a picnic blanket, much of it was overshadowed by trees.

'We could picnic on Hawks Down, up behind the castle,' she suggested. 'I can show you the garden afterwards. It's run wild and won't be comfortable for a picnic but Hawks Down has views over the sea and plenty of places to sit.'

Oscar and Jeremy had gone to join their friends on the tennis court and the maid had arrived with a tea tray, but Ada was enthusiastic about the plan. 'Mabel in the kitchen will make us a picnic, I'm sure. Just the four of us – you, me, Oscar and Jeremy.' Then she caught herself and looked at Carrie. 'I'm being presumptuous, Miss Marsh. Perhaps you have a young man you walk out with and he would be unhappy with this plan?'

Carrie smiled. 'No, I haven't. And, please, call me Carrie. I'm only Miss Marsh in school.'

The maid took away the flowers to arrange in a vase and they settled to their tea on the terrace, the gentle thwack of tennis balls providing a backdrop to their conversation. Carrie discovered that the three siblings were at home for the summer, before Oscar moved to London to take up a job in his father's office. Jeremy was going to study at Oxford.

'And you?' Carrie asked Ada.

Ada shrugged. 'I'm not sure. There aren't many things that Father and Mother agree on as being suitable for me, since I don't have talents in any particular area. I fear it will be good works for me, trailing in Mother's wake, until it's time to marry.'

Carrie knew she shouldn't have been surprised at Ada's description of what the future held for her, but she'd imagined her as too spirited to be happy to follow such a path. She took in the surroundings: the beautifully tended lawns and flower borders, the tennis court where the maid was now delivering drinks to the players, all overlooked by the beautiful house, sited to make the most of the sea views. Ada had been born into this and, she supposed, would naturally expect to take up the reins of a similar comfortable life elsewhere, perhaps with one of Oscar or Jeremy's friends. She looked with new eyes at the young men, now standing around with their drinks and ribbing each other about the match they had just played.

How different her own life had been, she thought.

CHAPTER THREE

Carrie's father, William, was away from home a good deal. At least, that was what her mother expected her to tell people. In fact, William hadn't lived at home for many years. He lived somewhere in Canterbury, although his address changed frequently. Carrie took a train to the city once or twice a year to meet him. They would walk on the city walls to a park or, if the weather was against them, to a café. Carrie usually paid for their tea and buttered buns, having gained the impression that her father was not well off. She also rather thought he might have another family in Canterbury but didn't like to ask outright. Otherwise, why not take her to his lodgings unless they were too squalid to show her? He was always clean and tidy, even if his clothes were well worn. When he picked up his teacup, she saw how the skin of his fingers was cracked and calloused, making her think his work must involve manual labour. Again, she didn't like to ask and she came away from their meetings angry with herself. She was nineteen years old and working as a teacher, she reflected, yet these simple questions seemed beyond her. Instead, Carrie regaled her father with tales from school, and reported on her mother's health. Her father posed the occasional question but seemed generally happy just to listen. Carrie suspected he was relieved when it was time for her to get back on the train.

When Carrie returned home, always a little tired after the

outing and the walk back from the station, her mother avoided any questions relating to her father, invariably leading to Carrie bursting out in irritation, 'Don't you want to know how Father was?'

Carrie wondered whether her mother's illness had come about as a result of her father telling her he planned to leave, or perhaps it had been intended to stop him doing so. If the latter was the case, it had failed. There was a ten-year age gap between her parents, her father being younger than her mother, who had given birth to Carrie when she was in her mid-thirties. Carrie thought you'd be hard pressed to tell now – he seemed tired and old whenever she saw him. Her mother, on the other hand, despite having declared herself an invalid shortly before her father had left, seemed little changed over time.

Carrie wasn't sure what was wrong with her mother. She was pale and droopy, and a little underweight due to her insistence on a frugal diet. How she spent the day while Carrie was teaching was a mystery to her daughter. As with everything related to her parents, she'd come to accept things the way they were. And even though her mother never asked after her father following her visits to Canterbury, Carrie still recounted what she could – which was very little.

She couldn't imagine what it would be like to be brought up as part of a family such as the Hadleys', in a large house where money, or the earning of it, wasn't a constant worry. Carrie and her mother continued to live in the cottage that had somehow remained on Mr Marsh's side of the family, even though the relative who had been the gardener at the Glen had long since died. Carrie's salary had to support them both, and if they hadn't had the cottage at such a cheap rent, they would never have managed. She supposed one advantage was that she had learnt to be resourceful and independent. She was certainly one of the few young women who rode around Castle Bay on a bicycle; she knew she was considered unfeminine by some for doing so. She had little patience with that judgement, glorying instead in the freedom it gave her, although the uneven nature of the local roads and the challenge of cycling in a long skirt meant she frequently feared being flung from the saddle.

The bicycle had belonged to Mrs Chambers's daughter, Violet, who had married and joined her husband in London. She had left it behind, intending to use it on her visits home, but the swift arrival of twins had scuppered her plan, and the bicycle had been rusting gently in Mrs Chambers's garden, until she had thought to offer it to Carrie.

'I shall never use it,' she declared, 'and neither will Violet. But it will save you the walk each day if you aren't too nervous to ride it.'

Grove Lane ran the full distance between the school and Carrie's home, apart from the last few yards, which involved taking a path leading off the lane to the house. The lane crossed a stretch of countryside bordered by fields with no footpath, making for a long, muddy walk on wet days. Carrie was grateful to have the bicycle to shorten her journeys.

The Monday before the planned picnic with the Hadleys, she had found herself labouring up the hill on the way home after school, a motor-car following close behind. The blind bend in the road meant it wasn't safe for the driver to overtake and she was thankful he'd stayed back. She could have dismounted and let him by, but then she would have lost momentum and would have had to walk the bicycle the rest of the way. She was glad to reach the point where the road widened, looking up to acknowledge the driver as the car swept past. It was open-topped and Oscar Hadley was at the wheel. He gave her a wave and a toot of the horn, grinning broadly, as he went on his way.

Carrie was indignant, her heart pounding from the exertion. The cheek of it, she thought, then wondered what Oscar had done to offend her. Nothing, she supposed, other than doubtless laugh at her as he followed her up the hill.

She'd forgotten about the incident by the time of the picnic, the demands of the classroom filling her thoughts for the remainder of the week. Saturday dawned fair, with the promise of better things to come, and Carrie went about her weekly household chores with a light heart. There was laundry to be done and the house to be cleaned, but as the morning progressed the dusting had become sketchy. Carrie promised herself she would make up for the deficiencies the following week.

Once the washing was hung on the line, she settled her mother in a chair in the garden, out of the direct sun and with a blanket to hand in case she grew chilly. She put a plate of ham sandwiches on the table beside her with a cup of tea.

'Are you going somewhere?' Mrs Marsh was regarding her daughter with suspicion. Carrie supposed she must have noticed her nervous agitation, which had increased as the morning wore on.

'I'm going out for a picnic with Ada Hadley and her family.' Carrie, conscious of the time, was keen to go and change.

'It's kind of her to invite you. Who else will be there?' Her mother had noticed her slight evasion, Carrie thought.

'Just Oscar and Jeremy, her brothers.'

Mrs Marsh frowned. 'Is it suitable for you to be out in the company of young men in this way?'

'Oh, Mother, they're Ada's brothers. It's not as though they're strangers.'

Carrie was exasperated. When her mother was young, such an outing would have required a chaperone, she supposed, but surely not now, in the second decade of the twentieth century. 'I'll have to hurry, or I'll be late. Have you everything you need? Go back inside if you get too hot or too cold.'

Carrie was already halfway through the kitchen door before her mother replied, in plaintive tones, 'A bit of company while I eat my lunch would be nice.'

She ignored her, although it gave her a pang of conscience. She would take care to be extra attentive on Sunday, she decided, as she hurried upstairs to change. She'd settled on a long dark skirt and her best blouse. Her reflection in the narrow, full-length mirror of the wardrobe showed her that she looked much as she did when she set off for school each morning. The blouse, though, made of fine cotton lawn, with pin tucks all around the bodice and full sleeves, was finer than anything she would wear in the classroom. She had saved up for a long time to buy the fabric and had imagined it would only ever be worn for Sunday best.

She took her straw hat from the peg in the hall, slipped the key to the Glen from its hook beside the back door and, without a backward glance at her mother in the garden, she left the house.

CHAPTER FOUR

Carrie's mood lifted with every step she took towards Hawksdown Lodge. The sun was shining, the breeze was light, and she slowed her pace so she wouldn't arrive flustered and overheated. She would have to retrace her steps to lead the party back to the picnic spot, but she preferred it that way. She had every intention of keeping secret where she lived – the contrast between Hawksdown Lodge and Ivy Cottage was just too great.

As she opened the gate into the Hadleys' garden, she saw that Ada and her brothers were already sitting on the terrace, a picnic basket and neatly folded blankets on the table beside them.

'Am I late?' Carrie hurried to join them, wondering whether she had miscalculated her arrival.

'Not at all.' Ada was quick to reassure her. 'Mother and Father have lunch guests so we were only too happy to excuse ourselves and sit out here.'

Oscar took up the picnic basket, Jeremy gathered the blankets and they set off, Carrie leading the way. She walked up the road with Ada who, it turned out, was keen to ask about her family.

'I haven't any siblings,' Carrie told her. She hesitated, then added, 'Actually, my mother and father don't live together any more. They parted about ten years ago and my father lives in Canterbury. My mother doesn't really like anyone to know.'

'I won't breathe a word,' Ada promised.

'And my mother is what you would describe as an invalid, I suppose.' Carrie wasn't sure it was right to spill the family secrets but she was surprised to discover it was a relief to share them. She'd never felt able to do so before.

They had begun the walk up the incline leading towards the path to her house and to Hawks Down, and at just about the spot where Oscar had overtaken her in his car, Carrie found him walking beside her and Ada.

'You must live around here,' he remarked. 'I passed you the other day.'

'You did,' Carrie said, reminded all at once of his laughter as he swept by. 'And, yes, I live close by.' She waved her hand in a vague manner, hoping he wouldn't persist in his questioning. They were now within a few feet of her garden gate.

The path narrowed and Ada stepped back to walk with Jeremy.

'Well, if you bicycle this way every day, you must keep fit,' Oscar said. 'Ada tells me you haven't played tennis before. Perhaps we can remedy that.'

Now they were safely beyond her front door, and passing the gate leading to the Glen. Carrie wondered about pointing it out to them, but feared they would clamour to go in. It was her intention to take them via a different route, and to leave by the gate. It was well hidden unless you knew what you were looking for, plants growing through the wrought ironwork so that it appeared to be completely overgrown. In fact, it opened just enough to allow one person at a time to squeeze through.

Oscar had fallen silent at her side. He seemed out of breath, which puzzled Carrie after his talk of tennis and fitness. The incline was almost at an end and within a few yards the path opened up onto a flat, grassy field, with views over the countryside to the west, and out to sea to the east. One or two parties were already there, sitting on the grass taking in the view while their children played around them.

'I never knew this was here!' Ada exclaimed. 'And we live just along the road. How clever of you to show us, Carrie.'

Carrie smiled, pleased by her reaction. 'Now choose your spot,' she offered. 'Sea view or countryside?'

Ada argued amicably with her brothers as they walked on. She favoured countryside, saying, 'We can see the sea from home whenever we want.'

Oscar and Jeremy preferred the sea view. 'We're much higher here,' Jeremy said. 'Look how far we can see along the coast. Even across to France.' He pointed to the faint blur of white cliffs on the horizon, caught by the sunshine.

Oscar turned to Carrie. 'You'll have to decide for us.'

She already had a spot in mind, tucked into a slight slope with a fine view over the valley. 'Here,' she said, stopping. 'We'll be sheltered if the wind picks up. And if you stand up, you can see the sea.'

'Very diplomatic.' Oscar was amused.

Jeremy laid out the blankets and Oscar set down the picnic basket, flexing his fingers and grimacing. 'That basket grew heavier with every step as we climbed the hill back there,' he complained. 'I thought I'd have to ask you to stop. Make sure you eat well, everyone. I don't want to have to carry it all back down.'

Ada was already unpacking the food and, as Carrie surveyed it, she was glad it hadn't fallen to her to provide. Marsh family picnics in the distant past had consisted of a sandwich wrapped in greaseproof paper, with perhaps a hard-boiled egg or a couple of tomatoes to enliven things.

The Hadley picnic included tomatoes and hard-boiled eggs, but also radishes and pickles, pork pies, crusty bread and three different cheeses. There were plates, knives and forks, gingham napkins and glass bottles of lemonade. No wonder Oscar had struggled on the way up, Carrie thought. She knelt on the blanket, swinging her legs sideways to sit as neatly as possible, to avoid exposing too much ankle. Ada handed out the plates, cutlery and napkins, and sliced the pork pie. Carrie was hungry but she held back to see whether there was some etiquette she should observe. Oscar, however, was busy tearing off pieces of bread and adding them to his plate along with chunks of cheese, a tomato and a slice of pork pie. She was glad she'd waited: she would have tried to slice the bread. She copied him and filled her plate.

The Hadleys were very good company. There was a great deal of laughter and teasing, and the food was consumed without ceremony and plenty of enjoyment. Carrie sat back a little and observed them, joining in when appropriate but happy just to absorb the atmosphere.

When it was clear that everyone had eaten their fill of the spread, Ada unwrapped a napkin she had set aside, releasing a delicious, delicate scent. Four fruits nestled in the folds of cloth, their soft fuzzy skins a creamy yellow blushed with pink.

'What are they?' Carrie couldn't stop herself asking, although the others didn't seem to question what was before them.

'Peaches,' Ada said. 'The gardener does very well with them in our greenhouse.'

She offered one to Carrie who bit into it, closing her eyes briefly in enjoyment at the sweetness and perfume. Juice dribbled down her chin and she reached for her napkin, keen not to spoil her blouse. As she looked up, her eyes caught Oscar's. He was watching her and the realisation brought a rush of colour to her cheeks.

CHAPTER FIVE

Carrie, keen to cover her confusion, said quickly, 'This is wonderful. I've never tasted a peach before.'

Ada appeared surprised. 'Then we must send you home with some. I fear we have grown used to them. Look, the boys aren't even going to eat theirs.'

Carrie saw that Ada had placed her peach on a plate, where she was cutting it into quarters. She was much less troubled by the juice, Carrie thought, fearing she had done the wrong thing in her ignorance.

Oscar, gathering up plates and leftover food into an unwieldy pile, glanced up to give Carrie a small smile. Their eyes locked once more, giving Carrie a disturbing thrill. She was sure Oscar was singling her out for attention but no one else seemed to have noticed.

'Shall we go and visit the Glen?' she said. She was reluctant to leave, but also unsettled. Her mother's words about impropriety came back to her. She broke Oscar's gaze and began to help clear up the picnic things.

With the basket repacked – badly but at least made lighter – everyone scrambled to their feet. Carrie led the way back across Hawks Down to where the fence of a property bordered the field. 'We're going over there,' she said, pointing to a five-barred gate marked 'Private'.

'Well, Carrie Marsh, you surprise me. Are you suggesting we break the law? And you a schoolteacher, too.'

Oscar's teasing made Carrie blush. She rather liked the idea of appearing more reckless than she was. Nevertheless, she couldn't help glancing around to make sure they weren't being observed. 'Over you go, one at a time, then wait for me in the bushes to the left,' she instructed.

They scrambled over in turn, Oscar and Jeremy having no trouble while Ada was hampered by her long skirt. Carrie checked again to make sure no one was watching, then made ready to hoist up her own skirt. She realised, just in time, that Oscar, having stowed the picnic basket, had returned to help her. Her surprise made her almost miss her footing as she climbed the gate. The hand she held out to Oscar was surely sticky with peach juice but, before she could protest, he had seized her around the waist and swept her over the top bar.

'Oh!' Carrie exclaimed, as he set her down. He strode away to collect the picnic basket as if nothing untoward had occurred. Carrie's legs were shaky as she showed them the faint path, narrow and overgrown, that led away from the gate.

Within a minute or two, they'd reached the rim of the Glen, which formed a wide, deep hollow, filled with trees interspersed with rose bushes and other flowering shrubs, all grown tall in an effort to reach the light.

'Where are we?' Jeremy asked. 'Why is it private?'

'We're in the grounds of Hawksdown Castle,' Carrie replied. 'Don't worry, we're a long way from the castle and hardly anyone stays there now. Even when they do, they don't come down here: the paths are mostly impassable.'

She beckoned to them to follow and led them single file down a path that had suffered the ravages of time. Tree roots snaked across it and thorny bushes reached out to tear at their clothes. Carrie

185

began to wonder at the wisdom of wearing her new blouse. Behind her, she could hear her companions' feet slipping and sliding on the loose scree and Oscar's exclamations as he struggled to stay upright while hampered by the basket. Carrie was glad when they finally reached the bottom. She hoped they'd think it worth the effort.

They stood in a little group, catching their breath, and Ada spun round slowly, head upturned.

'You can barely see the sky,' she said. 'It's as though we're in a green cave, or underwater. And it's so quiet.'

'You could hide down here and no one would ever find you.' Oscar sounded thoughtful.

'Carrie would,' Jeremy pointed out.

'Yes, I've got a key,' Carrie said, pulling it from her pocket and holding it out for them to see. It covered her hand from fingertip to palm, a shaft of rusting iron topped with a design of interlaced loops, a heavy lock piece at the base. 'It opens a gate up there.' She pointed to the side of the Glen opposite where they had entered. 'We'll leave that way. It's on the path we walked along earlier to reach Hawks Down.'

'I didn't notice anything,' Ada said.

'It's well hidden.' Carrie smiled. 'Do you want to look around now we're here? It's bigger than it seems, but be careful. It's uneven underfoot and it's easy to trip.'

She was content to wait for them there, but Oscar loitered after Ada and Jeremy set off to explore.

'Won't you show me around?' he asked.

Carrie wondered again at being singled out. She felt anxious, but not a little thrilled to be alone with him. She told Oscar to leave the basket and she led him in the opposite direction to Ada and Jeremy, thinking they would meet up as they circled the base of the Glen. Oscar followed close behind and she half expected to feel his hand on her shoulder, but he maintained a respectful distance as she ducked under low branches and eased her way past clumps of blackberry briars.

It's going to be impassable here before too long, she thought, just as a briar she hadn't noticed dangling from a tree became entangled in her hair.

'Ow!' she exclaimed, and Oscar was at her side in an instant.

'Hold still,' he commanded, his face very close to hers as he concentrated on unravelling the strands of her hair.

She could hardly breathe but reached up, trying to help. He grasped her hands, returning them gently to her sides.

'Leave it to me,' he said. 'You can't see what you're doing and you'll make it worse.'

Carrie stood, obedient. She could hear Ada and Jeremy's voices but couldn't tell how close they were. She drew breath, intending to call out to them, but Oscar laid a finger over her lips.

'Almost there,' he said.

Carrie felt the taut pulling of her hair ease and she was about to step away with a murmured, 'Thank you,' when Oscar caught her once more by the waist. This time, he pressed his lips to hers. Carrie, who had never been kissed, was too startled to know what to do. Just as she began to enjoy the feel of their warm pressure, Oscar stepped back.

'I hope you'll forgive me. I thought you might want to thank me.' He smiled and turned around just as Ada and Jeremy burst through the foliage and came to a halt, laughing, on the path in front of them.

CHAPTER SIX

'This place is wonderful.' Ada was full of enthusiasm. 'It must have been such a beautiful garden – you can tell by all the flowers still growing here. We're lucky to see it now. In another year or so I think it might be lost under all this.' She gestured at the foliage hemming them in, then shook herself, dislodging twigs and leaves that had caught in her hair and the folds of her skirt.

'We found an old hut,' Jeremy said. 'Come and see.' He turned and plunged back into the undergrowth.

'Wait for me,' Ada said, and followed him.

Oscar looked at Carrie. 'Let's go,' he said, and vanished after the others.

Carrie stood for a moment, trying to marshal her thoughts. She should be furious with Oscar, for taking such a liberty in kissing her, but she found she wasn't. She was intrigued and flattered by his attention, and not a little flustered. Perhaps this counted as normal behaviour among people like the Hadleys. Since he was acting as though nothing had happened, she supposed she must, too. She caught up with the siblings, standing in a group a little way off the path outside a wooden hut all but obscured by ferns and ivy. Jeremy had picked up a large stone and was striking the padlock on the door.

'What do you suppose is inside?' he said over his shoulder to Oscar.

'A skeleton,' his brother replied, adding, 'or maybe two,' as Ada gasped in horror.

'I think it's just the gardener's hut,' Carrie said. 'I expect his old tools are still in there.' She considered a moment, then added, 'There is a story associated with this place, though.'

'What sort of story?' Oscar's dark eyes were fixed on her.

'It's supposed to be haunted by a ghost. The ghost of a relative of mine, actually.' Carrie felt a little foolish as she shared this last piece of information.

'A relative!' Ada exclaimed. 'Oh, do tell.'

'She was my two, or maybe three times great-aunt – Meg Marsh,' Carrie said. 'She vanished in the castle gardens here, on the way to meet someone about a smuggling deal. I have her diary – it's been passed down through the family. She was never seen again after that night,' Carrie continued, 'and there was talk that she'd been murdered and buried here in the Glen. Some claim to have seen a white lady walking here in the darkness.'

Carrie had often played in the Glen as a child, before it became so overgrown. Back then, the garden still bore all the evidence of cultivation and was a much lighter place. Now, the telling of the tale, and the memory of the diary, which she had read once and put away, had given her goose-bumps and she shivered. She suspected the sunny day had given way to cloud.

'I think it's time to go,' she said, just stopping herself adding, 'My mother will be wondering where I am.'

Jeremy gave up on his attempts on the lock and dropped the stone. 'Which way back?' he asked.

Carrie led the way, following the path to retrieve the picnic basket, and continuing on until she spotted the steps leading up to the gate. She waited for everyone to catch up, then pointed upwards. 'Be very careful here,' she said. 'The steps are crumbling, so it's easy to slip.'

It was a steep climb and Ada was breathless by the time she reached the top. Even so, she managed to say, 'What an adventure! Thank you so much, Carrie.'

Carrie had inserted the key into the lock and was jiggling it to get some purchase. It yielded at last and she turned the key fully, pushing the gate open as far as it would go and gesturing for the Hadleys to step through. Then she followed, swiftly locking the gate behind her, thankful that no one was on the path to observe their actions. It was best that as few people as possible knew she had access to the Glen.

'I'll leave you now,' she said. 'You know the way back from here – just straight down the path onto Grove Lane and follow it home. Thank you so much for the picnic.'

As she'd climbed the steps, she'd made the decision to part from them at the gate. There was no point in walking back with them, only to turn and repeat the journey. She felt sure her mother was becoming fretful.

'You won't walk with us?' Ada asked. 'What about the peaches I promised you?'

'Thank you, but perhaps another time, if I may?' Carrie hoped she didn't sound presumptuous.

Oscar spoke up. 'I'll see Carrie home. You two go on and I'll catch you up.'

Ada nodded, and she and Jeremy set off down the path, leaving Carrie standing awkwardly at Oscar's side.

'Now, where to?' he asked.

What could she say? There was no point in lying. 'We're already here,' she said. 'I live just there.' She pointed to the cottage, set back a little way along the path, conscious of how mean it looked in comparison to Hawksdown Lodge.

'So close!' Oscar laughed. 'No wonder you know this place so well.' He put his palm flat against the gate to the Glen as he spoke.

'You can catch them up,' Carrie said, pointing down the path to where Ada and Jeremy were still visible.

'I wanted to spend a little more time with you, Carrie,' Oscar said. 'Shall we walk?' He indicated the path back up to Hawks Down.

Carrie bit her lip. She really needed to get home to her mother.

'Just a few minutes,' Oscar urged, seeing her hesitation.

Carrie nodded, feeling some trepidation at walking alone with him.

'I've enjoyed today,' Oscar said, turning to her as they walked. 'I hope we can have some more outings together.'

Carrie was about to agree, when he added, 'But I'd like to see you alone, as well. Just the two of us. Would you like that?'

It was an odd question, Carrie thought. She would very much like to see Oscar again, but the thought of seeing him alone both intrigued and terrified her. She wasn't sure where such a friendship could lead.

CHAPTER SEVEN

Carrie was out of breath by the time she hurried through the front door twenty minutes later, to find her mother querulous, as she had expected. She was sitting in the little front parlour, complaining of feeling a chill. It was still pleasantly warm outside and Carrie felt sure the room would quickly be stifling if she lit the fire, so she settled her with a blanket over her knees. She would bring in the washing and set potatoes to boil for her mother's supper, she thought, then see whether she needed to attend to the fire.

By the time she'd done these things, answering her mother's questions about the afternoon as best she could, she was hard-pressed to stay patient. She hadn't told Mrs Marsh about the visit to the Glen, for she'd made enough fuss about them picnicking in a public place and fretted over the possibility of damp grass. Carrie wondered whether the Hadley siblings had faced such questions. She suspected Mrs Hadley would have asked if they'd enjoyed themselves, then wandered off into the garden. Perhaps Oscar and Jeremy had decided on a game of tennis, while Ada had taken up a book in her room. Such imaginings occupied her as she attended to her mother's supper: a chop as a change from fish, with carrots and runner beans from the garden. She wanted to scream at the predictability of it all.

Her thoughts strayed to the Hadleys, and Oscar in particular, with great regularity over the next day or so. So, when she received an invitation in the form of a note that arrived in the middle of the week, penned in Ada's hand, she didn't hesitate to accept.

What a successful picnic! Oscar has a mind to drive us out on Saturday to the countryside and to lunch at the Rose. Do say you'll join us – I'm not sure I will go if you can't.

And so began a series of local expeditions that filled the summer. The countryside drive, followed by lunch in the garden of the Rose, was a great success, as was a clifftop walk at St Margaret's Bay, when the wind lifted Ada's straw hat from her head and carried it out to sea, causing consternation and laughter in equal measure. They took a trip to Margate to sit on the sandy beach and eat oysters and whelks and, as summer waned, to watch the hop-pickers at work on a farm near Canterbury, followed by lunch at the Stag and Hounds.

Carrie was never alone with Oscar. She found herself watching him covertly, to see whether he was studying her. He treated her with perfect friendliness and, after every outing, Carrie wondered whether he had held her hand a moment too long after handing her down from the car, or been extra solicitous in offering her his jacket when the wind off the sea had caught them by surprise in Margate.

She hadn't known how to reply to his question about seeing her alone, posed on Hawks Down, and had stuttered and stammered in reply. Had she lost her chance of being anything other than a friend to Oscar? She was frustrated by her lack of experience in handling such matters. She would have asked Ada for advice, but Oscar was her brother. If Ada disapproved, it would tip the balance of their relationship and jeopardise the outings that had become such a highlight of her life.

Carrie continued through the summer in an agony of indecision, looking forward to the outings but worrying about them afterwards, picking over every word and action. Until, at the beginning of September, Oscar announced he would soon be leaving to take up a position in his father's firm. Jeremy was soon to begin at Oxford. The summer's idyll was at an end.

The casual announcement was made in the garden of Hawksdown Lodge at the end of the third week of August, when the heat made them indolent and disinclined to do anything other than sit in the shade and drink lemonade. Oscar's words came as a terrible blow to Carrie, although she had always known their time together had a limit. At least her mother would be pleased, she thought bitterly.

Her mother didn't approve of Carrie's friendship with the Hadleys. 'People will talk,' she said. 'It's not right to be seen out, unchaperoned, with two young men.'

With each outing, Carrie had tried a different explanation: to strangers, they would appear to be a family group; they weren't doing anything untoward, just enjoying the seaside or countryside; they were always out in broad daylight.

'You haven't been out yourself in such a long time, Mother. The world has changed.'

Her mother couldn't really dispute this, but grumbled none-theless. It had been almost a relief that day to find their planned outing postponed due to the heat. Her mother didn't find it as unacceptable for her to be in the garden at Hawksdown Lodge – although her opinion would have changed had she known Mr and Mrs Hadley were away for the weekend.

Carrie stared into her glass, where a floating slice of lemon had turned into a life raft for a small black insect. She fished it out with a finger and looked up to see Oscar's eyes fixed on her. 'I'll miss our outings,' she said, returning his gaze. 'It's going to be very quiet here without you all.'

'I'll still be here,' Ada protested. 'For a while at least. But I agree. Hasn't it been the most glorious summer?'

There was silence for a while, each of the four wrapped up in their own thoughts.

Oscar was the first to speak. 'It's not over yet,' he said. 'We've still got next weekend.'

'Yes, we must do something special,' Ada said. 'And if we have a picnic, we'll have champagne instead of lemonade.'

"Why don't we do that now?' Oscar was on his feet. 'Mother and Father aren't here – they'll never notice.'

'Don't let Mabel or Maria catch you,' Ada warned.

'I won't,' he said. 'Carrie, come and help me. You can carry the glasses.'

Carrie had never drunk champagne before, but it wasn't the thought of doing so that made her heart beat fast as she obediently followed Oscar into the cool of the house. He went to the dining room and extracted four shallow bowl-shaped glasses from the cabinet.

'You take these and I'll get the champagne, some ice too. I doubt there's a chilled bottle.' He was talking half to himself as he turned towards the door. Then he checked himself and turned back, almost bumping into Carrie who followed close behind.

With both hands occupied in holding the glasses upside down by their stems, she was powerless to resist when he leant in and kissed her. She remembered the soft pressure on her lips from their previous kiss in the Glen and felt a rush of warmth and delight. She had longed for this. But then his kisses became harder and more insistent as one hand encircled her waist, pulling her to him. As the other brushed her breast she stiffened, pulled away and stepped back, alarmed.

Oscar, unperturbed, smiled. 'I hope we have chance to repeat this before I leave for London.' Then he turned towards the stairs to the kitchen, leaving Carrie scarlet in the face and still clutching the glasses, her mind in turmoil.

Chapter Eight

Carrie returned to their table in the shade, thankful that Ada appeared to be dozing and Jeremy had picked up a book. Neither paid her any attention and she was grateful, for it allowed her colour to subside.

Oscar sauntered out shortly afterwards, with a bottle of champagne in an ice bucket. 'Liven up, everyone,' he said. 'Refreshments are here.'

The popping of the champagne cork roused Ada, who grabbed a glass and held it out as the champagne fizzed from the bottle. She passed it to Carrie, who waited until everyone had one before preparing to take a sip. This was quickly forestalled by Oscar, still on his feet, who raised his glass and said, 'To summer friendships and pastures new.'

Carrie, the only one present who counted as a friend and not family, felt honoured by his words. The apparent attraction of pastures new was less pleasing. She took a tentative sip of champagne: she wasn't sure she liked the taste and it was a little warm, but everyone else seemed to enjoy it so she tried again. She would happily have set it aside if Oscar hadn't urged her to drink up so he could top up her glass.

A debate was raging across the table – for the following weekend, their final one together, should they stick to the plan postponed that weekend due to the heat? Or should they go to

Eastling House, a grand residence belonging to friends of their parents, where Oscar declared he had a mind to try out the maze?

After Oscar had refilled everyone's glass, he had talked them round to Eastling House, provided he could get the use of their father's car. By the time Carrie was ready to leave, feeling giddy and wondering at the wisdom of riding her bicycle, the outing was agreed for eleven the following Saturday morning.

During the week, Carrie's thoughts were much occupied by the planned trip. Would the weather hold? What would she wear? She longed for something new, in the fashionable, slimmer style she'd seen featured in a copy of the *Lady* at Hawksdown Lodge. But she could neither afford it nor see how it might be practical, so she must make do with what she had. Her best blouse would have to make yet another appearance.

Thankfully, the weather was fine but a little cooler, which was welcome. The Hadleys collected Carrie on Grove Lane, at the bottom of the path leading up to Hawks Down and her house. She was delighted to find herself seated in the front, next to Oscar.

Eastling House was nearly an hour's drive away: Carrie wished it could have been longer, despite the fine dust thrown up by the road and the wind that whipped her hair from its clips and out of her straw boater. Their arrival at their destination was greeted by the sort of furious debate Carrie had become accustomed to from the Hadleys. Should they look around the grounds first, or ask to be shown the house? Should they picnic before or after the maze?

She listened for a while then ventured, 'Perhaps we should save the house until the end. There are clouds building to the west – I think we might look at the grounds before it rains?'

She feared that being the voice of reason made her dull, but how else would anything be achieved? And so it was agreed – the picnic basket was left strapped to the car while they took a turn around the grounds, which had clearly suffered from the hot, dry spell. Carrie could barely concentrate while Ada chattered on. She was impatient, her thoughts racing ahead to the picnic. Could she manage things so that she was seated next to Oscar on the picnic blanket? It would surely be her last chance to be close to him, because Jeremy would undoubtedly take the front seat in the car on the journey home.

It was Jeremy, driven by hunger, who played into her hands. He stopped and said, 'I've had enough, at least until I've had something to eat.'

Ada, though, had set her heart on walking to the folly on the edge of the grounds and was disappointed and disposed to argue until Carrie stepped in and suggested, 'Why don't we have our picnic there?'

Oscar groaned. 'You'd have me walk back to the car and then all the way over there carrying that wretched basket?'

Carrie pointed to a gate in the hedge. 'I think you'll find that's a short-cut to where the car is parked,' she said. There were times when she regretted her schoolmistress practicality, fearing it didn't sit well with the happily disorganised Hadleys.

Jeremy went off to help Oscar, leaving Ada and Carrie to wander in the direction of the folly. Built in the style of a Greek temple, it was set on a mound, giving views back over the gardens towards the house. Oscar and Jeremy caught them up while they were still deciding on the best spot to sit, somewhere that would provide shade as well as a vista.

'I raised the hood on the motor,' Oscar said. 'We don't want damp seats for the journey home if it rains.'

Perhaps Oscar was more organised than she'd thought, Carrie reflected, as she helped Ada lay out the picnic, resolutely turning her back on the storm clouds building in the distance.

Mabel had done them proud: the picnic surpassed the one

they'd enjoyed on Hawks Down, but Mr Hadley had vetoed the champagne. Carrie didn't care – she preferred her mind unclouded. She was determined to make the most of every minute of this day, but the harder she sought to make it memorable, the more unsettled she became. Nothing was quite as she'd hoped and she found herself constantly wishing for the next thing. She was glad when Oscar said, 'Time to pack up and get this lot back to the motorcar if we're going to tackle the maze.'

Jeremy grimaced. He had been planning to settle down for a nap after refilling his plate several times. Ada and Carrie, though, made short work of tidying everything away and within the half-hour they were all standing at the entrance to the maze, regarding the alley of tall yew hedges before them.

Oscar took out his pocket watch. 'Ada and Jeremy, you get a thirty-second head start. Carrie and I will meet you in the middle in twenty minutes.'

Jeremy, who had shaken off his sleepiness and enjoyed a challenge, grabbed Ada's hand and they set off at a run, rounding the first corner and vanishing from sight.

Chapter Nine

B arely ten seconds had passed before Oscar took Carrie's hand.
'Off we go,' he said.

She didn't quibble, enjoying the sensation of his grip,
warm and firm.

'We'll take it in turns to choose the direction,' Oscar suggested.

Carrie was pleased by his offer, having expected him to take sole
charge. 'Let's go right,' she said, and they took the opposite route
to Jeremy and Ada.

'Left.'

'Right.'

'Right.'

'Left.'

Soon, having hit several dead ends, they were breathless with
laughter. They had no idea whether they were any closer to the
centre. Every so often they heard running footsteps and giggles,
recognisably those of Ada. Carrie wondered why they didn't come
across anyone else in the maze. A moment or two later, she had
the answer.

Enclosed within the narrow pathways, bounded by towering
yew, they hadn't noticed the darkening skies until a sudden flash
lit them both and an almost simultaneous clap of thunder made
Carrie cry out in alarm.

Oscar turned towards her, as another flash of lightning lit his features. He pulled her to him as the first heavy drops of rain fell. Carrie shivered violently, whether from the sudden drop in temperature or the anticipation of what was to come, she couldn't say. Then his lips were on hers and they kissed as the rain fell in a torrent, soaking them in an instant. Carrie's straw boater fell back and her hair was plastered to her head. She knew she was a bedraggled mess but nothing mattered other than that their kisses should continue. She clung to Oscar, her body pressed to his.

She was oblivious to everything beyond Oscar's embrace, until she became aware of Ada's voice, her tone colder than she'd ever heard.

'There you are,' she said.

Carrie pulled away from Oscar and turned to see Ada just a little way along the path, Jeremy following.

'It's time to go home,' Ada said. The set of her mouth and the impatient way in which she pushed her wet hair away from her face suggested she was offended, if not outraged, by what she had witnessed. She didn't look at Carrie.

There was no more to be said and, indeed, very little was spoken as they tried to leave the maze. Each of them took it in turns to lead the group, ceding their place as each promising avenue failed to deliver salvation. Carrie was unsure how they found their way out in the end. She only knew they were thoroughly wet and miserable by the time they reached the car. She squeezed into the back alongside a silent Ada, thankful that Oscar had had the foresight to raise the roof and that the hedge they were parked beside had offered some shelter. Even so, she feared the amount of water they had brought in with them must surely damage the upholstery.

Oscar sat awhile with the engine running, answering Jeremy's enquiry as to why they weren't leaving with a terse 'Because I can't see through the windscreen.'

The storm departed as rapidly as it had arrived and Oscar

conducted the return journey at a more sedate pace than he had favoured that morning. The unmade roads ran with water and puddles stretched right across, until suddenly all was dry again and the sun came out. Carrie kept her head turned to gaze out at the countryside and willed them home.

They sat in silence – a silence that seemed more ominous and unbreakable as time passed. Ada was displeased, that much was clear. Jeremy seemed oblivious to the atmosphere, and Oscar was concentrating on the road. It wasn't the kind of memorable end to the day that Carrie had hoped for.

Jeremy, who had dozed during the journey, had to be woken when the car stopped close to home to let Carrie out. Neither Oscar nor Ada spoke as she struggled out of the back seat so, once out in the roadway with Jeremy waiting, she leant back into the car.

'Thank you,' she said. 'Oscar, I do hope the position in the bank is to your liking. Perhaps I will see you when you are home on a visit.' She sent a look of mute appeal his way, but he kept his eyes fixed straight ahead, acknowledging her words with a small nod. She turned to Ada, still looking cross in the back seat, saying, 'I hope I see you soon.'

Receiving no answer from either of them she withdrew and turned to Jeremy. 'I hope you enjoy Oxford,' she said.

He beamed. 'I hope so, too.' He got back in and waved as they drove away. Carrie, forlornly watching their departure, rather thought Jeremy was the only one not to be aware of what had happened in the maze.

She trudged up the hill and turned in at her gate, steeling herself for her mother's reaction to her bedraggled appearance. It was as she had expected.

'Well, you're a sight for sore eyes.' Mrs Marsh was triumphant. 'Perhaps that will teach you to go gallivanting with those friends of yours, leaving your poor mother to fend for herself.'

Carrie bit back the retort that rose to her lips. She contented herself with 'I was caught in a thunderstorm. And I left your lunch out for you, all prepared, so you wouldn't need to do a thing.' She wondered if it was still there – a hard-boiled egg, three tomatoes, a small piece of cheese, a slice of bread and butter and an apple, on a green-rimmed plate under an upturned bowl – ignored by her mother, just to spite her.

Mrs Marsh was still determined to have the last word. 'Go and change out of those wet things or you'll catch your death of cold. You're due back to school on Monday – it won't sit well with Mrs Chambers if you're not there for your new pupils on their first day.'

There was some truth in that, Carrie thought, as she went to her room and stripped off her clothes, now damp rather than soaking. Even so, she felt cold and clammy and shivered as she pulled on her dressing-gown for a bit of warmth.

She'd barely given school a second thought over the holidays, being far too taken up with spending time at the Hadleys'. Now, though, she must turn her thoughts to the new term ahead and resign herself to a long wait before Oscar returned. Today had been such a mixture of euphoric moments and low points. Oscar seemed able to make her behave completely out of character, leaving her feeling overwrought and ashamed. And now she feared she'd spoilt her friendship with Ada. She pushed away the anxiety as best she could and went back downstairs, resigned to another unhappy evening with her mother. Maybe it was a good thing that Oscar would be away for a while.

CHAPTER TEN

The hot, sunny weather returned for Monday. The children were excited to be together again, although Carrie was sure some had seen each other over the holidays. Several were from farming communities on the edge of town and she had an idea they would have been at work, helping with the harvest or tending the animals, which they did in any case before coming to school. It wasn't unusual to see them removing straw, or worse, from their clothes at the start of the school day.

Carrie let the children have their heads for a few minutes, then clapped her hands to restore order. There were new arrivals in class, looking nervous and overwhelmed by all the noise and excitement.

'Welcome back, everyone. I hope you've enjoyed yourselves over the summer and you're ready for some hard work this term.'

She ignored their groans and began allocating seating. It was a good moment to separate pupils who had become disruptive during the previous term, and to give responsibility for the new pupils to trusted older ones. She would miss those who had left at the end of the summer term, having reached the age of twelve. The school was too small to keep them and she knew most would now be at work.

The day and, indeed, the week swept by. Carrie marvelled at how tired she was. She enjoyed it, though, and there was an advantage in being kept busy – it meant her thoughts couldn't stray to Oscar and Ada, and there was little time to dwell on what had happened when they last met.

By the time the weekend came, Carrie had to face up to the gap in her life left by Oscar's departure and Ada's coolness. What had she done before her life became involved with theirs? She thought about going to Hawksdown Lodge to see whether Ada was at home, but wasn't sure of her reception. She'd allowed herself to be swept along in the wake of the Hadleys, trying to work out how to behave as they did. She supposed she and Oscar had behaved with impropriety and had offended Ada. Was an apology required? Should she write? But how to begin? She spent her time looking out into the sunshine and wondering what each of the Hadleys was doing and whether they thought about her at all. She tried to devote herself to her mother in the way that Mrs Marsh wished, but without a great deal of success. After a weekend of domesticity and quiet reading, Carrie found herself longing for Monday morning and a return to the noise, bustle and life of the schoolroom.

Carrie had hoped it would become easier to forget about Oscar's departure, and the upset with Ada, as the days passed. In fact, while the schooldays settled into a routine, the events of the last day they had spent together continually crept back into her thoughts to torment her. By the time Friday came around again, Carrie found herself locking the school door with dread in her heart at the thought of the empty weekend before her. As she went around the corner to retrieve her bicycle from the caretaker, she stopped short at the sound of a familiar voice.

'Hello, Carrie.'

Carrie turned to find Ada standing there, very smart in a slim blue skirt, tapered just above the ankles, with a loose duster coat in the same fabric belted over the top.

'I told Mother I'd walk back from the station while she took the car, but I'm regretting it now. It's still warm and these shoes

205

pinch.' Ada looked down ruefully at her narrow cream leather T-bar shoes.

Lost for words, Carrie stayed silent. Ada was acting as though nothing was amiss between them.

'Are you settled back at school? It must be two weeks now.' Ada glanced up at the red-brick building, barely waiting for Carrie to nod before saying, 'Since Oscar and Jeremy left, Mother has had me go out with her every day, accompanying her to lunches, meeting people she believes will be advantageous, finding a role for me in her good works. It's exhausting.' Ada laughed, and a wave of relief rushed over Carrie. Perhaps she had been wrong about her friend being angry and avoiding her.

'We've been to Canterbury today. It was supposed to be for shopping, but we lunched with some dreadful woman who has a son Mother thinks would be the perfect match for me.' Ada made a face. 'I think she should let me be the judge of that. But enough of me. What have you been doing?'

They retrieved Carrie's bicycle and began to walk along Grove Lane towards Ada's gate. Carrie told Ada about the new term, being careful to recount one or two anecdotes she thought would amuse her. It was almost like old times, but not quite. Carrie wondered whether Ada's keenness to account for what she had been doing was to disguise that she had been angry, but had now come round. As Carrie made ready to depart for home, Ada said, 'If you're free tomorrow, perhaps we could meet and go for a walk. It's quiet without the boys at home.'

Carrie's heart leapt at the chance to escape her mother for a few hours and she readily agreed. She tried not to feel guilty that her second thought was that perhaps there would be news of Oscar, too.

CHAPTER ELEVEN

'I owe you an explanation.' Ada's words came out abruptly, while they were strolling on Hawks Down on Saturday afternoon under a blazing blue September sky. She pressed on before Carrie could speak. 'You must wonder why I acted as I did on our last afternoon together, at Eastling House. I wondered afterwards whether you thought I was angry with you, when I was actually upset with Oscar. I had no idea there was anything between you both and I assumed he was behaving badly.' She paused. 'I didn't want him to toy with you and upset what we had together. I felt as if you were my sister on our outings so to see Oscar with you came as a shock. It seemed wrong. Am I making any sense?' She gave Carrie a look of appeal.

'I just thought you disapproved. Of me,' Carrie said slowly.

'Oh, Carrie, I'm so sorry.' Ada was contrite. 'Not at all. I disapproved of Oscar. I thought he was taking advantage of you.' She sighed. 'I haven't been able to talk to him about it because he went to London. And Mother kept me so busy I wasn't able to see you, either.'

They walked on in silence while Carrie mulled over Ada's words. She'd made it plain she thought Oscar was at fault, and that she wasn't angry with her friend. But she hadn't asked about Carrie's feelings for Oscar. Should she make it clear that she hadn't been upset by his attentions – that she'd welcomed them, in fact? Ada spoke again before she'd managed to express her thoughts.

'He's coming home this evening, for a family lunch tomorrow,' Ada said. 'And he'll be here again the following weekend.'

Carrie thought she perceived a question in Ada's eyes. 'Perhaps we could walk together next weekend,' Carrie said. She tried to keep her emotions in check but she had an overwhelming sense of relief, both at Ada's explanation and also at the thought of seeing Oscar again. Excitement bubbled up and she feared she was prattling on during the rest of their walk.

She and Ada parted with a promise that her friend would let Carrie know of any plan for the following weekend. Carrie then had to get through the rest of that weekend, knowing that Oscar would be at home less than a mile away. It was an effort not to find an excuse to walk in the direction of Hawksdown Lodge, in the hope of catching sight of him, but she fought down the impulse. She tried to be a dutiful daughter instead and, when Monday came, she vowed to devote her thoughts and energies to teaching, safe in the knowledge that she would see Oscar and Ada at the weekend.

Yet by the time Friday arrived, with no word from Ada about a possible outing, Carrie's agitation grew. Should she go to Hawksdown Lodge and ask to speak to Ada? Or should she be patient until Saturday? By the end of school on Friday, she'd made up her mind to call in on Ada on the way home, but her heart was thumping as she wheeled her bicycle in at the gate of the Hadleys' house. It was sunny, with the faintest hint of a chill in the air, but no one was in the garden, or on the terrace. Carrie's spirits sank as she made her way around to the front door. The house had a deserted air – there was no car on the drive and it took some time before the maid answered her knock on the door.

'She's in London for the day, miss,' the maid said, in response to her request to see Ada. 'They're staying the night and they'll be back tomorrow. Who shall I say called?'

'Carrie. Miss Marsh,' Carrie said. She felt despondent. Had

Ada forgotten? She turned away and went back along the path to retrieve her bicycle. Head down, deep in thought, she didn't see the figure strolling up from the tennis courts until he was almost upon her.

'Hello, Carrie. Looking for Ada?'

There stood Oscar, tennis racket in hand as he idly bounced the ball on the path.

Surprised, unable for a moment to respond, Carrie found her voice at last. 'The maid said you were all in London.'

Oscar stopped what he was doing and turned his attention to her. 'Ada and Mother are in London but I'm here, as you can see.' He regarded her for a moment or two. 'How are you, Carrie?'

She remembered her manners and, brushing his enquiry away with 'Very well, thank you,' asked, 'Are you enjoying your new job? And London?'

Oscar made a face. 'It was always going to be difficult working for Father. He's hard on me, and the other people in the office resent me for being his son. They're worried I'll carry tales back to Father so they keep their distance.' He shrugged. 'I know I'll have to stick it out but I can't tell you how glad I am to be home.'

Carrie, touched that he'd shared a confidence with her, said, 'Ada thought we might do something together, the three of us, over the weekend.'

Oscar frowned. 'She didn't mention anything. She's away until tomorrow evening and we have guests for lunch on Sunday.'

Carrie's buoyant mood was deflated in an instant. Oscar must have seen the disappointment on her face because he said, 'Perhaps we could take a walk tomorrow.'

Carrie's heart said one thing even as her sensible side took over and said quite the opposite: 'I don't think we can. It will cause ... talk.'

Oscar rolled his eyes. 'I suppose you're right. If only Ada were here – I've a mind to see that secret garden of yours again.' They were walking towards Carrie's bicycle at the gate and he gave her a sideways look as he spoke.

It wouldn't be hard to manage discreetly, Carrie thought. Her spirits soared once more as impetuousness took over. 'I could meet you in there, at around eleven tomorrow morning,' she offered. 'Can you remember the way I showed you, over the gate on Hawks Down? I'll use the key to go in by the other.'

'Let's meet in the afternoon,' Oscar said. 'About three o'clock.' He turned back to the house, bouncing the ball in front of him.

Carrie wheeled her bicycle out of the gate. She was filled with excitement at the prospect of an afternoon with Oscar. Yet she couldn't shake off the disturbing feeling that he had taken control of the arrangement they had made. What had she just agreed to?

CHAPTER TWELVE

The feeling of unease, mixed with excitement, bothered Carrie through the hours she had to endure before she would see Oscar again. One minute she feared it was folly to have agreed to such a meeting, while at the next an insistent voice in her head told her that there was nothing wrong with breaking free from her dull, predictable existence. She was flattered that Oscar wanted to spend time with her. Could it mean that he hoped to make a match with her? If Ada's words of caution resurfaced – that she feared Oscar was taking advantage – she chose to push them away.

Carrie wished she could dress up for the occasion, but she had told her mother she was spending time with Ada. She had to wear a skirt and blouse that looked the part, and could only pay extra attention to her hair, even though it would be mainly hidden under her hat. Her heart was hammering by the time she slid the rusty key into the lock of the gate to the Glen. She checked to make sure no one was around before she slipped through, locking it behind her, then stood a moment looking down into the secret garden.

The foliage was yellowing and the flowers had faded: the roses had turned brown on the stems and some had fallen, to be replaced by plump red hips. The lush splendour of their visit just a few weeks ago had disappeared, to be replaced by a definite hint of autumn.

Was Oscar already there? Or had he forgotten? She peered into the depths, hoping for a glimpse of movement, but could see no sign. There was nothing for it but to make her way down the steps. If he was about he would hear her, she thought, as stones slipped from the crumbling steps and rolled down into the Glen. She reached the bottom and sat down to wait on a fallen log. She feared her mossy seat was damp and shivered. The sun didn't penetrate this far and the air was cool. She wished she'd worn something warmer than her thin jacket.

Minutes ticked by with no sign of Oscar. She was about to give up when the sound of someone crashing through the shrubs on the far side of the Glen, their progress interspersed with curses, caused her to jump to her feet, laughing in relief. He hadn't forgotten her after all.

'There you are.' Oscar appeared before her, somewhat dishevelled. 'Lunch was interminable – I was late and thought I'd try taking a direct route down. I won't be doing that again in a hurry.' He looked ruefully at his trousers and Carrie noticed a rent at the knee.

'I'd forgotten how lovely this place is.' He smiled, and Carrie's anxiety vanished. He didn't seem to see the signs of decay. 'I love autumn best of all, don't you?' he continued. 'It feels like the start of something. A new term – new beginnings. I always liked going back to school after the summer holidays.'

Carrie shook her head in wonder, then started to laugh. How strange he was! 'I prefer spring. Or maybe summer. Then I know the school holidays are about to start.'

'What shall we do? No one can see us here so we can't cause any gossip.'

Was he regarding her with a speculative gleam in his eyes? Carrie was alarmed by his words. 'Let's walk around,' she suggested, to distract him. 'It will have changed since our last visit.'

She walked at his side, pointing to anything she spotted to keep the conversation alive. A nest had fallen from a tree onto the path and she marvelled at how tiny it was, and perfectly woven. A tangle of briars supported a crop of late blackberries in a patch where the sun had penetrated, turning them deep purple. Carrie reached up on tiptoe and picked a handful. She tried one, then held them out on her palm for Oscar.

'Lovely and sweet,' she said.

He took one hesitantly, popped it in his mouth and immediately spat it out. 'Ugh. Too soft. I think there might have been something in it.'

His horrified expression made Carrie laugh but she looked doubtfully at the remaining blackberries and threw them away. 'For the birds,' she said.

Their explorations had brought them to the gardener's old hut. 'Let's see what's inside,' Oscar said, and before she could protest he'd seized the stone that still lay where Jeremy had dropped it, aiming a couple of blows at the padlock. It held, but the latch pulled free from the rotting wood and hung down, allowing the door to creak open.

Oscar peered inside. 'Just as he left it,' he said. 'Come and see.'

He stepped inside, leaving Carrie on the overgrown path. She could see the cobwebs inside the hut's window lifting in the breeze that entered for the first time in many years. She had no fondness for spiders but she forced herself to step through the doorway.

Before her eyes could adjust to the gloom, Oscar had caught her around the waist and pulled her to him, his mouth on hers. Carrie was startled and put her hands up to his chest to push him away but, moments later, she relaxed, her body responding to the memory of his previous kisses.

'That's better,' Oscar said, relinquishing her at last. He still held her around the waist, looking deep into her eyes, and Carrie, embarrassed, couldn't hold his gaze. Instead she laid her head on his chest, where she could hear the strong, regular beat of his heart.

'I've thought about you while I've been away, Carrie. I'm glad there's no awkwardness between us. And now we have the perfect place to meet and get to know each other better.'

His last words awakened Carrie's unease once more, but he turned her face up to his and kissed her again, until she forgot to worry. They continued in this way – kisses interspersed with desultory conversation – until Carrie said, with reluctance, that she had to leave. 'My mother will expect me home.' She hoped Oscar wouldn't be difficult but he let her go at once.

'Of course,' he said. He looked around the hut. 'It's a shame we can't make it more comfortable, but it will have to do,' he said. 'It will be the perfect hideaway as the weather gets colder.'

Carrie hadn't liked to question him but his confidence about future meetings emboldened her. 'Will you be back regularly from London, then?' she asked, tidying her hair and attempting to tuck it neatly back under her hat.

'I plan to be,' Oscar said. 'At least while Ada's at home. It's dull up in town at the weekends – everyone goes to the country.'

They had vacated the hut and Oscar had his back to her as he used a loose screw, found on the ground, to arrange the latch so it looked intact. Carrie frowned. If Ada was at home, it would be hard to arrange to see Oscar on his own. Could she content herself with seeing him only alongside his sister?

As if he'd read her mind, he straightened and turned to her. 'Let this be our secret. I'll need to find a way to get a message to you, so we can meet here in private. Perhaps in the evenings, if it proves difficult to get away at other times.'

His dark eyes were on her and Carrie barely knew what to say. Agreeing to continue their meetings would compromise her, but still she found herself suggesting a way to get word to her.

'The bricks at the top of our gatepost have come loose. You can lift off the cap as well as the first row beneath. You could slide a

214

note in there?' Would he be prepared to walk up Grove Lane to her house to do that?

'Perfect,' he said briskly. 'Now, I will leave the same way as I arrived, but on the path this time.' He began to laugh. 'Perhaps we will bump into each other at the top.'

Carrie shook her head. That would make a mockery of her attempts at secrecy. Oscar gave her one last, brief kiss and strode away, leaving her to scramble up the steps to the gate. She was grateful that he didn't appear before she'd locked the gate behind her and taken the few steps to her own garden path. She ducked under the ivy, which had formed an arch over the entrance, and checked the gatepost. It appeared intact, but it was easy to slide the top aside. She glanced at the front windows of the cottage to make sure her mother wasn't watching. Carrie had a feeling that, whether or not it was likely Oscar was at home, she would be checking every day to see if a note had arrived.

CHAPTER THIRTEEN

Oscar came home every weekend throughout October. Each morning and afternoon, even when he was undoubtedly still in London, Carrie checked for a note on her way to school and back. She looked for an edge of paper peeping out – it was only on Fridays, and at the weekend, that she permitted herself to lift the heavy top from the gatepost. Her heart leapt whenever a note was there.

The days and times of their meetings varied, but they were always arranged to suit Oscar. Carrie understood: he had to slip away from his family without arousing suspicion, while it was comparatively easy for her to make excuses to her mother. On Saturdays, she usually spent the afternoons at the Hadleys' house, going for a walk with Ada, sometimes with Oscar accompanying them. If the weather was changeable, they would take a drive. Ada sat in the front seat beside Oscar as they toured around, and Carrie watched him from the back, alert to his every word and gesture and sometimes catching his eye in the driver's mirror.

The few private meetings they had increasingly took place after dark as the evenings drew in. Carrie had been nervous of finding her way down the steps to the Glen in the pitch black, but Oscar had presented her with a flashlight, and she became sure-footed in her descent. They still arrived separately, although the chances of being spotted together on a dark autumn evening were slim.

Carrie knew it was wrong to meet in that way, and that she would be shamed if they were discovered. Before each meeting, she vowed to tell Oscar that they must stop but she found she was unable to give them up. The candles they lit at the gardener's hut to ease the darkness only made their trysts more exciting. Mrs Chambers at school and Ada had remarked on how well she looked of late. Carrie thought this was all down to her secret.

It was clear, though, that Oscar wanted more from her. Carrie had resisted his ardour so far but she knew she had a decision to make. If she refused him, would he give her up? Yet if she agreed to his desire, would he drop her afterwards? It felt like a hopeless choice to Carrie so she continued to evade the issue until, one Friday morning in early November, she found a note from Oscar, asking to meet her in the Glen at seven o'clock that evening. The last lines read:

My respect for you has grown with my love. Please don't make me wait any longer, Carrie. I can't endure it.

It was signed with kisses, as usual.

Carrie was in a fever of apprehension throughout the school day. The wind had picked up, whistling around the building and buffeting the children when they went into the yard to play. Back at their desks, they brought something of the wind's wildness with them and Carrie, distracted by her thoughts, struggled to keep order. She was relieved when it was time to bid them farewell, gather up their slates and collect her bicycle to make the journey home. The wind tangled her skirt around her legs and caused her to wobble dangerously as she pedalled. And was that rain she felt on her face? She would have a hard job convincing her mother she was going out again on a night like this to meet Ada.

Carrie dutifully saw to her mother's comfort, preparing her

invalid's meal as she did every evening. Her hands shook as she set the tray in front of her and she was sure her mother would notice, but she only complained that she had fancied a nice chop for a change. Carrie held back her irritation and promised to visit the butcher the next day, then hurried to her room to prepare. She attempted to tidy her hair, knowing it would be whipped into an unruly mess as soon as she stepped outside, then cleared away her mother's plate, taking the opportunity to slip the iron key to the Glen into her raincoat pocket.

As expected, her mother complained about her going out. 'No one will expect a visitor on a night like this. Listen to that wind – if a tree branch is torn off and you're struck down, who will come to look after me?'

Carrie almost laughed at her mother's selfish words and plaintive tone, and promised to take care. 'I'm sure one of the Hadleys will run me home if the wind doesn't ease. Don't worry, Mother, it sounds worse than it is.'

She made her escape before her mother could respond, pulling her raincoat tightly around her as she stepped outside. It was raining hard and her mother had spoken the truth about the potential for danger – the path was littered with twigs and larger branches. It was hard to hold onto the gate as she unlocked it, the wind seemingly intent on wrenching it out of her hands. Would Oscar really come out on a night like this? She hesitated at the top of the steps. They gleamed black and slick with rain, as the scurrying clouds intermittently parted to allow a shaft of moonlight to light her way. She realised, too late, that she had left the flashlight in her room. She would have to rely on the handrail to guide her safely down into the Glen.

Halfway down the steps, Carrie discovered that the rain had washed away the most damaged section, leaving a trail of rubble and slippery mud to negotiate. Even as she began to pick her way through, clinging to the handrail, she wondered how she would make her way up again. Great gusts of rain-filled wind buffeted her and whipped her hair across her face, half blinding her. She felt her feet slip from under her and let out a shriek, carried uselessly away on the wind.

The handrail swayed but held and Carrie regained her feet, heart beating fast. Her skirt and shoes must be ruined by the mud, she thought, just as the clouds parted and revealed the steps below. Thankfully, they appeared intact. Carrie shifted her weight to move down onto more solid footings, when a gleam of white caught her attention. Alongside the ruined steps, caught up in the mud slide, was a scattering of bones. Puzzled, she bent to take a closer look then recoiled, and took a wild step downwards to escape from them. She barely registered what she had seen: long bones with a nub of knuckle at the end, arching, narrower rib bones. She flung herself onwards, hardly caring whether she fell or not. Miraculously, she reached the bottom of the Glen in one piece, finding it more sheltered there. In her distress she didn't pause to look back, but pushed her way along the overgrown path, soaking her skirt further, in an effort to reach the hut as quickly as possible. She prayed Oscar would be there – she couldn't bear the thought that she was alone, after what she had just seen. Human bones, surely: those of Meg Marsh, missing these last hundred years and believed cruelly murdered.

CHAPTER FOURTEEN

arrie arrived at their meeting place, half drowned by the rain, shocked and shivering, desperate for words of comfort. 'There you are,' Oscar said. He sounded exasperated as he took her hand and pulled her into the hut.

He pushed her up against the closed door and she shuddered, convinced she could feel the sticky catch of spider threads in her hair. His hands were searching, pulling her blouse free from her waistband, undoing buttons. She gasped as cold fingers found warm flesh.

His face was pressed into her neck and she felt trapped, wounded by the events of the last half-hour. She burst into tears and attempted to push him away.

'What's the matter?' Oscar's face loomed over hers. She sobbed as she described how the steps had been partly washed away, and how she had slipped before seeing the gleam of white bones beside her in the mud.

'Please, not tonight,' Carrie said. She was almost incoherent as he tried to draw her back to him. She could see his expression in the dim light: brows knotted, lips pressed together.

Oscar was impatient. 'Don't be silly. I expect they were animal bones. Why would they be anything else? I imagine the dogs from the castle were buried here over the years. You know the sort of thing – little gravestones with "Faithful hound" and the name carved on them.'

Carrie barely noticed his attempt at an explanation. 'I think it must be Meg Marsh,' she hiccuped through her sobs. 'My ancestor – the one who's supposed to haunt this place. The one who was murdered by smugglers.'

She heard Oscar's sigh of exasperation before he collected himself and said, 'Why don't we go back and take a look to put your mind at rest?'

'No!' Carrie's fear was giving way to fury. Had he no respect for her feelings? Was he so intent on his own pleasure that he was prepared to ignore how upset she was? He hadn't relinquished his hold on her – he surely didn't intend to force himself on her?

At that very moment, Oscar appeared to grasp that the evening, and his plans, were ruined. He sighed again and held Carrie away from him, at arms' length. 'Better get you home before you catch a chill,' he said. 'We'll leave by my route and I'll walk you to your door.'

Carrie didn't argue. She had no intention of going anywhere near the steps again, and she didn't care if they were seen on the short journey home. She was shivering violently and all she longed to do was go home, wipe away the mud as best she could and climb into bed without alerting her mother to the state she was in.

They left the hut in silence, Oscar barely bothering to pretend the lock was in place. He took her hand over the uneven parts of the path but otherwise walked ahead of her. Carrie followed, hunched in misery, her thoughts whirling. The bones by the path had struck a terrible blow to her previous assurance. The events of that evening had prevented her making a terrible mistake, the sort of mistake it was rumoured Meg Marsh had made. She hoped she would be glad of what had happened in the days to come, but for now she was eager to be away from Oscar. She'd glimpsed a side to him that she didn't like.

Carrie's mother called to her as soon as she heard the front door open.

'I'm soaked. Let me get dry and then I'll come in to you,' Carrie called, hurrying past the door to the sitting room. Her voice trembled – she hoped her mother hadn't heard it. She dripped her way upstairs and stripped off her clothes. She couldn't stop shaking. Was it the result of getting so wet, or because of what had happened that evening? She wrapped a towel around her hair and used another to rub herself dry, trying to calm herself as she did so. Oscar had recovered himself and behaved well enough in escorting her home, she thought, but she knew in her heart she was making excuses for him.

Her mother's calls persisted from downstairs so she pulled on her nightdress and dressing-gown and went down to her.

'Look at you! I told you not to go out on a night like this,' Mrs Marsh scolded. 'Fine friends you have. They could at least have driven you home.'

Carrie, having forgotten the excuse she had given her mother, was momentarily confused. 'Mr Hadley needed the car,' she said, once she'd collected herself. 'What can I get for you, Mother?'

'I want a hot drink and then to go to bed,' her mother said. She scrutinised Carrie. 'Make yourself a drink, too, and come and sit by the fire.'

Carrie nodded and went to the kitchen, glad of a few minutes to compose herself. She heated milk in a pan on the gas ring, then made cocoa, and added extra sugar to her own cup. Perhaps it was shock that was making her shake so.

Her mother had lost interest in hearing about Carrie's evening, wishing instead to tell her about an article she had read in her periodical. Carrie settled herself on the worn velvet seat of the chair on the other side of the fireplace, absent-mindedly rubbing its scuffed wooden arms as she half listened to her mother. The coal scuttle would need to be filled in the morning, she thought, and kindling chopped. It helped to fill her mind with mundane things to calm her agitation. The hot, sweet drink was soothing, too. She had an overwhelming urge to sleep and blot out what had just happened. Before she could give in to it, though, her mother must be helped to bed and the cottage secured for the night.

Over the following week, Carrie checked daily to see whether a note had been left for her in the gatepost, even though she knew it was unlikely since Oscar would be back in London. Was she hoping for an apology or an explanation? She wasn't sure, and she faced the weekend with trepidation, wondering whether he would come home and send word to her. She half dreaded what he might say, but she waited in vain. No note came then, or during the next week. She saw Ada that weekend and her studiedly casual enquiry as to the whereabouts of Oscar received the reply that 'Father was keeping him busy and he's sent word that he's unlikely to be home before Christmas.'

Carrie's heart plummeted. Oscar had behaved in a callous fashion, yet she couldn't help herself: a part of her longed to see him. It was clear, though, that such a possibility wasn't open to her. There was nothing to be done other than put the incident, and her foolish behaviour, behind her.

CHAPTER FIFTEEN

Christmas came and went without their paths crossing. The week beforehand, Ada gave Carrie a small box wrapped in bright paper. She pressed it into her hand and Carrie gazed at it in consternation.

'I wasn't expecting anything. It's still a week away. I've come unprepared.' She was flustered and her words tumbled out. She knew she wouldn't be able to match a gift from Ada.

'It's just something small but I hope you'll like it. And, please, I don't want anything in return. Your company is enough.' Ada gave her a warm smile. 'We're going to be in London for Christmas so I knew this would be my last chance to see you.'

They were in front of the fire in the sitting room at Hawksdown Lodge, as dusk crept across the garden. It had been a glorious day, sunny and crisp. Carrie and Ada had walked along the seafront, returning with cheeks glowing, fingers and toes chilled. They'd warmed up with cocoa and Maria had banked up the fire. Carrie was reluctant to vacate her chair in the comfortable room to make the chilly walk home to a house so lacking in the warm, relaxed atmosphere that drew her to Hawksdown Lodge. It would soon be dark, though, and her mother would worry.

Clutching the little box, she rose to her feet. A wave of sadness washed over her. It would be a dismal Christmas without Ada's company. And, she was forced to admit, without Oscar's. It was as though she'd been holding her breath until his expected return and now she felt deflated. Would the family be at home for New Year? She was about to ask the question when Ada, standing in the hallway as Carrie buttoned her coat, suddenly said, her brow furrowed, 'Father's worried. He thinks war could be coming.'

'War?' Carrie was bewildered. 'Who with?'

'Something to do with a Balkan war, and Germany building up their troops. He heard it at the bank.' Ada shrugged. 'He thinks we might have to leave the house and move to London.' She glanced around her as she spoke, at the rugs on the polished parquet, the gilt-framed paintings and the collection of china vases displayed on the hall stand.

'But why would you have to leave here?' It made no sense to Carrie – she couldn't understand what Ada was telling her.

'He said we're too exposed here on the coast. Too close to enemy raids from Europe.' Ada had opened the door and they gazed out into the gathering darkness. Mr Hadley believed trouble was brewing somewhere beyond the waves they could hear breaking on the shore.

'Surely he's mistaken,' Carrie said. 'Perhaps it's just a rumour, something to cause the bank to ...' She trailed off, having no idea how a banking institution worked. 'It's Christmas. Let's not think of such things. And tell your father you can't possibly leave Hawksdown Lodge. What would I do without you?'

Ada hugged Carrie. 'I'm sure you're right. I expect it will all be forgotten by the time I come back. Happy Christmas, Carrie. And hurry home – it's turning very cold.'

She shut the door, leaving Carrie to hunch into her coat, winding her scarf one more time around her throat before she followed the path round to the gate that led onto Grove Lane. Not only must she resign herself to spending Christmas without Ada, but now there was the prospect of the family moving away to worry about.

There was little festive spirit in Carrie's heart as she hurried home, feeling the sting of a snow flurry on her cheeks.

Christmas passed quietly in Ivy Cottage. Carrie was attentive to her mother and tried to inject some festivity into the day. She was pleased with the swathes of holly and ivy she had collected from the garden and used to decorate the mantelpiece.

Her mother, though, declared her attempt a waste of time. 'The leaves will wizen and drop off without water. And think of all the insects you must have brought in.'

As a treat for Christmas lunch, Carrie had ordered a chicken from the butcher. She'd roasted it with parsnips and potatoes, and boiled some carrots to add colour to the plates. She'd been daring and bought a bottle of wine, adding some to the gravy and drinking a glass while she cooked. Carrie thought the table looked wonderful draped in a white cloth, a shaft of wintry sun sparkling on the silverware she'd polished to a shine. She was going to serve the meal on their best china, which usually languished in the dresser. Her mother couldn't fail to be impressed by the delicious aroma, she thought, as she helped her from the sitting-room fireside to the table. It seemed, however, there was plenty for her mother to find fault with.

'The cloth will be ruined if gravy gets on it,' she complained, before she'd even sat down.

'I'll be careful,' Carrie promised, holding back a sigh.

Mrs Marsh refused wine. 'Water's good enough for me, Christmas or not.' She picked suspiciously at her food. 'Where are the greens?' she asked. 'I need greens for my digestion.' After a few mouthfuls she put down her fork, declaring it all too rich for her.

Carrie, dismayed, tried to encourage her to eat. It felt very similar to dealing with difficult children at school, she thought. Her own appetite fled as she bit back all the things she wanted to say to her mother.

'I'll clear away the plates,' she said finally. 'Then I have something for you, before dessert.'

'I haven't anything for you.' Her mother was blunt.

'That's all right.' Carrie gathered up the plates and took them through to the kitchen, frowning at the amount of wasted food. Would the trifle she had made the previous evening, before venturing out to church, be any better received? First, though, she wanted to open Ada's present. She had saved it until now, because she had known that, as every year, there would be no gift from her mother.

She carried through the trifle and set it in the centre of the table. The layers of red jelly, yellow custard and white cream were displayed in another rarely seen family possession: a cut-glass bowl.

'Why have you used that? It belonged to my grandmother. It's worth good money. I don't want it getting chipped when it's washed up.' Her mother barely paused for breath before adding, 'And I hope you haven't put any sherry in that trifle. You know I never touch a drop.'

'No, Mother.' Carrie closed her eyes momentarily, gathering strength. 'There's no sherry. Shall I serve you some?' Her mother had a sweet tooth – she'd probably have two helpings, no matter how rich it was. And it would buy Carrie some time to look at her present from Ada in peace.

She took the little wrapped box from the dresser, and set a parcel beside her mother. She'd bought her a fine shawl, something she could wear when sitting by the fire when she often complained of a draught at her neck.

'What have you got there?' Mrs Marsh had already eaten most of her first bowl of trifle.

'It's from Ada. I don't know what it is. Shall we see?' Again, Carrie was reminded of talking to a child. She tore away the paper, to find a dark blue box embossed with gold lettering. Carrie noticed the words 'Bond Street' as she opened it. Inside, a pair of drop earrings nestled on a velvet cushion. Two gold leaves adorned with a tiny pearl topped the pale blue teardrop-shaped stones, which were rimmed with gold.

'Oh, look at them. How beautiful,' breathed Carrie, taking a moment to gaze at them before lifting one from the box.

Her mother sniffed. 'Paste, I expect. Is there more trifle?'

Carrie stopped herself snapping that the bowl was right in front of her. Instead, she rose from her seat and refilled her mother's dish.

'They're from Bond Street,' she remarked, sitting down again.

'Let me see.' Her mother, interested now, held out her hand for the box. As Carrie handed it over, she had a sudden flash of how different things might have been if she was sitting at the Hadleys' Christmas table. She imagined herself getting up and hugging Ada, then being unable to resist trying on the earrings and looking in the over-mantel mirror. They would all have eaten and drunk well, the family noisy and appreciative of their dinner and their gifts. Her heart ached: how she longed to be part of such a scene. Her mother seemed to have become even sourer over this past year. How much longer would she have to put up with it?

Then, feeling guilty for having such thoughts, especially at Christmas, she roused herself and said, 'Open your present, Mother.'

Mrs Marsh set down the jewel box. 'More money than sense, some people,' she said. 'Why would she buy you such things?'

'She's my friend.' Carrie spoke hotly. 'And I had nothing to give her in return. But open yours. I hope you'll like it.'

Mrs Marsh opened the parcel with great care, peeling the tape from the paper. 'You can use this again,' she said, with some satisfaction as she pushed the paper towards her daughter. Carrie forbore to comment.

Her mother unfolded a shawl from the box and shook it out.

'It's not too heavy. I thought you could put it around your neck when you sit by the fire. You know how draughty you find it in the winter.'

'It's a bit drab,' her mother commented. 'Didn't they have anything brighter?'

Carrie had chosen one in muted tones of ochre, green and gold from the selection at the draper's in Castle Bay. It had reminded her of an elegant scarf Mrs Hadley wore.

Making a great effort, she said, 'I can take it back and exchange it, if you like?'

'No, no, it will do.' Her mother paused and remembered her manners. 'Thank you, Carrie. I'll wear it now. I think I'll go back to the fire.'

Carrie helped her to her feet and settled her back in the sitting room, adding a few lumps of coal to the fire. She'd probably doze for a while, she thought. She went back to the table, served herself with trifle and poured another glass of wine. If she couldn't have the company and celebration she longed for, she would settle for solitude.

CHAPTER SIXTEEN

❧

Carrie longed for the new school term to begin, so she could escape her home. She made excuses to her mother about work needing to be done in the schoolroom and cycled there along Grove Lane, hoping for a glimpse of the Hadleys or their car. She could have called at the house, of course, but feared an encounter with Oscar when she was unprepared.

In fact, it was midway through January before she was to see Ada again. Carrie found her waiting outside the schoolroom door on a Friday at the end of the day, stamping her feet and blowing on her fingers to ward off the cold.

'Why didn't you come in?' Carrie exclaimed, locking the door. 'But how lovely to see you. I've missed you. And I didn't know where to write to thank you for my beautiful earrings.' She put a finger up to her ear to show her friend.

'You're wearing them to school.' Ada seemed surprised.

'Only on Fridays, to mark the end of the week.' Carrie made a wry face. 'It's about as exciting as life gets at the moment.' Although she was tired at the end of each week and glad to close the schoolroom door behind her, the thought of two days at home was never appealing.

'Well, I hope you'll spend some time with us this weekend.' Ada linked arms with Carrie as they walked around the corner to leave the schoolroom key and to collect her bicycle. 'Oscar and Jeremy are at home and we'd love you to come to lunch and, if it isn't too cold, for a bicycle ride first?'

Carrie's heart lurched at the thought of seeing Oscar again. They had had no communication for weeks now and she was fearful of how he might react. But she couldn't let that stop her spending time with Ada. 'Did you have a good Christmas? And New Year?' she asked, eager for news.

'Too many parties.' Ada sighed. 'I'm glad to be back here, where it's so much quieter.'

Carrie, who thought it was possible for life to be far too quiet, said nothing.

They'd reached Ada's gate and Carrie wondered whether she would invite her in, but she said, 'Come tomorrow after ten o'clock, with your bicycle. I was given one for Christmas and Oscar and Jeremy can use the old ones in the garage. I'm not very good at riding it yet but it will be fun.'

Ada went in at her gate, leaving Carrie to mount her bicycle and set off for home. She was both delighted and unnerved by the encounter, thoughts of the day to come filling her evening so that, daydreaming, she overcooked her mother's fish and vegetables and earned herself a scolding. It was only as she climbed into bed that a thought put an end to the uneasy feeling that clouded her anticipation. She need have no fear of seeing Oscar: he would, of course, behave as though nothing had happened because they had always been at pains to hide their relationship from Ada and Jeremy. Carrie would need to catch a moment alone with him if she wanted to discuss it, and she wasn't sure she did.

She presented herself at the Hadleys' door at ten minutes past ten the following morning, leaving her bicycle propped just inside the gate. The sky was grey, but it wasn't too cold, and she didn't think it would rain. She was wearing Ada's gift – she loved the way the sparkling blue droplets echoed the colour of her eyes and stood out against her brown hair, now caught up in a beret. Carrie was smiling to herself out of pure happiness when the door opened at her knock. She was expecting to see Maria, the maid, but Oscar stood there.

'Oh!' she exclaimed, then recovered herself. 'I wasn't expecting you.'

'I do live here.' Oscar appeared amused.

'I've come to see Ada. She mentioned a bicycle ride.' Carrie was flustered. Oscar looked as though he had only recently got out of bed. His hair was rumpled and his shirt collar awry under his pullover. He yawned, confirming her suspicions.

'I'm just about to have breakfast – I arrived very late last night. Jeremy might join you if he's about.' He turned and called, 'Ada,' over his shoulder, then said to Carrie, 'You'd better come in.'

Carrie, who'd been standing awkwardly on the doorstep, stepped gratefully inside. She saw that Oscar, padding in the direction of his breakfast, was in his socks.

'Make yourself at home,' he called, as he went.

He'd shown no sign of awkwardness – in fact, he'd been rather dismissive of her, Carrie thought. She loitered in the hall, feeling uncomfortable, until Ada came down the stairs.

'Why are you standing there? Did Maria let you in? Why didn't she show you into the drawing room?' Ada frowned in annoyance.

'I'm sorry if I'm early,' Carrie said. 'Oscar answered the door, but he's gone to have breakfast.'

'Oh, he's hopeless,' Ada said. 'Is he going to join us? I told him the plan last night. I'm ready. I'll see where Jeremy is.'

She hurried away, leaving Carrie still standing in the hall, contemplating the undeniable fact that Oscar had known about the bicycle ride, but chosen not to get up in time. She didn't have long to dwell on it: Ada arrived back with Jeremy in tow, and shortly before eleven they were on their way. Ada had needed a couple of practice laps of the tennis court before she announced she was happy, but Carrie noticed she was still wobbly as they set off along Grove Lane. Jeremy was encouraging, though, pedalling beside her while Carrie followed.

'Where are we going?' Carrie called, as Grove Lane gave way to open countryside, but if Ada and Jeremy heard her they didn't reply. Carrie didn't mind. They would arrive in Kingsdown before long and she suspected it would be too hilly for Ada after that. They could wind their way through the village, following the hill down to the sea.

It turned out exactly as she had suspected. They reached a cross-roads and Ada came to an inelegant halt, dragging her heels in the dust. 'My legs are aching,' she said. 'And this seat is terribly uncomfortable. I don't think I can go much further. Shall we turn back?'

Carrie explained how to reach the sea. 'It's just a few minutes away. Downhill,' she promised.

'Let's go.' Jeremy had begun slowly to pedal away. 'Otherwise it's a wasted journey.'

Carrie was riding alongside Ada, taking care not to crowd her. Her friend was concentrating hard, her knuckles white as she gripped the handlebars.

'You're doing well,' Carrie encouraged her. 'We'll have a rest by the sea before we go home.'

'I'll need a cushion before I get back on this thing again,' Ada said, grim-faced as she pedalled.

Barely five minutes later they reached Jeremy, who had thrown down his machine on a patch of grass opposite a row of cottages.

'The tide's out,' he said. 'Let's see what we can find in the rock pools.' He was striding over the pebbles before Ada had dismounted, wincing.

'Let's join Jeremy,' Carrie urged. 'It will take your mind off things.'

Ada gave her a look. 'It will take more than a rock pool to make me forget I've got to get back on that.' Then she laughed and took Carrie's arm, hobbling at her side until her cramped leg muscles eased.

They spent half an hour or so poking around in the pools, exclaiming as crabs scuttled out from their hiding places under the weedy fringes, and admiring the sea anemones, which waved their tentacles as Jeremy drizzled a little sand into the water. Carrie wandered away to sit on a rock and watch the brother and sister, two dark heads bent close together. It was peaceful – there was no one else on the beach. She couldn't help thinking how different it would have been if Oscar was with them. She would have been on constant watch for some sign from him, hoping to catch him alone to exchange a few words. As it was, she was happy to sit and observe for a while, ambling back just as Ada shivered and said, 'It's cold now. The wind has got up.'

Jeremy shaded his eyes and peered out to sea. 'The tide's turned. The pools will be filling soon. We can go back if you like.' He looked at Ada as he spoke.

She nodded, so Carrie followed them up the beach. Ada paused at a patch of sand in the middle of the pebbles. 'Let's write our names,' she suggested.

They were like a group of school children, Carrie thought, as they jostled each other for space, vying to see who could produce the best script. Ada wrote with the toe of her boot, producing a giant A with a tail flick. Jeremy found a pointed shell and executed his name in beautiful italics. Carrie used her finger and felt her effort was a scrawl in comparison, although she was proud of the curly flourish on her C.

'Now anyone who visits the beach will know we were here,' Ada proclaimed.

Jeremy smiled. 'The sea will have taken them in the next hour.

I expect everyone's settling down to lunch, in any case. And I'm starving.'

'I might have to walk home,' Ada moaned. 'I can't bear to get back on that thing.'

'This will make it better.' Jeremy pulled the red woollen scarf from his neck and wound it round and round Ada's saddle, tucking in the loose end. 'Now try it,' he said.

Ada climbed on as he held the bicycle, gingerly lowering herself onto the seat. 'Better!' she exclaimed. 'Thank you, Jeremy.'

Carrie was impressed by his thoughtfulness. They'd take the path by the sea as their route back to Hawksdown Lodge: it would save climbing the hill, but although it was flat it was bumpy. She hoped the scarf would provide enough padding for Ada but they progressed well, stopping twice to rewind the scarf when it worked loose. Carrie, too, was ready for lunch by the time they arrived at Hawksdown Lodge. She was prepared to see Oscar, but when they burst in through the front door Maria greeted them with the news that Mr and Mrs Hadley and Oscar were dining out.

'I'll serve your lunch now,' she said, leaving them to divest themselves of coats and jackets, and to wash their hands. Carrie had to hide her disappointment at Oscar's absence, but it was quickly forgotten. Ada and Jeremy were very good company, entertaining her with tales of their London Christmas and all the relatives who had descended on them. Carrie was sad to leave them at the end of the afternoon, with only mild regret at still not having spent much time with Oscar. She felt sure she would see him the following weekend, or the next, but it was to be midsummer before their paths crossed again.

CHAPTER SEVENTEEN

❧

As the weeks passed, Carrie thought less and less about Oscar. She still saw Ada most weekends, Jeremy sometimes joining them, but the chilly spring that year curtailed their outings. Ada was reluctant to take another bicycle ride but they walked into Castle Bay and watched the fishermen at work, puffing at their pipes as they mended their nets on the shingle. When the sun came out, the promenade was busy with residents and visitors taking the sea air. Whole families strolled together, young children helping each other along and occasionally sharing a ride with the youngest in the baby carriage. Brisk winds still blighted the coast, though, and the ladies had to hold onto the brims of their hats.

As summer finally brought some warmth, the families took to the shingle beach, picnicking in the shade of the many boats pulled up on the shore. The wooden bathing huts were rolled out of winter storage to take their place along the water's edge and deckchairs set out in rows to face the sea.

One hot Saturday afternoon in June, Ada and Carrie stopped a little way outside Castle Bay, daunted by the crowds ahead on the promenade. They stood and watched a group of small children paddling at the water's edge, the boys with their trousers rolled up and the girls with stockings removed and dresses hitched. Their mothers were settled close by on the beach, keeping watch.

'I almost forgot,' Ada said. 'My mother said she would like to hold another tea party for the school. Could you ask Mrs Chambers and arrange a date?'

'Of course,' Carrie said. 'That's very kind of Mrs Hadley.'

They watched the children splash and shriek for a little longer, then Ada turned to Carrie. 'Shall we?' she asked.

'Yes!' Carrie exclaimed. Then she looked doubtful. 'Not here, though. Let's go back towards your house. It will be quieter and it's less likely we'll be spotted by anyone who knows us.'

It appeared Ada was less worried by such concerns but she agreed to turn back and they walked on until they reached an empty stretch of beach without even a fishing boat in sight.

'This will do,' Carrie declared, and they picked their way over the stones to the water's edge. She unbuttoned her shoes and took a good look around before rolling down her stockings. Ada was less cautious and was already stepping into the sea by the time Carrie began to edge towards her, complaining how painful it was to walk on the shingle. The icy rush of the shallow waves caught her unawares and she gasped but it wasn't long before she was laughing and splashing Ada while attempting to stay upright as the stones slipped with the pull of the water.

After fifteen minutes they had both had enough, the hems of their skirts now soaked. They picked their way back to their discarded shoes and stockings and sat in companionable silence, watching the waves as their feet dried in the sun. Carrie had just finished rolling her stockings back on and smoothing her skirt, hoping the salt water hadn't stained it, when a shadow fell across them. She turned her head to see a man in a straw boater and a linen jacket standing between them and the sun. His face was shadowed but Ada recognised him at once.

'Hello, Oscar. If you'd been here a little earlier you could have joined us in there.' She gestured at the sea.

'I saw you as I was cycling back from Castle Bay,' Oscar said. 'You looked as though you were enjoying yourselves.'

How long had he been watching them? Carrie wondered, as he settled himself onto the warm stones beside her.

'Let's hope Mother didn't see you from an upstairs window,' he said. 'She'll have something to say about it if she did.'

Ada made a face. 'I don't see why. You and Jeremy were bathing this morning. Why can't I paddle?'

'Because you're a young lady.' Oscar laughed.

'I thought Amelia was going to join you this weekend?' Ada said. Carrie registered the spiteful tone of her voice before the import of her words struck home. Who was Amelia? She glanced between Ada and Oscar and saw Oscar flush.

'I'm not seeing Amelia any more,' Oscar said. He got to his feet. 'I'd better be on my way.' He glared at Ada but she ignored him, staring out to sea. He nodded to Carrie and crunched his way up the beach, feet sliding in the shingle.

'Amelia?' Carrie enquired, when he was out of earshot.

'Someone he's been seeing for a while. Mother thought an engagement might be announced soon but it appears not.' Ada gave her friend a sideways glance. Carrie stared out to sea and tried to gather her thoughts. She needed time to think. There was someone Oscar had been seeing 'for a while'. Did this include last year, she wondered, when she and Oscar had been meeting in the Glen? She felt as though she had been punched in the stomach. When Ada suggested it was time to go back, Carrie got swiftly to her feet. She was keen to get away.

'Have you met Amelia?' she asked, hoping her enquiry sounded casual.

'Yes, at Christmas.' Ada began to slide backwards on the steep upward slope of the beach and grabbed Carrie's arm. 'They hadn't known each other long. Just a few months.' She gave Carrie another sideways look.

'I see. Is she – was she nice?' Carrie asked, after a pause. A few months. Was that before she'd last met Oscar in the Glen?

Ada shrugged. 'Nice enough. She suited Oscar, I suppose. It's a shame.'

Carrie struggled to keep her composure. Why hadn't Ada mentioned any of this before? Then she remembered Ada's words after their outing to the maze at Eastling House, back in September. Had she been trying to warn her that Oscar was seeing someone? She'd mentioned being worried that he was toying with Carrie, and said she wanted to speak to him. Had she done that? Is that why Carrie had seen virtually nothing of Oscar since October?

She was glad to wave goodbye to Ada at her gate, and quick to decline her offer to come in for tea. 'I'll ask Mrs Chambers about a date for the school garden party,' she promised, then pedalled away on her bicycle, retrieved from just inside the gate. There was a lot to think about. Oscar had had a girlfriend for all these months. But now he didn't.

Chapter Eighteen

Mrs Chambers was delighted by Mrs Hadley's invitation and insisted Carrie take a note to Hawksdown Lodge that very day, after school.

'I've suggested a date in the last week of term, when the children are always too excited to settle to work,' she said. 'I hope it will be convenient.'

Happily, the day not only suited Mrs Hadley but dawned bright and sunny. As she bicycled to school that morning along Grove Lane, Carrie noticed how warm it was even at that early hour. She hoped it wouldn't be too hot for the children – perhaps Mrs Hadley would find a shady spot for the tables. Was it really just a year since she'd met Ada? she thought, as she wheeled her bicycle into the caretaker's yard. How her life had changed since she'd met the Hadleys ...

The children's excitement rose during the morning and it was hard to keep them occupied. Carrie was glad when the time came to assemble the two classes on Grove Lane and make the short walk to Hawksdown Lodge. Clouds that had rolled in from the west made the afternoon a little cooler, but Carrie cast a few anxious glances at the sky as they walked: was there a chance the party could be spoilt by rain? There was no time to dwell on it, though, for they had arrived at the Hadleys' garden gate and the children's chatter increased in volume as soon as they saw the tables set out in long rows.

The afternoon proceeded much as it had the previous year, with plates of sandwiches and cake, cordial to drink and then games. This time, Carrie was in charge as Ada was in London. That was a shame, Carrie thought, as the children had looked forward to seeing her again. The skies darkened further during the last game, a skipping race, and a terrific clap of thunder came out of nowhere. The children started to scream and Mrs Chambers had to shout a good deal in an attempt to restore order. Carrie hushed the younger ones and glanced anxiously at the sky. Was there enough time to hurry the children back to school? Or were they about to be soaked?

As she instructed them to form pairs, ready to walk back, she heard an unexpected voice in her ear. She turned in surprise to find Oscar standing there.

'Mother said to shelter in the garages and tennis pavilion if you like. Hopefully the storm will blow over before too long.'

Great drops of rain were falling as he spoke and Carrie nodded her thanks, quickly turning to Mrs Chambers to pass on the offer. Then she led the way down the garden to the garages, ushering inside whichever children were nearest, before urging the others on to the tennis pavilion.

As the rainfall grew in intensity and became a deluge, she could only hope that they had managed to gather everyone together. The tennis court was soon a mist of bouncing raindrops and the children, squashed into the pavilion, had lost their fear and cheered each time the thunder rolled. This was so frequent that Carrie began to fear all the noise in such a confined space would give her a splitting headache. To divert them, she told them to count after each lightning flash. 'Like this – one thousand, two thousand,' she said, before thunder cracked above them. 'Almost overhead,' she exclaimed. 'If we can reach five thousand, it's a mile away.'

It was another fifteen minutes before Carrie deemed the storm distant enough to allow them all to tumble, hot and sweaty, from the pavilion. The tennis court had begun to steam under the hot sun that had now broken through the clouds.

She led the children back to the garden where the tables were now a scene of devastation. Soggy sandwiches rested in puddles on the plates, while cups and glasses had overturned with the force of the rain. Mrs Chambers offered Mrs Hadley grateful thanks for the afternoon, and for allowing them to shelter.

'I'm only sorry we can't stay to help with the clearing up, but we must get the children back to school. We've had a lovely time, haven't we?' she said, turning to her pupils as she spoke.

'Yes, miss,' they chorused.

Carrie had little doubt they would remember this party for a very long time. She ushered them through the gate onto Grove Lane, surprised once more to find Oscar hurrying up just as she turned to shut it behind her.

'Carrie, I'd like to talk to you. Meet me tonight in the Glen, eight o'clock.' These words were uttered in a murmur, then he added in a normal tone, 'Goodbye, everyone.'

Carrie, startled, had no chance to reply. Neither did she have time to ponder what he'd said: the children must be walked back to school and a final register taken before they could be sent on their way. Afterwards, as she pedalled home, irritation flooded through her. There had been no word from Oscar for over nine months, she thought, but he imagines he can tell me to meet him. Not ask me, but tell me.

By the time she arrived at the cottage, she'd decided she wouldn't go. Let him wait for me, she thought. But then, as it drew closer to eight o'clock, curiosity got the better of her. That, and a wave of despair at the thought of the school summer holidays stretching before her, with just her mother's company to enjoy. Perhaps it wouldn't hurt to hear what Oscar had to say. It might alleviate any awkwardness and allow them – Jeremy and Ada, too – to meet just as they had the previous summer.

At a quarter to eight she took the gate key to the Glen from its hook in the kitchen. She hadn't been there since that awful night last November. Would the gate even open? The last rays of the sun lit the sky as she opened the front door, calling to her mother, 'I left something at the Hadleys' house. I won't be long.' She shut the door on her mother's response and hurried out, clutching the key as she walked the short distance to the gate. Her hand shook as she inserted the key in the lock. At first, it wouldn't turn but by means of pulling the handle hard towards her it began to inch round, with a grating sound.

When the gate finally creaked open, Carrie stepped through it to be confronted by a dense growth of vegetation covering the steps that led down into the bottom of the Glen. Too late, she remembered that rain had washed away a section of the steps. She would have to take the long way round. As she stepped back onto the path, locking the gate behind her, she saw the unmistakable figure of Oscar coming towards her.

Carrie stood and waited for him. If anyone saw them together, it was too bad. There was no way to avoid him.

'I'm sorry I'm late,' he said, out of breath from hurrying. 'Were you leaving already?' He seemed surprised.

'No, the steps are too overgrown to use.' They spoke easily to each other, as though the intervening months had never happened.

'Then we can walk there together,' Oscar said.

Carrie was about to suggest they might as well walk on Hawks Down instead, but as she fell into step beside him, she saw other couples there. Keen not to be recognised, she followed Oscar over the gate into the grounds of Hawksdown Castle. He vanished into the increasing gloom under the trees and she followed. Was he really intent on forcing a way down into the Glen? What did he have to say to her that would be worth all the effort?

CHAPTER NINETEEN

It was hard to follow a path down into the Glen, but not as impossible as Carrie had feared. Oscar, ahead of her, trampled down whatever lay across the path, but it was still a scramble over fallen saplings and piles of stones created by slippage from the steep sides. Carrie became determined to give Oscar a piece of her mind. Why had she even agreed to this? She supposed she hadn't: he had given her no choice.

Oscar was waiting for her outside the gardener's hut. It was even more tumbledown than she remembered it, the door hanging half off its hinges and creepers covering the roof. Carrie shook leaves from her hair and the folds of her skirt and brushed the shoulders of her blouse, ruefully noting she left dusty smears as she did so.

'I just wanted to say I'm sorry,' Oscar began.

Her irritation grew. Why had he needed to drag her all this way to deliver an apology? He could have done that anywhere.

'After I saw you at the beach, paddling with Ada, I fell to thinking about the Glen and the time we spent here. They were lovely memories – the peace, the solitude, just us here together, away from everyone.' Oscar looked around. 'Somehow it doesn't match up to my memory. It's become even more overgrown.'

'It was autumn when we met,' Carrie pointed out. 'The leaves had fallen.' There it was again, she thought wryly, her practical schoolteacher side. She was standing a little apart from Oscar and she'd stiffened when he'd referred to them being there together. Now was the time to say what needed to be said.

'Oscar, I'm glad you have such fond memories of this place. I'm sorry to say they don't match mine.' She glared at him and he looked surprised.

'The last time we met here, I was distressed – caught in that awful storm and then seeing the bones of Meg Marsh.' Carrie shuddered. She could have sworn Oscar rolled his eyes, so she plunged on. 'You weren't very sympathetic. And now I think I know why. You'd begun to see someone else, hadn't you? Amelia? Ada mentioned her, that time on the beach. So what exactly did you think you were doing with me?'

The words had tumbled out and Carrie came to a halt. She was hot and her hair was sticking to her brow. The storm hadn't cleared the air – it was still very close, especially here at the bottom of the Glen.

Oscar had opened his mouth to speak more than once, but Carrie had forged on with her speech. Now he looked as though he didn't know how to reply. He looked down, scuffing the toe of his shoe on the ground. 'It was my mother's doing. She's friendly with Amelia's family. She decided we would make the perfect match and threw us together at every opportunity. I went along with it at first. It was easy enough: I was spending most of my time in London.' He shrugged. 'But my heart wasn't in it. I had to break things off before I found myself pressured into a marriage that could never have worked.' He looked up at Carrie, ducking his head, like a small boy caught out in bad behaviour.

She was exasperated rather than mollified. She didn't really believe him. It was a plausible explanation, at least for the relationship with Amelia, but what did he intend by this conversation? 'You could have written,' she pointed out.

'You're right.' Oscar nodded thoughtfully. 'I intended to. I suppose I didn't feel particularly good about the way I'd behaved and I put it off and then . . .' he paused '. . . and then it was too late. Do you hate me for it?'

The direct question caught Carrie by surprise and she said the first words that came into her head. 'I don't hate you, no.'

'But . . .' Oscar prompted.

'But it really wasn't a nice way to behave,' Carrie said.

'And yet you're here.' Oscar had a quizzical look on his face.

Why was she there? Carrie thought. Oscar had hit on something she was barely admitting to herself. She still had feelings for him, despite everything. Before she could respond, he was speaking again.

'The world's changing, Carrie. Working at the bank, I know a lot of what's happening right now in Germany. There's a threat hanging over us.'

Carrie frowned. What was he talking about now? Was this to do with what Ada had reported her father saying at Christmas? Something about moving away, because of a threat. She'd hoped all that had been forgotten.

Oscar had stepped towards her and now he grasped her by the shoulders. He was animated, his cheeks flushed and his eyes sparkling. 'Can you forgive me, Carrie, for the last few months? Can we put it behind us and be friends again?'

He whispered the last words into her ear. Then he turned her face gently towards him and kissed her.

She made a motion to resist, half pulling away, but the sweet familiarity of his lips on hers aroused a flood of emotion. She'd missed this so much.

He held her to him then and she felt the beat of their hearts as she rested her head on his chest. Neither of them spoke for some time until Oscar roused himself to say, 'We must get you home. It's late.'

Carrie, looking around, saw how dark it had become. She'd told her mother she wouldn't be long. She was immediately anxious but Oscar had already turned and was leading the way out, holding out his hand behind him for her to grasp. As they followed the narrow path, rising higher out of the Glen, she saw it wasn't as dark as she'd thought. Perhaps she hadn't been away as long as she feared.

There was no sign of the other couples on Hawks Down as they climbed over the gate, but she thought she heard muffled laughter somewhere close by. Oscar didn't appear to have noticed, taking her arm on the path home under the trees. He stopped at her gate, raised her hand to his lips and kissed it.

'I'm glad we're friends again, Carrie,' he said softly, and strode away. Carrie lingered at the gate, watching until he was out of sight, listening to the night-time sounds around her. There was a rustling in the grass along the path edge and a dog barked somewhere on Grove Lane. She looked up at the sky, now clear of clouds with stars beginning to peep, more and more of them the longer she looked.

She still had no idea what Oscar had meant about the world changing. But her world had changed a little that evening and she was glad of it.

CHAPTER TWENTY

After that Carrie fell into the habit of seeing Oscar every week-end – sometimes in Ada's company, sometimes just the two of them down in the Glen, as before. Yet not quite as before, Carrie thought. She had been shocked when war with Germany was declared a little over two weeks after the school tea party. Oscar could talk of little else, but she noticed his conversation on the subject varied depending on who he was with. With his father the topic focused on the mechanics of war, and how the bank might be affected. With Ada and Carrie he mentioned friends of his who had joined up, as if testing the water for their opinion. It was only when he was alone with Carrie that he spoke of his determination to join the army as soon as possible, despite knowing his parents would be bitterly opposed.

Down in the Glen, they sat outside the hut on a fallen log, Oscar having declared the roof only too likely to collapse on them if they ventured inside. Carrie leant against him, only half listening as he talked of the need for as many as possible of his fellow men to sign up for the army was woefully undermanned.

'But how will they train everyone in time? And is it worth it? Surely this won't last.' Carrie still struggled to comprehend what was happening.

For the moment, life in Castle Bay went on much as before, although she had met Mrs Chambers in the street and she had seemed worried. 'I think we will have smaller classes next term,' she had said. 'If the farmhands sign up, the children will be kept back to help instead. And there isn't much I can say – we need the eggs and the milk, and the crops to be planted.'

Carrie had thought of all the children in her class who came in from the surrounding farms. Would she be able to persuade the families to let the children attend school part-time?

Oscar was stroking her arm in an absent-minded way as he talked, explaining how important it was to act now against the German troops who were advancing only too easily into France. He spoke with confidence about the role the British Army had to play, and how important it was to strike fast.

'Your father will never let you go,' Carrie said.

'He can't stop me,' Oscar said. 'I'm over twenty-one. He won't be happy, but it's my duty. The sooner we go, the sooner we'll be back.'

Then he kissed Carrie and she forgot, for a moment or two, to worry about his words. Later that night, at home in bed, she ran over what he said. She felt honoured he'd chosen to confide in her, while keeping his intentions secret from the rest of the family.

It came as a shock, then, when Carrie called in to the Hadleys on a beautiful September Saturday to collect Ada for a walk as arranged, only to find her in floods of tears. Maria had appeared upset when she opened the door, telling her she'd find Ada in her bedroom. As she climbed the stairs, Carrie caught a glimpse of Mr and Mrs Hadley in the dining room standing close together in earnest discussion. She'd knocked on Ada's closed door, waiting for her friend's response but hearing only sobs.

'Ada – what's wrong? May I come in?' Carrie hesitated, her hand on the door knob, wondering whether or not to enter.

The sobs subsided into snuffles and the door swung open to reveal Ada, still in her nightclothes, her hair loose, her eyes red and puffy from weeping.

'Whatever is the matter?' Carrie followed Ada into the bedroom.

Ada tried to speak but only a shuddering sigh escaped her lips.

'Are you ill? Should I fetch someone?' Carrie was worried. She'd never seen Ada in such distress.

'Oscar and Jeremy. They've joined up,' Ada blurted out, and it took a moment or two for Carrie to register what she meant.

She sat down suddenly on the edge of Ada's bed. 'Joined the army? Both of them? But – how? When?'

'There's been a big recruitment drive in Oxford and London. Father said hordes of young men were queuing to sign up in Trafalgar Square. He's lost all his young staff at the bank. I suppose Oscar and Jeremy got carried away, along with everyone else.'

'Can they change their mind? Can your father pull any strings?' To Carrie's mind, Mr Hadley was a very important person. He must surely know people in high places who could help.

Ada shrugged. 'They want to go. They said it's really important for the country and they'd be cowards not to be a part of it.'

'Are they here?' Carrie's mind was a whirl of emotion. 'Or have they left already?' Had Oscar gone without a word of farewell? A wave of horror swept over her at the thought.

'No, but it won't be long. They'll be told where to go for training and allowed a few days at home to say goodbye.' Ada's voice faltered at the last word.

'Oh, Ada.' Carrie got up and went over to where her friend stood in the window, gathering her into a hug. She gazed over Ada's shoulder to the view beyond. Oscar would be sailing across that sea in a matter of days, then marching away to who knew where? Saying goodbye to his family would be his priority, of course, but Carrie hoped and prayed she would have the chance to see him before he went. The sun sparkled on the waves but, for Carrie, the bright day that had seemed filled with such promise had now taken on a sombre hue.

Chapter Twenty-One

Carrie was filled with feverish anxiety each day after Ada had delivered the news about Oscar. Could she get in touch with him? Would he get in touch with her? Her journey to and from school took her past Hawksdown Lodge twice a day and she found it hard to resist the urge to stop and enquire if they had heard anything more. But she knew she must endure the agony of waiting. The Hadley family had a far greater claim on Oscar than she did.

She struggled to keep her class in order, although she welcomed the distraction her work provided. More than ten days passed before she had word, in the form of a letter delivered to Ivy Cottage. It was waiting for her on the kitchen table when she got home from school on Tuesday evening. Carrie picked it up and looked at the neatly written name and address. She knew at once who it was from and the London postmark confirmed it.

Her mother was waiting, too. 'Who has written to you?' she asked. Letters were a rarity at Ivy Cottage.

Carrie was unprepared. Her mind raced through the possibilities she could offer to satisfy her mother's curiosity. Ada? But why would she write when she lived close by? A mythical friend? But then she would have to invent a whole story to go with it. Something to do with school? But they would have addressed the letter there in that case. She would need to play for time.

'I don't know, Mother. I'll start preparing your meal and then I'll open it.' Carrie hoped her voice sounded calmer than she felt.

She went through to the kitchen and began banging pans around as though she was beginning to cook. Then she opened the letter as fast as her trembling fingers allowed.

Dear Carrie,

I know Ada has told you my news. I've been unable to return to Hawksdown Lodge since then but I've received the date to join the training camp now and I've been warned we'll sail straight after that. This weekend will be my last chance to visit the family.

I want to see you, too. There's a question I've longed to ask you these last few weeks, but I've stopped myself. Now it feels as though I may never have another chance.

Carrie, I hope it's not presumptuous of me, but would you agree to meet me in Dover? I don't know what lies ahead but I don't think I can bear to part in the Glen. I feel such an important moment should be celebrated as a special occasion.

I'll tell the family I have to leave a day earlier than I need to, on Saturday afternoon, and I'll book into the Station Hotel. We could have some dinner, spend the night. Will you come? Please say yes. Let me know by return and I will make the arrangements.

Your soldier,

Oscar

Carrie felt sick as she laid the letter on the table. When she'd read the words *There's a question I've longed to ask you these last few weeks* her heart had leapt. Was he going to ask her to marry him? She'd had to read the letter twice to understand what he was saying. He wanted her to spend the night in Dover. Spend the night with him. He thought he might not come back. Despite all his excitement when he'd talked to her about joining the army, he feared the worst. What had happened since he'd signed up to make him expect that? She wished she'd paid more attention to the news.

Her mother's voice, calling through from the sitting room, put paid to her musing.

'Well – who is it?'

Carrie, who until that moment had had no idea how to react to Oscar's request to meet in Dover, made a snap decision.

'It's from Ada, Mother,' she called back. 'She's in London but will be back at the weekend and she's invited me to stay at their house on Saturday night. They're having a small party.'

There, it was done. She'd set the whole thing in motion. She ignored her mother's mutterings from the front room and began to prepare dinner, her stomach churning. The letter had lain there all day. If she sent a reply tomorrow, would he get it before he left London to return home? She would have to hope so. And, if not, Fate would intervene. She would ask for him at the hotel on Saturday and, if he wasn't there, so be it.

That night, she wrote a brief note to Oscar, confirming that she would meet him. She would make a detour to post it on her way to school the following morning. Then she looked around her room, considering where to hide Oscar's letter. She'd destroyed any previous notes from him, tearing them into small pieces and burning them on the sitting-room fire. This one, though, felt momentous and she wanted to keep it. Yet she wasn't sure that her mother had believed her story about Ada's party. She would have to find a hiding place, in case she decided to snoop. Her bedroom, sparsely furnished as it was, offered few options. Between the pages of a book would most likely be the first place Mrs Marsh would look. Still undecided at bedtime, Carrie put the letter beneath her pillow. She would take it to school with her in the morning if she hadn't come up with a plan before then.

On Saturday, Carrie took the late-morning train from Hawksdown station. She walked along the Dover seafront while she waited for Oscar's train, trying to imagine every aspect of his journey to meet her.

The family would have seen him off at the station – she imagined tearful farewells. Then they would have got into the car and driven home. Would Mrs Hadley have worn black to say goodbye? Or would that have been seen as a bad omen? Her petrol-blue coat with the fur collar, then. Ada would have worn her new suit. If Jeremy was at home, would he have been too busy with his own preparations to go with his mother and sister? Would he and Oscar have wished each other luck?

Ada – how would she feel if she knew the deception being practised? Carrie blocked out the thought. Ada was her friend. She confided in her, but she couldn't share this. Ada would have warned her against it. Anyone would – she hadn't wanted to hear what they might say.

Carrie waited for Oscar at Dover station. By the time he arrived, she was no longer sure their plan was a good one. Away from their secret meeting places at home, she felt exposed. But she would go through with it. It was an agony of embarrassment, checking in at the Station Hotel as Mr and Mrs Hadley. She was sure the desk clerk raised an eyebrow, taking in Oscar's uniform, the shopping bag she'd had to repurpose as an overnight bag. The dinner was good – Oscar ate well but Carrie could barely get more than a few mouthfuls past her lips. The fizzy excitement she'd felt the night before and that morning – when she'd taken the train, thrilled to be having an adventure – had evaporated.

Oscar was excited, speculating about his regiment, the training he hoped for, when he might be sent to France. She supposed she'd imagined whispered words of love, a languorous entwining of limbs on the bed, a glass of champagne on the bedside table. Not soup, roast beef, strong cheese and a red wine that made her cough. And war talk, all this war talk.

CHAPTER TWENTY-TWO

The next morning, Carrie walked home from Hawksdown station, her mind filled with a jumble of thoughts. Earlier, she'd said a hasty goodbye to Oscar: he'd overslept and had had to rush to catch the train that would get him to London in time to make his connection for the training camp. She'd been awake for what felt like the whole night, while he lay snoring beside her. She didn't really know why he'd wanted her there the night before. Perhaps she'd read something into his letter that wasn't there. In any case, his excitement over going to war had apparently overcome any fear he might have felt about not coming back. After dinner, they'd gone up to their room and he'd pulled her onto the bed, kissing her and fumbling with clumsy fingers to remove her clothes so that she'd had to help him, to avoid the fabric ripping. Then, while she was attempting to cover her nakedness with the sheet, he'd launched himself at her in an unspeakable way, mercifully rolling off her and falling into a deep sleep barely a minute later. Her cheeks burnt at the memory.

She'd been thankful that the rush in the morning meant there was no time for embarrassment: he was too busy dressing and gathering his kit. She'd waved him off at the station, receiving a peck on the cheek and a promise to write. She'd watched the train out of sight before going to the station café while she waited for her train in the other direction.

Carrie ordered tea and kept her head down while she drank it, not wanting to catch anyone's eye in case they initiated a conversation. She had no wish to explain what she was doing in Dover. In any case, she was so tired she could barely string together a coherent sentence. Her carriage had been mercifully empty during the short journey to Hawksdown station and now she walked slowly up the hill towards home, attempting to marshal her thoughts before she saw her mother. She needed to prepare a story about Ada's party – descriptions of the food, the guests, their clothes – when all the time she felt sure the guilt of what she had actually been doing must be plain to see.

As she stepped through the door of Ivy Cottage, calling, 'I'm home, Mother,' she still felt unprepared. She expected Mrs Marsh would be angry at having been left to fend for herself overnight, even though Carrie had prepared her evening meal – a salad with cooked chicken and bread and butter, left under a bowl on the kitchen table. She'd left her breakfast, too.

She looked into the sitting room, expecting to see her mother in her usual chair, but she wasn't there. 'Mother!' she called again, worry stirring as she entered the kitchen. It was empty, but at least there was evidence the food had been eaten. She looked into the garden before mounting the stairs, wondering whether her mother had taken to her bed in a fit of pique. But there was no sign of her and Carrie began to panic. Where could she be? Mrs Marsh hadn't left the house, other than to go into the garden, for as long as Carrie could remember.

She was about to return downstairs to search for a note, when a slight noise in her own bedroom made her pause before she pushed open the door to find her mother sitting on the bed. 'There you are. I've been calling for you. Didn't you hear me?' Carrie's exasperation was replaced by a sense of foreboding when she saw what her mother held.

'A party at your friend's house, you said. I didn't believe you and this proves I was right.' Mrs Marsh brandished the letter in triumph. 'What sort of creature are you? Have you no shame?'

Carrie gazed in horror at Oscar's letter. She must have left it under her pillow. How could she have forgotten to hide it?

'Well?' her mother demanded. 'What have you got to say for yourself?' She barely paused before adding, 'He won't marry you, you know. He's taken his pleasure and gone. You'd better hope you haven't been caught or you'll never hold your head up around here again. I thought I'd brought you up better than that. This is what you get for mixing above your station. You and your fancy friends – putting ideas into your head.'

When had her mother found the letter? Carrie wondered. As soon as she had left the previous day? Or that morning? It felt as though she had been brooding on it and Carrie didn't know how to defend herself. If truth be told, she feared some of what her mother had said was true. Oscar had used her and she was stupid to have gone along with his plan. He didn't love her and she couldn't imagine why she'd ever entertained a notion that he might. To think she had imagined he was going to ask her to marry him.

A tear rolled down her cheek and her mother's eyes glittered in triumph. She ripped the letter in half, then into smaller pieces and Carrie didn't object. 'Here, take it,' Mrs Marsh said, throwing the pieces to the floor. 'This is what it's worth. Nothing. And that's what you are worth now, Carrie Marsh. You're like your father and the Marsh family before him – no good. There's a flaw that runs through the lot of you.'

She hauled herself to her feet and pushed past an unresisting Carrie, before making her way heavily down the stairs. Carrie was left to stare at the torn paper, scraps of Oscar's handwriting littering the floor. She wished she could turn back the clock, but to when? To before the letter arrived? To before she'd met Oscar? To before she'd met Ada?

She didn't regret meeting the Hadleys, she decided at last. But she did regret her foolishness in agreeing to meet Oscar in Dover. She'd made a stupid mistake and she would have to learn how to live with it, if she hoped to put it behind her and move on with her life.

PART THREE

CARRIE: 1917–18

CHAPTER ONE

Carrie was daydreaming at her desk, sited in the window on the first floor of St Aidan's hospital, giving her sweeping views through the leaded panes over the fields and up to Hawks Down. Sir Charles and his wife Millicent, the acting matron, would be back from their meeting soon and she needed to finish typing up the list of the latest admissions. The men had been accompanied, as usual, from France by nurses, one of whom had thrust the list – several pages of crumpled foolscap – into Carrie's hand with a muttered apology: 'Sorry, we had to leave in a hurry, under shelling. I had to go round taking the names as we travelled.' She'd paused. 'Some of them didn't make it. I've crossed those through.'

The handwriting was far from neat and Carrie feared the rust-brown marks on every page were bloodstains. She'd thanked the nurse, hurrying away before she saw the tears springing to Carrie's eyes. Oscar's name would have appeared on a list, too, but not one detailing those being transported back to England.

She turned her gaze into the large, airy room where she worked, usually with Sir Charles and his wife, Lady Rowlands, seated at the other desks. The walls were panelled in oak, and thick rugs muffled the sound on the polished parquet floor. Carrie knew the house to be one of the grandest in the area, although she'd been familiar only with the exterior, until Sir Charles had offered it as an auxiliary hospital, to help with the war effort. This morning she had the room to herself while they arranged to house the flood of new patients produced by the offensive at Messines.

Here, behind the heavy oak door, it was calm and peaceful, with just the sound of birdsong drifting through the open window, and there was little to suggest a country so heavily embroiled in battle. A cursory glance over the lawns might even fail to spot that the flowerbeds had been turned over to vegetables. It was June, and Carrie's concentration was disturbed further by the pleasing thought of seeing her daughter that evening, for her birthday. Evie was going to be two, and although Carrie knew she was unlikely to have any recollection of the day when she was older, she was determined to make it a special celebration.

She'd collected scraps of fabric from worn-out sheets, pieces that were too small to be turned into a pillow case or a blouse, and sewn them into a cloth doll, wearing a patchwork dress. And she'd persuaded the cook at the hospital to make her a tiny single cake while she was making the weekly sponge pudding for the men. It was sitting in her bag under the desk now, wrapped in greaseproof paper.

Cook had hunted around in one of the drawers of the huge dresser that ran the length of a wall in the basement kitchen and pulled out a box. 'There,' she said, triumphant. 'I knew I'd seen these somewhere.' The faded cardboard packet contained a handful of small cake candles, all previously used. She shook out two and gave them to Carrie. 'I'll have them back when you're finished,' she said, and Carrie nodded. The war had taught everyone the value of saving anything that had the smallest chance of being reused.

Two years old today. Carrie tried to stop her thoughts taking the route they had followed only too frequently since Evie's birth. Would time ever erase the horrors she associated with that day, and the events leading up to it? In the first six months of 1915 she had lost her teaching job, Oscar, her mother and her home.

It was just before Christmas 1914 when she'd had to admit to herself that she was going to have a baby. She'd had one brief letter from Oscar in that time, telling her he wasn't allowed to say where he was but that it was somewhere he hoped she'd never discover in her worst nightmares. He said it had become clear they wouldn't be home by Christmas, as had been suggested when he'd signed up. He could barely remember his life before this, he wrote. They spent day after day in trenches filled with mud, stench and rats, but the men managed to keep up their spirits. He'd wished her a happy Christmas and told her she could write using the army postal service, that letters addressed to him and his unit would find him.

She'd sent him what she hoped was an uplifting card and a note. She didn't know whether he'd ever got it, or the letter she'd sent when events began to happen, one after another, that left her reeling.

By February, she had begun to wonder how much longer she could conceal her figure under shapeless clothes. The sickness that had plagued her in the first months, sending her whey-faced into the classroom each morning, had disappeared, but the weight she lost as a result only made the swelling of her belly appear more pronounced. Once spring arrived, she feared she would no longer be able to hide under baggy cardigans and woollen shawls.

In the middle of March, her mother died. Their relationship had never recovered from Mrs Marsh's discovery of Oscar's letter: for weeks afterwards their conversation was limited to polite but frosty interchanges. Carrie continued to cook and provide for her mother as before, seeing no alternative, but her spirit shrivelled at the meanness of her existence. Unwilling to give her mother the satisfaction of being proved right, she went to great lengths to hide her pregnancy at home. Carrie was sure she must suspect but, if Mrs Marsh noticed her daughter's sickness, she never said a word. In any case, she had begun to keep to her room in the mornings and Carrie left her breakfast, covered, on the table for her.

One day, when winter still refused to give way to spring, she came home from school half frozen after a bicycle ride in a gale that surely blew directly from the Arctic, to find the breakfast plate still under the teacloth, untouched. She'd hurried upstairs as fast as her legs, stiff with cold, would allow. Her mother lay in bed, face turned to the wall in the icy room, and Carrie knew what she would find even before she bent over her. Mrs Marsh's eyes were wide open, but all resemblance to the woman Carrie had known had fled from her features.

She'd had to get back on her bicycle to go into Castle Bay and fetch the doctor. Back at Ivy Cottage, he'd listened to Carrie's description of her mother's last months, shaken his head and debated with himself over whether 'heart failure' was an adequate description for the death certificate.

'It was likely to be a cardiac arrest,' he said, standing in the kitchen and packing his bag, 'but with no recent medical history to go on, it will have to do.' He turned to leave, having refused Carrie's offer of a cup of tea. 'It might be advisable to make an appointment for a consultation, Miss Marsh.'

Carrie was puzzled by his words, and the emphasis on 'Miss', until he added, 'It looks as though your time is a month or two away. Am I right?' He raised his eyebrows and left.

Carrie had sat down on a kitchen chair and stared at the opposite wall. Her mother gone, with no chance to make up for the dreadful atmosphere that had reigned between them; the cottage surely lost to her, too. The Hawksdown Castle estate wasn't well managed but it seemed likely that the adult daughter of William Marsh, himself the son of the gardener who had once lived there, had even less right than her mother to remain as a tenant. And now the doctor had made it plain that her shameful condition was apparent.

That night, she wrote to Oscar, telling him he was going to be a father. Then, with her mother lying cold and still in the room above, Carrie put her head on the kitchen table and wept.

CHAPTER TWO

⮑

She'd posted the letter the following day on her way into school, where Mrs Chambers had scolded her and sent her home.

'There's so few children here now, what with some of them working on the farms and the parents of others keeping them at home, fretting about the Zeppelins coming. I can manage the two classes together perfectly well. Take a few days and come back when you're ready.'

Carrie had set about making the funeral arrangements for her mother. She'd written to her father, but since she hadn't seen him over the last year and he hadn't been in touch, she feared he was no longer at his old address. Even worse, had something happened to him, too? At the weekend, she decided to ask Ada whether she would come to the funeral to offer support.

She'd walked up to the front door at Hawksdown Lodge and stared, uncomprehending, at the black crêpe wrapped around the door knocker. As she raised her hand to the door, it dawned on her that it must signify a death in the family, and a wish not to be disturbed.

She backed away, fear clutching at her heart. Who had been struck down? She turned to leave, filled with a terrible anxiety, but had gone barely five steps before the door flew open and Ada called her back: 'Carrie! I saw you on the path and came down at once.'

She'd been weeping and her eyes were swollen but she still managed to look striking, Carrie thought, dressed in black with her hair falling around her shoulders.

'I came to tell you about my mother, then I saw . . .' Carrie gestured at the door. 'I didn't like to disturb you.'

Ada looked puzzled at the sight of the black crêpe. 'I suppose Maria put it there. Don't go, Carrie. Won't you come in?'

Carrie stepped through the door, fear clutching at her heart. She knew what Ada was going to say, even before the words came out of her mouth. Oscar was gone, lost in action at some battle on the front line. They'd received the telegram the previous day. Carrie remembered thinking that she should have known the instant that the father of her child had lost his life. Why hadn't she?

Then a great roaring had filled her ears and she'd fallen senseless to the ground. When she'd come to, she was lying on the couch in the drawing room. It was clear at once that Ada had seen her condition. Lying on her back as she was, there was no disguising it. She'd sobbed then, and told Ada everything – about her secret meetings with Oscar and spending the night with him before he left for the army. She hoped Ada didn't think badly of her, but feared she must.

Things had moved quickly after that. When Ada learnt that Mrs Marsh had died, too, she told Mrs Hadley about the baby: Oscar's child. What was to be done?

Mrs Hadley – who was vague only when it suited her – was, in fact, an expert organiser when the need arose, although previously she'd confined herself to committees, her children and her husband. She questioned Carrie coldly as to whether there could be any doubt that Oscar was the father. Receiving her vehement response, she had everything under control in a short space of time. Carrie was to leave her teaching job at once, before her condition was apparent to everyone. She would use the excuse of her mother's death and the subsequent loss of the cottage as a reason for leaving the area.

Mrs Hadley would find her a place to stay on a farm a safe distance away, where a local midwife would attend to her, having been told she was a distant relative of the farmer's wife. She would have to give up the baby to the Hadleys at birth, for them to bring up as their own. Mrs Hadley would say the baby belonged to a cousin, both parents tragically lost during the war. She seemed convinced the baby would be a boy and referred to it as such throughout. Carrie could be godmother and see her child regularly, but she would have no right to him and must keep their true relationship secret.

Once the plans were put in motion, Carrie had little say in the matter. The discovery that there would be a baby to maintain Oscar's direct line seemed to lift mother and daughter's spirits, easing their terrible grief. Carrie, in virtual hiding at Ivy Cottage, had no such relief. Oscar could never have known he was to have a child. Her letter couldn't have reached him before he was killed.

She attended her mother's funeral, Ada accompanying her to lend support. Carrie hoped that her father would show his face, but the service was conducted with the two of them as the sole mourners. Her mother, who had chosen to live as a recluse for so many years, had lost any friends and acquaintances she'd once had.

Carrie was told by Mrs Hadley that she couldn't attend the service to honour Oscar's memory, which was held a few days later. 'People will talk if they see you in your condition, unwed and upset. I don't want anyone to put two and two together once we have the baby living here. I'm sorry, Carrie, but that's as it must be.'

Mrs Hadley had been firm so Carrie had stayed at home and wept alone, for herself and for the baby to come as much as for Oscar. Ada came afterwards to see her, but Carrie's confession seemed to have splintered the friendship. Ada must have felt betrayed, Carrie supposed, with her brother and her best friend keeping their relationship hidden from her. Ada's final visit to Ivy Cottage was to tell her to prepare a bag: by the end of the week she would be moved to the farm Mrs Hadley had told her about.

'And pack anything you want to keep from the cottage,' Ada said. 'You won't be coming back here, Mother said. If there isn't too much, we can store a few boxes in the garage until you're settled again.'

Carrie thought her expression suggested she surely wouldn't want to keep anything. After she'd gone, Carrie was agitated. Where would she live? And what would she do? She would have to find work as soon as the baby was born to be able to afford a room of some sort. It would have to be nearby – she was determined to stay in touch with her child.

Sorting and clearing out their few possessions kept Carrie occupied in the remaining days in the cottage. All their years there had amounted to no more than three boxes by the time she'd finished. She was leaving the furniture, and was thankful to receive a few pounds from the landlord for doing so. Her already meagre savings had dwindled since she'd stopped work, and she was uncertain how she would support herself after the birth.

While going through her bookshelves, she had unearthed Meg Marsh's diary tucked behind a larger book. It had been passed down the generations, Carrie's father handing it to her a year or two before he left.

'You might as well have this,' he said. 'I've never bothered reading it, but it seems wrong to throw it out.'

Carrie had flicked through the pages at the time but paid little attention to it, other than to look for clues as to what might have happened to her ancestor. The family story of Meg's disappearance and death had travelled down the years, and the last entry held a tantalising hint of a secret buyer for her goods, but nothing more.

Now Carrie opened the battered cover again, the pages threatening to fall free from the perished binding, and began to read. She found lists of goods – muslin, silk, a shawl, a length of chintz, with prices written in a neat hand, then another price with a question mark beside it. Smuggled goods, of course – it was accepted in the family that the Marshes had been involved in smuggling a hundred years earlier, but it was rarely spoken about. Interspersed with the lists were Meg's diary entries – mostly short and seemingly written in haste, for the writing was less neat. The lists were dated, not so the personal entries.

A man, or perhaps a boy, called Joseph had given her a shell strung on a leather thong to wear round her neck. He'd kissed her, which earned an exclamation mark. She'd been frustrated by someone called Samuel, who spent his days at the inn and wasn't bringing in a wage. Meg had made an account of money going out and the little coming in, but the next entry read, 'The boat went out. I have bought so much.' Carrie wondered where the money had come from.

There was a longer entry that Carrie found painful to read. Meg had begun to mention 'B' – someone she met after working nights at the Fountain, a place that earned many mentions. There was little detail about the meetings. Perhaps Meg had feared the diary being read. In this longer entry, she confessed to having behaved in a way that she felt shamed her. She didn't spell out what had happened but Carrie experienced a jolt of recognition as she read her words. She would wager Meg had behaved exactly as she herself had when she had agreed to meet Oscar in Dover. Meg had vowed such a thing should never happen again. Carrie had felt the same way.

Tears were trickling down her cheeks as she read on, but she wiped them away impatiently. There had been too many tears. 'B' had become elusive, despite apparently promising marriage. Carrie

272

could feel the despair in the few words Meg set down. One entry was just a single line: 'He is to be married.'

There were no more lists of goods, she realised, with just one page left before the final entry. Here, it simply said, 'Eliza has a plan. She will bring up the baby as her own. It will be for the best.' Carrie wondered whether she was trying to convince herself. The words didn't confirm that the baby was Meg's, but it seemed the most likely explanation. Looking back through the pages once more, Carrie noticed that the greatest detail was reserved for what she supposed were Meg's dreams for her future: a description of a shop she imagined herself having one day, and the final entry, in which she spoke of the kid gloves she imagined somehow to be her route to better things.

Carrie sat back on her heels. Meg's path through life had been very different from her own, but she couldn't help seeing parallels. Had they both made unwise choices, falling for unsuitable men? She didn't like to think of Oscar in this way, but it was hard not to think otherwise. Had the mysterious 'B' been someone outside Meg's social class, just as Oscar was outside Carrie's? Her baby would be born out of wedlock, as Meg's would have been. She couldn't prevent a gasp escaping her lips at the thought of Meg's baby. What had happened? Had the baby been born when Meg had vanished – or not? Her blood ran cold at the thought of the bones in the Glen. She wanted to believe that Oscar had been right, that they weren't Meg's, but belonged to a dog or some other creature buried there, and that Meg had simply chosen to disappear. She shut the book and laid her hand on the cover. Let the parallels finish here, she thought. Let there be a happier ending for me, and Oscar's baby, than there had been for Meg.

Chapter Three

Her pains, which started in the middle of the night, had found Carrie totally unprepared for what was to come. She'd had to summon the farmer's wife, who wasn't happy at being disturbed. In fact, she'd been generally unpleasant throughout Carrie's stay on the farm despite Mrs Hadley's no doubt handsome payment to her. The parlour that Mrs Hadley had assured Carrie would be available to her had never materialised and the farmer's wife seemed determined to keep Carrie away from her husband and sons. It was as though she believed her very presence would corrupt them. Carrie spent most of her days moping alone in her bedroom. She had begun to welcome the thought of the birth as a release from all that, but when the midwife arrived, summoned by a farmhand as dawn broke, she examined Carrie, then frowned and shook her head.

'This is going to be a difficult one,' she said, as much to herself as to Carrie, who was too convulsed by painful contractions to do anything other than gasp, grip the bedclothes and look pleadingly at the midwife and the farmer's wife. After a hurried consultation, the farmhand was despatched again, this time to fetch the doctor. When he arrived, Carrie was already exhausted. And by the time her baby, a girl, made her appearance in the world many hours later, Carrie no longer knew whether either of them was alive or dead.

As it turned out, it was Carrie who was closer to death. The baby recovered quickly from the ordeal of birth but Carrie was so weak from loss of blood that, as Ada told her later, they'd been told to prepare for the worst. Mrs Hadley and Ada had arrived straight after the birth and taken the baby away. Carrie hadn't expected that. The farmer's wife had shown one rare moment of sympathy when she couldn't stem the flow of tears on discovering what had happened.

'You need all the rest you can get,' she'd told her. 'It's for the best: a baby crying and keeping you up half the night isn't going to help you get well. And it's better to get used to being without her, before you're too attached to her.'

Carrie, barely conscious, had caught just a glimpse of the baby as she left, a thatch of dark hair peeping out of the soft cream blanket that swaddled her.

'Mind you,' the farmer's wife added, 'I'm not sure Mrs Hadley was happy you presented her with a girl. From the look on her face, it was a boy she was after, to replace that lost son of hers.'

Did everyone assume she was without feelings? Carrie wondered. Did they expect her to give up the baby she had carried for nine months without a care, as an inconvenience she'd be glad to be without? To add to her woes, Oscar had vanished from her life before she'd even had chance to know him properly as a person and she'd been denied the chance to grieve him, her baby's father.

Small wonder, then, that Carrie kept her face turned to the wall in her farmhouse bedroom throughout the week of recuperation. Her body might be slowly mending but her mind wasn't keeping pace. After a week in the tender care of the farmer's wife, who never failed to point out what a nuisance it was to keep going up and down the stairs all day, she was well enough to leave the farm. The doctor, summoned to approve this, wasted no time in telling Carrie, 'There'll be no more children for you.

This one nearly killed you – another certainly will. Be sure to tell your husband.'

Weak and filled with misery, Carrie barely took in his words. When the farmer's wife puffed upstairs to tell her that Mrs Hadley and Ada would arrive to collect her that afternoon, that she should wash and dress and generally make herself presentable, it was at least an hour before Carrie could force herself to stir.

She appeared in the farmhouse kitchen, bag roughly packed and her print dress crumpled, only minutes before the Hadley motor-car drew up outside. Ada, looking worried, helped Carrie out and into the car. They sat in silence and waited while Mrs Hadley finished conducting her business, the smell of the leather upholstery making Carrie feel sick.

'How is the baby?' Carrie managed to rouse herself enough to ask.

'She's well,' Ada replied, her face lit by a smile. 'She may be tiny but she has a good pair of lungs.'

Carrie closed her eyes in pain at the thought of what she was missing. She wondered whether the baby missed her, too.

'Does she have a name?' she asked.

'Evelyn,' Ada answered. She looked embarrassed, perhaps worried that Carrie would be upset at having played no part in the choice. 'But we call her Evie.'

'Can I see her today?' Carrie asked.

'I'm sorry, Carrie. Mother doesn't think it's a good idea. But soon,' Ada added, seeing Carrie's expression. 'She's found a room for you in Castle Bay, somewhere you can rest and recover further. And there's a job waiting for you at St Aidan's hospital in Hawksdown, which has been turned over to nurse the war wounded.'

She reassured Carrie: 'They don't know anything about what has happened. They think you went away to look after a sick relative and fell ill yourself afterwards. Mother will give you the details.'

Mrs Hadley climbed into the car. Hearing herself mentioned, she turned to Carrie. 'Ada has told you what's happening, I take it? Good – then let's get back to Castle Bay and settle you in.'

Carrie, at her desk in the leaded window of the office at St Aidan's, remembered how Ada's hand had crept into hers, and stayed there, as the car carried them to Castle Bay.

Since then, Carrie had played the part of a dutiful godmother, making the agreed monthly visits to Hawksdown Lodge. At first they were a terrible trial from which she left weeping at her loss. After she had grown accustomed to the situation, they had become the highlight of her life. Her friendship with Ada had wavered: Mrs Hadley wouldn't countenance social visits to the house in addition to permitted ones and it became hard to keep the relationship alive. Evie, though, was a delight – she was a fierce little bundle of energy who defied her nursemaid at every opportunity. Carrie wondered whether that didn't, in fact, make her more like the little boy Mrs Hadley had wanted. But Mrs Hadley, having taken possession of Evie and arranged her christening with the family name, had seemingly lost interest in her. Often, the house was empty of anyone other than the nursemaid, the cook and Evie when Carrie went to visit, Mr and Mrs Hadley and Ada being in London. Carrie had to work hard to suppress the resentment that had arisen over recent months. Evie was the only child she would ever have and, by a cruel stroke of Fate, the woman who had taken control of her daughter's life appeared little interested in her.

Mrs Hadley would surely be there that night for Evie's birthday, Carrie thought, returning to her typing with a feeling of panic at the amount of time she'd wasted in daydreaming. She'd managed to add another page to the small pile of paper beside her when she heard Sir Charles's voice in the corridor, the quieter voice of his wife answering him. They'd want to know why she hadn't finished the work.

She'd have to use the excuse of struggling to decipher the handwriting, Carrie thought, turning to the next sheet. She cast her eyes down the list and a familiar name jumped out at her, despite the semi-illegible scrawl: Jeremy Hadley.

She was staring in disbelief, wondering whether it was a coincidence or whether this really was Oscar's brother, when Sir Charles and Lady Rowlands entered the room.

CHAPTER FOUR

'Are the lists ready?' Lady Rowlands appeared unusually flustered. 'I gather the evacuation had to be undertaken in a great hurry. Not all the procedures could be followed. We need to let families know as soon as possible about the soldiers brought here.' She frowned. 'And the list of the others, the ones who didn't make it, must be sent to the War Office.'

'Just a page or so left to type,' Carrie said, hoping Lady Rowlands wouldn't check. She stacked three new sheets of paper together, interleaved with carbons, and fed them into her typewriter, then ran her finger down the handwritten list in what she hoped appeared to be an efficient manner. 'The writing is hard to read, I'm afraid.'

'Hardly surprising, given what we've just heard of the journey they undertook to get here.' Millicent Rowlands had moved to her desk and was hunting through it in search of something. 'When you've finished, Carrie, give the list to Matron and she can fill in the ward details. They're busy getting the poor souls cleaned up and into bed. We seem to have more than the normal quota of battle-fatigue patients this time.'

Having found the piece of paper she was searching for, Lady Rowlands hurried away with it. Sir Charles was on the telephone, so Carrie returned to her typing. The list of names included the injuries assessed at the casualty clearing station in the field.

Against Jeremy Hadley's name was 'Bad break to right leg' and, in another hand, 'Battle fatigue'. Carrie knew only too well what that was. The soldiers called it shell-shock and St Aidan's had a ward devoted to it. She thought of the Jeremy she knew, on the tennis courts at Hawksdown Lodge, or flying down the hill on his bicycle at Kingsdown, and hoped the young man afflicted in this way wasn't him.

She didn't think she would have chance to find out any further information before it was time to leave her desk and go to see Evie at the Hadleys' house. Her role was very much office-based and when she ventured onto the wards it was only ever in search of Lady Rowlands, Sir Charles or Matron to deliver a message. It was unlikely she would be able to discover any more that day, not while the nurses and volunteers were busy settling in the new arrivals.

Carrie directed all her focus into working her way through the handwritten pages. The fact that the remainder of the list contained mostly crossings out meant she had completed the work more quickly than expected, but she was sad to see how many of the men had perished of their injuries on the journey home.

She did as Lady Rowlands had instructed, clipping the pages together and going in search of Matron. She wasn't at her desk and, as Carrie stood there, looking a little lost, a nearby nurse called, 'If you're looking for Matron, she's gone to Primrose Ward.'

Carrie nodded her thanks and hurried away down the corridor. Provided Matron hadn't moved on, this might be her opportunity to find out about Jeremy Hadley. Primrose Ward was for the shell-shock patients. They were housed in a separate building, away from the main hospital, for a good reason. Some of the soldiers were very vocal, crying out, singing or screaming. Others were silent, or sat huddled on their beds, shaking and repeating the same phrases over and over. Carrie had visited it only once before and the experience had stayed with her.

The noise reached her ears before she had even opened the double doors into the building. She had to stand for a moment or two in the corridor, preparing herself, before pressing on. Matron stood in the ward, conferring with one of the nurses, while others were trying to persuade some of the men back to their beds. The air of agitation affected Carrie so that she was hard pressed not to put her hands over her ears, turn and flee. But she walked with determination towards Matron, all the while allowing her eyes to flit from side to side in a hurried search for Jeremy.

'The list, Matron,' Carrie said, holding it out.

'You could have left it on my desk. This is no place for you, especially today. The men are unsettled by all the new arrivals.' Matron appeared more flustered than Carrie had ever seen her.

'There's a name on the list I recognise. A friend of my family. Hadley, Jeremy Hadley. He's in here.' Carrie blurted out the words almost before she knew what she was saying.

'I can't help you, I'm afraid.' Matron was irritated now. 'I have no idea yet who any of the new arrivals are. You'll be able to locate him when we've filled in the list.'

Disappointed, Carrie turned to leave. She should have known better. It was too chaotic in there to expect an answer today.

The nurse who had been talking to Matron fell into step beside her as she approached the exit. 'He's over there,' she said hastily.

Carrie slowed her step and followed the nurse's pointing finger. Lying motionless in a bed, face turned towards the wall, was a figure with dark hair. Could it really be Jeremy? She cast a glance over her shoulder: Matron was at the far end of the room, facing away, in discussion with another nurse.

'Can I go closer?' she asked.

The nurse shrugged. 'If you're quick. He won't know you. He's one of them that don't speak.'

She moved away and Carrie quickly threaded her way through

the nearest row of beds to reach the one pointed out to her. 'Jeremy,' she said tentatively.

He didn't respond so she bent over him. His eyes were closed so perhaps he was asleep, although that seemed unlikely amid all this noise. There was no mistaking him, though. This was definitely Oscar's brother.

CHAPTER FIVE

By the time Carrie arrived at Hawksdown Lodge at six o'clock, she was still uncertain whether or not to share the news about Jeremy. It would come as a terrible shock to the Hadleys yet, selfishly, she didn't want the celebration for Evie to be spoilt. She would have barely an hour to spend with her before bedtime. She would wait until she knew more, she decided, as she knocked at the door.

Ada opened it, Evie in her arms. 'Here she is,' she said to Evie. 'I told you she'd be here soon.' She turned to Carrie. 'She's been asking for you,' she explained.

Carrie's heart leapt at her words. Evie held out her arms and Carrie, still on the doorstep, put down her bag and gathered up her daughter.

'Happy birthday, Evie,' she said, then buried her nose in her daughter's hair, breathing in her scent. 'Have you had a lovely day?'

'She has.' Ada answered for her. 'She's been thoroughly spoilt, but she's been looking forward to seeing her godmother.'

Carrie thought about her own simple present, the doll in her bag, and bit her lip. But she looked into her daughter's face and said, 'Do you want to see what I have for you?'

'Come in and sit down.' Ada picked up Carrie's bag and ushered them into the drawing room.

'Your mother isn't here?' Carrie was surprised to find the room empty.

'She was, earlier, but she's gone back to London with Father. I wanted to stay with this little girl.'

Ada had her back to Carrie as she spoke. It gave Carrie time to compose her features. She was still angry with Mrs Hadley. Ada's mother had been determined that Evie should be brought up within the Hadley family, so why wouldn't she spend more time with her? The words of the farmer's wife came back to her: 'I'm not sure Mrs Hadley was happy you presented her with a girl. It was a boy she was after.' But she wouldn't waste the precious minutes with her daughter thinking about it. She settled Evie on the floor and pulled the two packages out of her bag.

'Which one first?' she asked.

Evie pointed solemnly.

'This one, then,' Carrie said, helping her tear off the wrapping. It was the paper her mother had insisted on saving from her Christmas present more than two years ago. Another memory to haunt her.

Evie cooed in delight when she saw the doll and hugged it to her chest.

'That's lovely,' Ada exclaimed. 'Did you make it, Carrie?'

'I did,' Carrie said. 'As I'm sure you can tell.'

'Not at all,' Ada protested. She turned to Evie. 'Say thank you.'

Evie could barely talk as yet but she whispered something and Carrie laughed and clapped, then kissed the top of her head.

'Now this one,' she said, picking up the remaining package. 'But I'll open it.'

She eased the greaseproof paper away from the little cake and rummaged in her pocket for the candles, poking them into the top of the soft sponge. 'There,' she said. 'Have you got a plate? And some matches?' she asked Ada.

Ada fetched matches from the mantelpiece and a plate from the china cabinet in the dining room. 'Did you make the cake, too?' She sounded impressed.

'It's a present from the cook at the hospital.' Carrie struck a match, being careful to keep the flame away from Evie, then lit the candles.

'Now we must blow them out,' she said.

Ada and Carrie both tried hard not to laugh as Evie puckered her lips and sucked in air.

'Puff out,' Carrie encouraged. 'Like this.'

She took Evie onto her lap while Ada picked up the plate and held it, so Carrie could blow out the candles. Evie turned to give her a questioning look.

'Yes, you can eat it now,' Carrie said, removing the candles and pocketing them.

'Be quick,' Ada warned. 'If Maisie sees you eating after your supper she'll be cross.'

Maisie was the nursemaid. Carrie had never thought her name suited her for it sounded happy and friendly and Maisie was anything but. She would undoubtedly disapprove of cake before bed, even on a birthday.

Carrie held out the cake to Evie. 'A bite for you,' she said. Evie took a big chunk out of the cake.

'A bite for me?' Ada asked, opening her mouth wide.

Evie looked from Ada to Carrie, as if weighing up the situation. She hesitated, then seized the remaining cake and stuffed it into her mouth, sending the two women into peals of laughter.

The rest of the hour passed too quickly for Carrie's liking. All too soon, Maisie arrived to carry Evie away to bed. Carrie stood up at once and picked up her bag, unwilling to listen to Evie's wails of distress as she was taken upstairs.

'Won't you stay?' Ada asked. 'We could eat something together.'

Carrie hesitated, torn. She would like nothing more. Food had become scarcer and more limited as the months passed and she had a feeling that the Hadleys' larder would provide something better than the soup waiting to be heated on the gas ring in her room in Castle Bay. She was enjoying spending time with Ada without the presence of Mrs Hadley, too.

But how could she sit with her friend without telling her that her brother was lying in a hospital bed close by? It would be completely wrong. She would have to wait until the family had been officially notified about Jeremy before she could do such a thing. So she turned to what she felt to be a pitiful reason to excuse herself.

'I'd love to, Ada. But your mother prefers we don't socialise, because of Evie, so . . .' Carrie shrugged and held out her hands, palms upwards, as if to say, 'What can I do?'

It was a low blow and she saw that Ada looked hurt, but she hardened her heart and made her way out of the house, trying not to listen to Evie's muffled sobs from upstairs.

She hurried away, waving briefly at Ada, who was now standing on the doorstep. She was tired: the highs and lows of the day had taken their toll. Tomorrow, though, she intended to make it her mission to discover more about Jeremy and how he had come to be at St Aidan's.

CHAPTER SIX

I t would be difficult to visit Jeremy in Primrose Ward, Carrie knew. Anyone other than regular volunteers and medical staff was discouraged from entering in case it upset the patients. But she discovered that those patients who suffered in silence, like Jeremy, were wheeled out onto the ward terrace every day, weather permitting. It was felt that the beauty and peace of the gardens was beneficial to souls tormented by what they'd experienced at the front.

Seizing her chance when the office was empty, Carrie had been able to examine the file of Jeremy's medical notes. She had gleaned the information that Jeremy's fracture, roughly set before he could make the journey back from France, was deemed better left alone now that his leg had started to heal, even though the doctor felt it wasn't the best job and he would be left with a limp.

She'd also been able to speak to the nurses who had accompanied the evacuees, although she'd had to act quickly as they were due to take leave before returning to France. They'd stayed at the hospital an extra day to help settle the new arrivals, as the sheer numbers threatened to overwhelm the regular staff. One of the volunteers explained why 'battle fatigue' had been added to Jeremy's name on the list of patients in a different hand.

'He was well enough when we left,' she said, 'in pain from his injury, of course, and every little movement jarred his leg despite the splint. But something about getting on board ship changed him. There were troops marching past as we waited on the quayside to embark – British troops, who'd just landed – and it was the noise of their boots, or maybe the shouts of their sergeant, I'm not sure. Anyway, it seems he started to shake and the next thing I know the men are calling me over to his stretcher, saying he'd had some sort of fit. Then he shuddered and just went still and quiet, as you see him now.'

She gestured to Jeremy, in his bed on the terrace. Carrie had persuaded Lady Rowlands and Matron to allow her to visit Jeremy on her lunch break. They'd made noises about it being highly irregular, that patients on Primrose Ward didn't have visitors, that she wasn't even family. Then Matron had flapped her hands, declaring she didn't have time to deal with it and she could visit as long as she didn't upset Jeremy or any of the other men. Carrie promised she wouldn't, determined to make it a regular event.

She sat quietly beside Jeremy on the first day, without saying a word. The following day, she decided to talk to him to see whether there was any reaction. He didn't appear to heed her as she described her days to him, being careful to stay clear of anything that might remind him of what he'd endured. If, indeed, he could hear her, which she began to wonder. Had the shelling made him deaf, perhaps? Then, by the end of the week, she noticed his eyes follow a swift, high in the sky, as it hunted insects. He turned his head very slightly when a blackbird poured out its song from a high bough. And one Monday, after she'd eaten a sandwich in her usual spot by his bed outside, a nurse stopped her as she left.

'I think he missed you at the weekend,' she said. 'I swear he kept looking to the side, to your empty seat. He didn't sleep as well as he had during the week, either.'

The news gave Carrie a terrific boost. Although her inclination was to see whether she could get Jeremy to respond to her, caution made her tread carefully. She didn't want to upset him and give Matron cause to ban her from visiting. So she carried on as before, chatting while she ate her lunch and sticking to topics she thought safe until one day, without thinking, she said, 'Do you remember that picnic we had, at the folly at Eastling, just before the thunderstorm struck?'

It was the sandwich she was eating that had reminded her – ham and mustard, a rare treat these days. Cook had found the ham (probably on the black market but no one liked to ask) and shared it out.

Jeremy turned his head and looked full at her – the first time he had done so. Carrie, caught by surprise, blurted out, 'Hello, Jeremy,' without thinking how silly that sounded. Instinct warned her that she'd raised a difficult topic, one that might stir memories of Oscar, lost at the front. Jeremy would have been informed of his death, Carrie felt sure, but would he remember? Did this awful shell-shock affect memory and, if so, would Jeremy have to discover the tragic news all over again? In haste to divert his thoughts, she tore off a piece of sandwich and offered it to him.

To her amazement, he took it. He chewed it slowly, staring at her all the time. She began to fear he might choke, since his head was barely raised by his pillow. But he swallowed it and turned to gaze, apparently unseeing, over the garden.

Carrie looked up to see one of the nurses watching her. She gave her a nod and a smile of encouragement before tucking in bedclothes and offering cheery words as she moved along the row of patients.

After that, Carrie made a point of always offering Jeremy some of her sandwich. Sometimes he took it, often he didn't, but she tried to see every interaction as a small victory. One day, about a month after Jeremy had been first admitted, Carrie took her usual seat at his side, wondering whether the long-lasting sunny weather was about to give way to rain, when he spoke.

'Hello, Carrie,' he said. He was looking straight at her and, for the first time, Carrie thought she could detect a glimmer in his eyes of the Jeremy she remembered.

CHAPTER SEVEN

Jeremy's progress after that was slow but steady. He began to interact with Carrie's previously one-sided conversations in a voice that was hoarse and croaky from lack of use. He didn't sound at all like the Jeremy Carrie remembered, or really look like him. His face had changed shape, but that was hardly surprising: after weeks of living off army rations and then being ill, he was much thinner. She'd had plenty of time to study him while he'd been silent and had reached the conclusion he was undeniably altered. Yet, as he became more animated with each passing day, she saw flashes of the boy – now a man – she had known.

She'd avoided referring to his family as much as possible, but she knew it was inevitable he would start asking after them. Matron had said that, despite his improvement, he would have to stay on Primrose Ward, the other wards being full after another influx of injured soldiers. They also needed to observe him for a while longer to make sure he didn't relapse.

In the meantime, Carrie had paid another visit to Hawksdown Lodge to see Evie. The Hadleys by now knew of Jeremy's presence at St Aidan's and were full of questions.

'Are his injuries serious?'

'Why can't we see him?'

'Do they look after the patients well?'

'Can you find out any news for us?'

The questions came thick and fast and Carrie answered as best she could. It was only too apparent that the family had no idea she had been seeing Jeremy daily. She was filled with indecision. Should she tell them? Would they be upset she hadn't told them earlier? Would they be angry with the hospital for allowing her to see him, but not them?

The memory of Matron's reservations over allowing Carrie to spend time with Jeremy made up her mind. She was making good progress with him and she didn't want the Hadleys – Mrs Hadley in particular – to storm down to the hospital and make a scene, which could jeopardise everything. If she had chance to talk to Ada alone in the near future, she would tell her something of it, she decided, but for now, she told them she would discover what she could before asking, politely, whether she could spend a little time with Evie, as arranged.

It was a lovely August Saturday and Maisie had been in the garden with Evie, sitting in the shade provided by a tree on the lawn. When Carrie went out to take her place, Maisie was rather more gracious about it than usual. Carrie thought she was glad to escape the heat to spend some time in the cool of the kitchen, and to have a break from minding a two-year-old.

Carrie had a deliciously long time with Evie that day – longer than usual. She suspected Mrs Hadley hoped she would furnish them with more details about Jeremy in return. Was it unfair to keep Jeremy to herself in this way? His family must be so worried about him. And yet, she thought, Jeremy appeared to be lacking in curiosity about them.

Even so, the week after her visit to Hawksdown Lodge, she began to introduce references to his family into the conversation. She started with Ada: she and Jeremy had been close. At first, he asked questions about how she was and what she was doing, but then he lapsed into silence. He still tired easily, Carrie knew, so she returned to chatting in her usual general fashion before taking her leave.

As the week progressed, she introduced his parents into the conversation. Again, he showed some curiosity before losing interest. He never asked why they didn't visit, which struck Carrie as odd. It was only when she was mulling over their conversation that the truth dawned: he didn't want his family to see him in the state he was in. Not so much because of his physical injuries, for he was more frequently on his feet now, even though he walked with a pronounced limp and the aid of a stick. And he was still gaunt, it was true, although Carrie had grown used to that. She surmised he didn't want to see them until his mind was healed and he was more like the energetic and engaging young man who had gone off to war.

Carrie wondered whether, in fact, he would ever be that person again – he had seen too many horrors ever to feel quite so easy about life – but he needed to reach that resolution on his own. She concentrated on helping him to get as well as possible, which was earning her commendation from his nurses. Matron was less sure.

'It's a shame all our young men can't have the benefit of so much undivided attention,' she said tartly. But she didn't forbid Carrie her visits.

Jeremy rarely mentioned the war, although occasionally he mentioned names unfamiliar to Carrie, which she took to be those of his fellow soldiers. During one of those conversations he said abruptly, 'You know about Oscar?'

'Yes, Jeremy. It happened some time ago now. Over two years.' Jeremy was still sometimes confused by time. He was silent and Carrie wondered whether this was the moment to tell him that Oscar had had a daughter, who was living with the Hadleys. Although perhaps he knew – had Mrs Hadley written to tell him?

She couldn't reveal she was that daughter's mother. But should she mention her? While she was debating it, he spoke again.

'You were close, weren't you?'

'Yes, we were. But it's a long time ago now.' Carrie, heart beating fast, realised she didn't want to discuss it with him.

He nodded. 'I'm sorry,' was all he said.

She thought later she should have told him how sorry she was that he had lost his brother. She supposed he must have learnt about it in France, taken aside by his commanding officer, who had delivered the news then left him to get on with it. It must have been awful, having no time to grieve. Had that played a part in the way he'd suffered?

Had she grieved for Oscar? The thought brought her up short. She wasn't sure she had. She'd had the worry of the coming baby, the loss of her mother and of the cottage. Everything had happened at once. Even in her long, lonely days at the farm, waiting for the baby to arrive, she wasn't sure she'd thought about Oscar. If she had, she suspected she would have shut down the thought as quickly as it had arrived. One thing was for sure, she couldn't tell Jeremy she'd had Oscar's baby. It wasn't just that Mrs Hadley had forbidden it. For a reason she wasn't yet ready to acknowledge to herself, she didn't want him to know.

Chapter Eight

Carrie found her days dominated by thoughts of Jeremy. She looked forward to every lunchtime, and felt quite bereft at being kept apart from him on Saturday and Sunday. There were no undertones to their chats, no wondering over what his words might mean. There was just an easy friendship, yet it was something more than that. Carrie found herself longing to pick up his hand, stroke his fingers, tell him everything would be all right, that she would help him to heal if he would let her. But she didn't want to shock him by saying something that might be unwelcome to him and possibly set him back. And, of course, she had secrets she couldn't share with him – her past relationship with Oscar and Evie's birth.

There was no doubt, though, that Jeremy looked forward to her visits. After all, why wouldn't he? Carrie reasoned. He had no other contact with the outside world, apart from the nurses, who barely had time to speak to him of anything other than medical matters. She had avoided mentioning anything to do with the war, fearful of causing distress, but the activities of the planes coming and going over the hospital couldn't be ignored. The long, flat stretch of grass that ran along the top of Hawks Down, where they had once picnicked, had become an air strip and small planes were frequently involved in sorties and reconnaissance over the Channel.

Increasingly, as Jeremy's health improved, he asked for news and

Carrie shared with him whatever she'd been able to glean from the papers. As he grew stronger, he became restless, saying he needed to get fitter faster so he could go back to join his company.

Carrie didn't know how to respond. Surely it was obvious to him that his damaged leg alone would prevent a return to frontline warfare. In fact, anything that brought him in contact with the sight and sound of battle came with the risk of a relapse into shell-shock. It would have to fall to a doctor, or his family, to break that news.

Now that his return home was imminent, she began to wonder whether he did, in fact, know anything of Evie. She still hadn't admitted to the Hadleys that she saw Jeremy almost daily – it had gone on for so long now that she didn't know how to explain her previous silence. Neither had she felt able to enquire of Jeremy whether he knew about Evie. He had never mentioned her, in the few conversations they'd had about his family.

One day, before she could stop herself, she blurted out, 'You know there's a new member of the family at Hawksdown Lodge?'

Jeremy appeared only mildly interested. 'Have they got a puppy? I suppose Jupiter and Juno must be getting old now.'

Carrie was shocked: he didn't know. And now she must continue what she'd started. 'No, not a puppy. A little girl, Evie. Oscar's daughter.'

'Oscar has a daughter?'

Carrie noticed he spoke of Oscar in the present, not the past, and hoped it was just a slip of the tongue and not confusion. 'Yes, she's going to give you quite the run-around. I'm her godmother,' she added, as an afterthought.

Jeremy lapsed into silence. Carrie had noticed his lack of enthusiasm for returning to Hawksdown Lodge but had hoped it would pass once he was more settled in his mind. She wondered whether to engage in some positive talk about what he could expect once he was home, to encourage him to look forward to it, but he burst out,

'It's going to be intolerable, being back home in all that comfort, when I know what the men are going through at the front. At least here I'm surrounded by others who know what it's like. I can't bear the idea of talking to Mother, Father and Ada about it. And I can't tell them the half of it anyway.' He stopped abruptly and Carrie was struggling to formulate the right response when he said, 'You understand, though. Working here, you can't help but know.'

'I'm sure your family will want to understand, too,' she offered, although even as she said it she wondered how true that was.

'So, a baby in the house.' Jeremy's mind had jumped back to her earlier words. 'Thank goodness for someone who knows nothing of war.' His tone was bitter and his next words caught Carrie off guard. 'Did you mind? You must have hoped you might marry Oscar one day.'

He'd assumed Oscar had married and Evie was the result, Carrie realised. And it dawned on her that she'd spoken out of turn. Mrs Hadley had told people that Evie was the daughter of distant cousins. Would she have given the same story to Jeremy? Or would she tell him the truth and, if so, the whole truth or part of it?

She felt sick, suddenly, at what she'd started with her foolish, unguarded words. She made a show of glancing at her watch and jumping to her feet, saying 'Oh, goodness, I have so much typing to finish before Sir Charles's meeting this afternoon. I must go.' She smoothed down her skirt, buttoned her jacket and gave Jeremy what she hoped was a convincing smile before she hurried away.

Carrie didn't go to visit Jeremy the next day. It was chilly outside and she told herself she had a cold coming on. It wouldn't be a good idea to sit outside, and she didn't want Jeremy to become sick and delay his discharge from hospital. Then it was the weekend and by Monday she had composed herself. If he asked her about Evie's mother, she'd say he must speak to his own mother about it and leave it at that. But when she presented herself at Primrose

Ward that lunchtime, the nurse on duty said, 'Carrie, Jeremy's gone home. Didn't you know?'

Carrie tried to disguise her shock. 'I knew it was soon, but ...' Had he left at the weekend? She'd missed her chance to say goodbye. She would see him when she went to visit Evie but it wouldn't be the same, somehow.

'His mother and father came to collect him. They were very insistent they could look after him at home, I understand. It's not as though we don't need his bed for someone else, I suppose, but still ...' The nurse shrugged. She gave Carrie a knowing look. 'You'll miss him.' It wasn't a question.

'Yes, I will.' Carrie knew her blush gave her away. She walked back through the hospital to her desk. How would she fill her lunch hour now? Although that wasn't really a problem – there was always extra typing to be done. She barely got through her work by the end of each week. And she could befriend another patient, perhaps. She'd ask Matron. But her heart wasn't in it, at least not yet. Jeremy wasn't just a patient to her, but he could never know her feelings. Even if Mrs Hadley hadn't already told him who Evie's mother was, Carrie would bear the burden of that secret. She would have to lie to maintain the illusion of whatever story Mrs Hadley had told and it would be wrong to hide such an important truth from Jeremy. Getting any closer to him was out of the question. It was the price she must pay for her past foolishness, the price that ensured she could stay in touch with her daughter.

Chapter Nine

It was a bitter late December morning as Carrie, filled with nervous excitement, approached Hawksdown Lodge. She was looking forward to her regular visit to see Evie, of course, but she hadn't seen Jeremy since he'd left hospital, at least two weeks earlier. Now it was nearly Christmas, the fourth with the country at war. It seemed inconceivable. Would they never be free of the threat from Germany? It seemed to have grown in the last year, with ever-increasing bombing raids mounted by small planes from across the sea. The skies were rarely free now from the buzz of engines as aircraft were scrambled from the aerodrome hastily created on Hawks Down.

Carrie had volunteered to spend Christmas Day at St Aidan's, helping to raise the spirits of those who couldn't be discharged to spend it at home with their families. It was preferable to being alone in her room, attempting a festive lunch on her single gas ring. In previous years, she'd been asked for Christmas with the Hadleys but there had been no invitation this year. She feared her thoughtless revelation about Evie's father being Oscar, rather than a distant cousin, might have upset Mrs Hadley.

The full force of a chill wind off the sea hit her as she turned in at the gate, causing her to shiver. It had become noticeably colder since Jeremy had left St Aidan's and she'd comforted herself that, even if he'd still been there, they would have had to abandon their lunchtime meetings on the terrace. Now, the thrill of being with him again was adding to her excitement at seeing Evie and giving her a Christmas gift. It had been hard to know what to buy for her. She had the sort of toys that Carrie could never afford to purchase – a rocking horse, a big box of wooden blocks and a stiff, grumpy-looking teddy bear. So, knowing how much Evie loved the doll Carrie had made for her birthday, she'd decided to make it some new clothes. She'd managed to get hold of a piece of material from one of the volunteers who had turned a pair of curtains into a dress, giving the leftover fabric to anyone who could make use of it. She'd made a jacket and a pinafore dress for the doll, and a blouse to go beneath it from a couple of handkerchiefs. These were neatly packed, with a bar of chocolate she had been saving for Evie. So many things were in short supply or available only erratically. When she'd seen the local shopkeeper unpacking a carton of chocolate she'd seized her chance. He was rationing the bars to one per regular customer: there was no question in Carrie's mind that it would be Evie's.

She rapped on the front door and waited, nervous until she heard Evie's excited voice from the inside.

'Let me open it! Let me – I can,' she was insisting.

The door swung open to reveal a smiling Jeremy with Evie in his arms, her smile as wide as his. Carrie was shocked: she hadn't been conscious of her daughter's resemblance to Oscar until she saw her face so close to Jeremy's. Their colouring, the shape of their eyes – the two brothers had been very alike and Evie's family resemblance was very clear.

She pulled herself together, saying 'Hello, poppet,' to her daughter and greeting Jeremy as she took Evie from his arms.

'Come and see the tree.' Evie, after giving Carrie a big kiss on the cheek, had demanded to be put down and was now tugging at her hand.

Carrie gave Jeremy an apologetic smile and did as she was told, uttering what she hoped were suitably impressed oohs and aahs as she circled the tree, a small fir cut from the garden and placed in the bay window. At least one ornament, and often two, hung from every branch.

'I did it,' Evie said proudly. 'Uncle Jeremy helped.'

Laughing, Carrie turned to Jeremy who had just limped into the room. 'I told you she'd keep you busy,' she said.

Mrs Hadley, unnoticed by Carrie until then, rose from her arm-chair by the fire, glass in hand. 'You never mentioned how much time you'd been spending with Jeremy in hospital,' she remarked. She might have intended to keep her tone neutral but it came out as an accusation, nevertheless.

Carrie coloured. 'I wasn't sure what to do,' she admitted. 'I didn't want to upset you because I knew no outside visitors were allowed on Primrose Ward.'

'Jeremy has told us he couldn't have coped without your visits to lift his spirits. We owe you thanks for helping him recover.' Despite her words, Mrs Hadley was unsmiling. 'A Christmas drink to celebrate?' she offered. 'We still have some spirits and I think I can find some sherry.'

'No, but thank you,' Carrie said. She wanted to make the most of her time with Evie and she'd made the mistake in the past of accepting a drink from Mrs Hadley. She knew only one way to mix them – strong.

'Well, I'll leave you both to catch up,' Mrs Hadley said, and left the room. Carrie heard her calling for Maria. To her surprise, Jeremy settled himself in the other high-backed chair by the fire. She'd assumed Mrs Hadley had meant herself and Evie, when she'd said 'you both'.

'I can't tell you how glad I am to see you,' Jeremy said, as Carrie knelt on the floor so that Evie could show her a wooden Noah's ark. 'I'm slowly going mad here.'

Carrie glanced up sharply.

Jeremy gave a wry smile. 'Sorry, poor choice of words. But I feel trapped. I've spent so much time doing nothing since I was injured.' He noticed Evie look up, perhaps worried by his tone. 'Good job I've got Evie here to keep me company.'

'Come and play, too, Uncle Jeremy. I'm going to get Poppet.' Evie had run from the room before either of them could respond.

'Poppet?' Carrie asked.

'Her doll,' Jeremy said. 'She's taken to changing its name every few days. Do you know, Mother was trying to tell me some story that Evie was the child of distant cousins – until I told her I knew she was Oscar's.' He looked indignant. 'I supposed she's used that story to save face but how ridiculous to try to tell me – *family* – a lie.' He shook his head.

He'd got up from the chair and now lowered himself, painfully, to sit on the floor beside Carrie. He began to arrange the painted wooden animals in neat pairs, nose to tail, leading up to the bottom of the ark's gangplank. After a moment or two, he looked up at Carrie and smiled. She felt a wave of relief. There was nothing in his face to suggest he had been told she was Evie's mother. For a moment, she was tempted to ask who the mother was, just to hear what story Mrs Hadley had invented. Then common sense intervened – Jeremy might not even have asked.

Evie burst back into the room with Poppet and Carrie pulled a package out of her bag. 'I've got a present for you and Poppet. It's for Christmas, but I think you should open it now.'

She'd probably have plenty of presents on Christmas Day, Carrie thought, and she really wanted to see her daughter's face as she opened it.

'Where will you be on Christmas Day?' Jeremy asked, as they watched Evie tearing the paper off her gift.

'At the hospital,' Carrie said. 'I'd like to be of some use.'

Jeremy looked as though he was about to speak but Evie was now exclaiming with delight over Poppet's new clothes.

'Can you put them on?' she asked, holding out her doll.

The next hour flew by as Jeremy made the doll dance, speaking in voices that he felt suited her appearance. Evie was in fits of laughter and Carrie couldn't stop smiling. Uncle Jeremy was as good a father to her as Oscar would have been. Even better, perhaps.

CHAPTER TEN

A fter each visit, Carrie found it painful to leave her daughter behind. She tried to memorise Evie's every word and action, for they had to sustain her until the next time. It was doubly difficult that day for she had to leave Jeremy, too. He brought Evie to the door to wave her off and said, 'It's a shame you can't join us on Christmas Day but I'm sure you'll bring a lot of joy to the men at St Aidan's. Come as soon as you can afterwards, won't you? Both Evie and I will be looking forward to seeing you.'

Carrie smiled and nodded, then stooped to kiss Evie goodbye. How on earth could she explain to Jeremy that she wasn't permitted to visit as freely as in the past? She'd only be able to make a limited number of excuses before he'd begin to wonder what was going on. She considered saying she'd had a disagreement with Mrs Hadley, but dismissed the idea at once. He'd be bound to ask his mother why they had fallen out. As she walked back to Castle Bay she made a determined effort to put the problem out of her mind until after Christmas. She would enjoy the memory of her visit in the meantime.

Christmas at St Aidan's was far jollier than she'd expected. The nursing staff were determined to make it a happy occasion for the patients too poorly to be sent home. Carrie spent Christmas Eve cutting out paper snowflakes and sprinkling them with glitter to decorate all the ward windows. Christmas Day found her at the hospital extra early, determined to help get the men ready for the day ahead. The church choir was coming to sing carols in the wards, then each of the men would receive a small gift, bought and wrapped by the local parishioners. The contents would be simple: tobacco, soap, a bar of chocolate, razor blades (but not on Primrose Ward). When so many people were struggling to get by it was a kind gesture, Carrie thought.

After that, the men would be offered a drink provided by the Hawksdown brewery, and then it would be time for lunch. In the afternoon, some of the nurses, along with the more able men, were putting on an entertainment. She'd listened in on the rehearsals and was looking forward to it. It was to be an irreverent take on hospital life and she expected a lot of laughter. It would be the perfect antidote to what so many of them had experienced.

The carol-singing, though, reduced her to tears. She'd expected the men to be restless: not all of them had religious beliefs or, if they had, war had shaken them. Yet you could have heard a pin drop as the choir's voices soared to the rafters, and many of the men joined in, with surprisingly strong baritones. At the end, all of the patients clapped respectfully, one or two cheering in a muted way. Then the choir members moved around the room, wishing all the men a happy Christmas and a speedy recovery.

After this had been repeated in the other main ward, Carrie walked with the choir to Primrose Ward. They'd been warned what to expect but it was still hard for one or two of them to suppress a gasp when they entered the room. The rocking and shouting that Carrie had grown accustomed to must have seemed threatening to the visitors. Matron calmly led the way to the front of the room where the choir arranged themselves. After the first few bars of 'O Little Town of Bethlehem' Carrie saw that some of the agitation was stilled in the men. Many gathered in a semi-circle in front of the singers, gazing in rapt attention. By the end of the carol, the underlying noise in the room had all but died away, to be replaced by attempts to join in by some of the men.

The choir sang a couple of extra carols, then moved around the ward, offering the season's greetings. Sometimes this was met with puzzlement, but many of the patients clasped their hands and thanked them in return. By the time Carrie left Primrose Ward to escort the choir back to see Sir Charles and Lady Rowlands, she had a lump in her throat.

Within half an hour, though, the solemnity was lifted as the gifts were distributed. The dispensing of small glasses of ale added to the lightening of the mood. Carrie helped to lay the tables in the big hall for those able to sit at them, and to hand around meals on trays for those who couldn't. She was amazed at how well Cook had managed to provide: chickens and vegetables had been procured from all the farms in the area. It seemed everyone had been able to spare something for the brave boys who'd suffered so much at the front. A delivery of tinned Christmas puddings, courtesy of the local War Comforts committee, rounded off the meal. They were liberally doused in ancient brandy that Sir Charles had found at the back of the cellar, then lit and paraded into the room to the sound of gasps, followed by applause.

Carrie returned to Primrose Ward to help. Many of the men took a lot of encouragement to eat. She thought that the delicious aroma of chicken, roast potatoes and gravy might do the trick, but it seemed not. She was persuading one of the very withdrawn patients to try just one mouthful of meat, chopped into tiny pieces and soaked in gravy, when word came that half of the nurses should go for their Christmas lunch.

'Off you go,' the ward sister said firmly to Carrie, removing the plate from her. 'I'll take over here. You go and enjoy your lunch. You deserve it – you'd have been spending the day with family if you hadn't volunteered.'

Carrie didn't argue, although as she walked along the corridor back to the hall, she reflected she'd far rather be where she was. She thought she might even have forgone lunch at the Hadleys, and precious time with Evie, to take part in this day.

The food was as delicious as it had looked when Carrie handed it out earlier, but her appetite was blunted. She supposed it was from having had her nose tantalised by the seductive aromas for the last hour or so. Her neighbour at the table, however, wasn't similarly afflicted. After casting several covert glances at the roast potatoes Carrie was neglecting, she asked her outright whether she wanted them.

'Please take them,' Carrie said, offloading them. Her appetite returned, though, for the Christmas pudding, a small slice covered with watery custard but delicious nonetheless. Sweet treats were rare, these days, and Carrie's neighbour was disappointed if she had hoped to see an extra portion coming her way. Lunch had been a triumph and the kitchen staff must be exhausted, she thought, but it wasn't over for them yet. There would be plates of sandwiches to make for the men's tea and possibly something else to go with them. Since America had entered the war earlier that year, they sometimes received deliveries of goods they hadn't seen before, or not for a long time.

Once lunch had been served to all and the tables cleared, a space was created at the front of the hall for the afternoon performance. Without a stage, the audience had to manage as best they could, craning over each other's shoulders. At least the patients had chairs, Carrie thought ruefully. Her feet were aching from the amount of time she'd spent on them that day. All the nursing staff and volunteers were standing at the back, apart from a few who'd remained on Primrose Ward to stay with those considered too unwell to join them in the hall.

A few minutes into the show, Carrie's tiredness was all but

forgotten, as the patients sent up the staff with friendly, but unerring, precision. Some were even clothed in uniforms borrowed for the occasion, which in itself was enough to provoke tears of laughter. The staff gave back as good as they got and Carrie's sides, as well as her feet, were aching by the time the performance was over.

The good humour was sustained by another serving of ale and, as darkness crept across the lawns, the wards were lit by Christmas lights that Sir Charles had discovered in the cellar, saved from a long ago pre-war Christmas party.

At six o'clock, the tables were set up again and sandwiches laid out, served with copious amounts of tea and jam tarts, which Cook had managed to create by preserving every soft fruit she could lay her hands on earlier that year. Card schools replaced the tea things but by eight o'clock Carrie was exhausted and many of the patients were grey with fatigue, too. It had been a long day for men still recovering from serious injuries and Matron clapped her hands to call a halt to the proceedings.

'Time to prepare for bed, everyone. Christmas is over for another year. I hope that next year, Christmas finds us all at peace once more. In the meantime, let's say a big thank-you to Cook in the kitchen, all her helpers, the nursing staff and volunteers who've come to spend the day at St Aidan's.'

The claps, cheers and wolf whistles could probably have been heard at Hawksdown Lodge, Carrie thought, such was the volume. Shortly afterwards, she was pedalling home on her bicycle, thankful for the clear starry skies. Street lights were a thing of the past under the blackout. It was a chilly night and the road sparkled with a light coating of frost. The exercise in the fresh air briefly invigorated her, but soon after she arrived at home she fell asleep on the bed, fully clothed, and didn't rouse until she was disturbed by the light streaming in through the window on Boxing Day morning.

CHAPTER ELEVEN

❦

Carrie spent Boxing Day alone in her room, still weary and only too well aware that many of the staff would be back on duty. Probably it would be a quiet day at the hospital, she thought: the men would be tired, too. Hopefully, they would take away good memories of the day when they were eventually discharged.

Her euphoria from the Christmas celebrations slipped away as the hours passed. The lack of anything to occupy her drove her to look through the few books stacked on her bedside table. There was Meg Marsh's diary – possibly even more battered than before. She turned the pages, thinking back to when she'd last read it. It was before she had given birth to Evie. Had Meg ever known what it was to have a child? Carrie had had no idea of what it would mean to her, but Evie had brought her so much joy – and heartache because of their circumstances. Her thoughts turned to Evie and Jeremy, and she longed to know what they were doing at Hawksdown Lodge. While Jeremy remained at home, it would be hard to obey Mrs Hadley's strictures. Perhaps she might be permitted to visit more frequently. She wasn't sure how it could be managed but she was determined to try. The thought gave her a little glow of optimism, which carried her along to bedtime.

Luck, in the form of Ada, provided the answer. For some weeks now, Ada had been volunteering as an auxiliary nurse in London, at King's College Hospital. Carrie had rarely seen her:

time off was limited and she frequently chose not to take it. It happened a lot at St Aidan's, too, where the volunteers worked way beyond their suggested hours, seeing the pressure the hospital was under.

So Carrie was surprised, then delighted, to find Ada waiting outside St Aidan's on Friday afternoon when she finished work. It was dark and cold and Carrie, intent on retrieving her bicycle to pedal home, didn't see the figure detach itself from the shadows of the wall where she'd been waiting until she spoke.

'Hello, Carrie. Happy Christmas. A bit late I know, but better late than never.'

Carrie, recognising Ada's voice at once, spun round. 'Ada! How long have you been waiting? Why on earth didn't you come in out of the cold?'

'I haven't been here long,' Ada replied. 'I needed some fresh air, went out for a walk and ended up here. It was five o'clock so I thought I'd wait to see whether you came out.'

Ada held out her arms and the two women hugged awkwardly across the bicycle then walked slowly down the hill, wheeling it between them and talking non-stop.

'How long will you be at home?' Carrie asked eventually, once she'd answered Ada's questions about Jeremy and the time he'd spent at St Aidan's.

Ada didn't answer immediately and they walked a little distance in silence, Carrie glancing at her every now and then in puzzlement.

'I'm not sure when I'll be going back. But soon, I hope,' she added hastily. 'They think I'm suffering some sort of nervous disorder. A bit like the men and their battle fatigue.' She gave a short laugh. 'You know how it is, Carrie. You work and work, mopping up blood, changing bandages, talking to the men, holding their hands through the night, trying to encourage them to believe they'll be going home soon. And then they die. One after another. Such a terrible waste. On the bus home, or in bed at night, when I closed my eyes, all I could see was row upon row of beds and I felt as though I couldn't help anyone any more. That's why I waited outside for you. I couldn't bear to go in.'

'Oh, Ada, I'm so sorry. They're right, you know. You must rest.' Carrie paused. 'It's not like that everywhere. Perhaps your hospital only takes the most serious cases. The ones we have here are mostly recovering from operations. And shell-shock. Jeremy must have told you about that?'

'Not much,' Ada said, to Carrie's surprise. 'But you must come and see us. Are you free this weekend? Evie is such a darling. She's a real antidote to all this.'

Carrie was pierced to the heart by her words. It was as if Ada had forgotten she was Evie's mother. Yet she was probably the only person with whom she could discuss the problem over visiting.

'I visited just before Christmas,' she said. 'You know the agreement with your mother . . .'

Ada gave an impatient sigh. 'Oh, for Heaven's sake. Both Jeremy and I want to see you. Mother will just have to accept it. I'll speak to her tonight. Please say you'll come tomorrow. I'll expect you at eleven and I hope you'll stay for lunch.'

They'd reached the gate of Hawksdown Lodge and, on impulse, Carrie stood on tiptoe and kissed Ada's cheek. 'Thank you,' she said, then got onto her bike and pedalled home, her heart filled with hope.

She presented herself at Hawksdown Lodge at just after eleven the next day, less sure of her welcome now she'd had a few hours to think about it. But Ada greeted her at the front door, hand in hand with Evie, and ushered her into the sitting room before Carrie could ask her anything.

'It looks like rain so I thought we'd stay in rather than go for a walk,' Ada said. Carrie was about to protest that it was fine and sunny, then saw Jeremy sitting by the fire. He was hunched over, as though in pain, and he waved his stick at her in greeting rather than getting up. Carrie, who had only just registered how gaunt and pale Ada was, now that she saw her in daylight, refrained from asking either of them how they were. Instead, she went to kneel beside Evie, who had been tugging silently at her hand and pointing to the toy farmyard laid out on the carpet.

'Have you had a lovely Christmas?' she asked her.

'Evie kept us all sane,' Jeremy said, before Evie could reply. He resumed staring into the fire so she turned her attention to the farmyard, wondering what the problem was. She didn't have to wait long to find out.

'He's had a letter,' Ada said. 'From the army, discharging him due to his injuries.'

Jeremy snorted to signify his contempt.

Carrie felt a huge wave of relief. She couldn't imagine how he would have coped if he'd been sent back to the front, still suffering from shell-shock. The injury to his leg had saved him from that, at least.

'There wasn't a desk job you could have done?' she asked.

'Apparently not.' Jeremy scowled.

Ada raised her eyebrows at Carrie and shook her head, which Carrie took as a sign not to continue the conversation.

'Was this from Father Christmas?' she asked Evie, pointing at the farm set.

'No,' Evie said. 'From Granny.'

Mrs Hadley was the least granny-like of grandmothers, Carrie thought, amazed that she'd allowed herself to be called that. She was always happy to indulge Evie with presents, though. Carrie glanced anxiously towards the door, wondering where she was now.

'Granny's gone to London, hasn't she, Evie?' Ada said, looking at Carrie as she spoke. 'She and Granddad are spending the week there.'

Evie nodded, busy herding the toy sheep into their pen. Carrie knew Ada had just given her the permission she needed to visit every day if she wanted to. It was a chance she wouldn't be turning down.

CHAPTER TWELVE

Carrie took advantage of Mr and Mrs Hadley's absence to spend most of the weekend at Hawksdown Lodge, and to visit every evening after work. She couldn't remember ever having felt so happy. She returned to her own room – with its dingy wallpaper, chipped brown paintwork and draughty windows – only to sleep. She supposed Maisie might mention her visits to Mrs Hadley, but the nursemaid wasn't party to the agreement with Carrie and, hopefully, Ada would deal with any problems that resulted.

Carrie wasn't the only one to benefit from the visits. After she had seen Evie tucked up in bed – a rare treat for both of them – she sat down to eat with Ada and Jeremy. They would stay at the table after it had been cleared, reminiscing about times before the war and wondering whether they would return to that carefree existence at any point in the years ahead. By the end of the week, Ada was less prone to start at the smallest noise – a log shifting in the fire, Maria's knock to announce supper – and Carrie thought she looked a little less gaunt.

'The sea air's doing me good,' Ada said. 'I'm even sleeping better.'

Carrie knew that while she was at work Ada made a point of persuading Jeremy to walk a little: around the garden or along the seafront, despite the bitter wind blowing in off the Channel. He seemed to have become resigned to his discharge from duty but at a loss as to what to do next.

'I can't go back to studying,' he said firmly. 'It would seem like a pointless indulgence now. In any case, if I was seen around Oxford I'd be thought a coward for not signing up. I'd be given white feathers every day.'

'Nonsense.' Ada was brisk. 'They'd see your stick. It's clear you've been wounded.'

Jeremy just shook his head.

Carrie had been glad he was neither returning to the front nor going back to his studies at university. She was happy to keep him close for as long as possible. And she could barely contain her excitement over the bit of news she brought with her on Friday evening at the end of her working week. When Maria showed her into the drawing room, though, she found Ada and Jeremy morose.

'Has something happened?' she asked, looking from one to the other.

'We've had a letter from Mother,' Ada said. 'She's staying up in town and she's volunteering at King's College Hospital – *my* hospital.'

Carrie was surprised but couldn't see the problem so she stayed silent.

'Can you imagine how that makes me feel?' Ada couldn't contain herself. 'I've had to leave but my mother is going to step into my shoes and play the selfless saviour.'

It was a bit tactless, Carrie thought, although no doubt well-meant. She could at least have volunteered at a different hospital.

'So now we're both stuck here feeling useless,' Jeremy said bitterly, 'while our mother leads the war effort.'

Carrie bit her lip to hold back a smile. 'Well, I did come here with news for one of you,' she said. 'And now I've heard this I might well have something for you both.'

Ada and Jeremy were regarding her with interest but just then Maisie ushered in Evie, fresh from her bath. Carrie smiled apologetically at them over Evie's head, then devoted the following half-hour to her daughter. Evie was eager to hear the next instalment of a story about Poppet, which Carrie was making up as she went along. Jeremy must wonder at her allowing Evie to take precedence over the adult conversation, she thought, casting one or two glances his way as she sat with Evie on her lap. But he was gazing into the fire and she couldn't read his expression, although she was happy to see the frown that had been creasing his brow when she arrived had all but disappeared.

As Evie, after a brief protest, was led away to bed, Jeremy said, 'You're quite a storyteller, you know. Evie loves your Poppet tales. I have to listen so I can retell them during the day – she demands it.'

Carrie blushed. 'I had no idea. I didn't even know you were listening. I just say whatever nonsense comes into my head.'

'You're too modest,' Jeremy said. 'Now, I'm impatient to know more about this interesting news.'

'As I said, there may be something for both of you,' Carrie said. 'But I thought of you first, Jeremy. Sir Charles was talking in the office about the aerodrome at Hawks Down. He's worried about the increasing noise and how it affects the hospital. It's going to be the permanent base for a squadron, apparently. They're putting a lot of temporary buildings on the field below the airstrip, for workers and for accommodation. They're going to need people with the right skills to deal with the War Office in London and co-ordinate with the telephonists who'll be in touch with all the airbases along the coast. I thought it might be something for you, Jeremy?'

He didn't look convinced but she pressed on: 'I know it's not active service but maybe it's as close to it as you can get at the moment. It sounds like important work.'

She turned to Ada, leaving Jeremy to ponder her words. 'Hearing you talk about your mother just now made me wonder whether you might consider volunteering at St Aidan's. I know

316

you're not ready yet,' she added hastily, seeing Ada's expression, 'but maybe in a few weeks' time. It won't be anything like the work you were doing. We take mainly convalescent patients, men needing just a few more weeks' rest and nursing.'

There was silence when she'd finished speaking. Carrie began to feel anxious. The opportunity at the aerodrome had seemed perfect for Jeremy and the idea of Ada becoming a volunteer at St Aidan's had only just struck her, but now she wondered whether her enthusiasm had been misplaced. Had she upset Jeremy or Ada? She cast a worried glance at the brother and sister.

Jeremy was the first to speak. 'I think you may have hit on something, Carrie. It's right on the doorstep . . . and I can't get very far, these days. Anything I can do there will be far better than sitting here all day, too miserable even to read a book. Who should I get in touch with?'

'I can speak to Sir Charles on Monday,' Carrie offered. It was evident from Jeremy's face that now he'd reached a decision he was impatient to act on it. 'Don't worry,' she reassured him. 'I don't think many people know about it yet.'

'It sounds perfect, Jeremy. I can't imagine anything would suit you better. You'll feel as though you're right back in the thick of it.' Ada's enthusiasm made Jeremy smile.

She turned to Carrie. 'You're a genius, Carrie. Jeremy and I can rub along very well here while Mother and Father stay in the flat in town. And I think I can volunteer at St Aidan's, if what you say is true. Not yet – I must give myself another week or two. But I feel more positive than I have in ages.'

If her friends were happy, then so was she, Carrie thought. Better than happy, really. She had the three people who mattered most to her close by, all safe under the same roof. And with Mr and Mrs Hadley away, she could see as much of them as she liked, work permitting, of course.

CHAPTER THIRTEEN

D espite the constant presence of war, the few months that followed were as settled and happy as they could be for Carrie. She approached Sir Charles for more information about work possibilities for Jeremy at the Hawks Down airbase. Within the week, Jeremy was ensconced there, collected and dropped home each day by one of the naval squadron vehicles. At first, he was uncharacteristically quiet in the evenings. He was tired, unaccustomed to a full day's desk work after his lengthy convalescence. But he declared himself delighted to be back among the chatter and banter of the men of the naval air squadrons and soon settled into the routine. The constant noise of the aircraft engines didn't cause any return of his shell-shock, as Carrie had half feared, perhaps because he'd grown used to it at a distance at St Aidan's. She supposed that, in any case, it was unlike the bombardment of the trenches where the men must have felt trapped and helpless, like sitting ducks.

Ada, too, flourished in her volunteer role. Carrie frequently saw her at work in the hospital, smart in her uniform of blue dress and crisp white collar, her dark hair hidden by the low brow of her cap. Matron had described her to Carrie as 'very competent', which was high praise indeed. She'd lost some of her volunteers, who had gone to France or moved on to other posts and she was pleased to have someone 'with solid experience behind her', as she put it.

The only drawback to these new arrangements, Carrie discovered, was that Ada, too, was tired in the evenings, so she felt obliged to depart as soon as the three of them had eaten. Once Ada had discovered that Carrie had just a single gas ring in her room she'd insisted she must join them to dine every evening. Carrie had put up only a token resistance.

Yet, although she saw Jeremy daily, there was no longer any opportunity to spend time with just the two of them together, often with Evie, and she missed it. At the end of February, a change to Ada's work rota altered all that. Ada had sailed through the probationary period and was moved to a week of night duties. Carrie had Jeremy all to herself after Evie had gone to bed.

On the first evening, she pushed her chair back as soon as they had eaten, preparing to leave, but Jeremy objected. 'Don't go yet,' he said. 'I've missed the chats we used to have, back at St Aidan's. Although I haven't missed the circumstances,' he added.

'You aren't tired?' Carrie was doubtful.

'No, not at all. I'm used to the routine now. I'd welcome some company.' Jeremy got to his feet. 'But let's go and sit by the fire. We'll be more comfortable there.'

Carrie began to wish she'd made more of an effort when she'd left the house that morning. It had been dark when she got up and she'd put on her only clean blouse and a skirt that didn't really match, hoping the thick cardigan she had buttoned over her outfit would pull it all together. Sitting by the fire, she'd have to unbutton the cardigan, if not remove it. She'd dragged a comb through her hair and twisted it up, pinning it in place without looking in a mirror. She'd barely registered her appearance in the washroom mirrors throughout what had been a busy day. Now she caught a glimpse of herself in the over-mantel mirror, and grimaced.

They sat and chatted a while about their respective days, then subsided into silence, gazing into the fire. It was companionable, though, and it was with reluctance Carrie registered that the clock on the mantelpiece read eight thirty. It was time to go home.

As if he was aware of her intentions, Jeremy said, 'Don't go yet. There's something I want to say.'

He hesitated, as if unsure how to proceed, and Carrie had a sudden premonition, which brought colour flooding to her cheeks. She almost begged him not to continue, but it was too late.

'I've so wanted the chance to talk to you like this – I've imagined it time and time again – but now I don't know how to begin. The thing is, you were so kind to me in hospital, so good, and I was so wrapped up in myself that I scarcely recognised how I'd begun to feel about you. It wasn't until I was back here that I realised how much I missed you. Not just because you were good and kind, but because I'd fallen in love, just a little bit. And that little bit grew, seeing you with Evie and now seeing you every day, until I knew that's what I wanted, more than anything. To be able to see you every day.' Jeremy stopped, seeing Carrie's face. 'Have I spoken out of turn? I thought … I hoped …'

'No, not out of turn.' Carrie was agonised. She was hearing exactly what she'd longed to hear, what she had daydreamed about. But it could never be. There was Evie, and the truth about their relationship, which Jeremy could never know. Unprepared, she stammered, 'Your parents, they'd never agree.'

Jeremy shrugged, dismissive. 'It's none of their business. I'm not going to find anyone like you among their suitable friends. Times are changing, Carrie. War has changed us, changed all the old rules.'

Not quite all of them, Carrie thought. Her life was already bound to the Hadleys, but not in any way that Jeremy would understand. So she said, 'Once the war is over, some things will go back to how they once were. Your parents will want you to finish your studies. And,' she paused, 'you're the eldest son now. It will be important to them that you marry well.'

There was silence, during which they stared into the fire once more. Carrie's heart was beating so hard, she thought Jeremy must surely hear it. Why had she just tried to talk him out of something she wanted more than anything else in the world? She stole a glance at him. His handsome face was set in a frown as he contemplated her words.

'Is it because of Oscar?' He turned suddenly and caught her looking at him. 'I know you liked him. And then there was the baby – Evie. That must have hurt.'

Her heart lurched – for a moment she thought he knew the truth. Then she realised he believed she was upset that she'd lost Oscar to some other girl.

'No, it's not Oscar,' she said gently. 'It's as I said – we're living in strange times but one day they'll be over and you'll know this can never be.'

Jeremy kept his dark eyes on her, hard to read in the flickering firelight, but didn't speak. Carrie, all at once in danger of weeping, had to look away.

'Well,' he said, at last, 'during these strange times I'm going to carry on thinking in the same way. And I'll hope to change your mind. But I don't want this conversation to spoil our friendship. Will you promise me it won't? I can't bear it if you refuse to come here each evening, as you have been doing. Please say you still will. Even if Ada isn't here.'

Carrie wished with all her heart she could promise more, but how could she when she had a secret she couldn't share with him, a secret that would, no doubt, change his opinion of her? For now, she would try to enjoy what she had, and hug the knowledge of Jeremy's feelings to her as a joy and a comfort. If only he knew how fully and completely those feelings were returned – but that could never be. If Mrs Hadley had an inkling of the way things were, she would no doubt enlighten Jeremy as to the true state of affairs.

So, as she got up to leave, she said, 'Of course I'll still come. But let's keep this just between us.' It was a question as much as a statement, but she was relieved when Jeremy nodded.

'Of course,' he said, managing to raise a smile. 'After all, I'm hardly going to spread it around that I've been turned down by the best girl I know.'

CHAPTER FOURTEEN

The weeks merged into one as winter turned into spring, with no sign of peace ahead. Jeremy didn't speak of his feelings again but Carrie held the knowledge within her. It felt like a precious gift, something she hardly dared to examine in any depth, fearful of destroying it, but it sustained her through the days of grinding routine.

At the hospital, Matron's public face was resolutely businesslike but the mask slipped when she was in the office with Sir Charles.

'We've been told to expect more casualties,' she said, her hands clasped tightly in front of her. 'But where are we to find the space to accommodate them?' She was asking Sir Charles to find more room in the house, when he had already given over the greater part of it to the auxiliary hospital. He either pretended not to hear her or was too caught up in the latest newspaper reports to pay proper attention.

He startled Matron and Carrie by thumping the table. 'Can you credit it?' He was red in the face and indignant. 'The Germans have pushed forward again. They've advanced by forty miles, it says here. What's going on out there?'

Carrie's heart plummeted. The beginning of the year had seen meat rationing come into force, followed by restrictions on the use of coal, gas and electricity in mid-March. Now, as they moved into

April, they seemed as far as ever from the end of the war – or, at least, from a victory in their favour.

The following day at the table, Jeremy was full of the news that a Royal Air Force had been created by combining the Royal Flying Corps and the Royal Naval Air Service. He seemed convinced that aeroplanes would be the solution to ending the war, given the British success in dogfights with the Germans. Ada and Carrie couldn't match his enthusiasm as they did their best to eat a meal not only lacking in meat but without any flavour at all.

'You'll see – it's good news,' Jeremy protested.

'It doesn't feel like it.' Ada sighed. 'It seems there will never be an end to any of it. It's been going on for so long. How much more can everyone take?'

They sank into gloomy contemplation and Carrie decided to leave earlier than usual. It was Monday, and the whole working week lay ahead, yet they were tired already. Perhaps tomorrow would be a better day, she thought, pedalling home through an evening chill that held little promise of spring. The sole of her shoe had started to peel away again and it was catching on the pedal. The cobbler said it wouldn't take another repair so she would have to buy new ones, if she could find anything suitable. Everything was in short supply. Not for the first time, she reminded herself she was lucky. Worn-out shoes were a minor inconvenience compared to fighting at the front, or having loved ones there.

The following evening Jeremy and Ada were no more cheerful. Mr Hadley had telephoned to say that Mrs Hadley had fallen ill and been forced to take time off from the hospital.

'He said it was just a cold,' Ada reported. 'He thinks they should come home for a few days to give her time to rest properly but she's insisting she'll be well enough to go back to work in a day or two.' She paused. 'I suppose I should go to London and look after her – I think that's what Father wants – but all the new admissions will be arriving here any day now. I don't want to let Matron down.'

Carrie sympathised. It was still considered a daughter's duty to give up whatever she was doing to nurse a sick mother. Any new-found independence due to the war effort counted for nothing against traditional family values.

Ada looked to Jeremy for advice but he shrugged. 'I don't know what to suggest. She might be annoyed if you turn up and it's nothing.'

Ada nodded, reassured. Then she sighed. 'I'll speak to Matron tomorrow. Perhaps I can manage to be away for a night or two.'

Carrie couldn't help glancing at Jeremy. It had been a while since Ada had done any night duties and she welcomed the idea of having Jeremy to herself once more. She caught him looking at her, too, and couldn't stop her colour rising.

Ada went reluctantly to London, taking very few items in her bag since she was determined to be home again as quickly as possible. In fact, she was away for four nights rather than two, but it hardly mattered to Carrie and Jeremy. Conscious that their time together would be limited, Carrie spent the day before their first evening alone in a fever of anticipation. It appeared that Jeremy felt the same because neither of them could do much justice to the meal Maria had prepared. When it was cleared away, Carrie went over to the fireside and stood gazing into the fire. Jeremy closed the door firmly and she knew he was coming up to stand behind her.

He turned her gently towards him, cupping her face in his hands, and said, 'I know what you said about after the war, and I respect that. But, Carrie, who knows how things will be then? What if we don't win?' He stopped, breathing shakily. 'I know you feel something for me. I can see it in your face.'

He was gazing into her eyes as he spoke, but Carrie could feel his uncertainty. He was worried he'd overstepped the mark. She didn't reply but leant slightly towards him and kissed him on the lips. She supposed it was by way of giving him permission. He was right, even though it didn't alter how things stood. There was still this awful unknowable secret between them. But with the increasing feeling that everything was going so badly, was it really so important to maintain her stance? Who could predict what the future might hold?

Jeremy kissed her, gently at first, then more deeply. Carrie was first to disengage. Memories of Oscar and their meetings in the Glen flooded back, and – out of nowhere – she was reminded of Meg Marsh's diary. Could she risk another unfortunate entanglement? Jeremy was a very different character from his brother, of course, but the deceit disturbed her. She'd broken her own rules in exchanging kisses with him and her conscience would allow her nothing further, not in the Hadleys' house, with Evie asleep upstairs.

The subsequent evenings followed the same pattern, with Carrie unable to stop herself yielding, then holding back, until she was glad to see Ada's bag in the hall when she called round at the weekend. Jeremy hadn't objected to the boundaries Carrie had laid out but she was finding them harder and harder to maintain.

Ada heard Carrie talking to Maria in the hallway and came down at once. 'How is your mother?' Carrie asked. 'Is she better now?'

'Much better than she was,' Ada said, 'although not really well enough to go back to work. But she insisted, so I took the first train home that I could. Has all been well at St Aidan's?'

Carrie hid a smile. She thought Ada hoped to hear they had barely managed without her, but Matron had simply juggled everyone's hours to suit the influx of new arrivals who had, in any case, been delayed due to reports of a German submarine patrolling the Channel.

'It's been busy,' she said. 'I'm sure Matron will be glad to have you back. And I'm delighted, too.' She gave Ada a hug and Evie, who had just come downstairs with Maisie, rushed to do the same. With a flood of emotion, Carrie felt as though she had all her family around her once more.

CHAPTER FIFTEEN

Ada, Jeremy and Carrie fought off the dip in their spirits as best they could and carried on with their routines, determined to make the best of things even though the army's fortunes showed no sign of improvement at the front.

As the days grew longer and sunnier, they went out into the garden although it was sadly neglected, the gardener having gone off to war. The tennis court was overrun with weeds and the net hung in tatters, due to their failure to take it down over winter. They pulled up the weeds and let the damaged net down even further, so that they could play with Evie on court.

'We'll soon be able to play doubles,' Jeremy said, after they'd spent half an hour out there. 'Evie and Ada against Carrie and me.'

An indignant Carrie was about to give him a tart rejoinder, thinking he was commenting on her tennis skills, which were limited at best, until it dawned on her he was referring to himself. It must be hard for him, she thought, once an athletic young man, able to dash easily around the court. Now, handicapped by his damaged leg, he confined himself for the most part to standing still.

When tennis palled, they turned their attentions to the flower-beds, pulling out the bindweed that had wound itself freely across the roses, threatening to smother them. Ada found the lawnmower rusting in the shed and they took it in turns to mow strips of lawn, annoyed by its screeching until Jeremy found a tin of oil in the garage. Some areas of grass had grown too long for the mower and, after a few attempts to tackle them with a scythe, Jeremy called a halt, declaring it far too dangerous.

'I don't want to damage my other leg. Or injure Evie,' he added, for she was always on the move and he was worried she would come up behind him as he swung the blade.

Carrie shuddered at the thought, and Ada said, 'We've got plenty of short grass to sit on now. We can leave the rest. Maybe we can borrow a sheep or a cow to eat it.'

Evie thought this was a fine idea, while Jeremy and Carrie howled with laughter and asked her just where she thought she was going to find this hungry animal.

'I'll ask a farmer, of course.' Ada appeared puzzled by their obtuseness.

They were still laughing when Maria brought out a blanket and a picnic basket. 'For all your hard work,' she said. She'd made fish-paste sandwiches and some oat biscuits, which were very chewy and not particularly sweet but went down well with the tea she'd put in a flask.

'A proper picnic.' Ada was beaming. 'Almost as good as the one we had ages ago, up on Hawks Down. Do you remember?'

Carrie did. Oscar had been with them then and they'd lain around on the grass that was now the airstrip, eating until they were full. There'd been peaches from this garden, too. She wondered what had happened to the tree. Everyone had gone quiet, and she supposed they were thinking along the same lines.

'Well, at least the garden looks much better,' Jeremy said, breaking the silence. 'It was beginning to resemble the Glen, don't you think?'

Now that Carrie lived in town and was no longer just a few yards from its entrance, she rarely thought about the Glen. It must be completely overgrown by now, she thought. It was another unwelcome memory, conjuring up as it did her meetings there with Oscar.

Evie, bored by the conversation, leapt up and began to chase a butterfly round the garden. The adults, delighted to be released from their memories, shouted encouragement. Ada began to pack away the picnic things and Carrie helped her, resisting the urge to lie on her back and gaze up at the cloudless sky. This was, in many ways, an idyll, she thought – as long as you could discount the horrors being enacted not far distant across the sea. With Mr and Mrs Hadley away for so long, they'd arranged things to suit themselves. They got along so well, the three of them there with Evie. Not for the first time she wished she could live like this, as a little family, for ever.

As June drew to a close, it became apparent that a shift in the balance of power in the war had taken place. The arrival of American troops had revitalised the Allies and, for once, the Germans found themselves weaker and pushed back.

While decisive victories were being talked of at the hospital, at the airbase and in the newspapers, Ada took another call from Mr Hadley. Mrs Hadley was ill again – seriously this time. She had a sickness that had arrived with some of the soldiers evacuated from France.

Ada came away from the telephone, her face pale. 'Father says that younger men seem to suffer the worst and the hospital told him that all the volunteers who had caught it had recovered. Apart from Mother.' She sounded agitated. 'I told her not to go back to work when she did. She was still weak. That must be why she's been hit so badly.'

'But what is it?' Jeremy asked. 'What is she suffering from?'

'A kind of influenza,' Ada said. 'I must go at once.'

Jeremy quickly established that only one train was leaving in the evening that would get her into London before midnight, so Ada flung a few things into a bag while he backed the rarely used car out of the garage. It was a struggle to manage the clutch with his injured leg, but he told Ada firmly, 'You'll miss the train if we don't take the car to the station.'

Carrie watched helplessly as they drove away, thankful for the moonlight as headlights weren't permitted in the blackout. She waited anxiously for Jeremy to return and met him in the drive as she wheeled her bicycle to the gate.

'She caught the train?' It was an unnecessary question, for Ada wasn't in the car.

Jeremy nodded.

'You must be very worried. Ada's doing the right thing in going to London. I hope she'll find your mother much improved when she gets there. You'll let me know if you hear anything?'

Jeremy nodded again, too distracted to speak, so Carrie pedalled away. Ada hadn't once mentioned concern over leaving her duties at St Aidan's, which told Carrie that the situation must be serious. Yet there had been other cases at King's College Hospital, Ada had said, so they must know how to treat it. Surely everything would be all right.

CHAPTER SIXTEEN

⁂

At St Aidan's the next morning, Carrie sought out Matron and informed her that Ada had been called away unexpectedly, explaining a little of the circumstances.

'I've heard about these cases. They've been reported around the country, but I hadn't known London was affected. We must pray it doesn't reach here.' Matron's expression was grave, but she was called away before Carrie, shocked, could ask her anything further.

She was on edge throughout the day but there was no news, although Carrie didn't think she would have been told even if there had been. She wasn't sure how welcome she would be at Hawksdown Lodge, but she went there anyway on the way home, hoping to find out if Ada had been in touch.

Maria ushered her into the drawing room, without a word, and she found Jeremy standing staring into the fireplace.

'Have you heard anything?' Carrie asked.

Jeremy turned to her, his face drawn and grey. 'Ada rang to say Mother isn't doing well. She's very feverish and doesn't know who Ada is. She thinks I ought to be there, but she promised to ring again shortly, so I'll have time to catch the last train.'

'Oh, Jeremy, I'm so sorry.' Carrie felt helpless. 'I hope you don't mind me calling in – I'd hoped to hear better things. I'll leave you now.'

'Don't go, not yet,' Jeremy said. 'Wait until Ada calls, will you?

I'll ask Maria to bring some tea.' He stopped. 'Or would you like to eat?'

'No, nothing to eat, thank you.' Carrie's stomach was knotted with anxiety. 'But of course I'll wait with you.'

Jeremy went into the hall to call Maria. Carrie thought he was glad of the distraction. She could see the telephone on the hall stand, the dull brass gleaming slightly in the lamplight. Just as he walked back past it, it rang. She saw him start, then grasp it and put the receiver to his ear.

'Hello?' Carrie could hear the anxiety in his voice. He had his back to her as he listened, so she couldn't read his face. She heard him say, 'No!' and he sagged a little, leaning against the table to steady himself.

She leapt to her feet and hurried through, in time to catch him saying, 'When? But how? Why?'

Tears rolled down his cheeks and Carrie didn't have to ask to know what had happened. She put out her hand and gently touched his arm.

'Shall I come?' he asked, and for a moment she wondered whether she'd guessed wrongly. He listened intently to the voice at the other end, then said, 'All right,' hung the receiver on the stand and returned it to the table.

He stood for a moment, gazing at the silent telephone, then turned and went into the drawing room. Carrie trailed after him, unsure whether she should slip away and leave him in peace.

'She's gone,' Jeremy said. 'Dead. I haven't seen her since January and now I never will. Some sort of flu. This *bloody* war . . .'

He rarely swore and seemed oblivious to Carrie's presence.

'I'm so sorry, Jeremy,' Carrie said. Her words barely seemed adequate. 'Will you go up to London? Or are Ada and your father coming here?'

'Not tonight,' Jeremy said. 'They'll telephone me in the morning, and we'll work out what to do then. I should have gone up with Ada yesterday. Why didn't I?'

'You weren't to know.' Carrie attempted to soothe his anguish. 'You thought she was just ill, that Ada would nurse her.'

'I suppose so.' Jeremy was on his feet, pacing the floor. 'But I should be there now, with Father and Ada. I should drive up.'

Carrie was alarmed. It was a long drive, not to be undertaken in a blackout by a man with a damaged leg. 'By the time you arrive they'll be asleep,' she reasoned. 'Why don't you take the first train in the morning? Then you can all come back together, if they decide to leave. Or stay there ... if not.' She'd nearly said, 'for the funeral,' but it seemed wrong to speak of such a thing so soon.

He sighed. 'I suppose you're right.' He wrung his hands. 'But I feel so helpless.'

Carrie wished she could ease his pain. She resorted to practical suggestions instead. 'Why don't you pack a bag?' she said. 'And try to get some rest. The first train is very early – just a few hours away, really. It's not that long until you'll be with them.'

Jeremy nodded, but Carrie thought there'd be no rest for him that night: he'd no doubt sit staring into the fire as it burnt down to ashes until it was time for him to take the car to the station.

'I'll go now,' she said. 'But if it's all right with you I'll call in tomorrow after work to see Evie. She'll be worried when you and Ada are missing. And I can ask Maria if there's any news.'

'Of course.' Jeremy seemed barely to hear her, his head no doubt full of the implications of Ada's news, so Carrie slipped out of the room with no further goodbye.

Everything had been turned upside down, she thought, as she bicycled home. What would this mean for her and Evie? It had been Mrs Hadley who had dictated their relationship. Ada knew the truth, but how much did Mr Hadley know? Would it affect how often she could see her daughter? In the past few weeks, she had become accustomed to seeing her every day if she wanted to. What if the family decided to live in London after the war? She tried, and failed, to imagine how she would cope. Then she scolded herself. It was no time to be thinking like this. A woman had just died – the mother of her two best friends in the world, and grandmother to her daughter. Her relationship with Mrs Hadley hadn't been the warmest, but that didn't alter the fact that this was a tragedy, which would no doubt affect all their lives.

CHAPTER SEVENTEEN

⁂

As promised, Carrie called in to Hawksdown Lodge each day after work, to spend time with Evie. Maisie was waiting for her on the second occasion.

'I'm working too many hours with everyone away. Miss Ada used to give me time off at weekends. Who am I supposed to speak to, now Mrs Hadley ain't around?'

Carrie glanced at Evie to see whether she was listening, and frowned at Maisie, who set her chin in a defiant way. 'Miss Hadley will be back in a week or so, I expect. In the meantime, I'm more than happy to take charge of Evie during the day at the weekend and you can have the time off.'

Maisie appeared mollified, for now. Carrie wondered whether anyone had told Evie that her grandmother was dead. It was a job for Ada or Jeremy, she decided. She would concentrate on making sure Evie was well entertained in their absence.

Maria provided picnic lunches for Saturday and Sunday, the weather being kind. Carrie thought she shouldn't take Evie away from home, though. Where would they go, other than to Castle Bay? Hawks Down was now an aerodrome and the beach lined with spools of barbed wire in many places. They would do just as well to make the most of what was on their doorstep.

They spent a good deal of time in the garden, picking flowers to fill the vases in the house. Carrie showed Evie how to press some of them, using two sheets of blotting paper she had taken from Mr Hadley's desk. She spread the flowers on one, placing the other on top. Then she sandwiched them between the pages of a newspaper and piled the heaviest books she could find in the library on top of that.

'You mustn't look until I tell you,' she warned Evie. 'A week at least, probably longer.'

They painted big, sploshy flowers onto watercolour paper that Carrie took from Ada's room. She was sure she wouldn't mind – Ada had entertained ideas of taking up painting before the war, but it had come to nothing.

She told Evie Poppet stories, while they lay on the picnic blanket, watching the clouds float over high in the sky. They went around the gardens with an empty jam jar, looking for insects. Carrie allowed Evie to keep a pale green caterpillar, mottled with black, in the jar overnight. They gave it lots of leaves to eat, before she covered the top of the jar with greaseproof paper begged from the kitchen. Carrie punched holes in the paper and secured it with an elastic band.

'Will it climb out in the night in my bedroom?' Evie was suddenly doubtful.

'The holes aren't big enough. It's just so that it can breathe,' Carrie explained.

To her relief, it was still alive on Sunday morning so she insisted they let it go, but a long way from the vegetable patch where they had found it.

On Sunday afternoon, Carrie let Evie take charge of the scoring while they patted the ball back and forth to each other on the tennis court. Evie's counting was erratic and it had reached 100/20 in Evie's favour when they heard the noise of a car's tyres on the drive.

Evie dropped her racquet and ran across the lawn, calling back to Carrie, 'It's Uncle Jeremy. And Auntie Ada. And Granddad!'

Carrie picked up the racquets and balls and returned them to the summerhouse, then took her time making her way to join them all. She was ill at ease – unsure how to express her condolences to Mr Hadley and suddenly worried in case they thought her presumptuous for being there. She could hear Evie's excited chatter as she drew closer, and Ada's occasional interjections of 'Goodness,' and 'How lovely.'

Ada, who was still sitting in the car with the door open, looked up at Carrie's approach. Carrie noticed the dark smudges under her eyes, but Ada gave her a bright smile and said, 'What a lovely time Evie's had. I've heard all about it. Thank you so much.'

Carrie reflected that it was odd, as Evie's mother, to be thanked in this way, then felt mean for the thought. She could tell her friend was exhausted.

Ada stood up. 'You must excuse Jeremy and Father. They've already gone inside. We're only here to collect a few things as we're going back tomorrow for the funeral.' She answered Carrie's unspoken question. 'We'll take Evie with us.'

Evie had run into the house in search of her beloved uncle Jeremy, so Carrie took the chance to say, 'I'm so very sorry, Ada. What a terrible shock for you all. If there's anything I can do . . .' She trailed off. 'I'm not sure whether Evie knows, by the way. She hasn't mentioned Granny, so I think she might suspect something, perhaps from overhearing Maria or Maisie talking. I didn't think it was my place to tell her.'

'Thank you, Carrie. So many people to tell.' Ada sighed. 'You know how it is, of course, having lost your own mother.'

Carrie could hardly say that there had been virtually no one to inform about her mother's death, or that she barely missed her. Instead she hugged Ada, telling her to go inside and that she would tidy up the picnic rug and leave. 'I hope the funeral goes well,' she added, thinking how inappropriate that sounded.

Ada waved a hand in acknowledgement as she went up the steps, leaving Carrie to clear up as promised, then collect her bicycle to return home. She felt a little cheated out of the rest of a precious afternoon with Evie, then grew angry with herself for having such uncharitable thoughts. When would they return to Hawksdown Lodge? she wondered. If the funeral was early the following week, perhaps they'd be back by the next weekend. She hoped so, anyway. Her life would be very empty without them.

CHAPTER EIGHTEEN

During the first week of the Hadleys' absence in late June, Carrie called in to Hawksdown Lodge daily, then reduced it to two or three times a week, always greeted by an apologetic shake of the head from Maria.

'Nothing, Carrie, I'm sorry. No news about when they're coming back.'

By August, she'd dropped her visits to weekly and was contemplating stopping altogether. The garden looked more unkempt each time she called, the picnic area long since overgrown, the few remaining roses borne on straggly stems, heaps of browning petals pooling in the flowerbeds. She missed Evie more than she could bear, plagued by memories of her daughter snuggling in her lap, warm head resting against her, wide brown eyes turned up towards her every now and then; her small, trusting hand grasping Carrie's as they walked together round the garden; her regular cries of 'Look, Carrie, look!' It felt as though Evie's ghost ran around the lawns every time Carrie visited. Had her worst fears been realised, and the family permanently removed themselves to London? And, if not, how much would Evie have changed when she came back?

It was a warm Saturday at the end of August when Carrie made one more visit to Hawksdown Lodge. She'd all but decided against doing so earlier that day, but it was one of the very few things she had to fill her weekend. She'd decided to walk over rather than cycle because it would take up more time.

She was surprised when her knock at the door was answered by a beaming Maria. 'Mr Hadley is back. Mr Jeremy, that is. He's asked me to let him know when you arrive. If you wait in the drawing room, I'll fetch him.'

'Where is he?' Carrie asked, surprise making her heart beat uncomfortably hard.

'He walked down the garden to the vegetable patch, I think.'

'I'll go and find him,' Carrie called over her shoulder as she ran down the steps. Had anyone else returned? She saw him, poking around in the foliage growing against the garden wall. He turned at her approach and waited for her to join him.

'Look, Carrie, peaches,' he said, pointing at the fruit hanging from the branches trained to grow flat against the wall. 'I must pick them before they're ruined.'

Carrie, puzzled by his behaviour, didn't know what to say. He'd been away for weeks, and he greeted her by talking about peaches?

Then he turned to her with a smile. 'I was remembering the picnic on Hawks Down, with Oscar. How you'd never tasted a peach before.' He reached out and plucked one from the tree, presenting it to her. It held the warmth from the sun as it rested in her palm, and she sniffed its wonderful, distinctive aroma.

'It's been too long, Carrie. I've missed you.' Jeremy was talking to the wall, gathering more peaches and laying them gently in a basket at his feet.

'How are you? Is anyone with you? Ada, your father, Evie?' Carrie felt sure she was gabbling.

'Not yet. I had to get back to work. They'll come in another week or so.' Jeremy looked at her. 'You seem disappointed, Carrie.'

How could she explain to him that it was Evie she longed to see above all? She couldn't, not without making him wonder at her reasons. So she said, 'I've missed you all, so much. It's been very quiet. I've been calling in regularly, hoping for news. Maria probably told you.'

'She did.' Jeremy smiled. 'Shall we sit and eat some of these?' He pointed to a bench that was in danger of being overwhelmed by the ivy overhanging the wall, then limped over and set the basket on the seat. Carrie followed him and they sat down, biting into the fruit, the juice threatening to dribble from hand to wrist to sleeve.

'There's a tap here, somewhere.' Jeremy looked around, then spotted it half hidden by the ivy. He rinsed his hands then returned with his handkerchief, soaked, for Carrie to use.

'What have you been doing in London? After your mother's funeral?' It seemed to Carrie as though all the ease they had once enjoyed in each other's company had slipped away in their weeks apart. The evenings by the fire, just the two of them, might never have taken place.

'Father needed a lot of support.' Jeremy had picked up another peach and bitten into it. 'He was angry over what had happened – well, very upset but it came out as anger towards the hospital. Then there were relatives to see, paperwork to sort out, things at the bank.'

'And Ada? And Evie? What did they do?'

Jeremy frowned. 'I suppose Ada took charge of running the household. And Evie went to the park most days with Maisie. I don't really know.' He stopped, then burst out, 'I hated it there, in town. It was too busy, too noisy, too dirty. I just wanted to be back here, working at the aerodrome, seeing you each evening, listening to you tell Poppet stories to Evie.'

'Has she asked about me?' Carrie couldn't stop herself.

'Every day.' Jeremy laughed. 'I'd have brought her back with me, but I couldn't abide the idea of having to bring Maisie, as well. I couldn't tell her I was coming here. I know she misses it, too.'

He held out another peach to Carrie but she shook her head, unwilling to face the stickiness. She thought Jeremy must have dropped something, for he suddenly lowered himself on one knee, clutching her leg for balance so that, startled, she gasped.

'Carrie, will you marry me? Please? The war is all but done, I'm sure of it. There's no one I'd rather have at my side for whatever lies ahead. I've been thinking about it non-stop while I've been away. We could bring up Evie as our own. With Mother gone, and Ada talking about studying to be a nurse, she won't have anyone, other than Maisie.' Jeremy paused. 'I'll have to get up now. It hurts too much to be on my knees like this.' He offered a smile, but Carrie could see the anxiety in his eyes as she helped him up.

When he was settled back on the bench, he turned to her. 'Well?' he asked. 'You haven't said a word. Should I be worried?'

Carrie's heart was racing. What if she said yes? Now that Mrs Hadley was dead, did Jeremy really need to know the truth about Evie, about her and Oscar? The brief moment of hope that flooded her was quickly quashed. She couldn't live a lie. It would eat away at her and at some point in the future something unforeseen would expose the truth.

'I can't, Jeremy,' Carrie said. 'I can't explain why. I'm so sorry. Nothing's really changed.'

Jeremy must have seen her hesitation, her indecision.

'Is it because of this?' He indicated his damaged leg, his mouth twisted into a bitter grimace.

'No!' Carrie was filled with horror. 'Of course it isn't.'

He looked unconvinced. 'Then, what?'

Carrie swallowed hard. Yet again, Jeremy had just offered her the very thing she most longed for in the world and, because of her own folly in the past, she'd been forced to turn him down. Although, of course, if she hadn't made such a mistake, Evie wouldn't have existed – which was unthinkable – and none of this would be happening.

'I love you,' she said simply. 'Truly, I do.' There, she had spoken her truth aloud. She saw the flash of hope on his face. 'But I'm not worthy of you, of your love.' A tear rolled down her cheek and she brushed it away irritably. Now was not the moment for self-pity. 'I – we– haven't been honest with you.'

He gave her a sharp look.

'About Evie, that is. You see, I'm her mother.' Carrie bit her lip as she saw Jeremy's expression change. She rushed on. 'It was just the once.' She closed her eyes at the memory of the hotel in Dover. 'Oscar never knew he was going to be a father. When your mother found out, she said she would bring up the child as one of the family. It wouldn't want for anything and I could still visit every now and then, as the godmother.'

She didn't dare look at Jeremy to see how he was taking this.

'I would have kept the baby for my own if I could but I had nowhere to live and I had to work … I'm so sorry. I wasn't allowed to tell anyone. I had to let you believe what your mother told you.'

She was trying hard not to speak ill of Mrs Hadley now she was gone, but the memories of her casual cruelties flooded back. How she appeared to lose interest as soon as Evie was born, handing over all her care to a nursemaid. Carrie would always remember the words of the farmer's wife. Mrs Hadley had wanted the baby to be a boy. And then there were the absences in London, and the restrictions on Carrie's visits. But Jeremy was speaking and she was forced to look at him.

'How dare you?' he asked. His face was suffused with rage and he could barely get his words out. 'All of you! I can't understand it. Was it because I'd been ill? Did you think telling me the truth would be too shocking, that it would cause a relapse?'

344

He was working himself up, Carrie could see. She put out her hand to touch his arm but he shook her off.

'Get off me! To think I fell in love with you. You're nothing but a cheap—' He stopped abruptly.

Carrie, filled with hurt and distress, didn't know what to do other than leap to her feet and run, tears blinding her. If only she'd brought her bicycle. She could have pedalled away somewhere – anywhere – and no one would have been able to see how upset she was. Grove Lane was, thankfully, quiet, and she turned into the little park that lay one street away from the school, hoping to gather her thoughts and compose herself before she went home. Agitated, she walked quickly around the park, then sat down on a bench.

Would she ever be able to see Evie again? And Jeremy – could she face him after the way he had reacted? She ran over the scene in her head – there were so many things she now wished she had said. If only Mrs Hadley hadn't decreed that Evie's true origins should be kept a secret. It would have been better if Jeremy had known the truth from the start. The thought of what she'd lost filled her with despair and she buried her head in her hands, tears seeping between her fingers. It was only when the park keeper came along the path, ringing his bell to warn of closing time, that she stood up wearily and began to make her way home.

CHAPTER NINETEEN

‹❦›

In the coming days, Carrie was tortured by the clumsy way in which she had turned down Jeremy's proposal, and by his reaction to her explanation. She longed to be able to ease the hurt she had inflicted and explain further, but it was impossible. She could only hope she hadn't inflicted yet more damage on his already troubled mind. It was an effort to get through each day: her spirit was crushed by all that had been said. She felt unable to visit Hawksdown Lodge, even though she was desperate to see whether or not Evie had returned. If Ada had stayed in London, as Jeremy had suggested, it would make sense for Evie to stay there, too. It was a thought she could hardly bear.

Matron, in the end, was the surprising source of the information she sought about the whereabouts of the family. She'd called in to the office to speak to Sir Charles and had stopped by Carrie's desk as she left. 'I'll be glad to see your friend back with us next week,' she said. Taking in the surprise on Carrie's face, she added, 'You didn't know?'

'No,' Carrie said. 'I'd heard she was thinking of staying in London and studying nursing. I didn't expect to see her back here.'

'Well, she telephoned yesterday. I gather the family is nervous about the influenza outbreak and feel they would be safer here.' Matron frowned. 'I only hope they don't bring any infection with them.' She swept away down the corridor, leaving Carrie to stare at her typewriter, filled with astonishment and hope.

She didn't dare call in at Hawksdown Lodge at the weekend, even though they must surely have returned. She must be patient and wait until she saw Ada at the hospital, then ask her whether she might visit Evie. She feared awkwardness with Jeremy, but it would have to be overcome.

Monday dawned, one of those September days that starts with a chill in the air but produces blazing blue skies and hot sunshine by lunchtime. Ada appeared at Carrie's desk in the late afternoon.

'You're back!' Carrie wanted to jump up and hug her friend but felt restrained by her uniform and the formality of a work situation. 'I felt sure you would stay in London and Jeremy seemed to think so, too. But here you are. Is your father back? And Evie, too?'

'Yes, we're all home. London began to feel too dangerous, with the flu epidemic, and after Mother . . .' Ada's face clouded. 'I must get back to my duties, but I wondered whether you would call in after work one evening? Evie is longing to see you.'

'I've missed her so,' Carrie said, her voice sounding tremulous to her ears. 'I could come tonight?' Did that sound over-eager? But Ada would understand.

Ada, already half out of the door, nodded and Carrie went back to her work. It was a struggle to focus for the rest of the working day. The clock hands seemed to creep around the dial, and she dreaded being given an urgent piece of typing at the last minute. At five o'clock on the dot, she pushed back her chair, picked up her bag and forced her arms into the sleeves of her jacket as she hurried from the room.

She waited outside for Ada. They hadn't arranged to meet, but if they walked to Hawksdown Lodge together, she could catch up on any news. Ten minutes passed, then another ten before Carrie, conscious of time passing and the approach of Evie's bedtime, was about to set off when Ada came out, almost running.

'Sorry,' she gasped. 'Last-minute problem. How are you, Carrie? What have you been doing?'

Carrie didn't know what to tell her. The answer was very little, other than work, but she said, 'I saw Jeremy and he said you were planning to stay in London and study nursing once the war is over.'

'I'd like to,' Ada replied, 'but now isn't the right time. Jeremy hated it in London, Evie was unhappy there and Father became so worried about the flu that it made no sense to stay. So here we are – for the time being. At least I'm getting good experience while I'm volunteering at St Aidan's.'

Carrie presumed Jeremy hadn't said anything of what had passed between them, since Ada mentioned his name quite easily. They had arrived at the gate to Hawksdown Lodge and Carrie walked through it with mixed feelings. She was excited to see Evie but worried at the thought of Jeremy's reaction.

Ada opened the front door and stepped into the hall, just as Jeremy was passing through.

'How was your day?' he asked.

'Busy,' she replied, pulling off her jacket and gloves, then standing aside to let Carrie enter, too.

Jeremy looked at her, nodded, and walked on. Carrie wished the earth could open up and swallow her. He'd cut her dead and now Ada was frowning in puzzlement.

'Have you two quarrelled?' she asked.

Carrie swallowed. What on earth could she say? A squeal from the top of the stairs saved her replying. Evie had spotted her and, before Maisie could protest, she ran down the stairs, dressed only in her underclothes. Carrie saw at once her legs had grown longer and lost their chubbiness. Her face was thinner and had changed shape, too. But she was still her lovely Evie and Carrie scooped her up, exclaiming, 'My goodness, how you've grown. It must be the London air. You'll soon be as tall as me.'

She knew she was talking nonsense, but it was all she could do not to break down in tears at the sight of her beautiful daughter after all these weeks.

'The London air is horrid and dirty and full of germs,' Evie said vehemently.

'Evie!' Ada said reprovingly.

'It's true. Granddad said so.'

'Goodness, you're heavy,' Carrie said, to change the subject. 'I'm going to have to put you down.'

She set her on the floor gently and Evie began to tug her towards the drawing room. 'Will you tell me a Poppet story? I've missed them so. Where's Uncle Jeremy? He'll want to listen, too.'

Carrie's heart sank. How could she visit Evie and avoid Jeremy – or have him avoid her – without causing upset?

Ada spoke up. 'Evie, Maisie's waiting for you. Go back upstairs and have your bath. Carrie will still be here once you're in your nightclothes. She can tell you a story then.'

The protesting Evie was persuaded back up the stairs and Ada ushered Carrie into the drawing room, shutting the door behind her.

'Carrie, there's something wrong. What is it? I can tell by the look on your face.'

Carrie couldn't help herself – she burst into tears. Everything she'd held in – how she'd missed Evie, how she'd found herself drawn to Jeremy, his attempts to woo her, her turning away from him, the proposal, the shock and upset of the aftermath – welled up and poured out in incoherent sobs. It made little sense to Ada, who tried to soothe her, saying, 'There, there,' occasionally and patting her back. Carrie lapsed into shuddering sighs interspersed with occasional sobs, then stopped altogether.

'I didn't understand much of that.' Ada was apologetic. 'Something about Evie and the hospital, Jeremy and me being in London, and you and Jeremy— Oh!' She stopped. 'I've been dense, haven't I? You and Jeremy – I didn't think. I never realised. Oh, Carrie.'

Carrie, deeply ashamed, hovered on the brink of further tears. What would Ada think of her? Entanglements with both of her brothers, and a child among it all.

'You've turned him down and he's upset with you.' Ada was following her own line of reasoning. 'Well, he'll have to know, won't he? With Mother gone, I don't see any point in carrying on with that silly cover-up.'

Before Carrie could speak, to say that she had already told him, there was a knock at the door and Maisie ushered Evie into the room. Carrie hurried to the window and stared, unseeing, into the garden. Her face was hot and wet, her eyes no doubt red and she felt shaky. She heard Ada say, 'Carrie's not feeling well. She'll tell you a Poppet story another day instead.'

Evie began to wail and Carrie, without turning around, said, 'It's all right. Honestly. I can still tell her a story.' She held out her hand, without looking back.

Evie ran across the room, tucking her small hand into Carrie's. 'Shall I tell you a Poppet story instead, to make you feel better?'

Evie's thoughtfulness nearly triggered another bout of sobbing. Carrie risked sneaking a look at her daughter, fearful of upsetting her. Evie didn't seem at all put out by her tear-blotched face so she gave her a wobbly smile and said, 'That would be lovely. I can't think of anything better.'

CHAPTER TWENTY

Evie's Poppet story, a rambling mix of several of Carrie's, served the purpose of making Carrie smile again. She managed a quick new story about how excited Poppet was to be back at Hawksdown Lodge, before Maisie appeared to announce bedtime, standing firm against all pleas for 'just one more story'.

Carrie resisted Ada's attempts to persuade her to stay once Evie had departed. 'I'll see you at St Aidan's,' she said, almost pushing past her friend in her haste to be gone. She feared seeing Jeremy again and was worried that Ada would try to broker some sort of peace between them. She was still shaken by her emotional outpouring and wished for nothing more than to retreat to her room in Castle Bay and think it over.

It wasn't until Wednesday that she crossed paths again with Ada at the hospital, by which time she had recovered her equilibrium.

'Can you wait for me after work? We can walk part of the way home together.' Ada was in a hurry, and it was said in passing. She was unsmiling and Carrie's heart sank. It didn't look as though she had good news to impart.

Her premonition proved correct. Ada barely waited until Carrie had retrieved her bicycle, wheeling it along as they walked, before she burst out, 'Jeremy is insufferable. I began to tell him about Evie, that you were her mother, not her godmother, and that Oscar was her father and he flew into a rage with me. He said he already knew, that you had told him, and asked whether we thought he was a child to have hidden the truth from him. I explained that it was Mother who had insisted on the cover-up, but he just carried on ranting about how foolish he felt, now he'd discovered that everyone apart from him knew the truth. I'm afraid you didn't escape, either.'

Ada cast a sideways glance at Carrie. 'I'm sorry, but it's better you know. He said you had encouraged him to fall for you, that you'd taken advantage of him when he was at his most vulnerable in hospital.' She stopped. 'And some not very nice things besides, but he spoke in anger.'

Carrie was stung. 'I didn't encourage him to fall for me,' she protested. 'Quite the opposite. I hid my feelings from him and discouraged him. When he persisted, I told him that your mother would never approve of a match between us, that she would want someone from a suitable family.' She stopped walking suddenly and Ada, who didn't notice at first, had to take a few steps back to join her.

'You mustn't believe what he said,' Carrie pleaded. 'When I visited him daily in hospital my only thought was to help him, Oscar's brother, get better. I hated having to hide it from you all because you weren't allowed inside, but I told myself I could at least be a friendly face. I didn't do that to make him fall in love with me. Or for personal gain.'

Despair washed over Carrie. How could she explain that her motives were entirely innocent, if Jeremy had decided the opposite? And how would all this affect her chances of maintaining contact with Evie?

'Well,' Ada said, as they resumed walking, 'I've told him that you still need to see Evie and he'll just have to make himself scarce if he doesn't want to see you.'

The light drizzle that had begun to fall as they left St Aidan's became heavier rain. Ada turned up her coat collar in an attempt to shield herself and, as she did so, skidded on the pavement. The leaves had begun to fall, becoming slippery in the rain and impossible to see in the gloom.

They walked a little way in silence, picking up their pace once they reached the flat surface of Grove Lane. As they neared Hawksdown Lodge, Ada returned to their previous conversation. 'I've told Jeremy you'll come to see Evie every Wednesday evening, starting next week, and we can work out how to manage a visit every other weekend, too.'

Carrie was glad that the dusk made it hard for Ada to see her face. A visit just once a week would be hard after the freedom of the summer, but it was better than nothing, especially after the family's absence of several weeks. She would make the best of it, so she thanked Ada, got onto her bicycle and pedalled away.

She was relieved, she supposed, that Jeremy knew the true state of things, but she hated him to think badly of her. It was just one more thing to bear, somehow made harder by the fact that winter was approaching. How she longed for better things.

The Wednesday visits were eagerly awaited by both Carrie and Evie. There was never any sign of Jeremy, and as the weeks passed, Carrie stopped worrying that he might appear and confront her over what he perceived as her deviousness. She was relieved by his ongoing absence, yet a part of her longed to see him, too.

Spirits lifted at St Aidan's, and throughout the country, as autumn progressed and talk turned to the end of the war. Carrie didn't trust the news at first, but Sir Charles insisted that everything pointed to an Allied victory, as the German forces suffered defeat after defeat. By the end of October, she dared to believe it was true.

They celebrated Armistice Day at the hospital on 11 November, with flags and cheers and great joy among the men, who now knew they wouldn't face being sent back to war. Carrie heard there were parades and celebrations in all the big towns and cities – even in Castle Bay, where people gathered on the seafront outside Broad Castle, overjoyed by no longer living in fear of what lay across the water. She felt a pang not to be part of those bigger celebrations, but she was happy enough to spend the day with the men who had received their injuries helping bring an end to the war.

Two days later, she visited Hawksdown Lodge, to find the atmosphere different there, too. Maria was wreathed in smiles when she opened the door to Carrie, surprising her by spontaneously embracing her. 'I hope you don't mind,' she said, 'but it's been such a long war. I'm so happy it's over.' She was still smiling, but Carrie could see the glint of tears in her eyes as she hugged her back.

'Go into the drawing room, please,' she said. 'Evie is there. Miss Ada is upstairs but will be down directly.'

Smiling in anticipation of seeing her daughter, Carrie opened the drawing-room door. Her attention was caught by a doll's house, painted pink and set on the table near the window. Evie was busy putting furniture into it and looked around as the door opened. To Carrie's horror, Jeremy was there too, sitting beside Evie.

CHAPTER TWENTY-ONE

Carrie, mindful of Evie, had to erase the distress from her face. 'What a lovely doll's house,' she said. 'You're a lucky girl, Evie.'

She focused her gaze on it, a simple box shape with a front that swung open to reveal the four rooms inside, two up and two down, and a central wooden staircase. The windows opened by turning tiny metal rings, another forming a knocker on the front door. There were roses painted around the door frame, and she could see patterned wallpaper on the inside walls, that looked not only familiar but also out of scale. Was this yet another expensive present for Evie, bought from a London toy shop?

'Look, Carrie.' Evie was pointing into the house and patting the seat beside her, so Carrie had no option. She had to sit down, thankful that Evie was between her and Jeremy, who nevertheless felt too close for comfort. 'Uncle Jeremy made it,' Evie said, beaming.

'You did?' Carrie's surprise at Evie's words meant she forgot her awkwardness to look straight at Jeremy over her daughter's head. 'I didn't know you were a carpenter.'

Jeremy laughed. 'Hardly. It was very straightforward. I enjoyed it. I might start a business now the war is over.'

He winked at Carrie and, despite herself, she laughed. She felt a rush of relief that his anger seemed to have gone and, delighted, she gave Evie a squeeze. It was a way of expressing her feelings.

Although she gave all her attention to Evie and the doll's house over the next hour, she couldn't help being aware of Jeremy's closeness. Several times their hands brushed against each other as they moved the furniture around at Evie's command; each time Carrie, conscious of the contact, pulled away.

'Who will live in the house?' Carrie asked Evie.

'Mice,' Evie replied, without hesitation. 'A family of mice.'

'Oh, no!' Carrie exclaimed. 'They'll gnaw the furniture and make a mess everywhere.'

Evie stared at her. 'Not real mice,' she said.

'Oh.' Carrie was at a loss. Then she had an idea. 'I could make you some mice,' she said. She was imagining them already: just a couple of inches high, mother mouse in a floral apron and father mouse in a jacket, the little ones without clothes but wearing bows on their heads or around their necks perhaps. She was mentally rummaging through her workbox for scraps of suitable fabric – she could use some brown flannel from a skirt ruined by her bicycle chain to make their bodies and heads. And she was sure she had saved some plain and patterned fabric pieces that had proved too small to turn into anything useful.

'When can you do it? Tomorrow?' Evie was delighted with the idea.

'No, Evie.' Carrie was laughing. 'I have to go to work tomorrow. Perhaps I'll make them at the weekend and I can bring them next week.'

It looked as though Evie's patience wouldn't stretch that far. She began to pout, and tears threatened until Jeremy promised he would make mouse beds for them, to be ready for their arrival. Another storm was averted, when Maisie arrived to announce bath time, by the promise of a Poppet and mouse story once Evie was in her nightclothes.

Carrie feared a return of frostiness from Jeremy as soon as Evie had gone, but he talked quite naturally about the aerodrome and their Armistice Day celebrations. In no time at all, an impatient Evie was returned to them after her bath and Carrie, feeling self-conscious, launched into her story. It was a long time since Jeremy had listened in. Evie was persuaded up to bed with kisses and promises that next time Carrie visited she would bring two members of the mouse family at the very least.

'Can't you come before next Wednesday?' Evie's plaintive voice as Maisie ushered her from the room caused Carrie briefly to close her eyes. How to explain the complications of their arrangements to an impatient three-and-a-half-year-old?

A brief silence followed her departure, then Carrie stood up. 'Goodnight, Jeremy. Please tell Ada I'm sorry to have missed her but I'll no doubt see her at the hospital.'

'Why don't you come back before Wednesday?' Jeremy asked.

Carrie frowned. Surely he and Ada had discussed the arrangement.

'I mean, why don't you come at the weekend? With or without mice.'

Carrie shook her head. 'Evie would be so disappointed if I came empty-handed. I won't have anything ready before Sunday afternoon, anyway.' She was going to add, 'And in any case, I'm not supposed to, as you well know,' but it seemed churlish, when Jeremy was disposed to be pleasant.

'Carrie, I'm sorry. I should never have said the things I did to you, and to Ada when she tried to intervene. I suppose she told you?' Jeremy raised a quizzical eyebrow.

Carrie nodded, silent.

'It was wrong of me. I spoke without thinking. I was angry, and perhaps hurt. Once I'd got over the shock, I saw what a terrible position this family had put you in. First Oscar, then Mother. I've had plenty of time to see how wrong I was.' Jeremy gazed at the floor, then looked up at Carrie. 'I don't think I would ever have got better if you hadn't taken such good care of me at the hospital. I don't mean nursing me. I mean taking care of my thoughts – my mind.'

Carrie attempted to speak but Jeremy rushed on: 'I can only think my reason hasn't fully recovered. Why would I have believed you set out to trap me when you refused me – more than once? You told me you couldn't marry me. Only my twisted mind, and hurt pride, if I'm honest, could have made me think badly of you.'

There was a silence, longer this time, which Carrie hardly dared break.

'The thing is, Carrie, my feelings haven't changed. Now that I've put those ridiculous thoughts out of my head, I know I still love you. I don't care what happened between you and Oscar. And I should never have spoken to you as I did about that. It was unforgivable. I felt foolish and I was lashing out.'

Jeremy was on his feet now, standing with his back to the fireplace, a contrite expression on his face. 'Nothing would make me happier than you agreeing to be my wife, and for Evie to live with us as our daughter.'

Carrie, hardly able to comprehend what she was hearing, began to weep. Jeremy was stricken. 'I'm sorry – I've upset you again. I hurt you, then I expect you to forgive me and agree to be my wife, when what do I have to offer you? I'm nothing but a clumsy fool.'

Carrie began to weep even harder, just as the door opened and Ada came into the room. She halted on the threshold when she saw Carrie's tears.

'Is everything all right?' she asked, concerned. She looked at Jeremy and annoyance crept over her face. 'You've upset her.' It came out as an accusation.

'No, I mean, yes. Everything is all right.' Carrie found her voice. 'After four very long years, everything is very much all right.' She went over to Jeremy and took his hand. 'You have so much to offer, Jeremy. Don't ever believe otherwise. Nothing would make me happier than to say yes.' She paused. 'But there is something else you should know.'

It was only as the full import of Jeremy's words struck home that she had remembered one final barrier to her happiness, and potentially to Jeremy's, too.

'If we married, there couldn't be – that is to say, I can't have – any more children.' She swallowed hard and waited.

Jeremy, whose expression had changed from joyful to apprehensive in a matter of moments, looked relieved. 'I think Evie – and Poppet – will make quite enough of a family for us, don't you?'

Ada, observing Carrie's tremulous smile and the look that passed between her and Jeremy, quietly withdrew from the room.

Evie would, at last be with her own mother, Jeremy would have a wife who understood him and who would care for him, no matter what the future held. And Carrie, after so much heartache, had the Hadley brother she deserved, the one who would love her in the best possible way.

PART FOUR

JOSEPH: 1817

CHAPTER ONE

Joseph, sitting on a low wall on Folkestone waterfront, was soaking up what he could of the March sunshine while ignoring the brisk wind coming off the sea. He didn't notice the strong fishy aroma, either. It wasn't as if he didn't experience both of them most days when he was fishing. Today, though, his boat was pulled up on the shingle around half a mile away and he was watching the comings and goings at the fish market. Barrows and wooden tables, piled with heaps of cockles and whelks, oysters, crabs and silver-skinned fish were all crammed into a small cobbled area on the quayside.

A few children darted between the stalls, stooping every now and then to pick up something. Joseph couldn't be sure what it was: he saw a gleam between the fingers of the child closest to him – fish scales? Or a coin that had slipped from the hands of a customer? He idly watched the child – a girl, he thought, from the long hair, although the clothes she was bundled up in gave no clue. Around three years old, he decided.

He lifted his gaze from the market and the waterfront to the surroundings of the town. Folkestone was very different from Castle Bay: cliffs sloped down to the shore and a Martello tower sat high on the eastern cliff, facing France. The narrow streets of the town rose steeply behind him, crowded with inns and taverns close to the water's edge, shops and cramped houses taking their place the higher you climbed.

Could he make his home there? Joseph wondered. It was busy down here along the quay, unlike Castle Bay, which had fallen on hard times once Napoleon had been vanquished and the soldiers had departed from the barracks. Until they left, Joseph hadn't realised how much business they had brought to the town. He'd experienced a brief moment of prosperity, supplying fish to the barracks' kitchen. He was glad he'd been careful with the money he'd earned – the business was gone as swiftly as it had arrived. And when his father died, carried away by a cough he couldn't shake off, Joseph had found nothing to keep him in Castle Bay.

He'd taken his boat up and down the coast, scratching a living where he could and finding little favour among the established fishermen, who'd lived in the same spot for generations and vigorously protected their fishing rights. Joseph had skill in finding and catching fish, that much he knew. If he could find the right place to settle, he'd do well for himself once more. But he hadn't found that place yet.

The stocks on the tables at the fish market had dwindled as the morning went on. The stallholders had been there since dawn, no doubt, and now they began to pack up, calling out reduced prices for whatever remained. The small child he'd noticed earlier was standing beside one of the barrows where a woman was sluicing water over the surface and scrubbing it vigorously with a brush. The child held out her palm and the woman bent over to see what was there. As she did so, Joseph caught the flash of mother-of-pearl from a shell, threaded on a leather lace, as it swung free from the neck of her blouse. He stared, startled by the sight. He'd given just such a thing to Meg, whom he'd once hoped would be his sweetheart. Instead, she'd been murdered, her bones buried in the quarry at the back of Hawksdown Castle.

He remembered the night she had gone missing only too well.

He had revisited it many times in his mind. He'd been aware that Meg had had secret meetings with Bartholomew Banks, the Lord Warden's son who lived at the castle, and was filled with jealousy. He'd seen him waiting for her outside the Fountain late at night, watched them walk away together. He couldn't stop himself following her when, late one evening, he saw her slipping through the streets, although it was torture to him. He'd taken care to stay in the shadows as she hurried through the lanes and alleyways. She'd taken the sea path out towards Hawksdown Castle, and he'd tracked the light of her lantern for as long as he could, until it vanished. He assumed she'd met Bartholomew then and, filled with rage at his own stupidity, he'd turned back to town.

It wasn't until he'd returned from his fishing trip the next day, stopping by the Fountain to quench his thirst, that he'd heard the news. Meg Marsh had gone missing. There was a rumour going around that she'd been seized by the Kingsdown gang, the smugglers from the next village along. It was said they wanted her for her contacts with the French fabric trade, having a mind to break into it themselves.

He waited until daylight the next day, then retraced his steps from the night he'd followed her, until he found her lantern set down beside the path. He'd feared the worst then. Were the rumours true? Had she been snatched from the path? Why hadn't she returned to collect the lantern if she was able to do so?

He'd gone to see Meg's family, to ask whether they'd heard from her. He'd found them in the kitchen, haggard as though they had barely slept or eaten. When he showed them the lantern and told them where he'd found it, Mrs Marsh had burst into tears.

'She's never spent as much as a night away from this house in all her seventeen years. To have left us without a word – I knew something wasn't right.'

Hesitant, Joseph mentioned the rumours that she might have

been taken by the Kingsdown gang. He didn't share with them what he knew of them, their vicious reputation and evil ways.

Eliza, sitting at the table with Samuel and Thomas on either side of her, shook her head. 'That doesn't make sense to me. She'd have been on her way to see Bartholomew. Even though he wanted nothing more to do with her, he was expecting her to bring goods to Hawksdown Castle so he could impress the fine ladies. And she needed the money, so she couldn't say no.'

Mrs Marsh, brow creased into a frown, looked as though she was about to speak but Joseph got in first. 'I thought she and Bartholomew . . .' He couldn't finish the sentence. It would reveal too much, how he'd spied on Meg over the previous months.

Eliza shook her head. 'Dropped her, didn't he, when he announced his marriage to that Eustacia Blythe? I wonder whether he found out about the baby . . .' A look of horror crossed her face. She was blushing. Thomas looked puzzled. Samuel was staring at the table, and Joseph couldn't read Mrs Marsh's expression.

Joseph bade them a hasty farewell, but Mrs Marsh barely waited for him to close the door behind him before she began to shout, 'Smuggled goods? I thought all that had stopped. What have I told you all? What was Meg thinking?'

That night, the story circulating in the Fountain had changed. Someone's cousin's neighbour had it on good authority that the Kingsdown gang hadn't taken Meg Marsh. But they had been asked by someone important in the town – no names were mentioned but everyone knew it was the Lord Warden's son – to get rid of an inconvenience to him. Dead and buried in the quarry at Hawksdown Castle was the verdict and, since Meg never came back and there were no rumoured sightings, the story stuck.

Joseph stayed away from the Marsh family, not sure what consolation he could bring to them. The knowledge of Meg's death – the horror of it – had played a part in his resolve to leave the area. He kept wondering what might have happened if he hadn't given up following her that night once her lantern light had vanished. What would he have heard or seen if he'd stayed on the sea path? Could he have prevented it?

He'd thought that, by moving away, he could lose the memory. And, slowly, he had – until that day.

CHAPTER TWO

⌘

When Joseph broke free of his memories, the market was all but over. Only two barrows remained, and the sun had gone, replaced by threatening clouds borne on the strong wind. The woman who had sparked his reverie had gone, too, taking her child and the barrow with her. Joseph, chilled and stiff from sitting, walked briskly up into the town. He explored a little further than the main street and, seeing the humble dwellings in the back streets, and the shops with little to offer for sale, he soon realised that, once away from the harbour, it was little more prosperous than Castle Bay. Perhaps he wouldn't stay, after all, but would take his boat further south and try his luck at the next town, or the next.

He returned to the inn, where he'd planned to spend one or two nights, and sat in the corner of the bar with his ale and a beef pie. He listened to the conversations around him without feeling the need to be drawn into them, then climbed the creaking wooden stairs to his shared bedroom. His fellow guest snored through the night and that, with his thoughts, kept Joseph from sleep until just before dawn. Woken shortly after by the noisy ablutions of his roommate, he put his pillow over his head in an attempt to gain another hour's sleep but to no avail. The quay below had come to life, resounding with shouts, dogs barking and gulls screaming, while doors banged in the inn and raised voices sounded in the yard.

His thoughts returned, as they had throughout the night, to the woman he had seen in the market, the shell on a lace around her neck, the child. He hadn't seen their faces, but he had caught a glimpse of the woman's hair. Her shawl had been over it, in an effort to keep at bay the persistent wind that plagued the seafront, but he remembered it was dark. The child had fairer hair: dirty, he thought, but lighter in colour. Even though he told himself that no doubt plenty of women living by the sea wore mother-of-pearl shells around their necks, he couldn't shake off the conviction it was Meg. He needed to see the woman again, to put his mind at rest.

He hauled himself from the bed and set about a cursory wash. Then he went downstairs and sought out the landlord, to ask whether the fish market took place each day. A shake of the head dashed his hopes.

'Next one's Friday,' the landlord said. 'Twice a week – Tuesdays and Fridays. You'll be staying on?'

Joseph shook his head. He saw little point in spending good money on a night like the one he'd just had. He'd rather sleep in his boat, although it was too early in the year for that to be practical. He postponed his plan to sail on around the coast and, after he'd paid a visit to his boat to check all was intact, he returned to the town to make the steep climb up the hill.

He'd seen a sign – rooms for rent – in the window of a tall house near the top of the street. By breakfast time, he'd taken one for a few days. He needed to fill his time until Friday, so he decided to explore, walking up and out of the town. He was enticed by the cliffs, Castle Bay being surrounded by flat land. It was only as he was treading the cliff path, stopping every now and then to take in the view, that he wondered whether he might have found the woman he sought somewhere in the streets of the town that day. He cursed himself for a fool, until he reminded himself he'd be assured of success at Friday's market. Then he concentrated on his enjoyment of the springy turf under his feet, the skylarks soaring above him, pouring out their song, and, far below, the sea busy with the comings and goings of small boats.

Friday, though, did not bring the resolution he hoped for. Early that morning, he strode down the hill to the quay, filled with excited anticipation. The market was already bustling when he arrived, but there was no sign of the woman and child he sought. Thinking they might have set up in a different spot, he walked up and down and round the edges, but with no luck. He asked one or two stallholders about them, but the answer was the same: a shrug of the shoulders and a shake of the head. Only one, who was less busy, having already sold most of her stock of shellfish, offered an insight.

'There's different folk here on Tuesdays. Me, I'm only here Fridays. I'm in Sandgate Tuesday, Hythe Saturday.'

Joseph thanked her, with a sinking heart. It hadn't occurred to him that the stallholders were anything other than local. Maybe the woman he sought didn't live in Folkestone after all. It was pointless staying any longer. He'd explored the town and the area around it, spent more money than he should on lodgings and food and earned not a penny. He'd have to spend the same sum again if he stayed. He should take his boat and leave, just as he'd planned.

But even as his reason told him to go, another part of him resisted. The wind had got up and he'd heard talk on the quay that a storm was coming. It was no time to take off into coastal waters he didn't know, he decided. He'd do better to wait it out and set off when it was more settled.

It was Monday before the wind eased a little and the lashing rain gave way to sunshine. The sea was no longer a seething mass of white-capped waves. He should move on, Joseph thought, yet would it hurt to wait a little longer? Just to see whether the woman appeared at the fish market the next day. If he left now, he would always wonder. So he counted down the hours, whiling away the day watching the sea from the cliffs or lying on the grass staring up into the blue void of the sky, wondering what it was made of, how high the birds flew. He'd never had time to ponder such things before, out on the water with the wind and the waves, the fish beneath him. He'd been looking down more than up and it was strange to have time on his hands and a new perspective.

CHAPTER THREE

Joseph woke on Tuesday morning to a scattering of rain against the windowpane. His thoughts turned at once to the market. Would she be there? Even if the weather was bad? He supposed business was business, whatever the weather, so he made himself ready and set off down the cobbled street. He would go to sea once he'd reassured himself this woman wasn't Meg who, as all Castle Bay knew, had come to an unfortunate end. He told himself that in half an hour's time he would be chiding himself for wasting a week in this place on a wild-goose chase.

As he came down to the seafront the market was hidden from view, but he could hear the cries of the stallholders, competing over their wares. The drizzly rain hadn't kept customers away and, breathing deeply to still the sudden panicked beating of his heart, he joined a small flow of people walking towards the quay.

He reached the low wall, his vantage point of a week previously, and scanned the market. He was half hoping not to see her, to be spared the disappointment of expectations dashed, ridiculous though they were. She was there, though, in exactly the same spot, her back to him and the shawl over her hair to keep off the rain, her child by her side.

He followed the wall until he reached steps to take him down, keeping his eyes fixed on the spot where she stood. She was serving customers as he approached, her face still turned away from him. At last, as they moved on, he stood before the barrow.

She turned to face him. 'What can I get you?'

Joseph wasn't sure whether the intake of breath was his or hers. It was Meg, just as he'd hardly dared believe. She looked older and her face was drawn and, as she raised her hand to her mouth to stifle a gasp, he saw her narrow wrist, her reddened fingers. She'd lost the liveliness from her dark eyes that he remembered so well. But it was Meg, all the same. There was no hiding, even if she'd wanted to. For the longest minute, they didn't speak. They held each other's gaze until Meg looked down and ruffled the hair of the child who, as if sensing something momentous, had tucked itself into the folds of her skirt.

'Annie, it's all right.'

So, his guess – a girl – had been right, Joseph thought. He became aware of a customer waiting behind him.

'I can't talk now,' Meg said. She looked anxious.

'I'll be up there.' Joseph indicated the wall, from where he'd watched her before.

Meg nodded, eyes darting to the customer then back to him, as though she could scarcely believe what she saw. Joseph made his way back to sit on the wall, hardly conscious of the drizzle that continued to fall. He couldn't take his eyes off Meg and wondered whether she felt the pressure of his gaze, for she glanced up regularly. He feared that if he looked away, even for a moment, he would see an empty space where her barrow stood and she and Annie would have vanished, lost to him for ever.

He thought, as he watched, that he should make a plan. But he had no idea what she was going to tell him. It struck him that she might be married now, and he tried to see whether a ring showed on her finger. She was too far away, and her movements too swift as she served customers, for him to tell.

His stomach rumbled. He hadn't had breakfast and he longed to visit the food stall on the other side of the market. Every now and then, enticing aromas drifted across: mackerel frying, soon to be daubed with mustard and slapped between two pieces of bread. He couldn't leave his spot, though. He couldn't be sure she would be there on his return.

At long last, the stallholders began to pack up. Joseph retraced his steps and stood helplessly by the barrow as Meg sluiced it down, scrubbing the surface to remove the sparkle of scales and the stink of fish.

'What can I do to help?' he asked.

Meg pushed her hair away from her forehead with the back of her hand. 'Nothing,' she said. 'But you can give me a hand to push the barrow to the shed.'

Joseph nodded. 'And then we can talk?'

'Yes.' The look Meg gave him was fearful, he thought. He wanted to reassure her, but kept quiet under the watchful gaze of Annie, once more clinging to her mother's skirts. Now he could see the child close up, he could see she had her mother's heart-shaped face and dark eyes, and nothing of the father in her at all. He saw that her hair wasn't dirty, just uncombed.

He was glad when the cleaning was done, and he could be useful at last. He seized the handles of the barrow and, surprised at how heavy and unwieldy it was, followed Meg as instructed. He remembered her narrow wrists and wondered she had the strength in them to push it on her own. He managed to negotiate a passage to the edge of the market, with Meg occasionally offering a guiding hand. They stopped outside one of a number of low wooden doors set into a wall. He'd noticed them before, assuming fishermen stored tackle there.

Meg fished in her pocket for a key, put it into the lock and pulled back the door. Joseph pushed the barrow into the dark, gloomy space, manoeuvred it against the wall, then hurried out. Meg locked up and stood looking at him.

Joseph still had no plan but, seeing they were close to the food stall, which was serving its final customers, he gestured to it. 'Shall we eat something?'

Annie's eyes widened and she almost left the safety of her mother's skirts. Joseph guessed the food stall wasn't something they ever visited. Meg bit her lip but nodded and, furnished with the last of the mackerel and the good wishes of the stallholder, who was glad to close for the day, Joseph searched around for somewhere to eat.

'We can go over there.' Meg pointed along the seafront. 'There's a bit of beach, and some rocks where we can sit.'

The drizzle had eased by the time they reached it, although the clouds remained. They had only gulls for company, wheeling and screeching overhead as Joseph divided up the mackerel and the bread.

There was silence while they perched on the rocks and ate – Joseph supposed they were both as hungry as he was. They rinsed the greasy aftermath from their fingers in a rock pool, then dried their hands on a clean handkerchief from Joseph's pocket.

'Go and play, Annie.' Meg spoke abruptly. 'Show Joseph how good you are at skimming stones.'

Annie, fortified by the food, seemed to feel it was safe to leave her mother. She slipped down from the rock and went to the water's edge, glancing back at them for approval as she did so. After a while, distracted by something a little way along the beach, she wandered off and Joseph turned to Meg.

'I knew about you and Bartholomew Banks. And the baby – Eliza told me. I believed you dead. The story in Castle Bay is that you were murdered, and your bones lie in the quarry at Hawksdown Castle. Your family believes it.' Joseph was troubled. Why hadn't Meg returned home?

Meg gazed out over the water as she spoke. 'That's what Bartholomew wanted everyone to think. He paid the Kingsdown smugglers to kidnap me, take me away from Castle Bay and make sure that I never went back.'

Joseph stiffened, wondering what new horror might be revealed.

Meg continued, 'They bundled me into a cart and dragged me off to Kingsdown with them. They took my package of goods for the ladies at the castle, and they went through it, talking about using me to get such fine things for them. But then they reckoned Bartholomew would get to hear of it and he wanted me gone from the area, never to return. He could make trouble for them and they knew it.'

Joseph, shocked, barely knew what to ask. 'Are you sure it was Bartholomew? Why would he do such a thing? Did he know about the baby?'

Meg shrugged. 'I hadn't told him. And I'd sworn Eliza and my mother to secrecy. I can only think that, after his marriage, he worried I might make trouble and wanted me out of his sight, permanently. But it had to be him – he'd arranged for me to go to the castle that night to show the ladies the run goods I could supply.'

She stopped speaking, to call to Annie to stay back from the water, warning her that the tide was coming in and she wasn't to get her feet wet.

'What happened next?' Joseph prompted.

Meg grimaced. 'They told me I was leaving the area and I wasn't to think about coming back – ever – if I knew what was good for my family. Then they shut me in a shed, locked up with tubs of rum and a few rats for company. It was the early hours by then and I was kept there until nightfall, gagged so I couldn't call for help. Then they blindfolded me. I feared the worst, thought they'd decided to kill me, but they put me in the cart again and drove it inland, uphill. I couldn't hear or smell the sea any more. I was bumped and shaken around for hours – I thought I'd be sick at best or lose the baby. It was near morning when we started to go downhill again, and I could tell we were nearing the sea.'

She paused, taking a deep breath. 'They pushed me out of the back of the cart while it was still moving and left me. I was still gagged and blindfolded. I banged my head as I fell. It was over there, near the quay.' She nodded in the direction of the fish market. 'I think I was knocked out. The next thing I remember is seeing the sky and someone asking me who I was and what happened. They'd taken off the gag as well as the blindfold, but I couldn't speak. I was too parched.

'It was the day of the fish market – the first stallholders had just arrived. They gave me some water and I told them I was called Sarah Adams – the first name that came into my head. I asked where I was, and they told me. They wanted to know who had done this to me. I said I'd been taken by men my husband owed money to – that he'd died at sea, and they thought my family would pay to get me back. But they couldn't find the money so the kidnappers had dumped me.' Meg shrugged. 'I'm not sure anyone believed me, but they helped me all the same. One of the stallholders, Abraham, said his wife wasn't well and I could help with the children in return for a roof over my head.'

She stopped again and looked down at her feet. Joseph saw she'd dug the toes of her boots deep into the sand and her hands were clasped tightly in her lap.

'His wife still isn't well. I do her job of running the stall once a week and the housework and child-minding the rest of the time. I take in laundry, too. He's been good to me, letting me stay and keep Annie with me, instead of sending us to the poorhouse.'

There was a long pause. This wasn't Meg as Joseph remembered her. The spirited girl was no more and he wondered at it. Had she been ill-used by Abraham? He shrank from asking, fearing what he would hear.

Meg spoke flatly. 'He's waiting for his wife to die, and then he'll want me to marry him. I've kept him away until now.' She was watching her daughter on the shore. 'I've been setting aside what little I can so I can take Annie away and we can start again somewhere new.'

'Why don't you go back to Castle Bay?' Joseph was puzzled.

'Bartholomew made his wishes clear – he wanted me gone. Of course I want to see my family, but I'm still too frightened of what he might do, to me or to them, if I go back. And I can hardly accuse him – who would believe my word against his?' She frowned. 'And there's Annie to think of. Eliza was going to pretend she was with child so she could take the baby and bring it up as her own. Then no one would suspect it was mine. If I'd gone back with the baby already born, the plan was ruined. And, anyway, once I'd had her, how could I give her up?'

Joseph couldn't miss the smile that spread over her face as she gazed at her daughter. What he wouldn't give to have such a look directed at him.

CHAPTER FOUR

Meg called to summon her daughter. 'Annie, we have to go. Abraham will be waiting.'

Joseph caught her arm. 'Don't go back.'

Meg, astonished, shook her head. 'I must. He'll be anxious – angry. Worried about his takings.'

'Tell him you met an old friend,' Joseph urged. 'Then, when you've given him the money, come back and meet me.'

Meg laughed, but without humour. 'You don't know what he's like.'

Annie was at her side now and Meg stood up. Joseph, seized with desperation, felt his chance slipping away.

'Meg, I thought I saw you here a week ago. I've stayed here all the time just to discover whether it was really you. I can't let you go now. I still care for you. We can all go away, leave here – together.'

Joseph's words tumbled out in disjointed sentences in his haste to make Meg understand. He wanted to reach for her hand but feared alarming her. She'd been ill-used too often by men.

'Joseph, I can't. Too much has happened ... And it's not just me, now.'

'I know.' Joseph smiled down at Annie. 'I'd care for both of you. Of course I would.'

Meg closed her eyes, a look of anguish on her face. Joseph wondered what he could say or do to persuade her.

'Don't go back,' he repeated. 'I've taken a room in town. You could stay there and I'll take another. Or we can leave together, tonight. My boat's here,' he added.

'You have your boat?' Meg stilled, before, agitated, she grasped her daughter's hand. 'Annie, we must hurry. We're late. We'll tell Abraham ...' She stopped, at a loss.

'We'll tell Abraham it took longer to sell everything because of the weather,' she decided. 'And then I'll say I wrenched my ankle on the way home and we had to stop and rest until it was better.' She bent down and looked into her daughter's eyes. 'You understand, Annie?'

'Yes, Mama.'

'And we won't mention meeting Joseph.'

They set off at a brisk pace, Annie skipping along beside them. Joseph, in a final attempt to change her mind, racked his brains.

'You were wearing my necklace, Meg. The shell on the leather lace. I saw it last week and that's when I suspected it was you.'

Meg stopped and her hand flew to her throat, colour rising to her cheeks.

'Are you wearing it now?' Joseph asked.

Annie piped up. 'Mama always wears it.'

Meg stared at the ground. 'It's all I have to remind me of home,' she whispered. 'Of better times.'

'And of someone who once loved you, and loves you still,' Joseph said. He put his hand on Meg's arm and, hardly daring to breathe, gently drew her to him.

She clung to him, then, and he could feel all her fierce resolve draining away as her body relaxed. She'd had to stay strong for so long, he thought. Her face was buried in his jacket, and he wondered whether she was weeping.

Annie was gazing up at them both, her face etched with worry. Joseph held out a hand to her and she hesitated a moment before taking it and allowing herself to be drawn into her mother's side.

Suddenly Meg pulled away from him. 'Annie, we have to go. Hurry.'

He could scarcely believe his ears. 'But, Meg ...' He was almost running to stay at her side.

She spoke quickly. 'We'll go home and take Abraham his money. And we'll stay there tonight but, before it gets light, we'll slip out and meet you here, at the quay. Then we'll go and find your boat and we'll sail to Portsmouth. We can get a ship there to take us to New South Wales. And we'll never come back.'

They were hurrying up the hill, but at Meg's final words Joseph, bewildered, stopped. It was a moment or two before she realised. 'Come on,' she said, impatient.

He hurried to catch her up. 'Whatever do you mean – New South Wales?'

'I've heard they need people to settle there. People with skills. You can catch fish. I can bake or maybe teach. We can sell your boat in Portsmouth and with that, and the money I've saved, we can buy our passage and still have enough for some land. We can start afresh. No Bartholomew Banks. No scandal. No Abraham.'

She stopped speaking, struck by a thought. 'Oh, but your father?'

Joseph shook his head. 'He died.'

'I'm sorry.' Meg gave Joseph a sideways glance. 'So there's no one to keep us here?'

'No,' Joseph agreed. He was still reeling from Meg's whirlwind of ideas.

'We go this way,' Meg said, pointing to a lane leading off to the left.

'I'm up there.' Joseph pointed up the hill. 'And I'll see you tomorrow on the quay, before dawn?'

Meg nodded. She was more like her old self, Joseph thought. Then he was seized by misgivings. 'Meg, I hope you meant it. I'll get you away from here, no matter what. But it would make me happier to know that you came with a glad heart, because of me, not just because I can provide an escape.'

He made a tentative step towards her, longing to take her in his arms again.

She held up a warning hand. 'Not here, Joseph. We're too near the house. If word gets back to Abraham I've been seen with a stranger . . .' She shuddered and lowered her voice. 'We'll see you tomorrow.'

She raised her hand and he thought she meant to blow him a kiss, but she touched her fingers to the shell necklace, smiled at him, then turned away.

Joseph watched her go, half intending to follow at a distance to see where they lived. Then, mindful of her words about Abraham, he turned and walked slowly up the hill, deep in thought. Would she really be there, with Annie, in the morning? Could they make their escape without Abraham discovering it? How far was it to Portsmouth? And after that – did he even want to leave this country, the only one he had ever known?'

These thoughts ran around his head throughout the rest of the long day and well into the night. Exhausted, he finally fell asleep only to wake a few hours later in a panic. Had dawn already broken? Had he missed them? But all was dark and quiet, both inside the house and out. He lay and listened to the thudding of his heart, then decided to get up and go to the waterfront to wait. He couldn't risk not being there at the right time.

He crept down the stairs and out of the house, boots and pack in his hand. He'd told his landlady he was leaving and paid his bill the previous day. He'd already decided that even if Meg and Annie didn't appear, he would go anyway.

The harbour clock showed half past three by the time he arrived at the quay. Sunrise was a long way off. Cats prowled, hoping to find a morsel of fish lodged in the cobbles of the market. Joseph sat on the wall and told himself it wasn't cold, that they would come. He had a hard job convincing himself on either count.

The clock struck four, then four thirty. The sky was no longer completely dark, and the town was stirring with the first signs of life. Joseph's gaze constantly strayed to the street leading down from the town, hoping to see Meg with a small figure at her side. By five, he was losing hope. He forced himself to stop watching the town, looking out to sea instead. If they didn't come, he'd decided to follow Meg's dream anyway. He'd sail to Portsmouth and take the ship on his own. He had no idea how she'd come by such an idea but, the more he thought about it, what did he have to lose?

Absorbed in his thoughts, he didn't notice the woman and child who'd arrived at his side on silent feet until Meg spoke. 'We must go. Abraham will be up any time now and he'll see we've left the house.' Meg glanced behind her, fearful. 'Where's your boat?' She looked around as though expecting to see it beside the quay.

Joseph, who could scarcely believe she was there, gestured westward along the shore. 'It's out there, on the shingle.'

Meg nodded and began to hurry in the direction he had pointed, Annie at her side. Joseph forced his cold, stiff limbs to life and followed her.

She didn't speak to him again until they reached the side of the boat, twenty minutes later. The tide was high, and Joseph was grateful. His boat wasn't large, but it would be heavy to haul into the water.

Meg lifted Annie into the boat, then said, 'Tell me what to do.'

He showed her the wooden spars stowed inside, and how to lay them parallel on the shingle, at intervals, until he'd hauled the boat close enough to the waves to slip into the sea. He had to rely on her to drag the spars back to him while he held the boat steady in the water. The hem of her skirt was drenched by the time he pulled her aboard, but she made no word of complaint. Annie was silent, white-faced.

It was only as the sails of *Early Dawn* caught the wind and they skimmed away from the shore that Joseph, who was beginning to wonder about Meg's reasons for coming with him, saw a change in her demeanour. She had been gazing back to land as he busied himself with setting the sails. Now she stood up carefully and made her way to his side, clinging to whatever she passed as she did.

'Joseph, I can never thank you enough.' She tried to smile but Joseph could see she was close to tears.

'You don't need to,' he said. 'But I hope, one day, when all this has faded from your mind,' he waved his hand back towards the shore, 'you might be able to consider me – to love me . . .' He stumbled over his words, unsure of how to continue.

She reached for his hand and turned her face up towards him, standing on tiptoe to kiss him gently on the lips. Then, glancing back at Annie, who was peering over the side, entranced by the water foaming past, she reached up and kissed him again. A longer kiss this time, enough to give him hope.

'I should never have stopped,' she said, and made her way back to Annie, putting an arm around her daughter's shoulders as the sun rose higher in the sky and turned the sea around them into glittering diamonds.

Joseph set a course parallel to shore and watched Folkestone fall away into the distance. Whatever hazards, difficulties or adventures lay ahead, he was ready for them. He felt he could face anything with Meg, and Annie, at his side. For the first time in three years, he allowed himself to feel the faint stirrings of happiness.

HISTORICAL NOTE

There is a great deal of proud interest in local history in this area of east Kent, with generations of families having been born and brought up here. To avoid causing upset over any liberties I may have taken while creating historical fiction set here, I've changed the names of the towns, and some streets, too. The town of Castle Bay is based on the seaside town of Deal, Broad Castle being Deal Castle. Hawksdown and Hawksdown Castle are based on the adjacent town of Walmer.

The Lord Warden lived at Walmer Castle (Hawksdown Castle in the book), although the Lord Warden in residence at that time didn't have a son involved in the smuggling trade. But the story of the hidden gloves, first mentioned in the Prologue, is true.

Throckings Hotel was actually known as the Three Kings Hotel, but misrecorded in the Pigot & Co. directory of the 1830s. I rather liked the name so I kept it.

During the First World War, there was an aerodrome on Hawks Hill (Hawks Down in the book), and an auxiliary hospital nearby, but the events I have portrayed are entirely fictional. Carrie's employment as a teacher would have fallen foul of the Education Act of 1905 had she been living in a city – rural areas appear to have taken a little more time to follow the new rules.

ACKNOWLEDGEMENTS

Thank you, as always, to my agent Kiran, at Keane Kataria for her unfailing words of wisdom and support, and to my editor, Eleanor Russell, at Piatkus for her encouragement and enthusiasm. Thanks are also due to Hazel Orme for bringing eagle-eyed clarity to *The Smuggler's Secret*.

My friends and family deserve acknowledgement, too, for their unfailing support, as does The Deal Bookshop, and David and Gemma in particular, for championing me as a local author.

LOVED
THE SMUGGLER'S SECRET?

DISCOVER MORE FROM LYNNE FRANCIS WITH
A MAID'S RUIN

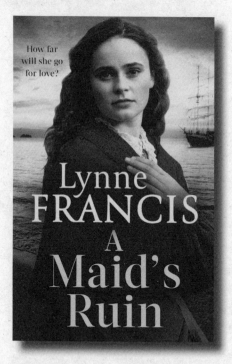